Rave reviews for E. C.  Book Apostle:

"In a grim world of m... ... primitive surgery, E. C. ... of one man's humanity as ... who like realism as wel... —Glenda ...

"A vivid, violent, and marvelously detailed historical fantasy set in the perilous world that is medieval England in the middle of a war. Elisha Barber wades through blood and battle in his pursuit of arcane knowledge—forbidden love—and dangerous magic."
—Sharon Shinn, author of *Troubled Waters*

"Ambrose's fantasy debut depicts a 14th-century England in which magic and fledgling science exist side by side. Elisha's struggle to bring relief to those in need is complicated by his own need for redemption and his innate fear of what he cannot understand. This beautifully told, painfully elegant story should appeal to fans of L.E. Modesitt's realistic fantasies as well as of the period fantasy of Guy Gavriel Kay."   —*Library Journal* (starred review)

"*Elisha Barber* is at its heart a story of resilience, of why we strive to be better, even when that journey seems pointless. As the start of a new series, the book sets a half-dozen plates spinning, and not a one wobbles for a second."
—San Francisco Book Review

"E.C. Ambrose has created an exciting, adventure-filled world that draws you in; you are able to picture not only the characters but the world they live in. *Elisha Magus* is fantasy at its best and I can't wait for the next book by E.C. Ambrose."   —Fresh Fiction

"I am really enjoying this series. After reading the first book I was eager to read [*Elisha Magus*]. It did not disappoint."   —Night Owl Reviews

"The historical milieu is detailed and brings the period into sharp focus. . . . The magical battles rivet readers' attention as Elisha fights for his life and sanity. Book three looms in the wings as Elisha learns to wield his powers and protect his chosen king."   —SFRevu

Novels of
The Dark Apostle
from E. C. Ambrose

ELISHA MANCER

BOOK FOUR OF

The Dark Apostle

E. C. AMBROSE

DAW BOOKS, INC.

DONALD A. WOLLHEIM, FOUNDER

375 Hudson Street, New York, NY 10014

ELIZABETH R. WOLLHEIM
SHEILA E. GILBERT
PUBLISHERS
www.dawbooks.com

First Printing, February 2017
1   2   3   4   5   6   7   8   9

**DAW TRADEMARK REGISTERED
U.S. PAT. AND TM. OFF. AND FOREIGN COUNTRIES
—MARCA REGISTRADA
HECHO EN U.S.A.**

PRINTED IN THE U.S.A.

ELISHA MANCER

"We are devoured by a secret ill: it is not life they are taking from us, it is goodness; we can neither live in virtue nor die with honor."

—Petrarch

Chapter 1

———— ❖ ————

Eight days out of Brussels, along the eastern bank of the river, the bulk of Cologne Cathedral grew upon the horizon. A steady drizzle shivered Elisha's skin with a hint of pain, his first sign of the mancers he had travelled across the Channel to find—and destroy. The vessel's captain strode back and forth while his men moved with efficiency, sometimes swinging outside the rails to judge the distance between their boat and the numerous others travelling or preparing to moor at the busy dockside. Smaller vessels shoved up onto the shingle to load and unload over the sides with a cacophony of shouting and gestures. Elisha leaned over the rail, then dodged sailors and scrambled to the far side as they came about to dock. Raindrops glazed his hands, the contact bringing that sense of a stranger's hurt. His awareness showed the presence of a magus, at least, and likely a mancer, given the excitement that accompanied the pain. Elisha needed to reach Emperor Ludwig, the father of King Thomas's slain first wife, to warn him about the mancers who stalked the crowns of Europe. After Ludwig's excommunication, a rival emperor, Charles, had been raised in opposition to Ludwig, perhaps by the mancers themselves. This inadvertent contact through the rain could be his chance to start uncovering their plan for the Holy Roman Empire, and give Ludwig what he needed in order to stop them.

He spun about. "Captain! Is there time to go ashore?"

The captain tipped his head back, squinting at the gloom that settled over both city and river. "We'll be off at Nones—that's maybe a couple of hours. Best you stay with the boat, if you don't know the city."

Elisha hesitated. The city wall stretched in both directions along the river, punctuated by towers and gates. It had to be two or three times as vast as London. Even the cathedral, though its spire stood unfinished, towered large enough to encompass St. Paul's and Westminster both. The boat pushed between a dozen others, making for a gate directly below the bulk of the church. "I think that is landmark enough," he answered, and the captain looked up again at the city this time before he grunted.

"Brace!" he shouted and each man caught hold of some fixed object while the oarsmen strained and shoved the boat aground.

Elisha swayed with the jolt, then stepped up on a chest near the rail and swung himself down to the shore.

"Are you going to see the magi, then?"

He turned back, startled, to find his fellow traveler Brother Gilles leaning on the rail above him.

Slipping back his velvet hat, Elisha was about to speak when the hat flew away, twirling in the breeze. He snatched after it too late and glared as it landed on the water with a ripple of burgundy silk, only to plunge beneath the keel of a passing boat. Really, the hat was just as well gone. After years of cheap woolens and bloody linen, the velvet had felt absurd and extravagant, a guise he had taken on—along with the title of "doctor"—when he had been granted the office of King Thomas's personal physician. He was no longer a king and still not a noble, but it should be enough to gain him an audience with the Holy Roman Emperor.

"Alas, my dear sir, you have misplaced your hat. What misfortune!" The round friar clucked his tongue, beaming down at him, hands hidden in the folds of his weighty robe. "But perhaps I have dismissed you too quickly, my good doctor, if you desire so fervently to view the holy shrine." The relics dealer had ignored him since their embarkation, when he learned Elisha had little respect for the bits of bone and other remnants he claimed to be from saints—and no inclination to pay for them.

But then, Elisha carried his own remnants, the talismans that gave him access to his magic. He wore only one talisman openly, the golden ring given him by King Thomas, and more precious than mere metal. Beneath his robes and tunic, he carried a stronger talisman: a vial of earth from the ground where his brother died. Like the other talismans among his things, this one strengthened the reach of magic, amplifying it like the belly of a drum making a single hide sound like thunder. And unlike the others, this talisman offered him a direct connection to the dirt floor of the workshop where his brother cut his own throat. If he needed to, Elisha could reach back through the tainted soil he carried and open the passage of his brother's death, the passage he thought of as the Valley of the Shadow. Elisha could summon himself to England through that howling place of pain and fear, and go home. If only he could summon himself to the Emperor Ludwig's side so readily, but no magic could be made where he had neither contact nor knowledge, and so the river remained the fastest way.

"You mentioned a holy shrine, the magi," Elisha prompted.

"Indeed. The three kings who witnessed the birth of our Lord"—Brother Gilles crossed himself—"have been translated here, their holy bones gathered into a magnificent shrine of gold."

Magi. Wise men. Brigit told Elisha the Biblical magi claimed that title to harken back to the wisdom of old. "I wouldn't miss it."

"I shall accompany you," the friar said grandly, heaving himself up and nearly falling as he jumped to the ground, his sandals squelching in the mud as Elisha caught him.

"Thank you, Brother, but I'm sure—"

"Nonsense! I, too, should like to pay my respects to such a holy place."

If need be, he could outpace the friar. For the moment, they moved on together, slogging up the muddy stones to the pavement that edged the wall and passing beneath the hard gaze of city guards. The gate cut off the rain, and he lost the sensation that drew him, then emerged again to find it stronger, coming from the direction of the cathedral itself. The friar stuck at Elisha's elbow, chattering about the other great relics of the area, lamenting the fact that he hadn't time to reach Aachen to venerate the dress of the Virgin and the Loincloth of Christ, not that these notable items were displayed, of course, but still the sense of their holiness lingered, did it not?

Elisha frowned, listening. Of course things worn or used by these holy figures would retain their connection—it was one of the basic principles of magic—and their bones or dust must be closer still, allowing ordinary people contact with the saints, as if they, too, understood the heart of magic.

A broad square opened out before them, with a few steps up to join it to another. Market stalls stood at the sides, while jugglers, tumblers and a dancing bear attracted small crowds in the steady drizzle. Up ahead, adjacent to the church entrance, the crowds cleared a large ring, and a man wailed in pain to the sound of whips slapping flesh. Elisha's jaw set, his own back, once beaten, tensed with the memory as he quickened his steps.

Within the ring of citizens a second ring of people shuffled, one after another, their garments torn down from their shoulders, each bearing a whip of many tails to lash the back of the one before him in the circle. Welts stood out against their shivering flesh, some struck so often that they bled, a thin stream of crimson trailing down to mingle with the rain. They moaned and shouted incoherently, lashing each other onward.

At the center of these miserable wretches a tall man loomed, wearing his tunic one-shouldered, the drape revealing his own beaten back. "Hear us, Almighty Lord! Let our suffering reach your ears as we drive out our mortal weakness!"

"Yes!" and "Amen!" cried some in the circle, and some of their audience as well. The lashes fell again and Elisha

flinched. Faith so often drove men to madness. He looked
away as they struck again, but their blood swirled into the
water, and he gave thanks for his boots to defend him
from feeling their pain. Even the sense of it in the stinging rain distracted him. A trained magus could control his
presence, containing his emotion beneath the skin, but
these *desolati*, those without magic, had no such skill.
Blood drifted in pink eddies around the friar's sandals
and moved in lazy circles inward. Elisha blinked and focused. His left eye overlaid the scene with shades, the
residue of those who had died here, endlessly shadowing
the moment of their deaths.

"Yea, Lord, from the deeps we call to Thee! From our
hearts, we call to Thee! We mortify this earthly flesh and
deny all earthly comforts for Thee!"

Extending his magical senses to understand what was
happening, Elisha also traced the paths of blood with his
eyes. The apparently ordinary ripples, disturbed by the
shuffling feet of the flagellants, swirled inexorably inward to lap the naked toes of their leader, as if he sucked
their pain through his bare skin. Withdrawing his awareness, Elisha backed out of the circle.

"Indeed, good doctor, it is disturbing—"

"Hear me, ye sinners all!" the leader thundered,
swinging about to face them, and power sparked in the
rain on Elisha's skin. "The Lord knows your hearts! The
Lord knows your sins! The Lord knows where you are,
He knows who you are! Fall upon your knees ye sinners
and despair!"

Dozens in the circle dropped to their knees. Over
their heads, the wild eyes of the flagellant leader caught
Elisha's glance. The leader raised his own lash and
smiled grimly. "Come, sinner," he pointed the whip at
Elisha. "Do you not kneel in the presence of the Lord?"

"It is not God who spurs you on," Elisha answered.

The leader swung his lash over his shoulder, the dozen
tails striping his own back. As they fell, the rain slapped
Elisha with the force of a hundred lashes, every blow
that fell upon the flagellants gathered and reflected by
their leader, the necromancer.

Elisha staggered and cried out, wiping the water from his face, cursing the loss of his stupid hat — ludicrous as it was, it had shielded him from this contact. His presence, felt through the rain, must have exposed him as a magus to the mancer who now struck at him. The lashes fell again, and Elisha's face and hands burned with pain. He stumbled and fled toward the nearest building. As long as he stayed in the rain, the mancer could make contact, delighting in the wanton use of his power. As long as the mancer stoked the agony of his followers, and they devoted their hearts and flesh to him, like living talismans, he commanded more power than Elisha could muster, lost as he was in a foreign land. The rain stopped abruptly as a lintel intervened overhead. Tripping over the threshold, Elisha fell headlong into the cathedral.

He rolled over, breathing hard, wiping his face and hands on his robe to dry off the tainted rain.

Concerned churchgoers leaned over him, and Elisha shook his head to fend them off, answering briefly in English, then recalling the German he had learned on the weeks-long voyage from England. A priest loomed in, then Brother Gilles patting his shoulder.

Pushing back, Elisha sat against the wall and finally caught his breath.

"My good doctor, you seem quite overcome," Gilles said, the heat of his hand soothing Elisha's damp confusion. "Are you then caught in sinning, or can you be so sensitive to the suffering of others?"

"Some of each, Brother." The murky depths of the church around them slowly clarified, its vast arches reaching upward, every surface of the ribs elaborately carved, framing slices of stained glass impossibly tall. How was such a building able to stand with so little stone in its walls? Incense lingered in the transept where he sat, and people shuffled by, many stopping to gawk at the rainbow walls and far-away ceiling. Workmen clattered at one end and stone dust lingered in the air.

"You seemed sensitive to my relics as well, sir." The friar pursed his lips. "Perhaps you would be willing to look them over with me. I do like to be certain of their authenticity, especially since I must present items suitable to the Emperor Ludwig and perhaps to the Holy Father himself. The rival emperor, Charles, is to meet with Ludwig at Trier to discuss terms and I know he is a very devout man. God willing, this journey could do much to enrich the coffers of my humble priory." A quick crossing of his chest followed this avowal. "Have you recovered sufficiently to visit the shrine of the Magi?"

"I think so," Elisha murmured, rising to his feet and allowing himself to be drawn into the shuffling line of pilgrims. They passed through bands of color shining down from the windows and came up to the rounded end of the circuit where the sudden glory of the golden shrine gleamed against dark wood. It rose on an altar high enough to pass beneath, and several men and women reached upward, pressing their fingertips to the underside as they prayed. The wealth of a city stood over his head, the holy bones of the Three Kings resting there. As he passed beneath, Elisha prayed for a way out of this cathedral. As long as the rain fell, as long as the mancer led his flagellants to beat themselves for his power, Elisha could be pinned here.

Bardolph, the German mancer who escaped the battle in England when Elisha saved Thomas, might have gone anywhere through the Valley of the Shadow, any place where he knew the dead and could make contact through a talisman. Had Bardolph spread word of Elisha's coming? Elisha could not know if the mancer flagellant recognized him as one who stood against them, or merely as a sensitive magus, to be scorned for his rejection of stronger magic, but he could not wait to be sure—he had to get back to the boat. Their journey would soon diverge from the Rhine and he could not navigate to Trier and the emperor on his own.

A rattling box was pushed in front of him by a smiling priest, and Elisha dropped in a coin to win his right to pass away.

"We do not have much time, sir, and should be going," Brother Gilles pointed out, leading the way toward the door where they had come in, but Elisha hesitated, seeing the rain and the crowds. He might cloak himself in death—would he be able to project a presence so unlike himself as to pass beneath the notice of the mancer?

When the friar turned to him with raised brows, Elisha said, "I can't go without a hat." He sounded like a vain fool, like just the kind of man he'd always hated.

"Ah, your unfortunate hat, I remember." The friar cocked his head. "We might exchange robes, sir. Mine has a hood."

"It's asking much of you, Brother."

"Nonsense. When we return to our vessel, you shall return the favor by examining my relics. I shouldn't like the emperors themselves to find my offerings wanting." The friar untied his belt and began wriggling out of his long woolen habit.

Elisha followed suit, smoothing down the layers of tunic and undershirt his supposed position as a royal physician required and shivering as he handed over his own wet robe.

"Do be careful, there are relics stitched in at the cuffs and collar." Brother Gilles, holding the robe given Elisha by the king himself, clearly considered his own bits of bone to be more valuable.

Mindful of the garment's saintly cargo, Elisha drew it on over his head and pulled up the hood. It hid his face and the ample sleeves gave him room to tuck in his hands. More than that, the garment hummed with fragments of the dead. It felt like a musical consort tuning up, a dozen different presences tingling against his skin, some chilly in the ordinary way of death, a few stinging with the cold of betrayal, murder, torture. Elisha took a deep breath to brace himself and opened to their touch, their influence mingling with his own. There could be no finer disguise than this, especially for a man who knew death. Elisha smiled grimly. "Thank you, Brother. Lead on."

With this web of relics draped over him, Elisha followed the friar out into the rain. He kept his own awareness thinly stretched, the pain and power of the flagellants' circle numbed by Gilles's robe. Cries of hurt and devotion echoed as they passed, and Elisha felt the tingle of the mancer's interest reaching toward the friar who wore his own robe, but it faded back again, then they moved beyond its reach and hurried down the steps.

By the time they reached the foreshore, the bells rang out behind them and the captain frowned as he heaved them both into the boat, men standing ready to push it back into the river.

Before they reached Trier a few days later, Elisha had acquired a handful of bone shards from the friar and carefully stitched them into his own clothing. He selected them based upon their different presences, arranging these fragments of death as an artist arranges his paints. Several of the friar's other offerings showed signs of medical intervention including saw marks and even wounds from the bombards at Dunbury. The friar's description of the ugly monk he had received them from matched Morag himself: apparently the mancer had a sideline in passing off parts of soldiers as relics of saints. Without participating in the death himself, Morag couldn't use these as talismans, so he seemed to have found another way to profit by them.

Many items in the collection sent the shock of murder straight to Elisha's center, and the friar did not even need to ask if they were genuine. They might not be the bones of the saints, but they were surely martyred. The supposed Arm of Saint Brendan, which Brother Gilles hoped to offer to the Emperor Ludwig, showed the marks of Elisha's own saw, but the friar merely mourned the sad circumstances of the monastery forced to let go of any part of their fabled saint, even if it must be by cutting.

Both men arrived at Trier the happier for having met—and the more prepared for what they must meet next: the Holy Roman Emperors. One emperor needed a relic to appease a pope, the other might well keep a retinue of necromancers to control the throne.

Chapter 2

❖

*A*fter it diverged from the heavy traffic of the Rhine, the Mosel River flowed between high sloped vineyards with castles every hundred yards, or so it seemed, and backed by hills thick with dark trees. Despite the heavy scent of grapes in the air, the entire land lay too quiet, waiting for war between the rival emperors. Unsettled by Emperor Ludwig's excommunication, the group of powerful nobles and churchmen who made such decisions had recently elected Charles in opposition to Ludwig. So far, Charles had apparently been patient, waiting for Ludwig to give up the throne of his own accord—or, Elisha suspected, under from the influence of the mancers. Curious that the mancers, who so enjoyed the horrors of battle, would be so patient as well. This was another movement in a dance whose pattern Elisha had not yet discerned.

When the valley widened at Trier, Elisha breathed more freely without those castles and the deep forest overshadowing his passage. The broad gray wall of the city stretched along the river toward an ancient bridge. The captain pointed out a cluster of pennants snapping over a brick tower just visible within the walls. "The Emperor Ludwig's banner flies. You're in luck."

Along the river stood a few squat round towers with cranes poking out of their rooftops. The vessel pushed in next to one of these, longshoremen making fast their bowline. With a groan and squeal, the roof of the round building rotated, the crane's lines lowering toward them, and the crew leapt to work tying off Brother Gilles's crate to be lifted ashore to a waiting oxcart. Elisha took up his own small chest and waited as a plank was laid from the gunwale to the base of the crane.

"Is that all?" Gilles asked, shaking his head. "My dear doctor, I don't know how you expect to make an imperial impression with such limited options."

"I'm not looking to be hired, Brother."

"No?" Gilles waited, but Elisha said no more, and the friar shrugged. "Perhaps we shall meet again in the emperor's halls."

Bidding him farewell, Elisha swayed across the plank to the solid shore. He crunched his way over the tiny clamshells that decked the muddy foreshore, the smoke of iron smelters clogging his throat until he coughed. From the shape and size of the wall, he expected Trier to be as vast and dense as Cologne, but once inside, found houses clustered on a few streets and separated by fields of grain where farmers wielded their scythes and flails. He walked steadily into town where the houses finally closed out the fields, and it started to feel more like home, with shops at the street level and two or three stories of living space above them. Here, the stone-built houses rose smoothly without the jutting levels of those in London, allowing broad bands of sky to show through. Layers of brick separated some floors while other houses were painted pink, orange, or red, with round-arched windows that seemed to smile down onto the streets.

The high red tower the captain had pointed out proved to be one end of a huge brick building that looked like half a church, round where the tower rose up a level higher than the rest. Smaller windows had been built into the large red-stone frames as if the current occupants took over an earlier structure. At the flat end of the building, where it joined with a lower cloister, stood a peaked wooden door cut into the brick. Elisha presented his travel documents—a letter dangling with the seals of King Thomas—to a guard who eyed him from the slit in his helmet, then took the parchment inside. Elisha set down his chest, shaking out his hands, and extended his senses in every direction.

A shiver of interest reached back to him, and he sensed a presence retreating from the gallery above.

At length, the soldier returned, this time sliding the bar to open the door beside him. "Leave that here," he directed, gesturing to the chest. Then he ushered Elisha inside—only to lead him through an opposite door until, disconcertingly, they were outdoors again. The old building's brick frame stood open to the sky while smaller workshops and stables lined its interior up to an elevated walkway patrolled by a few soldiers. A row of old windows gaped open between the rooftops of the new construction and the wooden supports of the soldier's walk as if the occupiers were not quite bold enough to fill this grand place. At the base of the tower, another soldier scrutinized him, then motioned them into a gap in the wall where a staircase spiraled upward inside its thickness. The dark forest, the city gates, the brick walls of this inside-out place, now this mouse hole of a staircase enclosed him, and a prickling unease tightened Elisha's shoulders. Soon, he would find Emperor Ludwig, deliver Thomas's greetings, and warn him about the mancer threat. After the encounter in Cologne, he expected the mancers to try to stop him—but perhaps they did not anticipate his mission after all.

The door swung open, soldiers bowing him through, and a happy voice called out, "So here is the emissary of our brother monarch, King Thomas. No, do not stand on ceremony, but tell us how things fare in England?"

Elisha straightened from his bow to find a man of about his own age, smiling broadly, arms open in welcome. It took a moment to realize the man had spoken in English, with a recognizably French accent. "Well, your—" But Elisha hesitated, frowning. This friendly blond fellow was far too young to be Ludwig, Thomas's father-in-law.

"Your Majesty will do." He continued to smile, a capelet of purple swishing at his knees as he rocked slightly. "You were expecting a different greeting, I presume. Or a different sovereign?" With this last, he switched to German, turning his hand to indicate his surroundings.

A chuckle swept the little gathering of soldiers and courtiers arrayed about a pair of tall chairs. A few dogs lounged around the first while a lovely woman clad in satin occupied the second chair, looking peevish. An older man with tonsured hair and a golden robe leaned to whisper to her. An archbishop. He straightened up and stalked nearer Elisha, looking him up and down. "Come, Charles, do not taunt the man. It is you who have chosen to raise the pennant of your enemy alongside your own."

The blond man—Emperor Charles IV—sighed. "Any day now, we expect the man who claims my crown, and we do wish him to feel welcome. His wife is pregnant— very much so—and they travel slowly. They have come so far as Heidelberg, but that is still a few days' journey away."

The archbishop took over as Charles resumed his throne. "His Majesty enjoys greeting foreigners because he delights to speak in other tongues." The old man did not smile, but maintained his air of appraisal. "We are preparing for our luncheon, and you shall join us, of course."

Elisha gave another bow. By rights, he had wandered into the enemy camp, yet they received him as a friend. Tension gathered in his neck, but he forced himself to smile. "Of course, Your Majesty, thank you." Already servants bustled about setting trestle tables and bringing up benches and chairs. "I expected to find—Duke Ludwig here," he began, employing a title Ludwig held undisputed.

"And so he should have been," Charles said, lounging in his throne as platters of food were placed before him. "If it were not for Margaret's pregnancy, I should guess that he is punishing me. Last time we arranged for such a meeting, it was I who was detained." He popped a handful of almonds in his mouth and crunched them down. "No matter. Baldwin is an excellent host." He tipped his head to the archbishop, who gave an almost imperceptible sigh. Hosting an emperor could not be any easier than hosting a king, especially under the present circumstances. Archbishop Baldwin. Elisha searched his memory for the information he'd been given before leaving England, and placed the name: Baldwin was not only the archbishop, but also Charles's uncle. A man to be reckoned with.

The lady let out a stream of elegant French, plucking at Charles's sleeve to draw him nearer. He gestured toward Elisha, answering in the same language, and Elisha caught a few words. "My wife, Blanche," Charles supplied with a note of apology. "She speaks no English, and little German, though she is learning." He smiled at her fondly. "But come, you must tell us the events in England. It has been a difficult year, has it not?"

Sinking into the offered chair, Elisha nearly laughed. A difficult year—and none could know it better. He chose his words with care, hoping he sounded a neutral party in the events of the past summer. "King Hugh died in June, at the battle of Dunbury, against a duke he considered to be in revolt." Elisha had killed the king, but this did not need to be shared. "We had believed that Prince Thomas turned traitor, but this proved false, so he succeeded his father, but his younger brother was killed."

"His brother and heir, if I am not mistaken," Charles mused. "Pity."

Elisha expanded his awareness through the room, the table and the floor. He let his left eye unfocus, distracted by the curving bits of shadow that clung to the relics he wore, bits of death forever stained by the shades of the living people they once had been. A mass of similar shadows rose and shifted in the corner where an ornate cabinet stood—likely some sort of travelling altar—tended by a pair of hooded monks.

Elisha had been too close to all of it to think in such political terms. It had never before been his world to understand, now he must at least try. He came here because he knew the mancers—not because this world made any sense to him. He brought his attention back to Charles and replied, "We found that his eldest daughter,

Alfleda, survived the attack that killed her mother. She had been taken as a hostage, but she has been restored to him."

"Hmm. Interesting. Has he spoken yet of her marriage prospects?"

Marriage? Alfleda was eight. Before Elisha could form an appropriate response, Charles continued, "Or perhaps, his own? Surely he shall be seeking a new wife, especially now that his heir has passed." Charles crossed himself with a languid grace.

The duke's daughter, Rosalynn, had married Thomas and been killed by a necromancer once she became pregnant with his child. She died believing that Elisha had killed her. Elisha took a swallow of the wine poured for him, letting it warm his throat before he answered, "King Thomas has recently re-married, but his wife is . . . not well. She may not recover." Brigit. Thomas married her at the depths of his grief, to give his realm an heir in the form of the child she already carried. His brother's child, so most believed. Elisha's chest tightened. Not merely his own child, also the heir to the crown of England. If it survived, if its mother's unwaking sleep could be prolonged until the baby could be delivered. And there was the matter of Thomas's confession, the hot, confusing weight of the king's admiration. Elisha took another drink—longer this time—and wished he knew how to change the subject.

"Pity," Charles repeated. "I have a sister of marriageable age who is being raised at court in Paris. The alliances could be quite valuable. But of course I wish his wife a swift recovery." He raised his goblet and cried, "To the health of the king of England, and of his bride!"

The gathering raised their goblets, echoed the blessing and drank.

"But you have not spoken of sorcery," Charles prompted, setting down his goblet and snapping for it to be refilled.

A sense of heightened awareness passed through the room, and Elisha resisted the urge to look around. Someone else wanted the answer to that question, someone in contact with this floor or this table. "There have been rumors, Your Majesty," Elisha said. "There are always rumors."

"Rumors only? My foster father, King Philippe of France, has lately been plagued by witches. He has set about a program to remove their taint completely, and he has been given to understand that England was already infested with diabolical magic."

"Hence his attempt at invasion." Elisha set down his goblet and met the gaze of the would-be emperor. "Which was firmly repelled."

Archbishop Baldwin tapped his knife upon his silver plate. "Please, gentlemen. We seek only polite conversation at meals. Surely such matters can wait a better time."

Charles, the affable emperor, was raised by the king of France, a king who was killing all of his magi—likely at the behest of the mancers. Charles himself might be under their influence; it behooved Elisha to tread carefully and quickly in the opposite direction. "I do appreciate your hospitality, Your Grace, and Your Majesty, but if Duke Ludwig is at Heidelberg, then I should make haste to see him there."

"You have only just arrived, and surely are tired from your journey. You must be our guest tonight, at least," Charles protested. "I promise I shall speak no more of France. There is bad blood between your great sovereigns, and it is not for us to resolve."

The archbishop gave an approving nod. "But you have told us nothing of yourself, sir. You are a doctor? An unusual choice for a messenger."

The rich food did not sit well in Elisha's stomach—or it might have been the conversation, fraught with dimensions he did not fully grasp—but he felt a little sour as he sought to explain why he had come, and realized that he had already given a reason. "We are concerned for King Thomas's queen, Your Grace. When I have discharged my duty to Duke Ludwig, I am to inquire of the local doctors about her condition."

Baldwin inclined his head gravely while Charles explained to Blanche. The pretty queen finally showed some color and spoke animatedly, something about a famous doctor. After a moment, Charles said, "My wife suggests that you must contact Guy de Chauliac, the personal physician of the Holy Father. I can, of course, give you letters of introduction should you wish to travel to Avignon to consult him. Also the university at Heidelberg may be of use to you." Charles toyed with a pheasant leg as he spoke, then glanced again at Elisha. "I myself shall found a university on my return to Prague. We shall be looking for the finest professors . . . if you know anyone you would recommend."

"I shall think on it, Your Majesty."

Charles pointed the bone at him, leaning forward. "You know that my competitor is under excommunication. You are not his subject — you have no obligation to speak with him at all — and in fact, as a Christian, you are obliged not to speak to him, to give him no comfort. Does your king not understand this?" He flung the bone away to be snapped up by a dog. In English, he said, "Ludwig is a despicable, unholy man. The Holy Father cannot abide him, nor can we. I hate to see you walk into such a meeting."

"What do you want from me, Your Majesty? If you wish me to betray my king's trust, it will not happen. If you think Thomas will abandon his father-in-law to support yourself, then you don't know how much he loved his wife."

Baldwin's brow furrowed, and Blanche drew back at Elisha's vehemence, her plaintive voice clearly asking for translation.

"Your Majesty," Elisha continued. "I am no diplomat. I cannot negotiate for King Thomas. Neither will I set aside his commands. Whatever offers you wish to make, I will take them back with me, but please ask no more of me than that."

"As a good Christian, it was my duty to warn you." Charles turned up his palms. "When you come to Ludwig, you shall see what you shall see, and perhaps then you shall carry my good wishes back to your king. We should like to offer you our hospitality, but we understand you may not accept. Please at least take a horse from my stable by the Southeast Gate." He gestured to a young man waiting on a stool nearby. "Clerk? A writ of safe passage. Add a note about the horse." He waved his hand and the clerk scurried up with the document, shaking, drying sand off the fresh ink of the amendment.

"Thank you, Your Majesty," Elisha said, tucking the document into the water-proof packet he carried beneath his robe.

"If this man reaches Ludwig, Your Majesty, there will be war," said a low, rough voice. The shadows parted by the corner cabinet, and Elisha stiffened. One of the monks approached, bowing, trailing the chill shade of death, a woman's tortured presence that draped the shoulders of her killer.

Chapter 3

❖

Charles cocked his head, watching the monk. "There has been war, there will be war again, and I shall win it. Have you not seen as much, Brother Henry?"

"I have seen many things, my liege. I have seen that this man is a liar." Brother Henry gestured, his hand still hidden beneath the coarse brown cloth of his habit. "His queen, the queen of England, ask him what he did to her."

Elisha rose from the table, the tingling sense of his own talismans swelled against his skin as he drew upon them, letting his flesh go cold. "Your Majesty—"

But Charles put up his hand for silence, his fair face troubled. "Tell me what you have seen, Brother." He pressed his hands together as if at prayer.

"I have seen the flames of a witch's pyre. I have seen a woman bathed in blood and crying for mercy. I see this man take her in his arms to kill her—all of this have I seen, my liege." The hooded figure shuddered, shoulders drawn up. "God revealed this woman to me in glory, crowned and clad as a bride for her marriage. She lies now as if for her funeral and witchcraft keeps her so."

"The queen went mad, Your Majesty. It was her mother who died upon that stake." Elisha's breath misted just a little. Magical assault he was prepared for, but this game of visions was a new weapon and a deadly one if it fell upon credulous ears.

Charles's dark eyes flared. "And you, doctor? What did you do to her?"

"I induced her to sleep, Your Majesty." This was near enough the truth.

"You claimed to come here seeking a cure." Charles pushed himself up.

"A cure for her madness, Your Majesty. You have my oath I do not wish her dead." He could assail the mancer with magic, but fifteen innocents shared the room with himself and the mancer—including an archbishop and a queen. Even if they were not harmed, if he manifested any magic, they would seize him or die trying. He had imagined the mancers controlled their monarchs as they had tried with Prince Alaric—openly offering power at a terrible cost. Yet Charles seemed truly driven by his faith: he may not know he was the tool of evil. Could Elisha twist the mancer's vision to reveal the truth? "God has granted you clear sight, but He may not have revealed all. Tell me, Brother, what else have you seen?"

The shade stirred at the mancer's back as he drew upon his power.

Elisha's palms grew damp as he waited for the reply.

"I have seen you steal the crown—taking it with your false-scarred hands!" The monk revealed his own hands at last, knobbed with age as if he clutched at power in Elisha's stead.

"Then you have seen, too, that I returned it, Brother. Or I should hardly be standing here as the king's messenger."

"It seems that the gaps in your news are larger than the news itself," Charles observed. "You dared to wear the crown of England?"

"It was given to me by the Archbishop of Canterbury, the prelate of the realm. Thomas had been taken by magic, and my regency was the only way to hold the kingdom until we brought him home."

Charles's eyes narrowed, and Elisha realized his mistake: he used the king's name without his title.

"He claims to you, my liege, that he cannot negotiate for England, he who wore that crown, who is the dearest companion of that king. Such visions I have seen! He is not to be trusted." Brother Henry loomed in a wavering of brown wool and deathly shadow.

Archbishop Baldwin cleared his throat, rubbing his neck with one hand. "You say, Brother, that this doctor usurped the crown, and in the next breath, that he is a boon companion of the king. It seems to me, that at least he speaks the truth when he says that God has not shown you all."

A thrill of hope strengthened Elisha's stance as the monk's hood twitched in the direction of the archbishop. The air chilled between the two religious men. The monk should apologize to his superior, yet the archbishop's hands trembled.

Charles resumed his easy smile. "I trust him neither more nor less than any other foreigner, Brother, but his explanations match what you have seen." He fit the ideal of the Christian king: martial intensity, high spirits, and unshakeable faith. People would be proud to follow him—no matter the cause. If the mancers could shape that faith to their ends, the empire would be lost. Elisha imagined a new crusade, led by an idealistic emperor with the deepest faith, and backed by the darkest power. Could this be the mancer's true plan, not merely controlling the thrones of the nations, but shepherding a new age of violence?

"My liege, did you not feel that chill that passed the room when I challenged him?" The monk moved sideways, retreating from Elisha, lifting from the folds of his habit a wooden cross embellished with roundels. He stood now as if sheltering behind the throne of the queen. "The scars, my liege, those false stigmata upon his hands—he knows more of magic than he says!"

"Stigmata?" Charles took a few steps closer. "May we see them, doctor? Do they bleed?"

"Look to your wife, Your Majesty," Elisha said in a low voice. "This man is no true monk. Beware false prophets."

Baldwin made a soft sound of approval.

"Brother Henry has been in our retinue for years, doctor, and his visions have always proven true," Charles said. "But you have not answered me. Do you indeed bear the wounds of Christ?"

"They are the brands of punishment, my liege," said the false monk. "'tis true that King Hugh died, but it was this man who slew him—I have seen it! Praise the lord!"

The mancer damned him not with lies but with the truth. Charles caught Elisha's wrist in a firm grip, drawing up his arm, then running his fingers over Elisha's hand, his gaze flashing back up. "His skin is cold as snow!"

"Look to your wife, he said! His hatred for the French drives him to her, Your Majesty! Just as he ruined the fleets of your father, he shall ruin her." Brother Henry raised his cross, his other hand gripping the queen's shoulder as if to defend her from Elisha's ill-will. Blackness roiled in the glass at the cross's center as the mancer prepared to strike in a way that only Elisha could see.

"No! Let her go," Elisha cried, twisting against Charles's grasp.

The soldiers started forward as he struggled with their king. Save the queen from the mancer's assault and reveal himself for a witch, or let her be lost—and be damned for it. Taunted by a mancer whose face he could not even see.

"Guards!" the emperor shouted.

A door at the side banged open, more soldiers clattering overhead, two emerging through the door. Elisha sent a snap of cold down his wrist. The emperor cried out and released him, stumbling back. Elisha mounted the table and launched himself toward the monk even as the queen wailed in pain. He seized the cross and the monk's fingers wrapping it, staggering them both. The throne fell, the queen tumbling out across his feet, her body quaking.

Cold, pain, and terror from the tainted cross stabbed into Elisha's left hand. Drawing up the strength of his talismans, he sought the grain of the wood and the gleam of the glass. The cross shattered and the monk shouted as the shred of skin, bone and hair—the talisman hidden at its center—fell away.

With his right hand, Elisha touched the queen, turning cold to heat, fear to strength, pain to healing. His flesh tensed and his heart felt torn—the cold rush of death gathered at his left and forced to serve life, his every bone and muscle for a moment embodying the doctrine of opposites and he screamed.

The woman stared up at him, clear-eyed and peaceful. Above, the monk rocked away, tearing free his hand, crabbed with cold and stung with slivers. Pinpricks of heat marked Elisha's palm, flecks of blood and not all of them his own. When the cross shattered, Brother Henry had been cut.

Shouts and contradictory orders flew around them. The mancer's blood gave him contact as well. Elisha let go of the queen, shaking off the hand she stretched up toward him lest she be caught in the mancer's counterattack. Swords plunged toward him, and he let himself fall dodging beneath them, scrambling on hands and knees, snatching for the monk's habit.

A shock of horror broke the room with a howling blast of cold as if winter tore through a gap in the air. Brother Henry opened the Valley wide, and conjured at the same time—but what? "No!" shrieked the mancer-monk, silhouetted against a backdrop of gold and red, a dancing wave of spirits: the Valley of the Shadow, the pathway through evil that would carry him away. He projected its fear and horrors, his flecks of blood carrying the vision beyond him to anyone who had been spattered, letting them see, through his contact, the realm normally only visible to necromancers—and to Elisha. "Do not threaten me with Hell! The Lord is my Shepherd—" he shrieked in Latin as he stepped away into the rift. Just for a moment, Elisha glimpsed beneath the hood, and saw the mancer's smile. Then the rift snapped shut and he was gone.

Chapter 4

❖

"Seize the English before he curses the queen!" "Where's Brother Henry gone?" "—he maketh me to lie down in green pastures—"

Voices broke over Elisha's head, shouts of fear and prayers, and a quiet murmur of French from below. He pushed himself up, dodging the fallen queen and ran for the door. A sword sliced along his robe, snicking his shoulder, then he was past, stumbling up the stairs onto the round path edging the tower roof. The remaining guards sprang upon him, but he dropped again to hands and knees propelling himself along the wall, stripping off the robe that tangled his legs and regaining his feet while they fought off his discarded garment.

Breathless, Elisha ran the length of the brick wall. Already, two men from the other end swiveled toward him, one raising a crossbow. Elisha turned and leapt the battlement. For a terrible moment, he fell, wind streaking through his hair, then his feet hit the roof of the cloister below, and he slithered down the tile, spreading himself out, his fingers scraping and finally snagging in the gaps between the tiles, arresting his slide.

A crossbow bolt cracked into the roof between his outstretched arms. Elisha glanced down then up, finding the roof peak not far above. He kept low, fumbling his way upward, gaining the peak, hurrying along perpendicular to the battlement. Another bolt cracked the tile to one side and a third struck sidelong and fell away. Too quickly, the end of the rooftop cut off his escape in that direction. To the right, another roof joined it, edging the cloister and leading parallel to the archers. Not good. Ahead, a broad space of barren ground and the city wall, tantalizingly close, still too far to jump. Elisha dropped, letting himself slide feet first down toward the outside.

Two stories down. He sucked in a breath as he hit the air, pulled his feet up, and fell.

Hitting hard on his side, the breath knocked from his lungs, Elisha gasped a moment on the ground. His ribs throbbed—something broken there, but nothing serious. He could still run. Staggering up, he strove for attunement, desperate to understand his surroundings, at least to locate his remaining talismans. The vial of stained earth bobbed at his chest, a few relics brushed his chest and arms where he had stitched them in—even his trews and hose were stitched with hairs and cloth—every thread made significant. He drew on them now, encouraging his ribs to heal, at the same time, erasing himself, imagining his own absence.

Limping along in the shadow of the buildings, Elisha forced his breath to even out, his heartbeat to slow. He could not deflect the gaze of any who had seen him fall, nor could he erase his own shadow in the fullness of the sun—but lurking here, cloaking himself with the memories of death he carried, he came as close as a man could to invisibility.

A shade unfurled in the strange vision of his left eye, a soldier enacting his death, the last moments of his fear and pain captured by the earth where he had fallen. Elisha drew strength from this man's dying to sustain his need. The soldier wore a skirt of metal, like many of the shades he had first seen in England. Other shades rose up here and there, the now-familiar misty forms of those who had died.

Elisha kept moving, dodging shadow to shadow as men hurried past, crying out to one another, searching—but they looked for a man bent on escape, not one in hiding. There would be no escape now, not until darkness gave him the means to cross the ground to the outer wall.

He sighed in relief as he passed into the shadow of the church, and found the ground no longer barren but thick with graves. He found a tilted mausoleum backed by gravestones and flattened himself into the gap between them, sinking down, the slight chill presences of the dead crowding round him like children. The pain of his ribs ached but no longer stung despite the insistent pressure of his lungs as he caught his breath.

Elisha worked his fingers through his hair, finding the indented scars of the operation that saved his life not long ago. Oh, yes, the mancers had known he was coming, and they knew how to defeat him: because they did not care for life, but they knew he did. His compassion would be his undoing. In trying to save Queen Blanche, he revealed his magic before the rival emperor and the archbishop, and dedicated himself aloud to England, and to Ludwig. Anything he had said would now be suspect. Brother Henry was right—war between the emperors would follow, now that Charles's visionary had apparently been torn from the earth by a demonic agent of the excommunicate Ludwig. Archbishop Baldwin seemed suspicious of the monk, but given the mancer's disappearance, and with prayer on his lips, he made himself appear to be a martyr before the court while he continued to pursue the mancer plans elsewhere.

Elisha had made a bloody mess of the moment, but he could not think of anything he might have done differently. Back down from the mancer's accusations? But the mancer manipulated Elisha into apparently attacking the queen. Should he have let the queen be taken? What defense could he have made when the monk claimed Elisha responsible? The queen herself might give evidence, but she was a woman who did not even speak the language. He found two mancers so far, neither of them Bardolph, and lost them both after revealing himself. He had undertaken his mission with the arrogance of knowledge and power, and already he had lost so much.

A murmur of voices rose in the graveyard, and in the gaps between the stones, he saw men and women gath-

ering, moving among the stones in the direction of the
church. Bells began to toll nearby, calling the faithful to
Evensong. Elisha tipped his head back against the stone.
Sunlight spread low and golden across the land—not
long now until night should fall. His direct strategy had
worked in that he had found a mancer in Charles's retinue, but now that one was gone, without leading him to
any others. He must learn to be as subtle as they, to seek
them out without being seen.

How many people would attend the service, and
would the emperor's party be among them? How many
other mancers might lurk to fill Brother Henry's place?

Elisha slipped off his doublet and outer tunic. He
turned the doublet inside out, showing its plain lining
rather than the rich pattern, and pulled it back on, then
tore the hem of his tunic into a few strips, binding his
palms and wrapping his head with the rest of the garment, rubbing dirt into the scraps. In the dim light, he
might pass for a workman, someone injured and in need.
It reminded him of Thomas at the ball, dressed in rags,
and aching with loneliness. Where would his friend be
now? Arguing with the barons, exchanging firm letters
with King Philippe of France? With Duke Randall dead
and Elisha gone, Thomas must be lonely once again.
That thought did not bear dwelling on. For a few minutes, Elisha imagined the man he had made himself
become—injured, but not destitute, definitely local. Was
there anything that revealed his origins? He thought
not—not as long as he did not speak and display his ignorance or his accent. He projected all of these things,
withdrawing his own presence and re-creating himself
into somebody else.

When the bells stilled, Elisha rose and shuffled toward
the church with the rest. Soldiers would be seeking him
at the walls and gates, not in their very midst, though
Charles and his queen would be well-defended, just in
case. As he passed among the graves, Elisha breathed in
death and kept it close beneath his skin. His left eye
glimpsed the shades that lingered—not so strong as
those in the places where they died, but nevertheless

giving notice of their silent presence. Here and there,
some shone with the gleam of the worthy death, those
like Martin Draper, whose death quelled the fire in London, or the witch Biddy, whose sacrifice allowed Princess
Alfleda to escape. Others flickered with the bleak agony
of injury and disease. The more he lingered among the
dead, the clearer these glimpses became. He would never
know them through the dread power of magical knowledge that the mancers gained in killing, but his way was
enough.

Among the worshippers, Elisha passed into the church,
a clean new building lit with a breathtaking sweep of
glass. He extended his senses, and swept the crowd with
his gaze, his right eye obscured by the dip of the bandage
he had formed of his tunic, his left seeking the residue of
murder that marked the mancers.

Beyond the rood screen, rich male voices broke out in
chant, resonating through the church. From time to time,
he heard the rise and fall of the celebrant's Latin and
recognized the voice of the archbishop. Elisha circulated
along the perimeter of the church, as if he followed the
steps of Christ through each station. There, at the front,
Emperor Charles's hair caught a rainbow of glittering
light. His wife clung to his arm, both perhaps still reeling
from the earlier fright and grateful for the chance to
pray. To the right, behind them, a soldier's bowed head
bore the gloom of a killer. Further back, one of the nobles carried a second shady cloak of murder. Both had
been present in the chamber that day, neither had any
strong reaction. The soldier had a sharp mustache and a
long nose, the noble was thickset, bearded, with a scar
that tracked from his left eye to the hidden corner of his
mouth. Elisha kept searching. Standing with a group who
looked like merchants, a short woman's feet flickered
with shades. She was harder to make out, and Elisha
couldn't be certain he would know her again.

Closer by, a young man swept the crowd with his gaze,
an almost brazen stroke of awareness, as if he rifled the
pockets of the gathered citizens. Elisha gave a prayer of
thanks for the young man's lack of discipline. Two or

three shades hovered in the young man's presence, one of them sharply limned, edged with fresh pain. Another . . . Elisha frowned and focused. A shade flickered in and out, faint even when it was discernable, bound to the man's twitchy right hand.

Beyond the screen, amens echoed, and the shuffling of feet indicated the service was over. The crowd parted, allowing passage for Charles and his retinue, including the two mancers closest to him.

Keeping his eye on the young man down the aisle, Elisha moved slowly against the current, stopping to kneel at a side altar as the young man went by. Elisha caught the slightly iron tang of blood and turned carefully. A partial imprint of a boot remained where the young man had been standing, a mark made in blood. Crossing himself and moving his lips as if praying, Elisha moved to kneel again by the mark, touching his finger to the blood. Hot with life, flickering with pain. For an instant, he felt again that unbearable stretching, torn between life and death. The mancer's victim lived—but not for much longer. He was ripe for the harvest, and his reaper would be coming soon.

Elisha closed his fist around the blood and pain. Leave now and take his knowledge to warn Ludwig. Stay and find this tortured soul who might lead him to the mancers' lair. If he went to Heidelberg, he left the threat behind to fester and grow. He had not come here merely for warnings, but for war. He had a chance to strike while they believed that he was gone—he'd be a fool not to seize the advantage. But a man's life hung suspended, somewhere close, a life that now lay in his hands to save, or to discard for the mancers' pleasure.

Concentrating to remember his projection, Elisha limped back to the church door, crossed himself, and returned to the graveyard. Crimson stained the horizon and the sky above deepened to indigo as the last stragglers made their way home. He found a recent burial, thick with the miasma of death and mourning, and used it to cast his deflection, wrapping his own life with death, his presence with absence. Then he opened himself to the blood that marked his palm. Pain echoed in his hand, throbbed across his back and forehead, seeming to ebb with each slow beat of his heart. His lungs strained in terrible gasps, his arms aching. Elisha forced himself to breathe normally, to know what the other felt without taking it on himself.

The victim hung in near-darkness, a feeble light revealing huge round shadows, a dirt floor. Damp clung to his skin and the musty smell of old wood mingled with the sweetness of fresh grapes. A vintner's workshop—far enough from the city that no one could hear the screams. Elisha's jaw tightened, but he felt no other presence there, no mancers. Surely, he could save this one man without sacrificing his larger mission. He took a deep breath, drawing in the death around him, taking his time to forge the armor beneath his skin, to shape his weapons: the cold, the horror of the grave, the decay that time wrought on every little thing, the death that lay beneath every surface of life—waiting to claim its next victim.

Only a few times had Elisha opened the Valley. To travel through it required a familiarity with death, knowledge of the destination, and contact with that destination in some form. He was sensitive enough, and his affinity with death meant that he could open the Valley without a murder. He had seen the Archbishop of Canterbury open it with fierce majesty, and the mancer Morag open it with perverse pleasure. The monk today had torn it deliberately, revealing the sense of what lay within to awe his witnesses. Elisha worked now with the patient intensity of a surgical strike. He breathed in death, found the contact that joined the blood on his hand with that of the living victim, and pulled himself through. The night whispered open, the wails of the dead caught in a gasp, their maelstrom of hurt and horror suspended as Elisha stepped through into an accepting silence, as if he were one of them. He felt the echoes of other presences, the remnant emotions of death, including the soaring joy and strength of Martin's sacrifice. For a moment, he sensed something else, a lingering presence, hot where the others were cold, familiar, but out of his reach, then he was beyond the Valley—emerging into the flickering glow of a hooded lantern showing the blood-stained earth floor of a vintner's warehouse.

Elisha listened, breath caught, every sense extended. A single life lingered at his back, fading with each labored breath. Pain echoed from the ground and mice nibbled at shadowed beams, their teeth resonating through wood. The great rounds of barrels stood around him, but he heard nothing—no shout of dismay nor hurrying step. Swallowing hard, Elisha looked up and stifled his cry, his heart thundering.

Christ hung upon the cross above him in the darkness, blood marking his wrists and feet, and oozing from the rend in his side. Blood tracked down his face into his beard. His frail chest rose, hitched, and fell. His eyes opened slowly and welled with tears.

Chapter 5

◆

For a moment, Elisha stared at the crucified man, held by his gaze as if he truly faced the son of God. But the blood that soaked Elisha's knees was recent, each ragged breath grated with fresh agony. Elisha's own scars burned in sympathy, his back remembering the scourge, his hands trembling as if once more pierced and pinned. The cold pall of death hovered close, its time almost at hand.

Breaking the trance, Elisha pushed himself to his feet, his head on a level with the victim's chest. The cross stuck up at an angle, held between the roof beams and the dirt floor with a few stones piled at its base.

Stripping the false bandages from his hands and head, Elisha allowed his grasp of death to recede, letting his hands warm again, reviving the instincts and training of the healer. "Don't be frightened," he said. He wet his lips and repeated the words, this time in German. Stepping into the shadow of the cross, Elisha put up his hand, bracing the victim's chest.

The man gasped, his heart lurching, and Elisha sent what comfort he could, steadying the rhythms of the ravaged body. Crowned with a wreath of thorns, the victim's head dangled just above Elisha's face and blood dripped from his forehead onto Elisha's cheek. "I'll take care of you," Elisha said, through contact and aloud. "I'll do what I can for you, do you understand?"

The man took a breath, his cracked lips moving, his

voice audible only through the magic of contact. "You are. With them."

"No," Elisha said, and the man winced at the fury in his single word. He spoke more gently. "I am their enemy. By all that's holy, if I have the power, I will stop them."

A spasm passed the weary face. "They will. Return. For me."

"I won't leave you."

Again, their eyes met.

"You're going to fall, I can't help that," Elisha told him quietly, "but I will catch you."

Elisha took his stance carefully, preparing to receive the man's weight. Across the shivering skin, he sent the softest urge, conjuring the end of iron and touching every nail with its small and silent death. The nails rusted, bent as they withered and sifted away in a powder stained like blood. The man's hands dropped, his body sagging into Elisha's arms. The crown of thorns tangled in his hair scraped down Elisha's cheek and scored his throat as the man's head lolled. Elisha sank beneath the weight, bringing them both to kneel. As the man gulped for breath, the strain of his stretched limbs and cramped chest finally released, Elisha merely held him. On the wall by the cross hung a spear, a scourge, a few knives and skinning blades, a hammer.

When the man's heartbeat ceased to pulse between life and death but moved, ever so slightly, nearer life, Elisha lay him down, trembling, on the dirt. He knew the man's injuries: they were known to every Christian and displayed in every church in the world. The worst of his condition was the time he had hung upon the cross. He might have been there for days, but Elisha had no power over starvation, exhaustion or weakness.

He rose quickly and crossed to the nearest of the huge barrels and found a taster's cup, cracking the tap and filling a cup of wine to bring to the stranger's lips. "Just a little for now." After he had taken a few sips, Elisha splashed the rest over his wounds to clean them. He needed this man stable enough to travel, and soon. If he carried him, then he need not worry about the wrists and feet just yet.

Elisha placed his hands to frame the wound at the stranger's side. He sent his senses inward, finding the depth of the wound, the severed muscle and skin, carved by the Roman spear. He choked his cry as he showed the flesh how to heal, using his own unbroken body as the model. For a moment, he felt they shared the wound—the victim's pain halved, Elisha's side abruptly pierced with a shaft of pain, then he closed the muscle, his medical mind providing the knowledge that knit together vessels and nerves, and finally skin. Shaking with the effort, Elisha withdrew his hands, straightening his back and flexing his shoulders.

The man's dark eyes regarded Elisha, tracing his features, fluttering closed then open again with a start.

With careful hands, Elisha removed the crown of thorns and cast it aside. He felt the other's exhaustion, confusion, fear, and wonder twisting together. "We need to go. Do you live in Trier?"

The slightest nod.

"I can bring you there. It will be awful, but swift, faster than horses." He bent to gather the man into his arms, then his skin tingled, and the stranger whimpered as terror shot through them both: the stranger had felt that sensation before.

Wind howled at Elisha's back, and his left eye caught the flare of wild light as the Valley opened. Elisha's head jerked up. "No," he whispered.

"—careless of you—all ye saints and martyrs!" said a voice.

Elisha rose and spun about, keeping himself between the Valley of the Shadow and the man its travelers had come for.

"Christ on the Cross!" cried the young man, then snarled, "Not any more. Fuck! What're you doing with my Jew?" He tossed down a bundle of linen.

"Shut up." The older man rapped his companion's head with bent knuckles that Elisha recognized. Brother Henry still wore his habit, with the hood tossed back to reveal a wizened face and a nest of silver hair around his tonsure. He narrowed his eyes at Elisha. "So the Lord has given you into my hands. Praise God." He crossed himself with fierce accuracy, then slid his hand into the opposite sleeve.

Power streamed up from the floor, from every death known by this terrible place, drawn by the monk as he gripped a scrap of skin in his hand. He had the knowledge Elisha lacked to tap the resonance of his slaughterhouse.

"Take your Christ," Brother Henry told the younger mancer. "And I shall take the English."

The blood on Elisha's skin flared to agony, but he had not released his grip on death and his armor held, deflecting the worst of the pain. Behind him, the prostrate victim, assaulted by the flow of the mancer's magic, screamed and thrashed, his hand locking around Elisha's ankle. That contact linked his need with Elisha's power, and Elisha struck back at the young mancer, reflecting the pain and then some, the victim's urgent will steeling his own.

The mancer howled and the darkness of murder swelled to his command to force away the contact Elisha had forged.

With a leap toward the opposite wall, Brother Henry seized a long knife, stained with old blood. An ominous mist swirled over the blade as he thrust.

Elisha dodged the blow, but fell, his ankle twisting from the victim's grasp. The monk lunged after him and Elisha scrambled away. Sending his awareness into the floor, Elisha seized the spilled blood of the earth and tried to tumble it, but it was too mingled with other deaths—deaths the mancers knew and held. The blade plunged again toward his chest. He rolled and struck the barrel hard, the breath knocked from his lungs. Cold sprang through Elisha's back and legs, the icy strength of death pinning him to the floor as the mancer squeezed his off-hand weapon, the stripped skin from one of his victims.

The barrel's tap stuck out over Elisha's head as he

tried to break away. He turned his attention from earth
to wood and brought forth the rot inherent in the oak.
The barrel groaned then collapsed, a flood of wine sluic-
ing over Elisha's face and figure. Some of it turned instantly to ice, crystals clinging to his clothes as the rest
rushed onward and forced his attacker back.

To Elisha's left side, the victim retreated from the
fight at a painful crawl, edging toward the wall of weapons.

Elisha sent heat and snapped free of the icy mud,
scrambling to his feet. The blade swung down, slashing
across his shoulders with a hard edge forged in murder.
It shot through his flesh, so sharp and fast he had no time
to scream. The force of every death it carried—a pregnant woman, a child, a priest—carved into him.

Arching away from the blade, mouth open, Elisha
dropped to his knees. His heart seized, his breath
stopped. The howling darkness tore at him from within.

Once before, the Valley had opened for him of its own
accord. That time, Martin's presence lingered there, lighting his way, if he chose to take it. Now, there was no light,
no flickering imagined Hell. The Valley seared into being, not outside, but within, reaching into him with an
intimate knowledge, a personal assault like nothing he
had ever felt before as the mancer conjured Elisha's own
death.

A spear cut across his startled vision followed by the
grunt of impact. His spear thrust, his desperate strength
utterly spent, the mancer's victim collapsed at Elisha's
side. Brother Henry tumbled against Elisha's feet, his
body jerking, the baying glee of death leaping free.

Elisha called it to him. Power rushed through his feet
and pushed back the pain. The deaths, the tortures, they
were not his own. He rejected the Valley that beckoned
him, and sealed it with the death of the man who tried to
kill him. He took a deep, cold breath. When the presence
of Brother Henry's companion flared hot with reaching,
with his fear and his desire, Elisha put up his hand and
brushed away this new assault.

Not since the battle of Dunbury, when he took the

power of his nephew's head and severed himself from
the mortal world, had Elisha felt so clear and distant.
The young mancer cried and cursed, his voice felt like
the ripples of tiny fish. He wanted something that lay at
Elisha's side. He would not have it. When the mancer
took his curving blade and grabbed the victim's leg, Elisha reached out a steady hand.

The young mancer pushed away, waving the bone of
some dead man as if to fend him off. At Elisha's touch, it
shattered.

The mancer's presence stilled as he conjured the Valley. It tore open, an echo of it answering from Elisha's
heart. Through Brother Henry's still form, Elisha
reached out and pulled it shut.

Spinning, eyes wide, the mancer gave a piteous squeak.

Elisha rose and seized his throat. With a sigh, he
breathed in the mancer's death.

Chapter 6

---❖---

Elisha let the body fall, his hand shaking. The wine-scented air filled his lungs again, his lips sweet with the earlier flood from the barrel. Attunement returned slowly, the flickering candle, the rasping breath of the only man who still lived. Elisha blinked, rubbing his face. No, surely he himself should be counted in that number. He could no longer be certain. The experience of the Valley opening within had both shaken him and filled him with a tremendous strength, but he did not know what it meant—save that he had taken a few steps nearer to that awful ecstasy of the necromancers.

He dropped down by the victim's tumbled form and touched his throat to look for life. Yes—there—stronger than when he had arrived. Thank God.

Gathering the man against his chest, Elisha stood unsteadily. He took a moment to knock down the lantern, setting free its little flame to flare up the old timbers of the workshop and dance madly across the surface of the wine. The blood he bore had washed away, but he no longer needed it—the man he carried gave him contact back to the church. He used the last of his magical strength to steel them both against the passage before he reached out through life and opened the Valley.

They stepped through into darkness, the victim stirring in his arms. Before he let go of the passage, Elisha borrowed a little of its bleak power. He felt the stinging

wounds that cut the man's feet and wrists and made
them whole.

Elisha staggered as they entered the church proper;
the vast space felt cold in a perfectly ordinary way. He let
the man's feet down to the ground, taking his weight
upon his shoulder. The patient roused at the touch of the
marble floor. "Where?" the man gasped.

"The church. The south transept. Can you walk?" He
braced the man's arm over his shoulders, his own arm
lying across the welts of the mancer's abuse.

"Barely."

Together, they shuffled down the aisle, a few candles
at the side altars lending their glow. Elisha leaned him
against the wall long enough to unbar the door and drag
it open. His muscles protested when he resumed his
place at the victim's side, as if bearing his own weight
were more than enough. The wound across his back,
healed though it was, still ached, the scrapes on his face
and neck stung when they stepped out into the night air.

"Where do you live?"

"You can't come there." The man's touch tingled with
his alarm. "I am a Jew."

"You are my patient, at least a little longer, just direct
me."

"Across the square and down a little." His raspy voice
gave out, and Elisha started walking, slowly, as his patient breathed.

At last they stopped before a door, and Elisha reached
out to knock, the sound echoing in the narrow street. He
knocked again, harder, and heard a muffled voice within,
then the sound of footsteps approaching. With a scraping
of metal, a little door opened at eye level, a light coming
close so the occupant could peer out, a girl who squinted
and tipped her head. "There are no loans now, sir. You
must come back another time."

"I need to see the master," Elisha said, and the girl
drew back, then slid shut the peephole and her footsteps
hurried away.

After a moment, the opening slid again, a brown eye

peered through, darkly ringed and red with lack of sleep, framed by a bushy eyebrow. "I am not giving loans just now, good sir. Do forgive me."

"I don't—" Elisha began, but the man at his side pressed his hand against the wood, leaning in.

"Father," he moaned.

The eyebrow rose, then the eye flooded with tears. A bar scraped and the door jerked open so quickly they nearly fell in. The man inside let loose a stream of joyous babble in a language that sounded like German, but wasn't. He pulled his son inside, touching his face with a trembling hand, shocked at the blood. "Elsa!" he bellowed. The servant girl started to turn toward the stairs, but steps already creaked from the next floor. "What is it, Jacob?" called a voice from above.

The victim swayed and Elisha caught his shoulder, urging him forward, toward a little bench in the hall where he sank down, his hands clasped in his father's, trying to answer, shaking his head.

Elisha caught the servant's eye. "Some water." He pointed to the victim, and she nodded, returning quickly with a pitcher and a glass nearly as fine as those on the emperor's table. She poured with shaking hands, then set down the pitcher, and held out the glass, smiling. "Don't let him drink too much," Elisha warned. "He'll be weak for a while yet, and his stomach may not handle it well."

An older woman appeared at the end of the hall, her hair covered, clad in a dressing gown of velvet which she clutched together with both hands. This small decorum fled her, tears streaming down her face, as she ran toward them.

Suddenly outside this family scene—in more ways than one—Elisha backed away. He leaned a moment on the doorframe. Weariness gripped him, but he knew of no safe place to sleep. Taking hold of the door, Elisha turned to go.

"Sir!" A tremulous hand touched his and withdrew, the old man smiling at him. "We cannot thank you enough. Nine days he has been gone. Nine! We never thought to see our Simeon again."

Elisha hesitated, wondering how to frame what had happened to Simeon. "Your son suffered greatly. He will be a long time recovering from this."

"But he tells me you have healed him." The old man regarded Elisha gravely.

"I am a doctor," Elisha told him, as if this were any decent answer. Across the street, a voice called out, and Elisha stiffened. In this city, he was a wanted man—both by the emperor and by the mancers. "I have to go."

The man's face sagged. "Of course, sir. It is a Jewish place. You have humbled yourself—"

"That's not why," Elisha said. "I'm a danger to you." He winced, the scrapes on his cheek burning. "Men are looking for me—I have to go."

The Jew studied Elisha's face as if in doubt, and Elisha supplied, "The emperor's men."

At that, the man reached out and took his arm, drawing him firmly inside and shutting the door behind him. "If the emperor's men are looking, sir, they will never search for you in Jacob's house." He touched his breast.

Elisha smiled faintly. Very likely, the man was right. Few Christians would take hospitality from Jews. Fewer Jews would offer it.

Simeon's mother draped her son's shoulders with her own robe, directing the servant to light a fire at the hearth and bring clothing, then she straightened, fists on hips. "He says," she swallowed, glancing down at where her son's feet stuck out from beneath the robe, a single ugly scar marking each. "He says they have done to him as some say we have done to your Christ."

"These men, the ones who took him, they don't care about God. Maybe they took him because he's a Jew—I don't know—but that's not what they want."

"What do they want?" She shot back at him, her voice strained by the years of suspicion that lay between their peoples.

"This," he said, gesturing from himself to her. "They want to create fear, they want hate, anything that gives them power. And they will do anything to get it." A wave of weakness passed through him, and he leaned against the wall, head tipped up.

"You do not know how it is for us," the woman replied stiffly. "You don't know how badly we are treated."

"No, I don't," Elisha answered, "but you were not treated so by me."

"These men," Simeon whispered, drawing their eyes back to him. "Whatever they were, they were not Christian."

Elisha came to kneel before him, touching his knee lightly. "Can you tell me what happened?"

Simeon took a few breaths. "It was late. I was on my way from the cranes. . . he came"—a slight shake of the head—"from nothing." He spread his fingers as if trying to encompass the emptiness. "He had a knife—not . . . not just a knife."

"A cursed blade," Elisha said, for such a knife had slashed open his back. Simeon's parents frowned at this, but their son gave a nod.

"He grabbed me. I offered my purse. But he," Simeon drew a shaky breath, "took me. Through pain, shrieking." His hand lifted toward his ear, his head bent, and Elisha felt the tremor of fear. Beneath his own tunic, clammy with wine, he carried a scrap of cloth Martin had given him—his first talisman—and conjured from it comfort, friendship, safety. Simeon relaxed a little. "He took me where you found me. He was not the only one."

While he took another sip of water, Elisha asked, "How many did you see? Would you know them again?"

"Six. They let me see their faces. That's how I knew I would die."

His mother, Elsa, sobbed and came to his side, clutching his shoulder.

"Six," Elisha echoed. "I've seen five, but two of those are dead."

"You killed them?" The father asked.

"One—Simeon killed the other. Without his courage, neither of us would be here."

Simeon breathed, "You gave me courage, when you

came." He rested his head on his mother's arm. "Thank you."

Sitting back on his heels, Elisha withdrew his touch. "You should sleep, take some broth if you can. Give it a day before you try solid food."

Elsa spoke again in that unfamiliar tongue, and, between herself and the servant, they brought Simeon toward the back of the house.

"Sir, take some comfort." Simeon's father, Jacob, led Elisha to the adjoining chamber where a fire warmed the room. "We have brought some clothes that may suit you."

"I'll need parchment and ink, if you have it."

"Of course," Jacob replied, but he arched an eyebrow at Elisha and waited.

With a sigh, uncertain how his plan would be received, Elisha said, "I need to warn the archbishop. He seems a worthy man—he was already suspicious of one of the men involved, and he's made them angry."

"You are the Englishman who came seeking the wrong emperor. There was talk of it at synagogue." He nodded as if this explained everything. "The archbishop is as close as my people have to an advocate before the emperor. And you? You are not merely a doctor. Not merely an Englishman." He crossed to a tall cabinet and found what Elisha needed, along with a tablet to write on, and offered the tools.

"I warned you it's dangerous to have me here. If you wish, I will go." Although, as the fire warmed him and the soft cushions of the couch enticed him, he wished his conscience clear to stay.

"I owe you the life of my son," Jacob told him. "Now sit."

Elisha sank gratefully onto a chair and took the writing things.

"I'll wake the cook to bring you food." Jacob's brow furrowed. "You look concerned."

Concerned? Elisha felt like weeping. He stared hopelessly down at the parchment. "I can write no German, and my Latin is weak."

Jacob slipped the tablet away again and tucked it under his arm. "Rest. Take some dry clothes. This will wait a little longer." He bowed his head, then left the room, shutting the door behind him.

After a moment, Elisha roused himself to strip off his wet things and lay them out by the hearth, plucking free a few of his talismans to tuck into the borrowed clothes. He had been without a talisman before—it was not a lesson any magus should need to learn more than once. The vial of earth from his brother's workshop still dangled at his chest and Thomas's ring remained on his hand. He sorted a fresh pair of hose, trews, tunic, and a short robe from the pile of fine woolens, dressing with numb fingers. Finding the oilcloth packet of Thomas's letters, Elisha stuffed in a few of his talismans and slipped it under his waist tie, beneath his tunic before he sank back into the pillows. He let his awareness spread to the door, a light touch like whiskers, ready to stir if anyone approached. The outer door opened and shut softly; Jacob and his servants moved in the hall. Beyond the far wall, Elsa fussed over Simeon, whose pain subsided with every moment he was home. Elisha let himself be comforted, and let his eyes slide shut.

When they opened, the archbishop himself was staring back.

Chapter 7

❖

Elisha stifled his cry and pushed himself up in his chair. How had the man come so close before he noticed? But the cross that dangled from Baldwin's chain might explain it, the relic within it serving a similar function as a talisman for a devout Christian. Once Elisha came alert, the archbishop's presence loomed with authority and curiosity. "Your Grace," Elisha managed.

At the archbishop's shoulder, Jacob patted the air, indicating that Elisha could relax. "I have told you he is our advocate. He has tried to locate Simeon these past days. I sent a servant to bring him the news."

"And to say that there was a tale I must hear," the archbishop added. "No need to be coy, Jacob."

"I am not coy, but contrite. This man saved my son's life, and now I have risked his by contacting you. If he is in danger because you are here, Your Grace, then I must make amends."

"For the sake of our trust, Jacob, I will give him an hour. And then, of duty to my nephew, I must act."

His nephew, Charles. Elisha's heart fell, and he doubted anything he said would sway the archbishop's intent.

"Eat, drink. Talk quickly," Jacob urged, indicating a tray at Elisha's side.

After a few swallows of wine that warmed his throat and made his tongue tingle, Elisha said, "Your nephew is under the influence of evil sorcerers who are helping him to take the empire, but not for the good of its people."

"I see." Baldwin settled on a chair, his silk gown crinkling as he folded his hands, the large ring on his hand winking. "King Philippe has said that sorcerers are attempting to kill himself and his family—is this related?"

Elisha chewed a piece of flatbread as he considered this. "King Philippe is killing innocent people who might have helped him against this evil. I must believe that the threat to France comes from those who claim to be on his side. In England, a group of them has already tried to seize the throne, at the cost of thousands of lives."

"And *you* stopped them." Archbishop Baldwin stared at him without expression.

"With the aid of the king and some others." Taking another sip, Elisha darted a glance at Jacob who stood to one side, hands at his back, listening.

"So it is lucky we have you to defend us."

Elisha nearly snorted his wine and slapped the glass back down. "It was luck that I was able to stop them in England—England is a small nation, an island I know well, and they did not expect my opposition. At least one mancer escaped from there to here, and another to France, Your Grace. Already, their tactics have changed. They know what I can do, and they know—" *How to hurt me*, he almost said, but held his tongue. The tone of this conversation was already dangerous enough.

"What can you do . . . Doctor?" The archbishop steepled his fingers. "Earlier today, I watched you send a man to Hell with a touch."

"No—you watched him stage a show for your benefit, and that of the emperor. You saw exactly what he wanted you to see. He was one of them, these sorcerers." Elisha knotted his fingers through his hair.

"Mancer? Is that the word? I do not know that word."

"Necromancers," Elisha spat. "Your Grace, ask Simeon when he recovers. Ask him what he saw and heard."

"Apparently, these men who took Simeon intended to make him, a Jew, suffer the wounds of our Lord." Archbishop Baldwin crossed himself. "This is terrible, of course, but not so far from the realm of possible crimes. Maintaining peace between our communities is not easy."

Jacob stirred, but did not speak.

"I do not see why your necromancers, if you will use this word, why they would do such a thing, if not from the hatred of their hearts. They are wicked sinners, to be sure, and we shall try to bring them to justice—" Jacob made a sound of frustration, but the archbishop ignored him and continued, "But they are not acting against our people, or even against our rightful emperor. You say one of them was in England. Then he is barely returned himself. How long was your own voyage, to come so far?" The archbishop smiled briefly, but the smile did not touch his eyes. "Jacob is a modest man, but his family is quite wealthy. Some of this money is raised through usury—forgive me, Jacob—and that angers many Christians, especially those who might have difficulty with their financial responsibilities. When we seek to assign blame for this dreadful matter, there is no need to cross boundaries of sea and spirit."

Snatching a slice of chicken from the tray, Elisha took a savage bite.

"I do not take you for a devout man, my good doctor. However, you yourself display such wounds, and have yet to explain them."

"A necromancer nailed me to the ground to kill me later," Elisha said. Already, the archbishop meant to capture him. He had no evidence of what he said—even the slaughterhouse he had burned to prevent the mancers' making use of it. He took another bite, more slowly. The archbishop had a point, at least in one respect: the mancers nailed a man to the cross—why? Not merely to craft new talismans for themselves—any terrible death could give them the horror they sought. At least, such power could be harnessed to the killer. But if he were right about what he had overheard in England, the power could be linked to any other mancer who shared in the crime.

Why torture a man that way? To forge relics, false holy items they could twist to their own ends. Emperor Charles collected relics, traveled with them, was devoted to the bones and bits of saints—or were they saints at all? He thought of Brother Gilles' crate of death: an arsenal to the mancers who created it. But then why let these things out of their own hands? Wouldn't they want to keep their talismans handy, the way the mancers of England had a stockpile of gruesome trophies to summon up their power?

Yes, the Archbishop was right: it had taken Elisha weeks to travel to Trier, but only because he possessed neither knowledge nor contact. He did not know any place here so well that he could open the Valley to travel to it, nor did he have the kind of strong contact required to do so—a contact made by following the presence of the dead. *They came from nothing*, Simeon had said. Elisha's throat went dry, and he dropped the meat, shrinking into his chair.

"What is it, doctor?" Jacob asked softly, but Elisha shook his head.

Kill a man—torture him first, create for him a death so terrible that the Valley of the Shadow howled its victory. Invite friends to share in the power of that death— all the mancers who could come, as they came when the Archbishop of Canterbury slew Rosalynn, as they came to share in Brigit's attempt to kill the nobility of England. She had conjured her mother's death in the memory of all those who had been present and made contact through a field sown with blood, building up to a final slaying that would kill every *desolati* in her audience. As the mancers would have come when Thomas was slain, his skin ripped from his body. Why? So they could spread talismans of those deaths and open the Valley anywhere the talismans might be, concealed in the open as the relics of saints. They might carry the relics themselves to specific churches, or simply allow believers like Gilles to extend their web. They could seed the world with sorrow, with the knowledge of those murders and contact forged in anguish. They came from nothing, with cursed knives, Simeon had said, and if they spread their talismans far enough, the Valley would take them wherever they pleased, emerging from churches, altars, crosses, to wreak what havoc they would. Elisha sought to find the mancers, but he sought in vain. If he were right, they could be anywhere in an instant, wielding a power that he alone recognized.

"Holy Mary, mother of God," Elisha whispered. Then he looked up, meeting Baldwin's curious stare. "They're manufacturing talismans, relics they can use to travel anywhere, to hurt people, as they have hurt Simeon."

"Manufactured relics?" The archbishop snorted. "Relics cannot be so easily distributed as that—they must come with certificates and miracles. Bones of the saints cannot be translated to another place unless the saint's will is to go." He spread his hands. "Relics are not merely beads in a market, doctor."

Beads in a market—no, flesh on a butcher's hook. "They would have made of Simeon another martyr, Your Grace, and spread his remains everywhere they wanted to go. The relics would act as a doorway to them, to use their magic wherever they will."

"Have you any proof of your claims? I have seen no evidence of magic aside from your own deeds, and I must weigh the rescue of Simeon against the expulsion of Brother Henry." The archbishop rose. "You speak nonsense and blasphemy."

Even this worthy man would not believe him. He had seen evidence aplenty, but only another witch would understand it. Elisha squeezed his eyes shut. The crown of thorns they forced Simeon to wear had torn Elisha's cheek and it burned like fire. He felt certain he had uncovered a part of the mancers' plan, but the archbishop was right—it still took time, patience, and even paperwork to insinuate relics across the nation. There must be more to the mancers' plot than simply forging a network for travel, though God knew that alone could be terrible.

"Forgive me, Your Grace, but you must go," Jacob said firmly.

With a rustle of silk, Archbishop Baldwin moved toward the door. "I fear I must tell you that I have already placed soldiers around this house, along the streets."

"You promised us an hour! This is a good man, Your Grace. The best of men—"

"Your son's return is certainly a good thing. However, I have witnessed strange events this day, and I will have them explained. Charles is threatened, and our peace along with him. I have made oaths to God, to the Holy Father, and to the emperor. A man who speaks as wildly of heresy as this one cannot simply be allowed to rest."

Their words washed over Elisha without touching his despair. He, too, had made an oath, sworn upon the flesh of a crucified man, that he would stop the mancers. Had he meant it only for the night? Only for that one man? And when the Valley of the Shadow opened in churches, for children, for *desolati* innocents, for Thomas and his daughter?

"I have taken advantage of your welcome, Jacob," the archbishop said, "and for that, you must forgive me. I pray you shall not allow it to stand between us. We are the men who keep this city at peace—let us not forget that, even in the face of these difficult events."

The silence weighed down, pressing at the scars in his skull.

"Yes, Your Grace. As ever, you speak wisdom." Jacob shifted his stance. "But I will ask you, for my sake, to keep this promise. Your men wait outside, they wait at my every door and window. Let me have the minutes that remain."

Minutes. If they had not washed the floor in the church, Elisha could go to Simeon and make contact. He could drag himself back through the Valley at least as far away as the church—and then what? He might have allies at Heidelberg—and he wasn't even sure how to escape Trier.

"Very well, Jacob. Such as they are, they are my gift to you." Silk rustled as the archbishop walked to the door, then the outside door swung open and shut, and Archbishop Baldwin murmured to someone outside, but moved no further.

"Come!" Jacob whispered fiercely, tugging Elisha to his feet.

Elisha shook his head dumbly. "Where is there to go?"

"Just come, and quietly." He pulled his arm through

Elisha's, their heads close together. "You'll emerge two blocks away. It's not far—not nearly far enough. Go with speed to the southeast corner of the city, to the ancient gate there. It's not a gate, it was something else—it doesn't matter. There are three curves to the front of the building—" As he spoke, he pulled Elisha along the hall, turning quickly to a narrow stair that led downward into a vaulted room full of casks and crates with herbs and baskets hung from the ceiling. They ducked beneath them, Jacob now propelling Elisha from behind, his hands lightly at Elisha's shoulders.

"—go to the one at the center, and there is a grate. It's iron, it's loose. Go through it. Don't take the first turning to the left, take the second one. It leads outside the walls." Jacob came forward, felt around in the dim light, and tugged on a peg in one of the beams. The section with the beam groaned open. Jacob retrieved the lantern by the stair and held it up to reveal a small stone chamber with steps leading down into a pool of water. In the lantern's light, Jacob's face looked craggy, his thick eyebrows shielding too much. "Don't touch the water. Please. It's been purified."

"I understand," Elisha murmured. Few could be as impure as he. His reflection in the pool rippled with shadows.

Jacob gripped his shoulder briefly. "No, I don't believe you do. But there is no time." Handing the lantern to Elisha he pulled a few pages from his sleeve. "A map. It's not good, not detailed, but it should get you to Heidelberg." He opened it and indicated Trier, then moved his hand slowly to Heidelberg to be sure Elisha knew the name.

"And this . . ." Jacob stared down at the folded note, tapped it on his hand, then held it out as well. "If you should again need help from a Jew, show him this. It might help."

Elisha accepted the documents, still bewildered. "Jacob . . . thank you."

"For what you have done tonight, there are no words. If my talking to the archbishop has brought more trouble for you, then I am deeply sorry."

"Won't this bring trouble for *you*?"

Jacob shrugged. "I will be upstairs when he returns. I will tell him you have vanished. He saw that happen to the monk earlier; he will be angry but not surprised." He pointed across the water. "You can walk along this edge, carefully. And that door leads to a tunnel beneath several houses. Go quietly." He searched Elisha's face, nodded once, then stepped back through the concealed door and closed it softly between them.

Elisha took a moment to look at the map, tucked both pages into his water-safe packet and edged his way around the pool. It was just large enough for a person to lie down, and steps led into it. The tunnel beyond was narrow and low; he walked in a stoop, finding two more doors into the passage before reaching one at the end. It emerged into a culvert with bushes edging a field behind some houses. The half-moon lent enough glow to the scene, and Elisha blew out the lantern, leaving it inside the passage. He spread his senses and cast a deflection that blossomed from his talismans. He took a moment to re-orient himself and started walking toward the southeast. After a time, he heard faint shouting behind him, orders to search again, most likely, and he prayed that Jacob's relationship with the archbishop would protect the Jew and his family.

The vast bulk of the gate rose up at last, with the rounded lobes that Jacob described, their tall arches open to the night beyond. It took some fumbling to find the iron grate, and when he did, he missed a step and slithered inside, recovering his balance. Then he reached up to pull the grate closed behind him. He stepped away into darkness, attuning himself as he walked into the dank tunnel, feeling the space that opened at the branchings, then finding the one to lead him out. The bricks closed in to either side, and, just as he feared Jacob had sent him astray, he reached a tumble of rubble with a gap at the top and clambered out to freedom.

Chapter 8

A few days found Elisha riding swiftly toward Heidel-berg on one of Charles's messenger's best horses. It had been a simple matter to rouse a stable boy and impress him with the imperial seal on a document nei-ther of them could read. He rode cloaked in death, bor-rowing strength from every shade that rose up in his vision, as he had when he crossed England after saving Thomas and realizing Alfleda was still alive, and in dan-ger. The shades here were not so thick as at home, per-haps because the hills and dense forest did not lend themselves to battles, but they were enough to hide him and to let him breathe in his power, staying alert. He slept only when he could find a grave to lie upon, to con-ceal him from notice, and every time, it troubled him to rest upon the dead.

Elisha dreamed of mancers: his hands impaled by a dagger as Morag prepared to flay his king, Elisha rising from his grave to find himself rooted by the dread power of Chanterelle's death, the Archbishop of Canterbury wearing Rosalynn's bloody skin, the stone table set with chains where Elisha claimed the right to kill Thomas in a ruse to set him free. Himself, hand laid upon the brow of King Hugh, withering him to dust. He dreamed of mancers emerging from the Valley into peaceful churches, seizing *desolati* who had no magic to defend them, torturing and killing, using their remains to seed a new destination where they could strike again, faster than anyone's power to strike back. His own horse—fast though she was—could never outrace them. He woke again, gasping, feeling the spike through his hands, tasting the earth of his own grave, mingled with the ashes of his friends. Sometimes, he pressed a lock of Thomas's hair between his palms and took comfort from its warmth. Sometimes, in the depths of a strange forest, that was not enough.

When he reached Heidelberg and left his horse outside, he passed over bridges and through gates, among the tradesmen and other visitors, and took the long trudge up toward a vast castle of red stone. Guards examined his papers at the gate, then summoned a man in a tabard bearing the emperor's arms—a steward of some sort—who examined Elisha, his hawkish features focused and unfriendly, especially as he noted Elisha's mismatched eyes. "You are the personal physician to King Thomas of England?"

"Aye, sir." Like the guards at the gate, this man's presence echoed with fragments of shades—not the thick darkness of a mancer, but rather the association with death that any fighting man might have. Elisha blinked them away.

"And you are carrying a letter from this king to his Majesty Ludwig, the emperor of the Romans? Fine. Give it to me, and you may go."

"Sir, I am commanded to give it to the emperor and no other." The hawkish man circled him, and Elisha resisted the urge to turn about in order to match his gaze.

"Well. I shall inform his Majesty that such a communication has been noted. You may go."

Elisha's fists clenched, and he eased them loose again. "I have come a very long way for this meeting, sir. Is there—"

"No. There is not. If you wish, you may take lodgings in town and inform us of your whereabouts. It may be that his Majesty's orders shall change." The man pivoted on one heel to go.

"Wait a minute—his orders?"

The steward walked away, allowing the guards to gesture Elisha back the way he had come.

"Wait! For the love of God," Elisha shouted after him, following a few steps until two pikes swung down with a clang to bar his way. "This is none of my doing—whatever the problem. At least give me something to tell the king."

The steward straightened his narrow shoulders, his feet coming together with a click. He twisted his neck, giving Elisha the benefit of his hard profile. "For two years, there has been no word from England. Not since the deaths of the princesses. His Majesty has no wish to acknowledge a king so lofty that he does not stoop to answer the pleas of a grieving father. Now. You may go!" His head snapped forward again and he stalked on.

Not since their deaths? It was unlike Thomas to ignore another man's pain, even in the depths of his own. Deaths! Elisha caught hold of the pikes, pinning them together to lean past. "Alfleda's not dead!" Elisha cried after the retreating steward. "She's alive."

The man stopped in mid-step and swung about, eyes wide. "Alfleda? The little princess?" He waved his hands to clear the guards from Elisha's path and came back to meet him, hands outstretched. "She is alive." He clapped his hands to his face. "Praise the Lord, and what shall I do?" Then light broke over his face, and he nearly laughed. "Come with me and tell me as we walk."

They moved into the open yard of the castle, hurrying toward the keep up a slope of red cobbles.

"The bandits who attacked Thomas's hunting lodge were hired men, starting a plot to disinherit him in favor of Alaric. Princess Anna fought them as best she could, although she lost her battle, but they took Alfleda away with them and brought her to a convent to be hidden."

"Villains!" spat the steward, then waved his hand, already walking so quickly Elisha half-ran to keep up with him. "What else?"

"I found evidence that she had not been killed, and was able to track her to the convent. The—villains— tried to stop me taking her, but we escaped with the help of some of the nuns, and I returned her to her father in London." For a moment, the memory of Thomas's joy, the glow of his brilliant blue eyes and the heat of his gratitude flooded Elisha's heart. "I assure you, sir, he would not have denied your master any news to ease his grief. It was the traitor Alaric who stood in the way, I'm sure of it."

"Hmm." The steward trotted upstairs, and Elisha followed breathlessly. "Wait here a moment—I'll see what can be done."

Elisha nodded, catching his breath enough to say, "Thank you," then the steward hurried away, leaving Elisha in a chamber furnished with a few couches and tables, and a hearth tended by a slight young woman who watched him sidelong.

After a while, Elisha sat, choosing a plain bench. He longed for a drink or a meal, his stomach growling as he recalled the regal welcome extended to him by the rival emperor. At last, voices approached down the corridor and Elisha rose stiffly, his days of riding and nights of visions settling into his bones as he waited. A pair of pages scurried in, holding wide the doors for the party that followed: the steward, a black-robed monk, and a few soldiers.

At the back of this procession came an older man with a woman's hand draped upon his arm, his eyes already narrowed, her gown filling out with her pregnant belly. She walked as one careful and heavy with child, her face weary but only a few years older than Elisha himself. Clearly, she was not also the mother of Anna, Thomas's first wife. She watched him impassively as they approached, then lowered herself onto the bench he had just vacated as Elisha knelt to the emperor.

His face hard-lined, his curly hair tangling over his shoulders, the emperor stared down at him. "My man Harald tells me you claim that my granddaughter is alive. Tell me again." He spoke German, but with a thick, unusual accent so that Elisha gave thanks for the depth of his attunement that allowed him to follow the sense of what was said.

Remaining on his knees, watching the emperor's face, Elisha repeated the story he had told the steward, but Ludwig's frown only deepened. "What you say makes no sense," the emperor growled. "William! Come, listen to this man and say if you find him to be a liar."

The monk emerged from the emperor's shadow, his tonsure flecked with age spots, his eyes troubled. "So you are my countryman who brings so much difficulty," the old monk sighed, in English.

Elisha took a moment to master his frustration, his relief at hearing his native tongue extinguished by the cold words it spoke. His extended senses noted the animosity of the whole gathering, the serving woman alone feeling kindly toward him, though she stood with a pitcher of water and did not approach. At least none of them had the sinister presence of mancers. "Brother, if this is true, I do not mean it so. My king sends me here with tidings and warnings both, and I do not understand why this court treats me with disdain."

"The reasons, sir, are several. Most recently, that you stopped first to visit with the upstart who claims the imperial crown. Prior to that, your king failed to answer the letters of the emperor, to whom he owes a filial duty, if not one of honor. For the emperor himself, he worries over the tidings from England already—without your person here to intrude upon his own problems."

"I went to Trier because I was told that the emperor was in residence—the upstart flies the emperor's banner in expectation of his arrival, and probably to draw in travelers like me." The upstart, on the other hand, was charming, interested, immediately seeking advantage for both parties. Pity he allied himself with necromancers. If Elisha had the chance to separate him from his bad advisors . . . Elisha swallowed his unruly thoughts. He found no mancers here, though he expected they would be on the watch for him in Heidelberg. For Thomas's sake, he tried to view Emperor Ludwig with patience, as a man first grieving, then ignored; a man beset as Brother William had said, with his own problems. "I have letters from King Thomas to the emperor."

William gave a thoughtful nod, then turned to the emperor and repeated all of this, almost in Elisha's own words but in German. He concluded, "It is possible that the man is lying. Perhaps you shall know more by the king's letters."

"Harald, get our letters," the emperor said, gesturing to the steward, who approached. Elisha brought out his packet, sorting through the parchments for the king's documents, and handed them over.

Raising the larger parchment to capture the light of the tall window, the steward examined its wax seal and ribbons. "It appears genuine."

"Very well. We shall read it after dinner." The emperor stared down at Elisha. "There are several hostels in town if you wish to linger. I shall find you if I require you further." He swallowed, his eyes shifting toward his wife and back, an edge of worry underlying his hard words. "If not, that is the message you may bring to your master." He put out his arm for her, and the woman heaved herself back up to seize it as she groaned her weariness.

"Your Majesty." Elisha pushed himself up to one knee. "I have information about some of your rival's allies. Information you must have in order to fight them."

"What do you know of battle?" the emperor asked. "You are a doctor, are you not? My rival's most important ally is the pope himself—Charles is not called the cleric's king for no reason, Doctor. Do you know how to defeat the Holy Father?"

A few people in the chamber flinched at this, their hands twitching as if they would cross themselves but feared their master's wrath at any expression of their faith. No wonder the man was excommunicate.

"We kings, we emperors, we rulers of men—we pretend to hold the power, when it is the priest at Avignon who holds the ear of God and the hearts of every nation. Bring me an army who can conquer that, Doctor, and I shall shower you with honors. I thought once I could defeat the power of the Church. Now I merely hope to bargain for my share of my own sovereignty. I should like to

ride to Rome in the Jubilee and be welcome there as one
day I hope to be welcome in Heaven."

The woman beside him gripped his arm and gave a
little smile. "You shall, my dear," she murmured, and the
emperor's face softened just a bit. "And your granddaughter lives. Surely this is a blessing."

"I will read the letters," Ludwig told her. "Harald will
see you out." The party swept away again with all ceremony.

As they departed, Elisha bowed his head, using it to
stifle a cough. His throat ached. A bitter old man, already
defeated, and Elisha must rally him against an enemy
that could not be met upon the battlefield—if he could
even gain another audience. Brother Gilles with his relics might serve better here—and likely he would be here
soon, to bring the gifts the emperor required in order to
curry favor with the Pope.

"Sir," came a hoarse whisper, and Elisha glanced up
to find the young serving woman standing nearby offering a cup.

"Thank you." He reached for the water and their fingers brushed, a tingle of awareness passing through him.
Elisha lifted his eyes to her face, his breath stopped. A
magus, but her touch came so tentatively that he couldn't
tell if it were unintentional or merely cautious. The water
cooled his throat and wet his lips. He drained it in a few
swallows and held it up for refilling. "The emperor mentioned hostels. Do you know of one to recommend?"

Long, dark hair framed her face, pretty but not overly
so, her brown gaze focused on him, then quickly lowered.
"There is the Unicorn, sir. Just by the Church of the Holy
Spirit—the one without a spire. It is my mother's inn,"
she told him, with a flash of a smile as if in apology for
recommending a family establishment. "Food is good—
except for dumplings."

At that, Elisha smiled, but his humor quickly faded.
He hadn't actually any money—it all remained with his
things in Jacob's house.

"Sir?" she said, and her brow furrowed. Not only a
magus, but a sensitive one, based on the subtle reaching

of her attention and her instant awareness of his emotions.

"I was caught by surprise in Trier, finding the wrong emperor." Elisha settled on the floor, rubbing his knees, letting the focus of his magical senses move between them so gently even she might not notice. "I left in a hurry, and had to leave my purse behind. I do have some ... talents ... I might exchange, if anyone in the family needs medical care."

At the word "talents," she flushed briefly with interest, but said only, "I'm sure an arrangement can be reached. My mother would not turn you away." Her glance darted toward the steward who lingered at the door.

"Then I am in your debt." He pushed himself to his feet and returned the cup. "I should be going."

"Go with God, and the river," she answered, giving a little curtsy.

Elisha glanced back at her, arrested by that curious phrase, and her presence warmed, her smile hidden by the sweep of her hair as she cradled the pitcher. "What's your name?"

"I'm Gretchen," she told him.

"Well met, Gretchen. Thanks again."

His first acquaintance with the local magi gave him both hope and direction in the face of his failure with the emperor.

"Come, sir," Harald said, all brusque business again as he led Elisha through the passages into the late afternoon and watched him exit past the pikemen at the gate. A man apparently loyal to his emperor in spite of anything else, Harald's presence rang with worry and regret, but he said nothing at all, even when Elisha said his farewells and suggested he might call again on the morrow. With Harald's dark eyes at his back, Elisha began the long descent, now one among many heading down, while only a handful climbed the slope, their long shadows forming tangled thickets of darkness. The shades of the dead lingered silently among them, moving through recreations of their deaths until Elisha blinked them away.

He would have to try again, hoping that Thomas's

letters had softened the emperor's anger. The stiff-necked old man even refused aid against his obvious enemy. Having met them both, Elisha no longer wondered at the support from the other nobles that resulted in Charles's election despite a sitting emperor already upon the throne. Elisha shook himself. Any emperor influenced by necromancers, even one so pleasant as Charles, could not help but create evil. Somehow, he must make Ludwig understand the true threat, not merely against his position, but against the lives and souls of his people.

Elisha's awareness stirred with an echo of his own presence, and he stopped, stepping aside from the flow of traffic, searching the crowd. Below, a young man pushed against that flow, a bundle clutched in his hand and his brow furrowed. Elisha focused his senses, finding the fear that hid beneath the prickly heat of anger. Unlikely to be a mancer, then, though he carried something of Elisha's with him. Elisha's left eye caught glimpses of shades that hung about him, but faintly, as if death were a stain that faded but could not be removed. The man glanced up toward the castle, catching Elisha's gaze as he pushed himself onward. His steps slowed as he studied Elisha more closely. "Are you the English doctor?"

"I am," Elisha answered.

"Good." The stranger dodged a woman with a handcart to join Elisha in the browning grass at the edge of the path, though he kept a wide space between them. "These are yours." He thrust out the bundle. "A mutual acquaintance asked me to bring them, if I could find you."

Elisha took the bundle and peered inside to see his belt wrapped about his medical pouch and purse. "Thank you—and give Jacob my thanks."

"I shall not," the other replied, his shoulders too square. "I have dealings with him as rarely as possible."

In point of fact, the man resembled Jacob, though his hair and beard were closely trimmed. An estranged cousin or some other relation? "I'm sorry to hear it. He seems a worthy man."

The stranger wet his lips and lied. "We may have had

some business together, but otherwise, I know nothing of him, and I'll thank you to remember it."

His acid words stung, but Elisha swallowed his annoyance. "As you wish." He gave a nod and started down again.

"If he gave you any messages," the man called after him, "you should burn them."

At that, Elisha turned. "I beg your pardon?"

"He's a foolish old man and worry for his son has enfeebled him. If he wrote you anything, it's only the raving of a father overcome with joy." He stared down the slope at Elisha, hands clutched behind him. "It means nothing."

On top of his failure with Ludwig, this was one insult too many. "It's nothing to do with you if he has," Elisha snapped back. "And how is Simeon?"

"Recovering." For an instant, a hint of relief broke the man's fierce presence, though his expression only hardened. "But I don't—"

"You don't associate with him, either, of course. Good luck with the emperor. Your humors are nicely aligned today: both choleric. Good day to you."

"God be with you!" the stranger shouted defiantly, as if it were a curse. Then he turned sharply away.

Elisha stalked down the hill, the bile returning to his own humor. His feet ached as he returned to the streets of the city, weaving between citizens on his way toward the Church of the Holy Spirit, to find the Unicorn. The huge church, cut of the same red stone as the castle, rose up from a cobbled square with the awnings of market stalls forming a skirt around its base. Scaffolds covered the apse of the church, and workmen moved about with trowels and stones. The towerless church enveloped an earlier structure, aging stone replaced with new, even as commerce bustled in its shadow.

Elisha paused in the shadow of the broad church steps, scanning the wooden signs that hung above the doorways all around him, and taking the moment to slip his belt back on beneath his outer tunic. Down an alley to the left, he spotted a swinging golden unicorn, carved rampant as if it would charge the chandler's sign across the way. A good meal and a rest would rouse his spirits, and he could hope the night would do the same for Ludwig. He started to emerge from the shadows, then froze and shifted back again.

A hooded man, one of many, to be sure, walked toward the door beneath the swinging unicorn, his arm in a sling of fabric across his chest. He exuded friendliness, but so strongly that it seemed as a spice laid upon rotten meat: clearly a projection.

Yanking open the door with his good arm, the man ducked beneath the swinging unicorn and shut the door behind him, not before Elisha recognized the cool, strong presence: Bardolph, the mancer who had escaped him back in England. While Elisha fought the other mancers to rescue Thomas, Bardolph left to fetch Brigit to claim the rescue for herself—and he never returned to the fight. Bardolph was one of the mancers who seized Thomas and Rosalynn, who slew the queen and readied the king to be skinned alive.

Chapter 9

❖

Elisha leaned back against the tall church steps, his heart racing, draping himself in a deep deflection. He had known Bardolph was German, had even expected to find him lurking somewhere, probably in the service of the upstart emperor, Charles. But seeing him enter the very inn that had been recommended by another magus left Elisha shaken and worried. Had the mancer spoken with Gretchen, or had he merely guessed where to look, anticipating that Elisha would seek out the company of magi? If Gretchen's family were not involved with the mancers, Elisha risked their lives to go there and confront Bardolph, bringing them into a conflict they had no part of. On the other hand, if they were colluding with his enemies, then he risked his own—and before he completed even the first part of his mission by telling Ludwig what he needed to know.

Elisha's head thumped back against the old stone, a drift of stone dust from the mason's work tickling his throat, reminding him of the water Gretchen offered. He so wanted to trust her. He needed that small kindness she gave him, but the need turned sour in his stomach. Of course the mancers would have spies in the stronghold of the emperor. Elisha refused to walk into their trap by going to the inn. But what was the alternative? He could hide in the church all night; already, the workmen packed their tools and draped cloth over the unfinished windows. Mass would not likely be held in the

half-made building, but in one of the older churches, so
he would have time and space. In the morning, he would
crawl back up the hill to prostrate himself before the
castle guards and try to convince them to let him in.

Around him, shopkeepers packed up their things and
closed their shutters while the crowds dispersed, many
heading to his right, toward the other steeples, until the
square stood nearly empty, the golden light of early evening shimmering on the red stone buildings, the chatter
of conversation ebbing to nothing. A few people
emerged from the Unicorn, a few more went in.

Elisha wrapped his fingers through his hair, binding
his useless hands. In England, men had feared him and
wooed him for his power, and here he must cower in a
church and wait upon an old man's whim. By God, he
was not made for this.

For what, then? For what did he have this dread affinity, this too-intimate knowledge of death, if it availed
him nothing? He felt like a shepherd in the moors,
watching a storm approach and helpless to do anything
about it but suffer the lashing rain. Luck or fate or divine
providence had brought him to Simeon at the moment
of his need. How many others wept or died in their dark
prisons while Elisha was powerless to save them? At any
moment, the necromancers might leap through the Valley to their forged relics to steal another victim, and Elisha still had little sense of the true nature of their plans.

Across town, a church bell rang for Vespers, and every
church took up the tolling, save the vacant one in the
center of the plaza. The people still trickling through the
streets hurried their steps, and a fellow with a few woolen
cowls slung upon a pole rested it on the ground, then
heaved it up again with a grunt. Elisha stepped out of the
shadows. "Here! Are those for sale?"

"Aye, sir," the man replied. "Only gray left, though."

"It's fine."

He slid one off the pole and handed it over while Elisha fished out a coin. The cowl draped his neck and he
pulled it up to cover his head, sending his face into shadows. The door at the Unicorn banged open and Bardolph

popped out, waving off a woman in an apron. "Come, Bardolph, you've not even—"

"It's Vespers. I'm sorry," he said over his shoulder as he hurried away from her.

Wiping her hands, she called after him, "Say a few for me, would you?" The mancer laughed, giving a slight wave with his good hand. The door banged shut again as she went inside, and Bardolph instantly changed direction, cutting across the square and bounding up the steps into the unused church so fast that he slipped and banged the elbow of his damaged arm on the entry. A ripple of anger broke his cool projection, then he pushed inside.

Casting a deflection to conceal his presence, Elisha ran after. He couldn't enter via the church door without drawing the attention of those inside, but the scaffold beckoned. Finding a mason's ramp, Elisha moved upward as quietly as he might, dodging the lashed uprights to make his way to the church wall. Tall frames of stone marked where stained glass would someday light the nave, but for now they stood open in the thick walls, draped over with lengths of cloth to keep out the weather. Elisha carefully slid between the wall and the cloth, moving it as little as possible to avoid letting in a telltale shaft of light. After a moment his eyes adjusted to the vast, dim space beyond. The aching presence of the dead filled the void, some whole and buried, their shades lingering, others fragmented, captive in the altars, bits of saints waiting to serve the prayers of sinners, and a few shades reenacting their deaths. Only one moved among them, his presence too sharp to be dead. Bardolph cut across the floor below, still fuming, until he entered a side aisle and Elisha could no longer see him.

Elisha dared to reach through the stone, extending his senses in a narrow path in search of those living feet, a tenuous contact at best. He felt the vibration of Bardolph's long stride, then the mancer halted. The hairs on Elisha's arms tingled as the Valley opened somewhere below; the brief howl of pain, grief, and fear, then it snapped shut and the sense of Bardolph was gone.

With a silent oath Elisha slapped the wall, stinging his palm.

Bardolph was in a hurry—the bells had been a signal for him, but not a call to prayer. This might be his best chance to learn more about the mancers' schemes. No longer concerned with silence now that his quarry had vanished, Elisha scrambled down the ramp and up the steps. A heavy lock hung upon the latch, but a careful glance showed the latch itself disconnected. Pushing inside, Elisha shut the door carefully behind him and ran down the aisle toward the chapel where Bardolph had opened the Valley. The church held little—only things too heavy to be moved to safer quarters for the duration of the work, like the baptismal font and main altar. A few side altars remained, bare of their altarpieces and cloths. Elisha slowed, glancing up to count windows and find where he had been standing, then he moved more cautiously toward the chapel at that end. Now that he was aware, fully present, the air chilled his skin when he came to the altar, and tension tightened his shoulders. He forced himself to relax. A step to either side, and the sensation vanished. Even here, immediately before the slab of marble, it faded as he reached to capture the feeling, to remember it. The altar looked like any other, without even the images of saints to identify its patron. Elisha ran his hands over the surface, disturbing the dust of the construction work and making it clear that Bardolph had not touched it so. He might have opened the Valley with a talisman he already had, but then he could have done it right inside the door—why cross the entire church to this very place?

Squatting, Elisha found marble columns at each corner, enabling a petitioner to crawl beneath and thus be closer to the saint whose relic made the altar holy. He tipped his head beneath it and looked up. A small panel was built into the lower surface of the slab near the front, embellished with carved acanthus leaves like those on a manuscript page, and emanating the sense of violent death too recent for any saint. He was right about the relics, bits of the murdered, planted as talismans to allow

their murderers easy transit. He rose again to stand before the altar and reached his hand beneath, his fingers
going numb with the chill of death when he slid back the
door. Inside it, wires held a finger bone in place. He recoiled: the finger had been severed from a living hand.

Bardolph passed this way, going to some pre-arranged
destination, the relic providing the connection he needed
to open the Valley. If Elisha would stop the mancers he
must know what they did, who they were, what they
planned, how they moved. Pressing his hand over the
bone, Elisha opened himself to the stirring of the dead.
He caught the memory of an old man, bound and frightened; hot, living hands holding him; his own son wielding
the knife.

Seven mancers slew this man—seven who could use
his death to travel the Valley. Would they all be waiting,
gathered in some distant place with Bardolph now
among them? Elisha's pulse thundered, his breathing
too sharp. Part of him urged patience, rest, find an inn
and report to the emperor. Or was it fear that urged his
retreat? If he lost this trail, when would he get another
chance?

Elisha breathed in dust and summoned power. His
sensitivity and his affinity with death allowed him to do
what the mancers could not: travel the Valley through a
death he had not committed. Knowledge flowed up his
arm, as if his own veins drew it onward to his heart. He
must be Death. He must be unknowable, invisible, silent.
He let himself go cold. When he opened the Valley, it
would be not a tearing, but the whisper of a familiar
path; the howling wind of this man's death must become
a soft voice that beckoned him to find the murderers.
None must feel his coming. Elisha wooed death with sorcery. He remembered his own near-dying and the holes
pierced through his skull resonated with the memory of
pain. He claimed the old man's death, tamed it, and
made it the blade that cut through the dim light of the
church into darkness. The Valley opened with a soundless, frozen mist, like a painting of Hell.

As he opened the Valley, he felt again that strange

tension, as if it were reaching back. He did not think it was only his near-death that made it so, but he had not the time to investigate.

In the blink of an eye, a dozen points of black, stained by this one death, stood out from the maelstrom of the Valley, but, as if the old man truly guided him, one felt more distinct than the rest. Elisha's skin burned with cold fire as he called upon the power there and reached toward that deepest night. Pinpricks of heat shimmered within. Elisha strained to hold himself in the Valley, caught between one place and another in the terrible nowhere of death that underlay both worlds. The effort made him tremble. Heat: the living. He reached more carefully to the edge of the ripple, further from the heat.

With a last wrenching of his heart, Elisha slid out again on the other side, soundless, sucking the cold into himself, his jaw so tightly clenched that his teeth ached. The Valley stroked across his skin, familiar, then gone.

For a moment, the silence throbbed against his ears.

Holding his breath, he stood in a dark forest rich with death—and made himself as nothing, his presence deflected.

Living voices broke into his numbness.

"—Vespers!" Bardolph had his back to Elisha, so close that a simple misstep would bring them both down.

"Look, Bardolph, when you were late, we assumed you were courting and didn't wish to be disturbed. And anyhow, it doesn't matter—we've made the harvest."

"For God's sake, you might have waited!" Bardolph snapped.

Someone else laughed. "You can barely hold the knife since you went over."

Elisha made himself breathe, if shallowly. God's sake? A necromancer dared call upon the name of God?

Elisha's left eye saw it first: the shade of a fresh death, swirling toward him, drawn by his affinity. He sealed himself against it, refusing to draw up that power. His ruined vision might be unique in all the magical curses of the world, but he could not risk another tracing the shades of death back to him. Four mancers formed a loose circle in a clearing of the woods, Bardolph on the outside with another confronting him—a thickset man with a huge ginger-colored beard, a man Elisha had last seen in the company of the Emperor Charles. Though he looked like any courtier, his form flickered with the shades of the dead, concentrated around the sword he wore, an elegant blade dense with the stain of murder. His hands, too, emitted that swirling darkness, the shades of those he had killed still marking to their killer.

Against a tree nearby, a slender young man lounged, richly dressed, with pale hair and eyes, his lips set in a prim line. His glance flickered with disdain from Bardolph's confrontation to the mancers who formed the circle. Each of the mancers carried the echoes of murder, shadows that draped their hands. Inside the circle, a table of stone ran with blood, a crimson corpse upon it, still glistening as, with a wet, tearing sound, the others peeled its skin. Her skin.

Elisha's stomach churned, but he knew it was too late.

"We voted," offered one of the knife men in a guttural accent.

"Do not take that tack with me," Bardolph replied. "Someone had to track the damned barber, that is why I'm late."

"You should've done the job in England and had him off our back once and for all," said a thin man, yanking the skin so hard that it tore. For a moment, they all stared at the dangling strip of hide. "Shit." He laid it carefully on the far side of the slab and worked more carefully over the dead girl's shoulder.

"I am sorry about your brother—I've said it over and over," Bardolph went on. "There was really nothing I could have done—"

"Nothing? You could've stayed in England to sort the barber there, couldn't you? Or gone back to Bruges to wait for him? You're the one who thought he'd cross the Channel to begin with!"

"There is no earthly way your brother's death was my fault. You are only angry you lost the chance to harvest him." Bardolph smacked the air with his good hand.

The mancer at the table straightened slowly, towering, his fleshing knife dripping blood. "Don't you dare say that. He was my brother."

"He was a fool," said the big bearded man amiably. "Don't complain, we all knew it. We thought he could manage the crucifixion—it was his own mistake tracking blood around that let the barber find his workshop."

"No," said the tall one. "The barber is a Judaizer; he must have known something about the Jew already, or he'd never have been able to get to the vintner's workshop by contact alone. Even by blood, it isn't enough."

"You have not been listening to me," said Bardolph, and some of his anger shifted away, his control returning. "The barber has a level of awareness most of you can't imagine. He can travel the dark road with deaths he hasn't caused or even shared. Can even your father do that, Conrad?"

The pale young man, Conrad, stiffened and aimed that fine glare at Bardolph. "There is no one like my father. Even I cannot yet master the way he can manipulate the paths of the dead." He spoke with a thick, unfamiliar accent.

A few rays of low sun struck beneath the table, casting long shadows back toward the denser forest, shielding Elisha, shimmering on the trickle of blood that crept across the barren ground between him and the table. A man who could manipulate the paths of the dead: the Valley. He breathed carefully, listening.

"That is precisely my point," said Bardolph. "You all persist in the belief that the barber is one of us, that he is simply working on a plan of his own, independent of Rome or Kaffa, and I tell you he is not. In his position would any one of you have let me live? No. If he's one of the Chosen, then something is terribly wrong. Look at what happened in London."

Rome, Elisha recognized, but what, or where, was Kaffa?

"Aside from the fact that the queen's gambit failed, leaving the crown in the hands of the blood heir, we don't really know what happened in London, do we?

That Frenchman Renart was there, but he left too early to tell us much." The bearded man folded his arms. "We can only guess at how it turned out."

"Based upon the fact that Wolfram and Federica never came home, it turned out very badly. Is that not enough for you, Eben?" Bardolph regarded the bearded man.

"You should have been there to find out!" snarled the tall man, thrusting his knife in Bardolph's direction.

"I would've been dead, too, and you would never have known about the threat."

"One barber," scoffed the bearded man, Eben. "How much of a threat could he be? I saw him at Trier where Henry got him to run for his life." He toyed with the hilt of his sword, cold steel gleaming from colder shadows.

"You were the one who supported the new English candidate to begin with, a queen without royal blood," said the tall man. "When their prince died, they should have gone for the daughter. Jonathan should have governed his followers better."

"You think the English could be ready for Rome if they had to work with a child?" Conrad made a dismissive sound. "Rome will be the culmination of a decade's planning. Better to leave the English out of it entirely if they haven't a firm hold on their throne."

So the mancers planned something important for Rome, and a Frenchman named Renart was involved. Elisha clung to every scrap of information they spilled.

"Jonathan intended a regency on her behalf." Eben sighed and shook his head. "We're going to miss him the next couple of years. He was a great mind."

"He would've been a hide worth taking," Conrad agreed. "My father still speaks of him."

"See? The barber didn't even harvest him," Bardolph pointed out. "He is not like us. Besides, the new queen was a magus, a powerful one, and one willing to partner with us. We will be stronger if we maintain our connection with the other magi."

Back in England, before Brigit's arrival, Bardolph had spoken this way, of bonds with the magi. Perhaps those at the Unicorn were, indeed, working with the mancers, just as Brigit had been.

"There's only one of them you want to connect with," said the tall man, giving a thrust of his hips that made his meaning clear.

Eben opened his hands, a crackle of darkness stretching between them that cut short the other's irritation. "A magi queen, who is already with child? Bardolph is right about that much at least: For our purposes, she's perfect—we just need to get her back."

"Agreed, but you're not going to find her by standing around here bickering." A man at the feet of the corpse straightened his spine, groaning. "I'd like to get this done and get on home, right? You'll argue 'til Rome at this rate. I'm sick of hearing it, and my wife's waiting for me."

"Your man makes a good point. I have an important meeting in the morning." Conrad inclined his head with the grace of one who expects others to bow to him.

Eben met his nod evenly, not bowing a single inch more. "You're sure you do not wish to join in?"

"I wish I could, but my father would know it. He finds this sort of thing unbearably vulgar." Conrad made an elegant turn, the Valley sliding open like a lady's bed curtain, to welcome him inside.

"Are all the Italians so insufferable?" said the tall man. "Maybe I'm glad they don't join."

"They hardly need to work toward Rome—Conrad's father already owns it," said Eben. "Pity he lacks his father's sensitivity, though. We could use a few more like that."

"Help me roll her," said a woman who stood on the other side. She and the tall man took hold of the body, then the woman hesitated, frowning, shifting her grip. "None of you has got a new talisman, have you?"

Elisha's hand, steadying him against the ground, shivered with a touch of Death. Blood seeped around his fingers. Blood that had run in slow rivulets from the altar and now linked him with every mancer at the table. He glanced up and the woman met his gaze with a cry of surprise.

Chapter 10

❖

Elisha sprang up, bowling over Bardolph so that the mancer's head thunked against a tree. Elisha seized the cold power that flowed around him, his left eye clearly seeing the shadow that dripped from the murderers' hands and clung about their arms. With the strength of the Valley still bound against his living flesh, Elisha forced the contact. The mancers screamed, the woman spinning, wiping her arms where the dead girl's blood withered her skin. Her fingers writhed, rotted and tumbled away, the pallor of her fear swiftly overtaken by the gray of ancient skin. The three knifemen with her likewise howled their agony, two twisting and dancing, desperate to strip the stain from their arms before it carried their deaths too deep. The third man lunged away from the table and spun, launching his bloodied knife.

The blade arced through the air, following the paths of blood, diverting Elisha's focus to the weapon itself. He reached through the blood to contact the blade, slowing it enough to dodge and knock it from the air. Before they could recover, Elisha stamped on the knife, pinning it down. From the Valley, Elisha conjured Death, his fell hound, to rend the mancers soul from body. For a moment, their lives held out—long enough for one to seize a wineskin and sluice the blood away, but the others, perhaps not recognizing the threat, reacted too slowly, and Death raced through them, stopping their hearts.

Three voices cut short, one mancer flung across the dead girl's body as if, at the last moment, he begged for her forgiveness.

The fourth man backed away from the table, shaking the dregs from the wineskin over his arms. He stared at Elisha, his thin lips parting to a triumphant grin.

Bardolph shifted, scrambling up—but Elisha had already gone, snatching himself through the Valley as Morag used to do. For that moment of his absence, he imagined their relief and confusion—just as he had felt the first night he knew this was possible—and the howls of the dead voices became chants of excitement, urging him on. Brigit, he thought. That touch in the Valley reminded him of her, and now it was as if her voice encouraged him.

Elisha stepped through the Valley to the far side of the table, caught the man by the shoulder as if to steady him, and sank the ice of death into his heart. The man's back arched, his breath broken as he collapsed to Elisha's feet.

Across the way, Bardolph, a dagger in hand, turned from the place where Elisha had been, darting his glance around. He arrived too late to participate in the kill, and Eben the nobleman abstained, both of them unmarked by blood. Eben gave a single nod, his dark eyes on Elisha's face.

Bardolph straightened, dagger extended, his injured arm held close. "Now, Eben—now! Between the two of us, surely," but his voice quavered.

"Do you think so," Eben murmured. "Do you really?" His own hand slipped to his belt, the other snatching Bardolph's wrist. With a shriek, the Valley tore open, and Eben yanked Bardolph through, but his dark eyes remained steady, calculating, then they were gone.

Elisha swayed, panting. He stumbled, then reached through the girl's death to the Valley, searching the howling chaos. For an instant, he sensed the heat of their two lives, then it faded, and he let go, standing alone in the forest, the earth bathed in blood, with the four dead mancers sprawled about the girl they had murdered, the posthumous weapon of her own vengeance. So fast, so many dead.

Elisha's heart thundered and his legs shook. He longed to step back to the church, to sink to his knees and ask for absolution—not for killing those who died, but for that thrill he felt when he had done it.

Spreading his awareness, he knelt by the first mancer. Like the mancers of England, this man carried the skin of his first victim, a tattered thing, aged with use. He also carried a knuckle of the old man whose death had brought Elisha here from the church, and a half-dozen relics of other victims. Elisha did not take the time to know their deaths. Instead, he carefully searched the other three mancers gathering their brutal talismans. He lay them out at the dead girl's feet, averting his gaze as if she had any modesty remaining. Sorting the relics, he found they shared several victims, an unholy communion that allowed the mancers to gather here through their knowledge of the murders.

One of the dead mancers claimed Elisha must have had prior knowledge of Simeon, the Jew they crucified, in order to follow the man's blood to the vintner's. The only reason to share in such a harvest was to share the power it conferred. The mancers needed to understand the death in order to exploit it. Elisha's sensitivity combined with his compassion gave him the advantage: He could track these remnants to their matches, even through the lives and deaths of strangers.

At last, he raised his eyes to the girl's face. Sometimes, the dead appeared at peace, composed by those who prepared them for burial. Some, like Martin or Biddy, even carried the gleam of hope, their willing sacrifice serving a greater cause. This girl lay on her side, half-flayed, blood dripping from her long, wavy hair. He could touch her, or simply allow her blood to communicate the terror and pain of her last moments, but he could not read enough of her that way to know her name, where she lived or who might search the streets to find their daughter. Would it be better for them to find her, like this, or for her simply to have vanished?

Eben and Bardolph knew his power, and would guess how he came to be here. If they still carried their talismans of the old man who brought him, they were greater fools than they seemed. Seven pairs of hands took part in that slaying, and three of them were dead—the female mancer must have been linked to the table through some other talisman. Bardolph and Eben would soon warn their compatriots and gather strength against Elisha. Unless he moved against them first.

Elisha gripped the knuckle bone and stepped into the Valley. Again, the darker points directed him to the dead man's bones. Most lay cold, alone, probably hidden in churches waiting to be used. Two talismans of the victim mingled with the heat of the living. He slid through the Valley and emerged in a narrow street, into the path of a stout man who stumbled, his sleeve torn so that a few things tumbled free along with the talisman that drew Elisha here.

Turning, growling, the man said, "You might've washed up before you came."

"Sorry," Elisha said.

He had thick lips and bristling brows. He did not look like a murderer, nor did he carry the depth of shades Elisha had come to expect. "What do you want anyway? I wasn't expecting anyone."

"Just to talk," Elisha told him.

The man's features furrowed. "English, are you? Heard you lost your candidate."

"We've got a new one," Elisha told him.

"Can't hurt, can it? That kind of thing just makes 'em more ripe for harvest." The fellow grinned, then bent down to gather his things—bones and bits of leather, each flickering with the chill of death. "You be more careful, though. Next time just give it a shiver and let the other fellow answer. Some o' them aren't as forgiving as me."

Elisha stared down at the velvet cap on the man's head. He looked for the moment like any wealthy man who spilled his purse, except the coin he carried was paid in blood. Every item he picked up carried a thrust of fear and pain. No doubt, Elisha reeked of it.

"Here," said the mancer, holding up a patch of dried skin. "Can you smell that?" He brought it to his nose and smiled. "A man never forgets his first, eh?"

Since he slew King Hugh back in England, Elisha had been at pains to insist he was no assassin, no dealer in death. Tonight, quenched in the dead girl's blood, drawn by the old man's pain, Elisha renounced that claim. He reached out a fistful of cold, touched the nape of the man's neck, and the stiff bolt of death passed from his hand. The man's thick lips gaped, his eyes rolling up to stare, then Elisha stepped away, letting the man fall to the street, his first talisman clutched in his hand, the relic of a woman's breast, the nipple showing dark against the freckled skin.

His shade roiled to Elisha's touch as he withdrew into the Valley, carrying that power too close to his heart.

Summoning himself through the Valley with another of the relics from the stone table, Elisha met the woman merchant from Trier. She fought, landing a blow with a fire iron that numbed his arm, but did not stop his touch.

Six more times Elisha crossed the Valley, employing the talismans of those he had slain in the forest to bring justice to the killers. As he travelled, the Valley's chaotic presence felt more acute, no longer a chill miasma he passed through, but rather a clinging, constrictive smoke, as if it sought to inhibit his passage.

A few mancers had time or breath to scream as Elisha dispatched them. One, he met on a dock where the man held a child beneath the water. The man died. The child met Elisha's gaze, and fled, his terror as plain as his desperate cries.

The last, he met in a church. Before the altar a woman knelt, hands clasped, three talismans laid before her: the bone that drew Elisha to her presence, a patch of skin no longer recognizable, and a hand, desiccated with age. At his arrival, she jerked and looked up, her face streaked with tears. Rage, fear, glee he had met this night, but sorrow unnerved him despite the evidence of her complicity in the slaying. The power of the deaths he wrought gathered around him, spanning the altar like unholy wings.

The mancer gasped, her hands trembling, then broke

into a tearful smile as her eyes slid shut, head tipped back. "Come, Lord—I've waited so long." She spread her arms to embrace her death.

Elisha hesitated, staring at her exposed throat, framed by braids of dark hair streaked with silver. She looked a few years older than he, and would have been lovely, but for the grief and fear that marked her face. Many of the others took him for one of them at first and exposed their wickedness. When they knew he was not, he expected violence, the violence with which these people lived—the violence with which they killed.

Her eyes opened and she stared up at him, then tipped her head. "Why do you hesitate, Lord? Are you not here to slay me?"

For a moment, in the brightness of her gaze, he wanted to deny it, but the power of death roiled in his palm, waiting the chance to strike again, as if the dead mancers urged him on.

"Please!" she pushed herself forward and he drew back a pace. "Please, Lord," she continued, her voice falling, "If you don't, I'll return to them, I will—they'll never let me go."

Elisha spread his hands, death swirling about him. "If you don't want to do this, why would you return?"

With a shake of her head, the woman searched his face and figure again. "You must know what they would do to me; I deserve to be punished—God knows—*you* know, I deserve it." She stroked the dried, dead hand, then held it up to him. "I'm wicked, Lord, I have always been wicked. You saw fit to send my husband to punish my wickedness. And when I—" She faltered, bit her lip, then continued. "When I denied his punishment, you sent *them*." She dropped her gaze to the bone and the scrap of flesh with a shudder. "Strike me dead, Lord," she whispered, "surely Hell can be no worse than this."

"Who do you take me for?" he said at last.

She clasped her hands again, the mummified hand still between them as she cowered and her voice sank so low that only his magical senses carried her words. "Lord Uriel, the angel of repentance."

Lord Uriel, the archangel, the guardian of Hell.

He closed his fist, extinguishing the darkness. "Your husband beat you," he murmured, sorting through all that she had said.

She gave a tiny nod.

"You took his hand. It gives you strength," he said. "Power."

She flinched, but nodded again. "I never meant to, Lord, I know that sorcery is wrong, I know that. I never meant—"

As if she had recalled with whom she argued, she broke off, shrinking back.

"And they found you." The dead hand, the talisman of murder, would have drawn the mancers just as in the New Forest of England they were drawn to the child's head he once carried in a jar. He hoped for a miracle, for the power of resurrection, and found death instead. But when the mancers sent Morag to recruit him, he rejected them, while this woman, expecting her punishment, accepted what they made of her. Pity soured his strength. Was she wicked? Had she been, before her husband's beatings drove her to his death? Who was he to stand in judgment?

Uriel. The angel of repentance. Elisha wet his lips. "Repent," he said softly. "And sin no more."

Her head shot up, but Elisha retreated, snapping into the Valley. It seized him, a sudden sharp presence swelling around him—a presence both austere and terrifying, the touch of a distant mind that stroked over him, piercing and probing, closing the Valley around him as if that distant one could fling a cloak over his head and smother him. Elisha sealed himself, coiling the weapon of Death into an armor beneath his skin, repelling that touch and struggling free of the Valley.

He stumbled into the Church of the Holy Spirit, the moon glowing through the cloth-covered windows, and caught himself on the altar, his arm throbbing as the cold strength of the dead left him merely flesh once more. Gasping for breath, Elisha sought attunement, the first discipline of the magus, to know the place he occupied, to know himself. That one, that presence in the Valley, knew the passage of the dead. It was not roused immediately, only as Elisha sped on his mission of death, slaying mancers and opening the Valley again and again in service to his cause. Could a magus be attuned to the Valley itself, aware of those who passed through it? A mancer could, a person of immense power and sensitivity. Conrad named his father the master of the paths of the dead, also, if Eben were right, the master of Rome. A master among mancers, the warden of the Valley—a man Elisha hoped he never had to face. But if he would stop their plans for Rome, then he must go there, to the very nest of his greatest opponent.

The woman from Trier had likely been on the alert because she knew what he had done in the vineyard. The others, unprepared, had no chance to fight back.

How many had he slain tonight? Eleven? Twelve? As many as he killed in England to save the crown. Surely he was in the right—this was a war, an invasion of evil, insidious and secret, slaying where it would. Someone had to fight back. Avenging angel indeed.

Elisha fought for his own breath, then slumped to his knees. Killers all, even if he did not catch them in the act. Murderers, just like him. Fatigue throbbed in his temples and shivered his limbs. At first the transits had been, not easy perhaps, but a familiar resistance—as the warden grew aware of his activities, it became harder, the warden's search for him building like friction against Elisha's magic and wearing him down.

Elisha's head rested against the altar that concealed the old man's finger, his eyes squeezed shut, his skull aching, the tortured voices of the Valley still ringing in his ears and in his flesh. How many mancers were there? One of those he slew tonight called out in a language he did not even recognize. He could stand hip-deep in slaughter and he could not kill them all. The warden nearly caught him this time, after a dozen slayings. Next time, he would be ready for Elisha, expecting the assault, even if the individual mancers did not.

The weight of the dead bore him down, their screams,

their curses echoing in his ears, and he remembered the woman who prayed for death, to free her from the slaughter she felt compelled to embrace.

His body succumbed to sleep, to dream of an endless Valley, lined with the shades of those he killed, jeering voices that multiplied around him. One of the men at the stone table spoke of his wife who would be waiting for him—waiting forever, as wolves devoured his body, along with his victim's.

It was not guilt that stirred his dreams, for when he woke and tried remorse, he saw again the bloodied corpse of the dead girl, the startled face of the child who would not be drowned that night, the gratitude of Simeon's father, and certainty settled in his bones. And yet . . . his own behavior appalled him. His anatomical knowledge turned to knowing where to touch to be closest to the heart or to the veins. And through it all, he pulsed with righteous wrath, the hunter's joy, not so different from the joy the mancers found in their slaughter.

His own hands bore only the blood of the victim, yet they seemed distant, the hands of a stranger. He remembered learning magic, elated at this skill even as he worried over what might happen if his witchcraft were discovered. Brigit wooed him to her cause, hoping for his support because she knew that his power could be this, a stroke of death in the darkness, without warning, without hope of escape. These last months, in Thomas's behalf, he reconciled himself to power, to being feared as a knight should be, for the strength of arms he wielded in a righteous cause. Now, with Brigit lying as one entombed, and Thomas far away in England, Elisha had become a foreigner, even to himself: he wore a Jew's clothes, spoke the German language, parlayed with emperors, slept among the dead, slew his enemies out of hand.

For a time, this night, he reveled in his strength. Viewed more clearly, he knew the hunt must fail. Bardolph and Eben would be making their own plans, calling upon the ones who remained, and the warden of the Valley would be on the alert. Had the warden gathered knowledge enough to recognize Elisha's presence when he merely used the Valley, without the added power of his killings? The presence of the woman he recognized from Trier, and the foreign mancers, their references to the mancers of England and France, suggested they worked as guilds, halls of murderers, linked across the distance to the others of their awful trade. He had damaged their brotherhood tonight, but he could not bring it down that way: never again would they be caught unprepared.

Diplomacy, trying to warn Archbishop Baldwin and Emperor Ludwig availed him nothing, and this, too, had failed. He could not win in single combat. He would meet an opponent who countered him with strengths he could not imagine: the warden would be waiting, like a cutthroat in a darkened alley. His fight was just, and he was doomed.

Chapter 11

———————— ✦ ————————

$\mathcal{B}$y the time the sounds of market filtered through the hollow church, Elisha's body ached all over. Wounds, he could heal, but the exhaustion of his effort and of sleeping on a stone floor could not be resolved through magic. Pushing himself up, stripping off the tunic stiffened with blood, Elisha smoothed his undershirt and tried to brace himself for the long walk. He edged cautiously around the door, squinting despite the pall of mist that obscured the early sun. His left arm throbbed from elbow to wrist from the blow of the mancer's fire iron. The cowl at his neck felt too hot against his stiff neck, and he slipped it off to tuck through his belt. His enemies would be alert for his power, not his face. If they knew his weakness, they might well strike him now.

Sighing, he moved between the first of the carters and vendors setting out their wares. The warmth of Martin's talisman, the long strip of cloth the draper had pressed upon him like a lady's favor to a knight before Elisha first set off for war, hovered at his chest. He let its strength flow, calling up his awareness, preparing to shield himself in other ways.

"Hallo! We thought to see you last night," called a cheerful voice, and Elisha looked up to find Gretchen a few paces away. She tipped her head and frowned at him. "You ought to have come, really. Wherever you slept doesn't appear to have done you well."

Kindness. Again. But he sensed no duplicity in her,

only a soft concern. "The night has served me ill, Fraulein. If there is a basin and a meal on offer, I'd be grateful."

"I can't come with you—I'm only down for some herbs the empress hopes to soothe her. But tell them I sent you, and they'll take care of you." She gave him a nod of encouragement—more forward outside of the imperial presence.

"How does she with child?"

"Not well." Her brightness died away, and she hugged her basket. "She can hardly hold her stomach, but we know she's got to eat more. She's weak all the time it seems."

Elisha poked through his medical pouch and found the packet Mordecai gave him for the voyage. "Ginger. It can help."

Gretchen accepted it and tucked it in with the others. "Thank you." She bobbed a curtsy. "I'd best be on."

"I'll be along myself in a while."

"I hope his Majesty treats you more patiently this time." She gave a nod and hurried away.

Only a few patrons occupied the Unicorn's common room, served by the aproned woman Elisha had seen calling after Bardolph the evening before. Wearing a bonnet that concealed her hair and echoed the roundness of her face, she put out a platter of cheese on one table before turning to him, her expression shifting from expectant to concerned in the space of a breath.

"Gretchen sent me," he told her, and the innkeeper's wariness withdrew into a smile that resembled her daughter's—though the hard lines did not ease around her eyes. "I'd like a chamber for washing, then breakfast. A razor, if you've got one," Elisha added with a smile of his own—another item he'd never have been without in England. The last barbering he'd done was to prepare Thomas to be king.

"This way. She did say we'd be looking for a foreigner." She bustled down a crooked corridor toward the back.

"Was anyone else looking for me? I thought I saw an

acquaintance of mine leaving last night, but I wasn't able to catch him." True enough: she needn't know what Elisha would do when he caught him.

She ushered him through a door. "Nobody asking," she said. "What's he like?"

"Tall, sharp, bearded. Carries his arm in a sling. I know him as Bardolph."

"Oh, my, yes. No wonder you couldn't catch him—he didn't stay long—but he didn't mention he was looking for anyone."

Elisha ducked into the chamber. A broad brickwork, emanating warmth, marked the center of one wall, with the rattle of cookery next door. The bathing chamber backed up to the kitchen, then. She rustled out again and returned with a basin and toweling, setting them out on a table. A young man followed with a great, steamy pitcher of water, then gave a nod and departed.

"Always off to church, that Bardolph," said the innkeeper. "It's a wonder he's not turned cleric."

"Is he so devout? I've not known him long."

The innkeeper hesitated, then shut the door and faced him. "Peace of the river to you, stranger."

Elisha caught his breath, the tendrils of her awareness stroking him through the floor. His left eye saw the remnants of sorrow and deaths that touched her, including two infant shades that gathered soft and gray about her, lives that she had lost, but no lives that she had taken. "And to you, I would say—but I am a stranger. If there are ways . . . for our people, I do not know them here. Will you stay and talk with me?"

"We were speaking of Bardolph," she began, "but do take your ease. We avoid names, here, unless they're needed or widely known. We do go to the river. We greet each other as you've heard, and yes, 'also to you,' would be a fair reply."

Elisha stripped off his undershirt, shifting his belt so he need not remove it and risk abandoning his property all over again. If she made anything of his scars, she did not say so. He washed the last of the blood from his hands. By now, it was so dry and mingled with the dirt of his night's work that he doubted any would mark it for what it was. "And Bardolph?" he prompted. Water rinsed away some of his exhaustion, and he faced his weary reflection in the small mirror, taking up the razor to shape his beard into a German point.

"He was always one for the Mass, but I think he's grown more fervent. He's been that worried lately, the more so since he came home. You know that he was sent on a charge for the emperor?"

"It's how we met," Elisha answered, carefully avoiding a lie as the keeper's anxiety and warmth edged around him. "I gather he had a hard time of it."

"Oh, he did, sir. Came back with that injury. Don't know what happened, exactly, and he won't say." She tilted her chin, watching him in the mirror. "Do you know what happened? Seems he's been praying even more now."

As well he would, since the churches he attended were his connection to the other mancers. "It's not for me to tell you of his trouble, mistress, but I can say Bardolph's lucky to be alive." Elisha's blue eyes stared back at him from the mirror, his face leaner than it had been. He turned the other cheek to shave. "Is he family?"

"Was a time I thought he and Gretchen might be a match. May still be," she chuckled, then her mood sobered, her presence radiating worry. "Even so, there's few enough of us that we're all like family here. Used to be more."

Elisha cleaned the razor, watching her in the mirror. "What happened?"

"Hard to say." She wrung her hands in her apron. "Seems like some of our friends moved away. Don't know where. I'd've thought they'd just go upriver."

"So that they could still talk with you," he said softly, and she gave a nod.

He thought of the dead girl in the forest, and the remnants of the others slain there. How many had been magi? Love, loyalty, betrayal made their awful talismans that much stronger. How many had been taken there by those they trusted, those few who shared their magical secret—or rather, who they thought shared it? In France, the king's assassin targeted the magi, weakening any force that might stand against the mancers, sowing distrust among those who might recognize what was happening. This woman knew Bardolph as a magus, but the more she spoke, the more he felt certain she did not know the depth of his secrets.

"Do you know something of this, sir?"

Drying his hands and face, Elisha pulled his tunic back on. "It's hard for me to know how much to say, mistress. My guess would be your friends are dead."

She flinched back from him, bumping the door, her dark eyes wide and every force of her awareness bent upon him.

"In France the king campaigns against us, at the behest of others who are no friends of his, not if he knew them truly."

"What has that to do with us? The French are always squabbling among themselves, or, if you'll pardon my saying it, with you English." Her hands tucked into her apron, the lines around her eyes deepening.

"I came here to warn the emperor that these enemies are spreading, that they have designs upon his throne, as they have claimed the throne of France, as they have tried to claim England. There is a larger plan at work here, and I have set myself to discover it, to stop it if I can."

"I don't care for France or England, or even—God help me!—the emperor. I want to know what's become of my friends." A ripple of power stirred the air around her, and Elisha suddenly realized she had a talisman worked into her apron, as Mordecai had woven hairs of his dead family into his prayer shawl.

He put up his hands. "Don't send me your anger, mistress. Have you seen the mobs who go about beating themselves? They are harnessed to magic, and they are not alone."

"Harnessed?" Her eyes widened. "Can it be so? Like living talismans. That's awful!" She crossed herself.

"Bardolph," he began, still debating with himself how

much to say. "I fear he may have fallen in with bad company, mistress."

"Oh, Good Heavens—he's in danger?"

Elisha replaced the razor, lying it atop the toweling, dodging the mirror, his black hair sliding damp over his shoulders. "He knows his danger, mistress. He's brought it on himself."

"Beg pardon?" Her power crackled in the air around him, an impending storm. "What are you suggesting?"

He turned, arms folded, pressing his own linked talismans close against his chest. He could accept her hospitality and send Bardolph his good wishes, but the thought soured his stomach. She and her daughter were good people, they deserved warning—especially if he were right about what was happening to the local magi. "Whatever he was to you before, mistress, Bardolph has been complicit in crimes in England, and here as well. Be wary of him and of anything he tells you. If he calls for Gretchen, don't let them go anywhere alone."

Her lips parted, and she shook herself. "I thought you were his friend, and here am I gossiping away. Are all English such two-faced fiends?"

"How can I know whom to trust, mistress? Have you felt any lie in me?" He offered her his hand. "Come—tell me what you feel."

She thrust out her hand and laid it over his. "You masked yourself to come here."

"Bardolph's friends will kill me if they find me."

"As you would kill him." She stared back at Elisha, her flesh humming with power.

"The bell at Vespers last night called him to a murder, mistress, a murder he seemed sorry to miss."

"Are you mad?" she asked, but at a murmur. She could feel his urgency, his fear, above all, his sincerity. Tempted as he was to send her the scene he had witnessed, he feared that would be too much—revealing his own power and its source, and likely convincing her she had been duped by a witch much stronger than she.

"Take me how you will, mistress, but take care with Bardolph."

Shaken, she pulled back her hand, then yanked open the door at her back. "I think you've stayed your welcome here, sir."

Taking a coin from his purse, Elisha gave a slight bow. She snatched the coin and coldly escorted him back to the door.

Still tired, aching and hungry, Elisha faced the day having alienated the only magi he had met who weren't trying to kill him. It must be time to meet the emperor.

Chapter 12

❖

The market provided him a meal he could take in hand while he joined the line of folk trudging up toward the emperor's castle, shining red and distant upon its hill. Apparently, the guards had received no orders to keep him out, and he was brought to a passage to wait with a number of people—all clad in velvets and silks, with sleeves that swooped to form pouches heavy with coin. Elisha's own garb barely suited the marketplace, and then only if he were a laborer. Among this company, he wished he had taken the time to purchase new clothes. They'd have been used and fit poorly, but he would stand out less. As it was, the others glanced him over as he passed, sometimes sending servants from their little groups to ward him off in case he wanted something from them.

"—heard the empress is faring poorly with the baby. Shouldn't wonder if court is delayed," one lord remarked.

At the door, a man clad in heavy woolens stained from travel argued with the guards, trying Latin and another language before he sputtered in poor German, "The tribune of Rome send me with invitation for your king! He is not to keep waiting." At his side, the Italian mancer, Conrad, stood tall and resplendent in velvets, his presence utterly courtly, though shades of the dead slithered in his wake.

"You cannot demand entrance from an emperor,"

said Conrad. "Even I could not do so," but his tone implied that was exactly what he wished to do. A mancer, yes, but one clearly on the outside of the emperor's circle. Elisha buried his awareness deeply, grateful that Conrad had left last night before he could have seen Elisha's face. Nonetheless, he quickly moved further from the door where Conrad waited.

Across the way, a cluster of merchants eyed their betters with speculation. Another joined them breathlessly, still straightening a cap. "Did you hear about von Werner? Found in the street this morning he was, stone cold dead!"

"Holy Mary," murmured one, and crossed herself.

"Murdered for coin, I'll warrant," said another, drawing his blue robes closer at his chest, his other hand resting over his purse.

"Nay, that's the madness of it, his wallet was full, and his sleeve, too. Rings and chains and all, still there for any to see. Looks as if he'd died of pure fright, and with a saintly relic in his fist."

Elisha paused to rearrange his shirt, listening.

The man in blue snorted, but the woman crossed herself again. "Visited by the devil himself, I shouldn't wonder if he'd made some bargain, with how busy his shop's been lately."

"No need to speak ill of the dead, Mateza," the man in blue said dryly, "or it might be we're scrutinizing your success now that von Werner's passed on."

Snapping her mouth shut, she looked away, shooting a frown at Elisha who moved to a space across from a lesser door. A servant approached Conrad and the messenger with him, escorting them away down the corridor, and Elisha relaxed a little.

"Are you following me?" demanded an acid voice from Elisha's right, and he found himself face to face with Jacob's surly relation whom he'd met on his descent the day before.

"If I were, I might've slept better. Did they bed you here in the castle?"

The stranger stiffened—as if it were possible for him

to be more tense—and replied, "As it happens, I was given leave to pass the night. I am a craftsman, summoned here by their majesties. As such, I have their respect." His lips parted as if to say more, and Elisha caught an edge of fear.

"You think I would spoil that respect?" Elisha shook his head. "Good God, why should I make any man's life more difficult? I don't know why you've taken against me, or against our mutual acquaintance in Trier. If you're so concerned, then feel free to pretend we've never met."

"That suits me well," the stranger replied, turning from Elisha.

A booming voice announced Brother Gilles' approach, his friar's robes carrying him through the crowd. "Ah, my dear doctor! But you seem to have fallen in status, my friend." He put out his hands to clasp Elisha's hand between them and shake it vigorously.

"You don't know the half of it, Brother."

"My relics and I have just arrived, and I even gathered a few more on my journey. Here." He reached out to pin something to Elisha's shirt. "A gift for you! A nail trimming of Santa Lucia! Don't trouble yourself," he said as Elisha reached as if to remove it, "I have more. I paused to make this trade, but the emperor sent a man on ahead to meet me. It's the arm of Saint Brendan he's wanting." The friar grinned, and Elisha wondered what price might be set upon the arm of a saint. "I understand he's sent for the finest goldsmith of Aachen to make the reliquary, but I've yet to—"

The caustic stranger, Jacob's relative, who had begun slipping away once the friar began to speak, checked his movement, squared his shoulders, and executed a sharp pivot that left his long over-sleeves swinging. The others faced him, Gilles with confusion, Elisha with a sinking feeling that the fellow was about to confirm. "That would be myself, Brother. Isaac Burghussen, at your service." He gave a short bow, introducing himself by the name of his town in the German tradition.

"Well met!" cried the friar, seizing Isaac's hand. "And you've already met the good doctor. Excellent. Perhaps this evening we shall have a merry feast together, and my friend shall tell me what brings him to this lowly state."

Immediately, both of them started to shake their heads. "We have met, Brother, but he doesn't like me," Elisha said.

Isaac scowled. "That's not it at all, I simply—"

"Peace, Friend," Elisha interjected, touching the man's sleeve. "I have no intention of coming between you in your business."

"There are other goldsmiths," the friar said, "if his spirit is not suited to such a holy task." He managed to look stern.

Isaac's face turned a sickly shade, his mouth twisting. "Please, Brother, we've only just met. I have children at home, and this commission could mean a good deal to my family." His presence echoed with old shades that hovered near him with fear. No mere transaction should set a man so on edge.

"Peace," said Elisha again, this time projecting the word, letting the sense of peace fill his touch and radiate from his presence. "Herr Burghussen is an excellent goldsmith, Brother, and the emperor will be well-pleased with his work, as will the Lord and the saint it honors." He pointed toward the goldsmith's chest where a rich gold pendant dangled on a chain. An intricate pattern of tiny beads edged a cross of exquisite workmanship. "See for yourself, Brother. Don't let our journey together affect your judgment when it comes to the work of God."

"Amen," said the friar, leaning forward to squint at the cross. "May I?"

"Yes, of course." The goldsmith slipped the chain over his head and laid the piece on the friar's hand. "This technique is called granulation. It requires very careful soldering."

"And to add it to a work already so finely wrought. One twitch of the flame and all of your work would be ruined." The tonsured head and the curly one nearly touched as the two of them bent over the cross.

Elisha edged to the right, leaving the pair to their excitement over the work to come. The great doors groaned open and Harald stepped through, clad in his royal tabard, his entrance silencing the hall at once. "His Majesty, by the Grace of God, the Holy Roman Emperor thanks you for your patience, and is pleased to say that his good queen fares much better. She appreciates your prayers and good wishes."

A cheer greeted this pronouncement and the assembled nobles and merchants began to press forward toward the chamber beyond, but Harald had not moved from his place and two pikemen stood to either side.

"His Majesty begs your patience a little longer. There is one among you who should be dealt with and sent off with no further delay." Harald swept the crowd with a hard stare. "Elisha Physician, approach!"

Elisha's teeth ground at the tone of this summons. Brother Gilles murmured something soothing while Isaac merely stepped away, once again distancing himself. Had he been allowed through the gate only to suffer this humiliation before all those expecting an audience? God! He wouldn't blame Thomas if he had deliberately snubbed his father-in-law. Elisha stalked forward past the silent, supercilious faces. "Attend the emperor!" Harald called out as they marched forward together, then dropped to one knee.

A painted lattice, marked with stars of gold, spread up the walls and covered the beams of the high ceiling, with chevrons of blue draping down toward the thrones of their majesties. The emperor leaned back in his seat, glaring. "I should have sent you away without seeing you, but for this." He tipped his head toward the empress, who smiled.

"My girl Gretchen brought me a basket of herbs this morning," she said. "Among them was a packet labeled in English, from you. I have not heard before about the use of ginger. Of course, we have some in our own kitchen, and I shall be sure to keep it well stocked. It is the first thing that has settled my poor condition." She gazed down at him, and the steward gave him a nudge.

"I am pleased to have been of use to you, Your Majesty. It seems my visit has not been entirely in vain."

"No, indeed, Doctor. You give me hope for the child." Her smile turned tremulous, and she flicked a glance at her husband, but he stared sternly ahead as if carved in stone.

"If you are strong enough, Your Majesty, try to walk daily," Elisha offered.

At this, she lifted an edge of her gown to reveal her feet propped on a little stool before her, her ankles swollen above the slippers she wore.

"May I?" At her nod, Elisha moved forward on his knees to come to her feet, gently working the slipper from one foot, then the other, wincing at the sight of the bands worn into her hose from the tight shoes. Calling upon the talisman of Martin's friendship, Elisha summoned warmth to his hands, and comfort.

"My physician von Stubben says that he would bleed me but not during the pregnancy."

"Certainly not," Elisha said, a little too harshly, then clasped his hands gently over her other foot, calming himself to send her his healing. "Forgive me, Your Majesty. Have one of your girls rub them lightly with oil of roses and lavender. And don't let vanity keep you from larger shoes," he said more quietly.

"No," she said, "You're right." She gazed down to where he knelt at her feet, touching her. "You defy what I imagine of physicians, Doctor."

Elisha stiffened, expecting the usual criticism of the barbering trade. "My training has been more in the practical than in the philosophical, Your Majesty. If I affront you, please forgive me."

"No, Doctor, you do not. It is rather a relief to speak with a medical man who considers my feet and not merely my stars. They prescribed a visit to Bad Stollhein for the healing salts. Do you agree?"

Elisha thought furiously, wondering how to parlay the empress's favor into a chance to stay near and keep watch over the emperor and his family. "Salts are known to have a good effect, Your Majesty, and a salt bath, in particular, can support the body in a way that you may find soothing to your back and legs."

"Plans are made to proceed there on the morrow," the emperor said. "Are you satisfied now, my dear?"

Sending comfort and vigor into the empress's feet, Elisha took his chance. "Your Majesty, if you would have me, I should be willing to accompany you there and assist in your care during the journey."

She let out a sigh and nodded. "I would be delighted, good doctor, to have your advice."

The emperor's lips formed a straight line in his thick beard, and he growled low in his throat. Empress Margaret's face colored, but she lifted her chin. "Pray you join my barge at the river in the morning. We shall not sail too early, I fear, but you will be welcome at any time you arrive." She said these last words with precision, and Ludwig's hand tightened on the arm of his throne. "Before you depart . . ." She motioned to Gretchen, who knelt by her daïs along with a few other servants and ladies, and whispered something in the girl's ear that sent her hurrying from the room.

The empress shifted forward on her seat. "Pay no heed to my husband. I fear he has many things to worry him."

The side door opened again, and a servant came through; expecting Gretchen's return, Elisha found himself disappointed to see a girl he did not recognize. She carried a bundle which she held out to him as the door swung shut behind her. Decorously, he replaced the empress's hem before he rose to accept the bundle.

"In thanks for your care, we give you this. Our autumn can be cold here, Doctor, especially upon the river. Allow my gratitude to keep you warm."

Indeed, the closing door had let in a draft of chill air that tingled his skin. From the bundle, he unfolded a short cape, hooded and lined with fur. As it unfurled, he sensed a quiver of excitement, and he envisioned Gretchen, taking it up to bring it here, then giving it to another. What could have delighted her and distracted her from her mistress? "I thank you, Your Majesty."

"If you're done bestowing largesse, darling," the emperor interjected, "then I believe the barber can go. Harald shall escort you to the gate."

"On the morrow, Doctor," said the empress.

Elisha bowed himself from their presence, his bent head concealing his surprise. Barber—yet those he knew here called him "Doctor." Perhaps Thomas's letters had revealed more than Elisha would wish.

As the steward led him through the crowd, Harald said, "I'm sorry his Majesty is no more kindly disposed toward you. I had hoped for better, as, I'm sure, did you."

"I hoped to tell him about his enemies. He doesn't even know what he's facing."

The steward glanced at him sidelong, then gave a half-nod. "It may be that the empress's favor will bring you favor with his Majesty as well."

They came to the stairs leading down to the main gate, and Elisha stopped him. "Is there a man in the emperor's employ called Bardolph? Tall, handsome, recently injured his arm."

"He's a royal messenger—why do you ask?"

"He's dangerous. He's working with enemies of the empire."

The steward's eyes flared. "Charles?"

Elisha shook his head. "Worse than Charles, though they are in league with him."

"Bardolph came in this morning, just after you arrived, in fact." The steward sighed and shook his head. "Looking for his leman, unless I miss my mark."

"Gretchen." The thrill of her excitement clinging to the cape, the sharp draft that disturbed him shortly after it was delivered. He'd taken it for the breeze of the closing door—not for the subtle opening of the Valley itself. Damnation! Bardolph had found her. "Where did he go? Where would he look for her?"

"The queen's chambers, but—"

"Take me there, now." He caught Harald's arm, sending his urgency. "Please, it could be her life if you don't."

Harald thrust up his chin. "Unhand me, sir, or I shall call the guard to expel you."

"You don't understand." Elisha shook his head, draw-ing the man with him, the steward resisting as Elisha moved them from the aisle where servants and courtiers lingered. "The emperor is the target of sorcery. There are witches working with Charles to bring down your master and send the empire into ruin. Bardolph is one of them, and Gretchen is in danger because she spoke to me. You've got to help me find them!"

Shaking him off, Harald took a step back. "I caught a glimpse of Bardolph's hand when he returned. The injury . . . it's not natural. It's as if his arm has aged a hundred years. Come, this way."

He ran back the way they had come, Elisha on his heels, dodging the richly dressed courtiers, hearing Brother Gilles call out to him, but he waved away the question. They rounded a corner and stopped before a door guarded by another pair of pikemen. "Did the em-peror's messenger Bardolph come by here?"

"Aye, steward, he's within."

Harald pushed open the door to an empty chamber and closed it again at their backs. Elisha moved ahead of him, spreading his senses, tossing down the cape that hampered his arms. Rich carpets covered the stone floors to match tapestries on every wall, on chairs, tables, cush-ions. A door led to the side, presumably into the cham-ber where the rulers held court, and a second door stood open at the back. Both men crossed quickly to find the revealed bedchamber likewise empty.

"They couldn't've gone through the court chamber — I should have seen, unless they went in after I left with you," Harald muttered while Elisha knelt, breathing care-fully, and set his hand to the floor, sinking his awareness into every detail. He swept the room with his gaze, and his left eye caught a shimmer of darkness, like a whiff of smoke that dissipates when a candle is extinguished. Stalking forward, he focused on the place, the unmistak-able sign that the Valley had been there, opened by a con-tact with death. It had touched him with its chill even in the other room. There was no sign of relics here, though something occupied the corner chapel he glimpsed from his position on the floor. Bardolph must have carried his talisman with him. Elisha sank to his knees, head bowed. How to track him?

"What is it?"

The slightest hint of warmth edged his fingers. A few tiny drops of blood marked the floor. Gretchen's blood. Would that presence in the Valley which opposed Elisha find him now? Could he let an innocent woman die to avoid that risk?

"Doctor?"

"I'm sorry," Elisha said, then he summoned his strength from every talisman, seized the steward about the shoulders and sent him sleep, an exhaustion of body and mind. At least the steward wouldn't see him vanish into nothing. Harald collapsed into his arms, and Elisha laid him gently on the carpet, then ripped open the Valley and sprang inside.

Chapter 13

───────◇───────

℮lisha held himself in the passage, dampening the dead voices that howled at his ears as if he led a chorus of Hell's jongleurs. A ripple passed before him, a span of heat that cut across the writhing madness, like a stone dropped in a river.

Far off in the rushing torrent of the Valley, Elisha felt the echo of Gretchen's living presence. Whatever malevolent force had noticed him the last time was absent now. Others crowded around him, the shades of those he had killed, linking him to Bardolph in this chain of sorrows. Elisha ignored them, paring down his contacts to that one, the living girl swept away through this awful country of the dead. Taking a deep breath, drawing in the dead to defend him, Elisha reached back. Contact.

The Valley sprang open, tumbling him into a grassy meadow to trip over a pair of bodies. Elisha stumbled a few steps as the bodies stirred, one shouting, the other crying out. Flushed, they stared up at him, Gretchen pushing her skirts about, her bodice askew, Bardolph glaring, wiping his mouth.

She looked completely unharmed—lovely in her flush, if rather startled by his arrival. A tiny scratch on her arm was her only sign of injury, but she wore no bonds, and he carried no weapons. None that could be seen, in any case. "What are you doing here?" Gretchen asked.

"Spying on me," Bardolph grumbled. He put out his

hands—gloved in fine leather to conceal the damage—
and helped her up. "Why can't you leave me alone?"

"I don't understand." She clung to her lover, her eyes
tracing Elisha's form, then her face hardened. Her presence buzzed with worry, her awareness brushing over his,
sparking like steel struck against flint. She tugged Bardolph's arm, drawing him away from Elisha. "You've
come with murder in your heart, Doctor—I can read it.
Why?"

Elisha swallowed, the dark power chanting at his
flesh, urging him to the attack in spite of his confusion.
He stilled his hands, resisting. "I have reason to believe
you are in danger."

"Who would put me at risk, sir?" She laughed a little,
then glanced at Bardolph. "You don't mean—?"

"He took against me when we were in England, and
we'd barely met. It was he who maimed me," Bardolph
told her.

"Is this true?" She reached out toward Elisha, seeking
contact and confirmation, but Bardolph grabbed her, his
left hand barely flexible.

"Don't touch him! To touch him is death."

The pent-up power shivered his muscles, but to move
against Bardolph meant exposing Gretchen to that
power and confirming all that Bardolph claimed.

Gretchen leaned back against Bardolph's chest, her
cheeks gone pale. "It is true," she breathed, "I can feel it!
Take us, Bardolph—take us away! He means to kill you."

"I'm not afraid to meet him, not with you beside me."

"No! He's too strong." Even as she said it, she wrapped
a fist around a tiny pouch that hung at her throat, her
talisman. All sense of her presence vanished, shrouded
by her own power. "What are you?"

Elisha gave a slight shake of his head. "You have
nothing to fear from me, Fraulein. Your lover is a murderer. I struck him when he tried to kill my king. I followed him here because I feared he would kill you."

"You are mad! Bardolph and I are to marry!" She
glanced back at her lover.

"Watch out!" Bardolph shouted, leaping backward

and taking her with him. Elisha lunged toward them, expecting the chill opening of the Valley, catching the wild look in the girl's eyes.

Something pierced his awareness, an instant before an arrow slammed into his back. Elisha spun about with the force of the blow, gasping, then choking as blood filled his mouth.

A second arrow ripped through his side, then a third.

A fourth furrowed his right arm as he tried to dodge, but they came from all sides. Pain shot through him and he tumbled to his knees, trying to catch himself on the left before jamming the arrows deeper still. Two feathered shafts stuck from his chest. Long, smooth, pale wood stained by spreading rings of blood. One at his back.

Elisha pitched sideways, trying to scream.

All the strength that he had mustered—strength to slay a mancer or to defend himself against magic— turned inward as Death leapt within the man who would be its master. Already, his hands and feet numbed, his limbs shuddered. His body curled around the wounds.

Tramping feet vibrated through his flesh, jiggling shards of pain that radiated from each embedded shaft.

"You were right, messenger," grunted the archer who stared down at Elisha. "He's not dead, though." He touched the bow hanging over his shoulder.

Elisha sobbed, tears streaking his face. His own death might open the Valley and take him straight to Hell. His left hand fumbled toward his belt.

"Hey!" the archer stuck his foot out, kicking aside Elisha's hand, then reaching down to grab the belt. He jerked on it, rolling and lifting Elisha from the ground before letting him fall back to earth. He struck hard, crying out as the shaft in his back shoved in deeper and snapped.

"No weapons to speak of. Grope all ye want." The man straightened from his cursory search, signaling to his unseen companions.

"Bardolph?" wailed Gretchen's voice.

Elisha rolled to the side, breathless.

"We thought he'd try again to kill me, dearest. I ought to have . . ."

But Elisha could not hear for the pounding of his blood. Desperately, he tried to marshal his scattering thoughts, to send his awareness back inside and judge the injuries. One arrow pierced his lung. One had nicked his heart. If he sealed the vessels, he might stop the bleeding, but he could not heal without pulling the shafts.

Something stung his chest, like the bite of an insect to insult a dying man.

The black tide welled up, a howling filling his ears and echoing in his skull. Elisha mastered his hands, groping toward the arrows in his chest.

With a low growl, the archer pulled out a knife.

Death's laughter rang through Elisha's body. His questing hand snagged on that stinging thing: the little pin with Lucia's nail trimmings. *"Don't trouble over it,"* Brother Gilles had told him, *"I have more."*

Elisha pressed it to his chest, and fell into the Valley as the archer's knife swung down toward his throat. The swirling abyss rose up all around him, enfolding him in cold comfort. The taunting faces of the dead mancers showed plainly against the background of shades. He sought for Martin instead, conjuring the warmth of his triumphant sacrifice to ward off death, to hold it at bay a moment longer. Brother Gilles. His wooden crate. The fingernails of a dead girl, given him as the remnants of a saint.

Wood cracked, and Elisha spilled onto a stone floor, straw and bones scattering around him.

"By the Rood!" cried a startled voice.

"Of all the—that's your doctor."

Footsteps vibrated through Elisha where he lay crumpled. "Help me," he gasped. "Help me," but he could not be sure they heard.

"How did he—he's bleeding. Shot through with arrows."

"Oh!" Gilles groaned, then the floor thumped, and he spoke no more. Elisha had chosen a fainter for his savior. He wept, his trembling hands refusing to obey.

Isaac's hand clasped his shoulder. "He's alive! Brother Gilles?" And a muttered curse in the language of the Jews. "I'll go for help," Isaac said, bringing his face very near. Elisha's right eye saw his fear. His left eye saw a tunnel of darkness as if the Valley never closed. It sucked at his heart, frosting his lips.

"No," Elisha breathed, backing this urgency with a plea from flesh to flesh. "Push the shafts through. Break the feathers, pull the points." He gulped, spat blood, then tried again, "Please. I can heal this."

Isaac started shaking his head, drawing back, but Elisha seized his hand, keeping it close. "If you go, it'll be too late."

Elisha's hand slipped away, his arm twitching like a thing already dead.

Dark eyes growing darker, the goldsmith pressed his lips together hard, then reached for the first shaft. "You're sure?"

A nod—or a tremor. Crimson pulsed across Elisha's vision.

Isaac winced, then pushed the arrow. With a slicing of flesh it thrust through Elisha's back. He cried out silently, then clamped his jaw and his eyes shut, turning inward. Wood cracked, then the shaft tugged against him. Elisha sank deep into himself, for the first lessons, the barbering of so long ago, to the anatomies he studied with Mordecai when learning his Latin. He urged his flesh to heal. As Isaac drew out the shaft, Elisha's awareness pursued it, sealing, bonding, fixing, and patching: vessels to their mates, flesh to flesh, skin to skin. The arrow clattered aside.

The heat of Isaac's touch shifted to the next, and Elisha followed, forgetting all but this. By the third shaft, the one already broken, the trembling of pain had become that of weakness, of too much spell-casting, and too much lost blood. He gagged, spat, and lay still, shivering, his forehead resting on the stone, his eyes still shut.

"Gracious Lord, what has happened here?" mumbled Brother Gilles.

"Something like a miracle," Isaac answered.

"Does he live?" Another hand, more hesitant, touched Elisha's shoulder and back, a finger stroked gently over the puckered skin of his fresh scars. "Saints be praised! The Lord delivered him here, to be healed through these relics. Can you say which saint provided the remedy? Oh, it is a miracle! The emperor will be so pleased. What did you see?"

For a moment, no one spoke. Elisha's rough breathing echoed in his ears. Someday, likely soon, he would have to move or speak, but the hard ground and the prickly reality of the straw beneath his palm was enough for now.

"Herr Burghussen? Can you tell me what you saw? This will be important for the accounts. I must write a report for the Holy Father."

Isaac's voice sounded subdued. "I really can't say."

"He appeared from nowhere! As we spoke of the—I see! You and I, we are planning a most ingenious reliquary for the arm of Saint Brendan. Surely, this miracle is a sign of his approval."

"What I'd like to know," Isaac said, with a hint of his former acid, "is how he came to be shot full of arrows."

A loud rapping echoed in the chamber, and Elisha caught his breath. If Bardolph came now—

The rapping sounded again, and Brother Gilles moved to the door.

"Brother. I'm looking for that English doctor." The voice of the steward, Harald, whom Elisha had sent to sleep in the queen's chamber.

"But he is here! There has been a miracle, sir. The doctor was beset and shot with arrows, and the Lord transported him to me, to my chest of relics, to be cured by his association with the arm of Saint Brendan."

Footsteps approached, then the steward cried, "Holy Mary!"

"I don't know that the Virgin interceded here, but it may be so."

Elisha trembled as he gulped for breath. He must answer them, he must speak, but the agony still echoed through him, and his breath caught in his freshly healed chest as if scars impeded his lungs. He shuddered against the floor.

"The cape, sir, please," said Isaac's imperious voice. "The cape," he repeated more firmly, then a dense warmth of fur and wool draped Elisha's shoulders, the weight of it embracing him. Slowly, his breath evened. The steward and the friar shared their conversation, the one dismayed, the other fervent with his faith.

By taking Gretchen, just there and in that way, Bardolph lured him through the Valley to die, to be shot by arrows, a weapon he could not combat with his power. The archers carried no magic of their own. They were *desolati*, not magi, certainly not mancers. "The messenger," they called Bardolph. Imperial men, in service to the mancers. "I have to go," Elisha gasped.

"Pardon?" Isaac's voice came closer as Elisha's eyes flickered open.

"I have to go. I can't stay here. Too many enemies." He got one hand under him and tried to push himself up, the cape sliding.

Isaac caught him about the shoulders and steadied him. "Easy, Doctor. Surely you should know that a man can't expect such a rapid recovery, even through the intervention of the saints."

Elisha's head swam, and he paused, letting his vision clear as he parsed out what the goldsmith was saying. "I know," he whispered. "I need to find a place to recover." But where? He clasped his other hand over his head as if he could squeeze it into compliance. He knew no one in this city save a goldsmith, an innkeeper and an emperor united in their low opinion of him; a friar convinced he was a miracle; and any number of mancers or their allies set to slay him. The empress might take him in—but he would not be safe inside the castle, not in his condition. He had to leave, and he had no place to go, nowhere in this city would he be either safe or welcome. Damnation.

Releasing him, the goldsmith eased away and came around to squat in front of him, careful to take up his velvet sleeves so they would not drag. His dark eyes studied Elisha's face.

"Is he conscious? Excellent!" Brother Gilles loomed up at Isaac's side, grinning. "Do tell me, Doctor, what happened? How did you come to be here and in such a state? How did you call upon the saints to help you? Come, Steward, and hear the tale!" Gilles flapped his hand toward the other man.

"Truly, it shall be a tale of wonders, I am sure—perhaps explaining a curious fit that took me not long ago," the steward replied. "But we should also call for priests and physicians, should we not?"

"My enemies laid a trap for me," Elisha said, barely above a whisper. "They linger still. I am too weak to meet them now. If they find me here, I'll die." He let his hand creep out to a pool of his own blood. With the last of his strength he smothered his presence with the impression of his own death.

"Goodness!" cried the friar.

"All the more reason to fetch the emperor's men," the steward said. "I shall return—"

"No," Elisha begged. "My enemies are among them."

"Gentlemen," Isaac snapped, sweeping himself up so quickly that they moved back from him. "It is clear to me that this man is in no state to respond to your questions. He cannot recover if he fears the very men you would bring to question or protect him." Isaac paused, and the steward gave a short nod. "If it please both church and state, I shall convey him to his friends in the city, and send word when he is ready for an examination."

Brother Gilles's round face collapsed into misery, and he sighed. "You may well be right, good friend. I shall prepare an account of what I have witnessed, and we will be ready for the doctor's testimony when he is more able."

"He is now a member of the party of the Empress Margaret, until she arrives at Bad Stollhein at least," the steward said, rather sharply. "We must investigate who dared assault him under those circumstances. In the meantime, I can escort you to the gate."

"Are you able to walk, Doctor?" Isaac asked, bending down again, holding out his hand.

Elisha took it, pulling himself up with far too much support from the slight goldsmith. He swayed on his feet and straightened, then slowly shook his head, still not letting go of Isaac's arm. "I cannot manage the hill," he murmured, then met the man's gaze. "Nor have I friends to go to."

Isaac gripped his arm in return. "Of course you have, Doctor. You've merely forgotten them in your recent injured state."

Elisha frowned, but the goldsmith said no more, though a slight shake of his head urged Elisha's silence. With their help, he made it through the door, down a corridor to a lower gate near the kitchens. Thank God there were no stairs here as there were at the main entrance. Here, the steward left them, suggesting Elisha send word to the barge in the morning to inform them of his condition. Isaac bargained with a carter who drove his oxen homeward after delivering butts of flour to the castle kitchen, and they two climbed into the back of the cart. Elisha sagged back, bundled into the cape the queen had given him, and stared at the deep gray turmoil of the sky.

The cart swayed back and forth, bumping down the road, and Isaac scooted near, crossing his legs at the ankle. "You still have your letter from Jacob, I trust."

It took a moment to place the name, then Elisha nodded. "I can't read it," he answered honestly. "I did not think you cared for me, sir."

Isaac's eyes cut away toward the carter on his bench, then back. "It is not for your own sake I treated you so, believe me. I have seen wonders this day, Doctor."

The raw hurt that pulsed through the goldsmith's presence touched Elisha's raw senses, and he dredged up a little power to seal himself from the other man's emotions. "You owe me no explanation, sir." Elisha swallowed, his throat still dry. "Rather, I owe you—"

"Don't," the goldsmith said, putting up his hand to forestall more talk. "Rest."

Elisha knew not where they went, but shut his eyes, sinking into the near-sleep of healing, his frayed senses still spread, his ebbing power bent on concealing himself.

Their departure through the lower gate should help in that regard. Pray Brother Gilles did not trumpet the miracle too widely just yet.

Shade reached over Elisha's face, and he opened his eyes to see the tops of painted plaster houses and stone buildings cutting the sky in his view. Isaac rose and braced his arms against the back of the bench to speak to the carter.

The fellow gave an oath. "But that's the Judengasse— you're sure?"

Isaac shrugged broadly. "I know it, friend, but there's a doctor can help him recover, or so he says. I swore I'd see him safely down, after that, I'm well away, believe you me."

The two shared a chuckle. "Well, and they do have some learned men, I've heard," the carter replied. "Don't know as I'd want one of 'em touching me or mine."

"God forbid," Isaac replied fervently, crossing himself.

The cart made a few turns, then lurched to a halt, and Elisha pushed himself to sitting, his head a little more clear now. Isaac stepped by and jumped to the ground, reaching up to help Elisha to the ground and settle the cape over his shoulders. The carter lashed his animals onward rather than wait a moment longer in a street of Jews and the cart rumbled away. Isaac rapped the doorknocker on a house painted the gold of deer hide. A girl opened the door. "Yessir?"

"I've come in the name of Jacob of Trier, to see your master."

"Yessir." She opened the door wider to let them in, Elisha moving slowly as his muscles shivered, Isaac supporting him under one elbow.

The servant led them to a well-appointed chamber with a fire already lit, and Elisha sagged into a sling chair. "What shall I tell the rabbi, sirs?"

Rabbi? Elisha thought, but Isaac turned to him. "Doctor, the letter that Jacob gave you, he'll want to see it."

Elisha untangled his oilcloth packet, with Isaac's help sorting out the two pages Jacob had given him, which the goldsmith turned over to the girl. She hurried away, only to return a few minutes later bearing a tray of wine and goblets. "He says to be comfortable, and he'll be with you soon." Leaving the tray, she curtsied and left them.

"Red wine," Isaac observed. "What should you have in your condition?"

"Red wine is perfect," Elisha said, feeling thirsty just at the thought, but given how much blood he had lost— "watered, if you can. Red meat would be even better."

Isaac moved about the room and returned with a larger pitcher and a mug. Clearly, he knew his way around this house. Elisha studied his movements, trying to reconcile this familiarity with his vehement anger against Jacob, not to mention the attitude he shared with the carter. Then the word came to mind. As Isaac poured him a tall draught of watered wine, Elisha leaned forward to receive it. "Converso, aren't you?" A flash of fear and fury broke Elisha's numbness, and the goldsmith's face turned pale.

Chapter 14

❖

Isaac replaced the pitcher with a hard click, barely under control, then he sat abruptly, his hands knotting together. "Yes, I am."

Elisha took a long swallow, grateful for the warmth and wetness, then focused on his reluctant savior, a Jew who had renounced his own faith to claim the Christian God, probably to improve his own trade, given the showy cross he now wore. "If you're found here, with Jews . . ."

"I'll be accused of Judaizing, reverting to my old ways." The edge of anger returned to Isaac's voice, although his fear had not passed.

"That's why you were angry at Jacob for asking you to bring my things." Elisha's voice strengthened with each swallow. "I'm grateful you brought me here, but you need not stay. I say again that I would do nothing to endanger your livelihood or your commission from the emperor."

"Thank you for that," Isaac murmured, never raising his gaze from his clasped hands. "I should go. I am no more welcome here than the rabbi would be at church." His velvet sleeves rippled, but he showed no sign of leaving.

"I'll think no less of you for going, nor would any man."

"Except my kin." The goldsmith shook his head, his dark curls bobbing. "No. The rabbi will be—"

"Don't speak of me as if I don't live in my own house, converso," thundered the rabbi himself, a barrel-chested man dressed head to toe in black, his gray beard curling thickly over his chest. He strode into the room, commanding it in an instant, as if he possessed a magic so strong he could bend the place to his presence. The priests at Elisha's burial held a power like that, the strength of their conviction blazing through them when they feared that he would use dark magic against them, even from the grave.

Elisha and Isaac sat up straight immediately, though the goldsmith kept his eyes downcast.

"Forgive me, Rabbi, I meant no disrespect."

"For you to be here, in my hall, is disrespect. No more, nor less than what you did in that church, before that cross."

Isaac flinched, then lifted his head, his steel returning. "You know the circumstances, Rabbi. You know what brought me there."

"You should have gone with your family rather than to shame them like this."

The goldsmith gave a cry, pushed himself up, and stalked toward the door. Then he whirled. "No, Rabbi, you are not rid of me so easily." He shot out his finger as if it were a weapon. "Not before I have witnessed to Jacob's words."

"Jacob is an old man gone mad with grief, and overcome by his son's return." For the first time, the rabbi lifted a shaggy eyebrow at Elisha, scanning and dismissing him in an instant. "Jacob does well for us in Trier, and we hope he'll continue to do so, but this"—he waved the parchment—"this is only a mistake to be scraped away and overwritten. Perhaps it may be suitable for writing a bill to haul garbage. Or perhaps to record your riches." He flipped the pages into Isaac's face and they fluttered toward the floor.

"Will neither of you tell me what he said?" Elisha asked.

Isaac ducked to retrieve the letter. "I have not read it, of course, but Jacob was too much in awe to be silent. He made claims for you, Doctor, for powers no man can manufacture. He calls you a wonder-worker."

Elisha recoiled with confusion and not a little anger. He expected Jacob's message to include an introduction, perhaps a recommendation, not a claim of miraculous powers; he'd counted on Jacob's discretion, and the thought of his dangerous power being discussed, especially in a letter Jacob knew Elisha could not read, rankled him.

Isaac continued, "I have seen it myself, Rabbi, and you must know I have no reason to put faith in anything of the Jews." Acid. Anger that covered his pain. Elisha wished he could reach out right then and work a wonder, healing the goldsmith of his grief.

"You. What have you seen?" The rabbi flicked his fingers, then, just as Isaac began to speak, turned his back and strolled to the fire to warm his hands.

With a movement of his jaw, as if he forced his teeth apart to speak, Isaac began again. "I have been to the castle of the emperor, Rabbi. He has granted me a commission that—" A pause. "It's not important. In any event, I met with a collaborator to discuss the work that must be done—"

"What is this thing you will not tell me of? You reek with pride at your imperial commission, but you won't speak of it? How great a thing can it be if you are ashamed to say it?" The rabbi spoke as if to himself, musing, dismissing Isaac's work by his very lack of vehemence. The casual rejection stung Elisha on Isaac's behalf, and goaded the goldsmith into speaking.

"As I say," Isaac continued, firmly, "I met with my collaborator, and this man appeared from nowhere, pierced by arrows and running with blood. He fell to the floor, and we were shocked at his appearance, his being there at all, but also at his injuries."

The rabbi's back stiffened, and he made a derisive sound, but he did not interrupt again.

"I bent to help him, Rabbi, to see what could be done. He asked me"—a glance at Elisha, a hint of worry—"he begged me to pull the arrows, and claimed that he could heal the wounds. He said that, if I went for help, it would be too late. Given how much blood had spilled, and the placement of the arrows. I . . . did not believe that anything could aid him, and so I did as he bid me. I pushed the shafts through his flesh. I broke off the feathers, and drew out the points. And as I did so . . . his flesh . . . he was healed, Rabbi. I cannot account for it."

The rabbi, who had gone still, snorted, and turned, his eyes narrowed. "You cannot account for it. Perhaps it's you who are the wonder-worker, converso. Perhaps you have this mystic power in your hands." He wriggled his thick fingers.

Isaac was no friend of Elisha's, only an acquaintance in the right place, at the right time, taking this slight risk—or so Elisha had thought—of seeing him safely to the Jewish quarter where Jacob's message might bring him favor. As a converso, Isaac risked suspicion to be seen in such a place, and now he endured the rabbi's scorn. For what? To convince the rabbi of Elisha's powers, powers that Elisha would just as soon keep quiet.

"No, if I had such power, I would be no converso. As God is my witness," he spat, employing the oath of a Christian. Then, more softly but with the precision of his trade, he said, "As you are my witness."

The rabbi reared back at Isaac's oath, then growled, "I might have sympathy for the child you were, but no child of the righteous would have done as you did."

Suppressing the spike of fury that dominated his presence, Elisha pushed himself to his feet, the cape sliding from his back. "We did not come for your approval, Rabbi, or for your condemnation. Surely there is a Christian inn or a pagan hovel that will show us more kindness."

The rabbi stared at him, gaze flickering over Elisha's chest. Holes edged in blood pierced the undershirt Jacob had given him. Swaying only a little, Elisha snatched up his new cloak, flinging it over his shoulders as he turned for the door. Isaac's features softened, his forehead creasing in concern as Elisha approached.

Shaking his head, Elisha murmured, "You've done nothing to deserve such abuse."

"You don't know—" Isaac began, but Elisha took his arm, his rough fingers catching on silk.

"Nothing you have done deserves this, master gold-smith, not when you fight on my behalf. Whatever Jacob said of me, it's not important. Let's go."

Isaac's eyes grew suddenly moist, and he breathed a few words in that strange language of the Jews. "Jacob was right," he said in German. "Forgive me, Doctor, we should never have come here." He straightened, taking Elisha's weight on his arm.

"Why are you doing this, you Christians?" the rabbi said. "Why forge yourselves a *lamed-vovnik*—why now?"

Elisha kept moving, ignoring the rabbi's foreign words, but Isaac stood rooted to the spot, an edge of white showing at his eyes. Then he braced Elisha with his other hand, his fear and anger flowing freely through the contact, and faced the rabbi. "How could you, Rabbi? And how dare you? You kill him with your words. Is this what ha-Shem asks of you? Whether or not you believe it, any man of humility would at the very least keep silent."

A wave of weakness swept Elisha's body, and he swayed, the cape sliding away, his forehead dropping to Isaac's shoulder. The goldsmith put up his hand, cradling Elisha's head with unexpected tenderness. "Please, Rabbi," Isaac said, very gently, as if he hated to disturb Elisha's rest, "have your servant call us a cart. If you have any mercy—"

The floor boards creaked, and Elisha's eyes fluttered open to a glimpse of the rabbi's black shoe tips, poking between his own round, brown boots and the goldsmith's pointed, painted leather; then a firm, unfriendly hand touched his back, fingers probing the torn cloth, brushing over the puckered scars. Elisha jerked, his elbow rising to ward off the intrusion, but it was Isaac who knocked away the rabbi's hand.

"Do you think he wanted this?" Isaac shouted, and other footsteps rustled in the hall, the entire household summoned by raised voices. "I've no idea what he is, Rabbi, but he is no fraud."

Elisha recovered himself, reluctantly giving up the comfort of Isaac's support to straighten and prop himself against the door arch. Two women and a few children clustered around in the corridor, gaping. Elisha ventured a smile, and the children giggled, scurrying away.

"And Simeon?" the rabbi asked in a strained voice. "You saw your cousin's wounds?"

"I saw his scars, Rabbi," said Isaac at his most acidic. "I heard Simeon's story from his own lips. No man would invent such suffering. Like you, I denied it. I did not believe it could be true."

"Please, master goldsmith," Elisha interrupted, "I need to go."

The rabbi put out his hands, pulsing them gently in the air. "Wait, please," he said, his manner chastened at last. "I don't know how to ask your forgiveness. I have treated you shamefully, as your host, if nothing more. What you need is rest and safety, and I did not offer them. I was . . . angered by Jacob's letter. Pay it no mind."

Isaac hesitated, his protective stance unaltered. "Are you fit to travel, Doctor?"

Where else would he go? Looking from one of them to the other, Elisha said, "In faith, no."

"Please, sit." The rabbi gestured them back toward the chamber. "My girl will bring you a meal and prepare a bed. I need . . . there are books I must consult." He made a vague motion of his hand. "I will return."

"Thank you." Elisha returned to the comfortable chair he had abandoned a few minutes earlier and sank gratefully back into it, his hands shaking. He pressed them together, then slid them up, locking his arms across his chest, shoulders sagging.

"Herr Doctor." Isaac came to Elisha's side, pouring a fresh goblet of wine, topping it with water, retrieving the cape to cover Elisha's shoulders and securing it with a pin that he plucked from his own velvet robe.

Elisha stirred himself to drink as the trembling retreated. "I don't know what to make of you, master goldsmith."

"Nor I, you." Isaac retreated to a chair of his own, dodging the conversation by summoning one of the children and speaking at length in that other language.

Leaning against a cushioned arm of the chair, Elisha shut his eyes and let himself drift, using only enough strength to ward himself against intrusion. He remembered all too well his last visit with a family of Jews, opening his eyes to the sight of the Archbishop of Trier, Emperor Charles's uncle and a man he had made an enemy. It would not happen again.

An older woman arrived some time later, with servants who laid Elisha's meal. She talked with Isaac in the stiff, formal tones of a hostess with an unwelcome guest. They spoke of the palace and exchanged news of mutual acquaintances in Trier, Aachen, and Isaac's home at Burghussen while Elisha devoured flat breads, meat, and peas prepared with unfamiliar herbs. By the end of the meal, his dizziness ebbed away, leaving him weary but clear-headed, strong enough to walk to the bed they had made up for him in an adjoining chamber. Every moment he stayed could put these people at risk, and left him no closer to finding or avoiding his enemies, but he needed rest. He must be ready in the morning to join the royal entourage, and prepared for whatever he might find when he got there.

Elisha began the work of attunement, understanding the place around him so that he could properly guard himself as he slept, but the small, dark room felt thick with absence: he thought of Mordecai, the first Jew he had ever met, the one who taught him so much, who showed how wrong folk were when they condemned the Jews. Mordecai watched over the silent Brigit, nurturing the baby that grew inside of her, and concealing both from Elisha's enemies, who sought her still. And he thought of Thomas, Ludwig's son-by-marriage, Elisha's king, Elisha's friend. The lock of his hair Elisha carried still felt warm, a comfort that reminded him of Thomas's keen gaze and rare smile—and his utter faith in Elisha. Like the Jews here, Thomas believed Elisha was holy. Elisha remembered the short time he himself had been king. One long afternoon, he sat after Sunday Mass and blessed and healed, imparting whatever strength he could to a line of supplicants that seemed unending.

Tonight, outside his chamber, strangers who prayed to a God he did not recognize spoke in a language he did not know. The warmth of Isaac's comfort faded in the darkness, returning Elisha to his customary chill. He lay in the dark, the vial of British soil pressing against a fresh scar upon his chest, tempting him to spill it, to conjure himself to London, back to Mordecai and the baby, back to Thomas, back home. Not since he lay inside his grave had Elisha felt so terribly alone.

Chapter 15

❖

Heated voices woke Elisha, long after the candle at his bedside burned to nothing. Isaac and the rabbi, going at it again. By God, what fury lay between them? His few hours rest and the good meal gave Elisha strength to face the storm in the next room. Why was it so important to them whether he was or was not this wonder-worker Jacob claimed him to be? The rabbi noticed him first, falling silent. The goldsmith stood opposite, arms folded so tightly they creased wrinkles into his velvet, the gold cross on his chest winking in the firelight.

"What is it you think that I am?" Elisha walked forward, fit enough, but empty of patience for the Jews' quarrel. He poured himself a glass of unwatered wine, a sweet richness worthy of Thomas's table.

"Lamed-vov," said the rabbi simply, and Isaac erupted from his place by the wall.

"Stop saying that!"

Elisha frowned. "If you're the one who believes in whatever that is, why does it matter whether he says it?"

Smoke drifted between them from lanterns and fire, their dark eyes locked upon each other. "You're going to have to tell him what it means, Christian," said the rabbi, running his fingers through his beard. "You can see he won't leave it alone."

Isaac winced, and finally pushed away from the wall. "Jacob said that your works show you to be one of a few—"

"—thirty-six," the rabbi interrupted, earning another black look from the goldsmith.

"A few men of each generation who strive to defend the righteous and suffer greatly on behalf of those they aid. They are given mystic skills to use in this cause, gifts of healing, and ways to travel that defy explanation. The name he keeps saying is simply the number. If one of them falls and ha-Shem cannot replace him with a man equally worthy, the world will end."

"And you think I'm one of them." Elisha stared at the scars on the backs of his hands, the scars the mancer-archbishop used to convince the people of London that Elisha was holy, a worthy king. "These thirty-six, do they rule your people?"

Both men looked shocked, the rabbi's hand frozen in the tangle of his beard, the goldsmith shaking his head urgently. "Of course not. To do their work, they must be secret. Even from themselves." He dodged Elisha's gaze. "Some legends say that, if one of them is revealed, it means his death."

"Ah." To be holy to the Christians meant reverence and power. To be holy to the Jews meant to be invisible, on pain of death. And Isaac the goldsmith vented his fury whenever the rabbi named Elisha with that word, "lamed-vov"—the goldsmith strove to save his life; the rabbi, angry that Elisha was not even a Jew, taunted him with a name that served as a curse. Elisha drained his glass. "I'm grateful for your hospitality, Rabbi, and you, Isaac, for bringing me, but I should go. My enemies have mystic powers, too." He gave a slight smile.

"Let him go, then," said the rabbi, folding his hands behind him, perhaps to control the stroking of his beard.

Isaac took a step before the door. "But if he is, Rabbi, then we should give him all aid—his cause is our own. The very fact he is revealed shows that a terrible time is coming. The hidden ones don't emerge for every imperial dispute."

"Look," Elisha began, but Isaac shook his head gently.

"You had nowhere to go tonight, did you? You fell as

if from the sky, grievously wounded, and in need. Cold as death."

The rabbi's breath hissed in.

"The stories say that some of—these people—are so frozen by the suffering they relieve that they must be cradled in the hand of ha-Shem for a thousand years before they are warm again."

Elisha reeled, his eyes squeezing shut against the sudden sting of tears. The cold that assailed him, he had invited it in. He took it to himself every time he called upon his power and felt it sink into his heart. It was not sacred, not a thing of compassion—God would not take Elisha into His hand after all that he had done. But if Elisha were terrible and mighty, then his enemies were more dreadful still, and he still did not know their plans. The mancers set kings upon their thrones, to what end? Not for the just rule of the people, that much was certain. For war, for pain, for the suffering of thousands. For a moment, Elisha envisioned the world—England, France, the cities of Italy, the Holy Roman Empire, and beyond— linked in a maelstrom of pain that swept power back to the mancers, just as the master in his ring of flagellants gathered their misery and reveled in it.

Worse was coming, just as Isaac feared, and Elisha seemed to be the only man trying to fight, but he could not do this alone. Elisha shivered. A thousand years of warmth. Christ, would that it could be!

"You mentioned aid," Elisha said carefully.

Isaac's eyes lit up, his face aglow with a new kind of ferocity. "There are Jews in every city of the Empire, and beyond. You need never worry where you will rest or eat or hide. Through commerce and through faith, we spread news as fast as the emperor's riders. Jacob meant to give you all this when he wrote his letter. If the rabbi were to write you one, if he were to speak about you, thousands would listen."

The rabbi rumbled behind them.

Isaac said "we" when he spoke of the Jews. He was still a man of two hearts. "Information?" Elisha asked. "I need to know about things like what happened to

Simeon, disappearances, people who can't be trusted, places where people are taken, the flagellant cults and where they go."

"These inquiries," said the rabbi, his presence swelling slowly with faith and worry, "if my people were known to be asking, to be thinking of these things, we would be accused ourselves. It's dangerous, these things you wish to know."

Elisha faced the old man. "Even if they never asked a thing, Rabbi, but simply told me what they already know. My enemies work by rumor and silence. They think they can prey upon your people because nobody will care, because you'll be too afraid to say anything. They want hatred and fear between us. Even if I learn only what's being whispered in the market, that can be an aid to me." As he spoke, Elisha realized he placed himself in the position of accepting the title that Jacob claimed for him, if only in return for the information that would help him try to stop what was happening. "I'm not holy, but I do have skills not given to many."

"Scars, and blood, and ... other men's words," the rabbi began, raising an eyebrow to Isaac, "I don't know if this is enough."

"You want proof." Elisha put out his hand to forestall Isaac's protest. "Is there someone in need of healing?"

"You are a doctor in any case," the rabbi replied. "Perhaps you have medicines more efficacious than those we know."

"No medicine can heal—" Isaac began, but trailed off at Elisha's sigh.

"Can you give me Kefitzat ha-Derech?" The rabbi folded his hands, a prim smile on his lips.

"Not if I don't know what that is." Elisha's fists clenched.

"Kefitzat ha-Derech," Isaac echoed. "It means folding the way." He pinched his fingers on both hands as if drawing a thread straight between them, then brought them together. "It means ha-Shem brings you from one place to another without passing in between."

The Valley of the Shadow, but for these people, it had

a name. During their stay on the Isle of Wight, he remembered Mordecai's joy at finding a Jewish book and
scouring it for information—for this name, for any sign
that this Hellish mode of travel came not from the fiend,
but from above.

"It requires blood, some connection between where I
am and where I must go. When you saw me appear, Isaac,
I used the bit of a relic that Brother Gilles had given me,
and I knew where I wanted to go."

"You drew yourself to the friar's chamber?" Isaac
cocked his head, and Elisha smiled grimly.

"It was not for the friar's sake—I had to have a connection to a place I did not think my enemies could follow. There are many connections we share, places they
can travel at will."

"So you are not the only one with this skill," the rabbi
observed.

"I'm not—and the others are far from righteous. They
can travel only where they have killed someone, or to
the places where they've hidden parts of the corpse."

The old man's deep eyes narrowed, but he did not
comment.

"You do have demons, don't you, in your version of
the Bible?" Elisha asked.

"Granted. So, you need connection, a relic." The rabbi
stalked about the room, took up an object the size of a
fist and carried it over, cradled in his hand and placed it
in Elisha's palm. "Take me here."

An irregular rock with one smooth side, perhaps
chipped from a dressed stone, it was pale gray, clean of
any dust or marking. "I can't work with this," Elisha said,
turning it over in his hand.

"If you're not what you claim—"

"I claim nothing," Elisha snapped back, enclosing the
stone in his fist, wrapping it in his awareness. It felt warm,
inviting his inquiry. He forced himself to focus on it. "I
work with the living and the dead, with blood and bones,
this . . ."

"Many have shed blood for this stone," said the rabbi.
"I have done so myself."

With a quick movement, Elisha reached out and caught the rabbi's hand with his left, the stone clenched in his right. Again, he felt the strength of the rabbi's faith, and his connection to the stone. Memories stirred the old man's skin. He resisted Elisha's grip, but did not pull away—he had the strength of a soldier beneath a scholar's air. A stone that he and others bled for. A plain of rubble, small bits of stone, surrounded by high stone walls, thick, arched gates passing inside—a place he must not go, for fear of ha-Shem's might. Why carry a stone from a place forbidden? For he had carried it, a long, long way. The stone echoed with the rabbi's anger, fear, faith, despair, hope, layered over that of a thousand others. It rang very softly with the memory of the rabbi's tears. Elisha caught his breath. When the rabbi bent his thought upon that place, a distant ruin on a sun-soaked hill, Elisha felt the way. Through the grief that joined the living man with his youthful tears, Elisha opened the Valley and let them be sucked away.

The torrent of fear and pain swelled around him, and Elisha realized his mistake. He swept back his own awareness, armoring himself and the rabbi with the chill he carried close to his heart, deflecting the horror of the Valley. He should have prepared the man for what they would feel—then he thought of Sabetha, the nun he had carried through the Valley, using its power to heal her. She declared it a beautiful place, so perhaps the rabbi's faith, too, would defend him.

Elisha stumbled as they struck, his heart beating madly with the chaos of the Valley. The rabbi stood rigidly beside him, utterly arrested by the experience. They stood together in a shadowed darkness on a path of rubble, the barest edge of light creeping over the towering wall beside them.

"Doctor, you have taken me through Gehenna itself." The revulsion in that single word delivered its meaning closely enough.

"Aye," Elisha said, matching the rabbi's hushed tone. "Forgive me for not warning you."

Then came the sound that Elisha never thought to

hear: the rabbi laughed. His free hand cupped over Elisha's fist, the stone between them, and he gripped Elisha with joy, with fear, with a resounding fullness of spirit that shot gold into the black thoughts that assailed him. Not letting go, the rabbi looked up and gave a soft cry—as if no utterance would be enough to encompass his emotion. The pale light of dawn showed the wall of dressed stone, three arches piercing it nearby, a few tufts of weeds marking the trail. Dry air seared Elisha's nose and throat with incense that wafted on the breeze.

"The sages say that Kefitzat Ha-Derech moves through the air of the demons. I felt the terror of that passage, as if I should be stripped spirit from bone, then you were beside me, all around me. Forgive you?" He laughed again, a sound both bright and painful. "You are real. You are here," he whispered, followed by a reverent string of syllables Elisha knew as prayer though he did not know the words.

Looking away, withdrawing his awareness from that disconcerting grip, Elisha asked, "Where are we?" He let his awareness spread around him, through the rock, through the wall, through the dry air of a distant desert. Somewhere below, a church bell rang. Lauds, the prayer of dawn. Echoes tremored through the air and stone, as if a thousand church bells tolled the hour throughout time. Yes, men had bled for these stones, fought to claim them and died to defend them. Men bargained for peace with any who won those battles. They bargained to be allowed to come, at almost any cost. And now Elisha stood, an unexpected pilgrim, in the company of a Jew at the very center of the world: the walls of Jerusalem.

Chapter 16

❖

"**We should go**," he breathed.

"Yes, yes," the rabbi echoed with a sniff as if he held back tears.

Elisha recaptured his image of the rabbi's chamber and all of its appointments. Knowledge, he had. Contact? His blood, drying on the toes of the goldsmith's shoes. He wrapped them both in the frigid cloak of death, banishing the mad whirling of the shades, and slid through the Valley, emerging to the goldsmith's startled cry. Releasing the stone to the rabbi's grasp, Elisha stepped away from him, trembling with the force of the other man's emotion. He did not ask if the rabbi were satisfied with this evidence. He did not need to.

The rabbi drew the stone close to his breast. "I need pen and ink, sheaves of paper. There's much to do."

"Where did you take him?" Isaac asked, but Elisha shook his head, reaching for the wine, and the goldsmith let the question rest.

The rabbi tugged a bell pull, summoning a yawning servant who snapped awake to fetch the supplies his master required. The rabbi prepared his writing desk, glancing at Elisha from time to time, then quickly away.

"Do you know the stories of your namesake?" the rabbi asked abruptly. "His bones, even, bring healing, according to the Torah. He was destined to perform twice as many miracles as his mentor. Twice as many!"

The Biblical Elisha's mentor was the confusingly

named Elijah. Elisha's own mentor was a Jewish surgeon, also a magus. Twice as many miracles. No doubt Mordecai knew that, but saw no need to mention it. Mordecai was not a man for destiny. What would he make of this, Elisha's strange fulfillment of a Jewish legend? Someday, they would sit together in the solar in their manor on the Isle of Wight and tell each other all that had passed during their separation. "I know that Elisha healed a river, and that he kept a lamp full of oil."

"Trifles! There are wonder workers who have been able to breathe life into a man when he lies as if dead," the rabbi said, his pen poised. "Enough—you know better than I what you can do. I shall tell them of your mantle, that's fitting. And the pin, if you may keep it. Goldsmith?"

"Of course." Isaac's shadowed eyes closed, and he stifled a yawn. "I should go."

"I will write those things in the letters, as well as a little about you, so they will know whom to seek, or who shall be seeking them." A hint of his former gruffness returned, and he added, "I will not tell them what Jacob said. There's no need to say such things, but the fact you are revealed, this tells me the danger my people are facing."

"The danger we all face," Elisha said, "if the mancers succeed."

"You made him a believer," Isaac observed.

"Aye." Elisha took another swallow of wine, letting it warm him from the inside out.

"But *you* are not."

Elisha waved a hand over his body, his ruined shirt and scuffed boots, his scarred chest and the secrets he carried close to his heart. "I live with this—with all of it. I never hoped for it, never studied for it. You want me to be holy, but I don't know how. All I can do—" He broke off, Mordecai's voice echoing through the rivers of memory, then he spoke the remembered words aloud. "All I can do is to soldier on in my own battle, until I fall beneath the enemy." *Or rise again in a way I cannot foresee.* His own voice, so naïve, followed Mordecai's musing with the arrogance of his youth—had it been only a few short months ago?

"Tell us about the enemy," the rabbi demanded as he wrote. "What do we face?"

Taking a deep breath, Elisha settled himself in his chair, and the goldsmith took a place alongside, not without a glance at the door. Outside, dawn rose slowly as Elisha told them what he could—all that he knew of the mancers, how they traveled, whom they killed and how, and how they wielded the power of their crimes. Sometimes, the scratching of the pen stopped, the rabbi's head bent as he listened, then he nodded and jabbed the pen into fresh ink, writing all the more fiercely. Around them, the household roused, the scent of a cook fire wafting down the corridor, the sound of footfalls overhead, and Elisha fell silent.

"So they wish for Charles to be emperor." The rabbi sighed, ran his fingers through his beard. "We don't know what to hope for. Archbishop Baldwin of Trier, Charles's uncle, seems a good man, willing to protect us."

Isaac slammed his fist against the arm of his chair. "No, not always." For a moment, they stared at each other. The old tension returned to the room.

"Be that as it may," Elisha said, "the archbishop already suspected or worried about Charles's retinue. It's worth maintaining that alliance as long as possible."

"Through him, to the pope, eh?" the rabbi said. "Your church is so powerful it's a bit hard to see how even influencing a dozen monarchs could bring about the madness these mancers desire."

Elisha blinked at that. The rabbi's point was not one Elisha had considered before, but in truth, the mighty Church reigned over all, over every nation where the Christian faith held sway. If the mancers truly worked toward chaos and terror on the scale Elisha imagined, then even if they controlled many of the nations, even if they manufactured wars between peoples, they could not rule the world without also bringing down the church itself. How would they go about it? A band of mancers, like the one in England which had tried to bring down

Thomas, could dominate a single crown, certainly, but no single band could dominate every parish, bishopric, and see. Planting tainted relics—their own talismans—in individual churches would give them a pathway to terror, to be sure, but still on a local level. Even by working together, they would be hard-pressed to assault enough of those spiritual domains to bring the Church into their power. What kind of attack could be employed against the Church itself, the root of the shared faith that made Christendom so powerful?

The mancers he overheard in the forest spoke of being ready for Rome: that must be the key to their joint assault upon the Church. The thought of that made Elisha's mouth go dry. Warning Ludwig could not be enough. Defending any single realm could do no more than delay the mancers. It was not merely their plot against the crowns that he must pursue, but their plot against the cross. More than the breaking of any one kingdom—after all, kings and even emperors came and went by succession, revolution or invasion—the collapse of the Church itself would destroy the world forever. What could possibly shatter the faith of millions? Elisha did not know, but he had no doubt the mancers would do it. He had to get to Rome and break the mancers' plot before it could break the world.

Aloud, he said, "The power of the Church is great, indeed, but the mancers are planning to subvert it. I don't yet know what they plan, but the pope has close ties to the king of France, who's already under mancer control, and Charles is under their sway as well. The Church may not know there is evil afoot until it's too late."

"Because the evil pretends to be righteous," Isaac said. "I should go." He stalked toward the door, ripples of buried pain flickering through his agitated presence.

Elisha rose and followed. At the door, he set his hand on the goldsmith's shoulder, their eyes nearly on a level, the goldsmith's self-loathing laid bared in his haunted face.

"You are not evil," Elisha murmured.

"You don't know that." Isaac traced the door with his eyes, his hand gripping the latch, his knuckles white.

"Look at me, Isaac. I've killed a dozen people since I came to your country. For the things I've done in my own land, my soul is damned a hundred times over. If I can still strive for the good, then so can you."

"But you're—what you are. I have turned my back on ha-Shem. Turned my back on God. Even the gentiles trust my faith only because they have need of my skill."

"It's the same with me. I'm a threat even to those I would save."

Isaac winced, his arm tensing beneath Elisha's grip. "They came in the night," he said. "They woke up the household, made us go out into the street." His throat worked, and the fractured images of a child's memory touched Elisha's mind—parents, a sister, two brothers. "There had been some trouble—I don't know what, but Jews were blamed. We had to stay inside, to stay quiet and hope they passed us by—but they came. They demanded that my parents should convert, and killed them when they refused. They gave the baby to somebody's wife to raise him as a Christian." Isaac's voice broke, his eyes closed, brows drawn up in anguish. "One of them took my sister aside. I never saw her again, but I heard her screams. My brother fought back when they took the baby. They cut him down." Isaac's short breaths echoed in the space between them.

"But you survived."

A single, shaky nod. "I called out when they came to me, when my brother's blood ran down my face. 'Christ and all his saints defend me!' I cried it over and over. I heard it in the market, or from the maids—I don't know why it came to me then, except I did not want to die."

Any devout Christian would say the prayer came true, that the boy's conversion at such a moment could only be the strength of God's intervention. But the horror of the night flowed through Isaac's skin, the desperation of his cry, the terror he felt every time he bent a knee in church and feared that Christ would know his heart was still a Jew's. Elisha sent comfort through his contact. If he might dream of a thousand years in the palm of God, then let at least a few of those be given to Isaac, to cradle the child that still hid behind his eyes. "You did what you had to do, to live."

The goldsmith drew a long breath and expelled it before his eyes flickered open, blinking away the memories. Then he tipped his head, and a wave of relief spread through the contact. "Or what I had to do to be here, now. To do what I could for you. God be with you."

"And also with you," Elisha answered as the converso let himself out into the quiet street, hurrying away before he could be seen in a neighborhood of Jews.

The rabbi's servants fed him well, clothed him in fresh garments appropriate to the chill, and even helped to stitch his collection of relics and talismans into various secret places in the fabric. The rabbi handed over a new letter, the sort of bland but significant introduction Elisha had believed that Jacob had written, one that would open doors otherwise closed to a Christian. Other letters went out by the servants' hands, traveling ahead of Elisha to the surrounding towns and cities, to anywhere someone might be able to help, to the places the rabbi knew, where the flagellants had been or where his wife and servants heard rumors of evil. Elisha walked alone no longer. He was gathering allies, people who would stand with him against the threat he feared that only he could see. The spiritual significance they assigned to him had opened up this chance. He must discharge his duty to Thomas's kin by marriage, then hurry on to Rome. He stepped down from the rabbi's door and made his way to meet the emperor, armed with knowledge, armored with hope.

Chapter 17

❖

At the riverside, the usual bustle of merchants and tradesmen gave way to a crowd of imperial functionaries—soldiers, servants, porters, ladies-in-waiting. Given the assault after yesterday's audience, and Harald's arrival to witness its aftermath, Elisha could not be certain what he faced. As he approached, he deflected his presence with a variety of talismans, making himself invisible to other magi and mancers alike. Hooded and cloaked, Bardolph lurked in the imperial retinue, flashes of tension streaking his own deflected presence. Elisha had rattled him. Good. Unfortunately, also mutual. The scars from his arrow wounds felt lumpy and caught the fabric of his new clothes.

Pulling up his hood, Elisha projected eagerness, curiosity, hoping he might be mistaken for a student from the university. He angled away from Bardolph's position, but Gretchen, clad in a traveling cloak, stood by the plank up to the imperial barge, her features pale—a magus, and a sensitive. He needed to get aboard, to stay close to Ludwig, but how to dodge the watchers? On the foreshore of the river, a dozen men stood ready with poles to push the boat off the shore and into the river's flow. A few ropes already led to oxen on the other side to pull the barge along.

On board, a pavilion took up the center of the vessel, pennants flicking, posts bound by guy lines to various pegs such that the boatmen grumbled and tripped, and a few of them had taken to the outside, clinging to the edge of the deck while they slid their feet along a ridge that stuck out to provide a bumper against docks or other boats.

The pavilion sidewall nearest the shore had been tied back, showing cushions and seats but no sign of the empress. Then a horn sounded up the street, and faces turned in that direction, expectant, as the crowds parted for the empress, riding a fine gray palfrey and accompanied by a few more guards.

Catching his breath, Elisha edged closer to the river, grabbed one of the knobs on the deck of the barge and pulled himself up to the bumper, absorbing the bounce of the boat. He worked his way around the back, over the river, only to meet another man coming his way. "Damned ropes," Elisha muttered, hoping his accent would be taken for only that of another part of Germany.

The sailor grunted at him, and Elisha climbed on deck behind the pavilion, where he busied himself checking the lashing of a few chests as if he'd come with the imperial party. The barge swayed, dipping a bit toward shore as more people boarded, and he sat heavily. Women's voices spoke within, solicitous of the empress's well-being, and the cold tone of a physician warned her against a surfeit of ginger.

"Where is my Englishman?" Margaret inquired.

"You've heard the stories, Your Majesty," answered one of the ladies. "Under the circumstances, I expect he is closeted with any number of priests."

"He is not blessed, Your Majesty, believe me," said Gretchen stiffly.

Her mistress replied, "Do not let a personal quarrel stand between you and the servants of the Lord." After a moment, Margaret continued, "In short, do not take my husband for an example in your dealings with the Church." A few ladies tittered.

"You are feeling better," said the first lady. "But I do fear that your Englishman, for one reason and another, will not be coming. It may simply be that he wishes to remain close to the palace and to his Majesty."

At that, Elisha's heart sank. He'd been expecting Ludwig to come, but of course, the emperor had a hundred other worries—taking his wife to a salt bath couldn't rate very highly compared with avoiding war with his rival. He rose and moved back toward the side of the barge, preparing to return the way he had come. The empress might favor him, but if he were a hundred miles from her husband, then he would be of little use in preventing the danger to come.

With a scraping of wood and a shout from the captain, the barge rocked and pushed toward the water. Elisha stumbled and fell, his foot splashing into the river below, soaking him to the knee.

"—as dangerous as all that." A voice, in the water. A magus.

"Even if he's not, we owe it to the Unicorn to keep an eye out, and so we shall."

"Thank you all. My daughter's safely off now, but her betrothed must remain. There are few enough of us as it is, we've got to preserve marriages of the blood."

"He must be hiding someplace in town. We'll find him and get word to you at once."

His deflection intact, Elisha hoped they had taken his startled intrusion for that of any desolati, and pulled his foot back to the bumper as a sailor reached down to steady him. "What's happened to you, man?"

"Lost my footing during the launch." He caught the strong grasp and let himself be pulled back on deck, glad to be leaving Heidelberg behind. A stranger's word would count for naught with the magi hereabouts—and any word they carried to the Unicorn would go straight to Bardolph. For good or ill, he'd joined the empress's crew now. "Thanks," he told the sailor, who had already turned back to his work.

At the riverside, where the oxen pulled their barge, a few dozen guards rode along as well, while the ladies took their ease upon the water. Elisha reached for attunement, keeping his touch light. He searched first for any sign of death. A bundle of shades at the near corner of the pavilion distracted him, but there was no life associated with them—not talismans, then—at least, not those carried by a mancer. Probably the empress's portable altar or reliquary. He caught the tingle of raised awareness not far beyond, recognizing Gretchen's presence, a fierce energy, pride, a hint of fear alongside desire. She missed Bardolph. In a rustle of skirts, she slid around the corner, staring along the short side of the pavilion directly at him.

Elisha met her gaze, then gave a slight bow. "Come, Fraulein, we should talk."

"Talk? With you? What are you?" She swallowed, lifting a hand to the talisman amulet she wore, the other hand resting on a sheathed dagger at her side. She darted a glance toward the water, but she could not reach it easily to send her message.

Stepping around a line toward her, Elisha kept his hands low and visible. "You do not know me, Fraulein, not at all. And you do not know your leman as well as you think."

She drew the dagger, causing a murmur from the two sailors at the stern, and one of them rose. "Now, Fraulein," the sailor began.

"Do you want them to hear your business, Fraulein?" Elisha's empty hands were more dangerous than her little knife could ever be, but the sailors could not know it. "Your mistress seems pleased to have my aid, Fraulein. I should be pleased to continue to give it."

A new, softer worry slid through her presence. "Come, then, and tell me your lies." She retreated toward the stern, perching on a long crate and tipping her head to indicate that he should join her, but she did not put away the dagger.

Elisha sat, folding his hands, elbows propped on his legs, and pitched his voice very low. "Did he tell you why he planned the ambush?"

"You're his enemy—I knew it from your appearance in the meadow. Your heart was full of murder, of hatred for him, and—" But she stopped, and set her jaw.

"And?" he prompted, but she stared at the striped wall of the pavilion. "And concern for you," he supplied.

"I didn't come there because I hate him, but because I feared for you. You must have felt it. There was a drop of blood in the queen's chamber that led me to follow. How were you injured?"

"There was a pin in the cloak, and it stuck me when Bardolph took it—" Her cheeks colored as she broke off.

There had been no pin in the cloak, not until he received the one from Isaac. "He appeared from nowhere and told you to let someone else take it to your mistress. Then he took you to the meadow. How did you get there?"

Her eyes narrowed as she glanced aside at Elisha. "Why ask me? You did it, too."

Elisha shook his head. "I followed you, through contact with your blood. But he had contact already with that place, through someone else's blood or bone."

Gretchen laughed. "We go there all the time. Not usually that way, of course."

Taken aback, Elisha said, "Wait a moment—you think he's such a great witch that he can travel to places he knows well, with no more contact than familiarity?"

Her face lit as she tossed back her hair. "He's very powerful."

No wonder her mother craved the marriage as much as she did. "And you felt no fear when he took you through the Valley?"

"The what? You mean the passage when we went from the palace?" For a moment, the worry returned. "It was a little frightening, but I'm sure he did not mean it so. He said I would get used to it, that it was only the newness that scared me."

Even from a foot away, Elisha felt the rising heat of her body. Bardolph shielded her from the Valley somehow—likely with her desire for him. She sensed the fear but wanted him so badly she ignored it. When they married, would Bardolph reveal what he was? "Why at that moment, Fraulein, when you waited on her majesty's court?"

"He's away so often on the emperor's business, we must take our moments when we can." Gretchen's dagger glittered in the spreading sun of morning. "You really believe that he nicked my skin on purpose, just so he could lure you to the meadow? To our private place?"

"Your private place that was already ringed by archers, Fraulein."

One of the sailors passed by, and she dropped her voice even lower. "You must be extremely arrogant."

Elisha burst out laughing. Arrogant. By God, he had been, long ago, arrogant about the skill in his hands—but the skill he now commanded terrified him. Any pride he took from his talent for death rested in his ability to fight back against the mancers. He laughed so hard that he wanted to weep.

Gretchen and the sailors stared, perplexed.

"Gretchen! Who—?" The lady's voice called, and Elisha swung about to face her, stifling his laughter. The prayerful mancer he had spared on the night of his slaughter stood there, all blood draining from her face. Elisha just had time to leap up before she fainted into his arms.

Chapter 18

❖

"**Margravine Katherine!**" Gretchen leapt up as well, brandishing her dagger at Elisha. "What have you done to her?"

"So far, I've prevented her from falling," he snapped back, then gathered the limp stranger into his arms as a few other women peered around the pavilion. "Is there a comfortable place to settle her?" he asked as they blinked at him.

"Doctor!" Empress Margaret's expression moved from surprise to delight. "Here, use our bedding." She put out an arm to hold back the canvas wall, but two of her ladies took hold, allowing her to precede Elisha into the pavilion. "Do put away your knife, Gretchen. Footing is uneven on ship."

Elisha did not see if she obeyed. He lay the fallen woman on a pile of blankets where the empress indicated, and set his fingers at her wrist to check her pulse, but her eyelids fluttered and she started awake with a gasp. He drew back his presence in an instant, but let his hand linger there for the sake of their witnesses.

"I did not think to see you so." Deep gray eyes regarded him from a handsome face, wisps of silvered hair escaping her skewed veil. She felt warm beneath his touch, but a hint of steel lurked below. Her voice, soft and despairing, stung his flesh. *"You'll wish you had killed me."* Then she gulped a breath, withdrawing her hand and holding it close.

Elisha gaped at her, glad that no other could see his face, but the thought had been so fleeting, he wasn't even sure she'd meant to say it.

"What's the trouble, Your Majesty?" asked the gruff voice of one of the physicians, edging between the stricken Margravine Katherine and the wall so that he could scowl at Elisha.

"My dear Katherine, are you quite well?" Margaret stood by, tried to stoop, and groaned, pressing a hand to her back.

"Please, Your Majesty—" Elisha began.

"Don't, Your Majesty—" said Katherine at the same moment. Their eyes met and glanced away.

"It was the sight of him," Gretchen said, as she brought forward a seat and helped the empress to be comfortable. "She merely looked at him and fell, as if he'd struck her."

Elisha wet his lips, but Katherine said, "We met at church, Your Majesty. To see him here was a surprise." She managed a smile. "Not an unpleasant one, Your Majesty. It's only . . . I feared he had heard my confession."

A few of the ladies laughed at that, and Katherine fluttered a hand, dismissing their laughter. "Even a widow has her secrets."

At the empress's side, Gretchen knelt, her hands clasped upon the arm of the chair. "Your Majesty, you are not hearing me. This man is a danger."

"If good Brother Gilles is to be believed, this man is a miracle." The queen's round face and prim lips held both humor and curiosity. "We did not think to see you here, after yesterday's misadventure." The smile left her, something of her husband's hardness taking its place.

Elisha took a deep breath. "My task remains undone, Your Majesty."

The empress crossed herself, the jewels on her finger glinting. "The abbess Hildegard once said something similar, when she returned from a trance in which she was taken for dead. She attributed the words to the Holy Ghost."

Shaking this off, he plunged ahead. "Your husband

faces dangers he does not understand, Your Majesty."
Tentatively, he spread his awareness again, hoping for a
sign from Katherine before he said any more. Did she
repent of turning mancer? Had they truly lured her in by
way of her husband's murder? He sensed the cold well
of her husband's death entwined deeply through her
presence from the talisman she wore bound under her
tight bodice, pressed beneath her breasts.

"So you did not offer to attend me for my own sake,"
the empress replied, then the smile returned to her lips
if not to her eyes. "As the consort of an emperor, I have
come to expect that."

Chastened, Elisha bowed his head, but she reached
out—Gretchen's presence shooting with tension—and
touched his face, drawing his gaze back to her. He felt
her concern, the weight of majesty as heavy as the burden of the child she carried. "Forgive me," he said.

"Do not trouble yourself, Doctor. You may not have
come for my sake, but I shall jealously keep you for your
own. You have already rendered me service." Her fingertips just reached the furred edge of the cloak she had
given him as she withdrew her hand.

Turning on her side, Katherine propped herself up.
"Shall we play at courts of love, Majesty? He is a handsome one."

Elisha caught his breath, suddenly worried over what
the empress had meant about keeping him. A net of fem-
inine laughter rippled around him, trapping him on the
barge, committed to his mission. Gretchen's anger and
suspicion barely penetrated.

"Gretchen, bring my looking glass! Surely the doctor
should see his own face—he is the very image of shock."

An unaccustomed heat warmed his cheeks, and he
stammered, "I fear I haven't the stomach for such a
game, Your Majesty."

"The stomach? Is it not the liver where love resides?"
asked another of the women, a blond with crooked teeth.
She waved to the physician. "Doctor von Stubben. Does
not love emanate from the liver through the eyes?"

Withdrawing from his examination of Katherine, the

physician scowled all the more. "I recommend a drink of wine while you recover, my lady. And that you do not trouble yourself for games of love."

The other women clapped their hands, beginning to rearrange their cushions and seats to cluster around the empress. "Doctor Emerick, have you an opinion?" Empress Margaret addressed the second, younger physician, and he moved forward with a bow.

"Well, Your Majesty, the effect of the gaze upon the object of love is well-known, of course. It can create all manner of sensations—"

"Like fainting?" asked the blond, with an arch of her brows toward Katherine.

"Indeed," said the physician. "Fainting is one of the primary symptoms of the dart—" he went on, raising his voice as the women laughed yet louder. "At the sight of the beloved, the heart may go still, or it may race as if during a great exertion—"

Beyond the tossing heads and ribboned headdresses of the laughing ladies, Elisha glimpsed the running water and considered springing up from his place to throw himself from their company. Good God! He had heard tell of Courts of Love and such games as noble ladies might play, but never imagined they might be applied to himself. The more the physician spoke, the more the ladies laughed, and Emerick's own grin threatened to interrupt his monologue: clearly, he enjoyed being the expert while the grumpy von Stubben muttered and returned to his chair at the far end of the pavilion, ostentatiously opening a scroll.

A light touch against his leg brought Elisha back from fantasies of escape. *"Forgive me, Doctor. I should not have distracted them so."* Katherine. *"I didn't know you would take it so ill. You are not used to such attentions."*

Not since he had left the whorehouses where he used to work as a barber—and then, he had known how to take the banter of whores. But of ladies so high-born he should not even be among them? *"No, I'm not."*

"I imagined with your bearing and your skills, that you must be surrounded by flattery. Forgive me twice over for

placing you in such a position." The warmth of her voice, the regret and amusement, lent a sexual cast to the word "skills" that only deepened his embarrassment.

Elisha put up his hands. "Your Majesty, your humor at my expense denies the urgency of my message."

Katherine's touch withdrew, and she sat up, scooting forward on the blankets, taking a moment to flick her skirts down over the stretch of her leg. "The doctor is a foreigner in our midst, my friends. We must not take advantage."

A few women covered their smiles with long, pale fingers, rings—and a few eyes—winking. The empress clapped her hands for silence, and the giggles finally ran down, the young physician bowing and retreating. "Katherine is correct, of course. Later, the doctor and I shall discuss his message—" She gave a little gasp, a spasm of pain crossing her face, and everyone stilled at once, leaning toward her. After a moment, her face relaxed, her hand lifting from her pregnant belly. "No, not yet, my friends, no need to worry." She took a sip from a goblet Gretchen held out, then continued. "Later, the message. For now, I feel weary. I think a story would serve me better than a game. Agnes?"

The blond with the crooked teeth began a tale of a minstrel who lost his love when he succumbed to a mountain enchantress. She had a rich voice and accented her telling with fitting gestures and expressions. Still, by the time the minstrel sought repentance and was denied by the pope himself, the empress's chin rested on her chest, sleeping gently. Gretchen stared at Elisha, but said no more against him as the day wore on. At Nones, the bargemen pulled in to shore where the party of soldiers paced them, and a group of women from a local village came aboard to lay out cold meats and cheeses. The doctors fussed over Margaret's choices, but she pointedly asked Elisha's opinion, and he did his best to supply a good one, encouraging the health of both mother and child. She did not seek his company, nor ask him any further about his message. The journey to Bad Stollhein would take four days or more. Four days of stories, laughter, and revelry. Elisha might have to leap into the river after all.

These sour thoughts accompanied his preparation for bed, taking his allotted blankets and cushions outside the pavilion where the men would sleep on deck while the ladies bedded down inside. The evening's chill stung his face as he curled onto his side, draping the empress's cloak over him so that the fur warmed his skin. Just as carefully, he extended his senses over the sleeping sailors, the ladies both restless and peaceful.

He woke with the moon high overhead as Gretchen crept toward the mooring lines. She sat on the edge of the boat, turned to lower herself onto the bumper, and Elisha slipped forward, silent as death, to catch her arm before she could dip her bare toes into the water. *"I beg of you, Fraulein, do not betray me."*

Her arm taut with fear, she stared up at him, her foot swaying over the water. *"If you are as innocent as you claim, then let me go."*

"If my enemies find me, they'll kill me—you know that."

"As you would have killed Bardolph."

He felt the sudden spark of her excitement, then she started screaming, beating at him with her hand, twisting against him. Astonished, he let go, and she plunged into the water, flailing and shrieking. On the shore nearby, lanterns flared and soldiers shouted.

Her arms thrashed as she struggled to keep her face above water, gasping, then disappearing beneath the surface. Again, her face appeared, wreathed by tangles of dark hair. "Help! I can't swim!" Her pale arm waved. Elisha tensed to jump in, but the dark water reminded him of the Thames and she did not want his rescue—never mind the fact that he could not swim either. Was she willing to die just to get him arrested? "Fraulein!" he shouted after her.

One of the soldiers leapt in, splashing as if he had little greater skill than she did in the water, his arms reaching for her. She flailed toward him, and he caught her wrist, dragging her closer. Dark water washed over their heads, then the soldier pushed her up again, taking her head on his shoulder as he floundered toward the bank. His fellows on shore leaned down to help, and she coughed violently as they pulled her up the bank. Elisha let himself breathe again. Gretchen alive could still cause him trouble, but he did not wish her dead.

"He pushed me!" she cried as her savior patted her back. "He wants to drown me."

Lights shone over his shoulder, then Katherine caught his arm. "Good gracious, again? Gretchen, my dear girl. I cannot conceal you any longer."

"What is it, Katherine? What's happened?" The empress, wrapped in furs, appeared beside them, squinting.

"It's Gretchen," Katherine sighed. "She walks at night, as if in a trance. I did not want to alarm you, so I have hidden her affliction."

Across the short span of water, Gretchen turned from her soldier-rescuer, waving an arm. "Your Majesty! That mad English doctor threw me in!"

"Oh, dear. She must have disturbed the doctor, as well as myself, and a good thing, too—I saw him try to stop her falling overboard! I should have foreseen the difficulties for her on a boat." Katherine leaned toward the empress and whispered, "I'm sorry I did not tell you before—I did not wish to spoil her prospects."

Empress Margaret's eyes narrowed. "Indeed, but she is now to marry Bardolph, one of my husband's messengers."

Katherine faced the empress squarely. "Of your mercy, Your Majesty, do not tell him. Surely, with no ill having come of it, she is not too wayward. Please—I should never have revealed her except for her accusations against the doctor."

"But you don't think she is a witch?"

"No," said Elisha at once, overcoming his surprise at hearing Katherine's pleas. "Your Majesty, I know that Gretchen means well." He stopped short of confirming Katherine's lie, but neither could he bring himself to deny it. "She has taken against me because of my difficulties with her betrothed, but there is no evil in her."

The empress murmured, "There have been so many problems with the pregnancy, that I have wondered if someone close to me intends me harm."

Katherine said. "If it worries you at all, then simply send her home. Surely a good husband will tame her wandering."

"Very wise, Katherine." The empress smiled broadly. "It shall be as you say." To the shore, she called, "Come, bargemen, bring us near that I may alight and speak with the girl."

The shore crew pulled the lines and the sailors pushed the plank between so the empress could walk down it. She greeted her maidservant, taking her hands, and speaking to her in a hushed tone. Gretchen's cry of upset echoed across the water—failing to shake the empress's cool resolve. Problems in pregnancy and accusations of witchcraft all too often wove together, but it was to Katherine that Elisha looked. Gretchen might love unwisely, but she did care for her mistress—she should not lose her position and reputation because of her suspicions of him.

He set his hand firmly on Katherine's shoulder. *"My lady, you've as much as accused that girl of witchcraft."*

"You would rather have been expelled from the barge? And what of the mission you mentioned?"

"You know the truth of my mission, lady—you were almost a part of it."

"And I may yet be," she answered, turning to face him, covering his hand with her own, strengthening the contact. *"Don't withdraw, Doctor, I can feel it in you. I worry you. I am of your enemy, and yet I defend you. You don't trust me, as well you should not."* Moonlight limned her face, tears glinting in her eyes. *"Repent, you told me, and sin no more. By God, I am trying. I am trying so very hard."* She shook her head, flicking away the tears, then pressing the back of her hand against her mouth. *"It's never been a struggle for you, has it? Using death, but only in service to life."*

Elisha's throat felt dry, her hand almost as cold as his own. *"Do not think me so pure, lady. That night I hunted your kind—"*

"Murderers!" She clutched his fingers. *"Why do you think I took you for an angel? We deserve to die, we who kill for power."*

An angel. He was anything but, and yet ... she saw him, that night, saw his purpose, not merely that he wielded death, but that he did so in the cause of life. *"Truly, lady, is that why you killed?"*

She did not answer, but withdrew her hand, covering her face, shaking beneath his touch. Elisha sent her comfort, strength, the will to turn away from evil. In two small steps, with a sway of her skirts, she leaned against him, her forehead to his shoulder, weeping. *"Help me,"* begged her tears, *"Be the angel of my repentance."*

He thought of Rowena, Brigit's mother, using the power of her death to transform into an angel as the flames of the stake rose around her. His cheek warmed as if at the stroke of her golden wing, the touch that turned his life and set him on the course of healing, and of killing. Were all angels at once so bright and so terrible?

She quaked against him, in despair. Elisha slid his arms around her, the cold shock of her talisman pressing close between their hearts.

Chapter 19

❖

$\mathcal{B}$y morning, Gretchen was gone—back to Bardolph in the nest of Elisha's enemies, but unable to disparage him to the empress any longer. Empress Margaret's return to the barge had interrupted his moment with Katherine, but he hoped for the chance to talk with her again, to find out all she could tell him about the mancers—surely she would give him that much, as sign of her repentance. The empress had raised her brows at her lady as the embrace broke apart, and though Katherine quickly explained that she'd only been overcome by fears for Gretchen's prospects, the empress clearly believed none of it. Away from the shadow of her husband, the empress proved to be a formidable woman, the discomfort of her pregnancy offering little impediment to her mind.

That afternoon, talk turned to pilgrimage, and to the sorry state of Rome, the heart of the Church and the key to whatever the mancers had planned. Elisha listened intently. He knelt rubbing the empress's feet with oil of lavender that perfumed the pavilion so strongly it masked the lingering scents of their nuncheon. "If Rome is so dangerous, why talk of going there?" he asked finally.

"Ludwig must be crowned emperor there, by the hand of the pope. The archbishop of Mainz has crowned him already, of course, but with the challenger gaining strength, Ludwig must be seen to have the support of both worldly and spiritual powers."

Elisha cocked his head. "But the pope is in France, isn't he?"

She radiated suppressed frustration. "For now, but he has declared a Jubilee just two years hence—he must return to Rome before then, and Ludwig hopes to be crowned at that same time. The last time he was in Rome, shortly after our marriage, I fear my husband undertook some tasks that made him unpopular with the Church. What better place for his reconciliation than the very place of his downfall?"

The city where Ludwig tried to proclaim his own pope, Elisha recalled.

"And anyone who makes the pilgrimage there shall be granted an indulgence against her sins," Agnes offered, with a wink in Katherine's direction. "Then you need not fear your confessions shall be overheard."

Katherine laughed, but she cast a shaded glance at Elisha, as if they shared a flirtation.

"In any event, I shall go," Agnes continued. "That madman who calls himself the tribune of Rome nonetheless seems to be making things safer. Already, thousands of people are planning their journeys, perhaps hundreds of thousands. I have seen maps for sale in the market."

"I hope you shall be there in my company, Agnes, and that of my husband." Empress Margaret shooed Elisha from her hem with one hand and found her goblet. "The tribune persists in inviting Ludwig to Rome, but he is lowborn for all of his claims. Even with the Holy Father's support, a madman is still a madman. Do you know, he bathes nightly in the Emperor Constantine's own tub, right outside the church that holds part of the very Cross itself?"

The ladies giggled at that, and speculated about the appearance and outlook of Cola di Rienzi, the innkeeper's son who had liberated the city and claimed the title of tribune—what, precisely, he might do in that tub. Elisha thought of the mancers in the clearing, talking about Rome: who would be ready for it, and who would not. The Pope must return there before the Jubilee, and thousands would flock to the city. The mancers worked quietly now, securing the thrones of several nations, but it was the rabbi who pointed out the problem of the Church. In England, Brigit claimed she could deliver the nobility, and tried to do so by killing most of them with her magical connection to the past. Such a gutting of the natural order would cause chaos, but the people would turn to the Church, and, even with a few churchmen in the power of the mancers, the clerics were too numerous to gather and ruin in the same fashion. Or were they?

The Church, with its network of cardinals, archbishops, bishops, priests, and holy houses, held sway over the people of many nations even more surely than the kings. Any one kingdom might fall, any nation might make war upon another, but how could the mancers bring down the Church itself? Unless the pope himself were in their sway, summoning his flock to Rome to lay them out for the mancers' pleasure.

Focusing his awareness on Katherine but keeping his eyes on the homely Agnes, Elisha said, "I should like one of those maps—I might have need of an indulgence myself."

"You, Doctor? You have sins? Do tell!"

Katherine's presence remained steady, unengaged in talk of Rome from what he could tell. "I used to work in Coppice Alley—the street of whores," Elisha announced.

This elicited a gasp from the ladies, then they eagerly shuffled their seats forward, shifting their embroidery, to listen. He told of bawdy monks and cuckolds, even the incident that convinced his brother to marry the lovely whore Helena, when she was accused of witchcraft. His presence must have echoed the sad ending of that tale—the ending he did not speak of—for Katherine's calm broke to a sympathetic warmth, her expression speculative.

"Ah, Doctor," said Empress Margaret, "I am ever more glad you have joined our company. Tomorrow, we disembark and take to horseback to finish our travel. I shall arrange for a private chamber where we may speak of more important things."

Elisha raised his own goblet to her and took a swallow of the rich red wine. As it filled his skull, he remembered the fight in the vintner's and taking Simeon home. On the morrow, he could tell the empress what he knew. Should he wait to speak with Ludwig directly with her aid, or move on ahead of the mancers—to Rome? Anticipation rushed through his body—at last, he might outpace his enemies. He had a chance to break their plans before they could spring their trap.

During the evening meal, Elisha took an excuse to touch Katherine's hand and communicate his desire to talk with her. After darkness fell, she crept to his place on the stern, motioning for him to stay down, then, trembling with fear and hope, she laid herself down with her arm wrapping his shoulder and her face pressed to his back. *"We are chaste,"* she said to his warming skin, *"yet we make a fine picture for any who happen to see."*

Elisha swallowed hard, but still he responded to her touch, to her closeness. He thought of Thomas's keen stare with a hopeless wish, and mastered himself to answer her.

Before he could frame a reply, she echoed his despair. *"You have a love,"* she said. *"I'm sorry if I cause you grief for your—but it is not a lady."* Surprise stiffened her arm, even as he tried to bury his response.

"Please, lady, do not ask more of me than you already have."

"No, forgive me." Her fist relaxed, her breath sighing against him. *"But you are not averse to ladies."*

Elisha pulled away from her, rolling to his back. "I did not ask you here for this—it is a convenient ruse, but no more. Do not ask it of me." He spoke harshly, and for a moment, seeing her face made silver by the moon, he thought that she would cry again. He was not sure he could resist her tears, but she pressed her lips together, and tentatively settled her fingers on his wrist.

"They want me to seduce you."

Their eyes locked across the gap between them.

"They wish me to use my body and my pain to distract you from your purpose, and to force you to reveal your

knowledge and your skills." She gave a tiny, tired laugh. *"I am no seductress. I am no enchantress in the mountain ready to lure you away—I have no such power."*

"You say you repent, lady, and that you want my help to do so. Help me unravel their plans."

Her breath quickened and she gave a nod, but her fingers tightened, just a little. *"There is one among the soldiers on the far bank. He watches over me, over both of us. They worry already because you did not kill me— that's why they believed this—my—my closeness—would affect you."*

"Do you tell them all? How much do they know about me?"

"Don't be angry—you knew I was one of them."

His anger wasn't for her, but for himself, for last night when he wanted to believe her, for the treacherous heat in his body when she drew so near. If he hadn't been so lonely, eager for someone who could understand the burdens of magic, would he even let Katherine approach? He carefully steeled himself against her, building his walls, allowing only the contact of her hand upon him, his jaw clenched.

"They cannot know my thoughts, not like this. If I allow it, they can feel what I feel, through a talisman we share."

A nudge of that talisman would get their attention, as he had done with the old man's bones when he hunted down her colleagues that dark night. *"Do they expect you to betray them?"*

Her thumb pressed hard against him with a bolt of fear. *"They have my children."*

For a moment, he couldn't breathe, as if her grip had pressed the air from his chest.

"I have killed only once with them. I attended another, but I could not bring myself—they have gatherings, and a few of the more important mancers circulate among them, so that a few participate with the other gatherings and take more talismans. They take as victims those who will not be missed, or those who become suspicious. These gatherings, they link like rings of mail, like a great armor

of horrors." Her hand trembled, her presence still shot with fear as she babbled into his skin. "*I have heard the leaders speak of Rome, but they say little to those who have only one or two murders. There is Eben, you've met him, yes? And a tonsured Frenchman, Renart. And a young Italian with very bright hair whose name I do not know.*"

Leaders. He would need to see them. If she opened herself to him, she could send the images. Slayings. Elisha rolled to face her and caught her shoulder, their noses nearly touching. "*Stop, Katherine, stop. They have your children?*"

She gave a jerky nod. "*Two sons and a daughter. I've searched, but I can't find them. I should have taken more care. I was the only one from the murder I shared who survived the night when you went hunting. It worries them.*" She turned her face to the deck, dodging his stare. "*They—I must do what they say. I must try.*" He sensed her stab of grief and despair. The enemy weighed the lives of children against Elisha's heart, because he could not bring himself to kill a mancer who prayed for such release.

"*Nudge your talisman,*" he told her. "*Send them this.*"

She blinked at him in the darkness, her uncertainty palpable, though her hand crept toward a pool of death that hung at her waist. A hint of the Valley tingled between them, a hint of interest from beyond.

Elisha knotted his hand through her hair and rolled her to her back, his body pressing against her. He kissed her, sending her his need, his longing, his aloneness. Her heart soared, and a rush of gratitude flowed between them.

Chapter 20

———— ❖ ————

Strange to have spent months loving those he rarely dared to touch, and now to spend a day in touching a woman he did not love. Each brush of their fingers conveyed their conversation and suggested to all that they grew in feeling for each other. She sent him images of the mancers she knew—not many, and most of these, aside from Eben, Conrad and Bardolph, were now dead by Elisha's hand. The barge neared the dock where they would disembark and proceed by horse to the salt baths, and the ladies lounged with their needlework, speculating about the Empress Margaret's baby and what it might be like. The empress turned wistful, saying, "I bid farewell to most of my children in Holland when I returned here to be with Ludwig, though I miss them dearly. The littlest is already three years old—she'll be so grown when I see them again!" She stroked the fullness of her belly and smiled down at it. "This one shall be the tenth—I feel it is a boy."

"Another Ludwig, then?" Lady Agnes inquired.

"Yes, I think so."

"What about you, Katherine? Will your family ride down to meet us?"

"Not this time," she murmured, but her throat worked.

"Your home is here?" Elisha asked, gently, with a touch that sent his concern.

"My husband held the land around the salt mines on behalf of the emperor." Katherine's eyes scanned the riverbank and the gathering crowd of soldiers, horses and porters. "Since his death, I am privileged to hold the lands as margravine in my own stead."

"No privilege, Katherine, but merely a sound decision," the empress said, then to Elisha, "She is an excellent manager of the estate and the mine." Again, her gaze took on that cool speculation. "I thought you might know this. If, that is, you are courting my lady Katherine with honorable intent."

"Courting is rather a strong description, surely." Katherine laughed, but the pink warmth of her cheeks colored her denial.

"Your Majesty," Elisha said stiffly, "I did not come here looking for either company or wealth." He had no idea how to deflect the empress's interest in this subject without damaging either his reputation or the lady's.

"I can give you company," Agnes announced, "but not wealth." She shrugged broadly. "And there are few enough men who seek my company. Truly, sir, with my devilish nose and your witch's eyes, our children would be quite remarkable." She made a grotesque face, rolling back her own eyes, then grinning.

Everyone laughed at that, but Empress Margaret took a long moment to turn her gaze away from Elisha's discomfiture. With a chatter of complaint about leaving their cushions and excitement about the salt baths, the ladies began packing away their stitching as the bargemen guided the ship toward the dock. Elisha emerged first from the pavilion, leaving the ladies and their awkward conversation. A church steeple of brown stone echoed the dark, spiked shapes of the forest encroaching against the town, murky despite the autumn sun. And beyond that rose a towering darkness, jagged at first with trees, then stone. Higher still, the stone turned misty, with pinnacles of white. Clouds drifted up there, some of them snagged on the peaks.

For the first time, Katherine gave a sparkle of genuine laughter. "The Alps. If you do wish to go to Rome, you shall have to pass them."

"It can't be done," Elisha breathed, staring up at the

forbidding slopes. Unless he had some way to forge a
contact in Rome itself, and some knowledge of where
that contact would bring him, he could not use the Valley
to travel there. Instead, he would be forced to go as other
men, to ride or climb through those terrible peaks. They
must still be many miles away, and he hated to imagine
how tall they must be in truth.

"You will find a way." Then she took his hand. *"That's
him,"* she said within his flesh, as one of the soldiers made
his way up the plank to the barge, giving a little bow.

"Margravine, please inform the empress that all is
ready," the soldier announced.

Katherine need not have pointed him out: a dozen or
more shades hovered round the soldier, darkening his
shadow and obscuring his hands.

"I'll tell her," Katherine replied brusquely.

The soldier bowed again, and departed with his entourage of spirits, apparently taking no notice of Elisha
at all.

As the lady turned to go, Elisha caught her shoulder.
"Will you ride by me? We still have much to discuss."

Her brow furrowed. *"It would be difficult to maintain
contact."*

"The empress and Lady Agnes have convinced me
that I don't know nearly enough about you, Margravine,"
he pressed.

"Of course," she murmured, with a smile.

In moments, all the ladies issued down the ramp to
the riverside dock and spread out to be helped to their
mounts. The empress herself, holding her back with one
hand and supported by Katherine, came after. Doctor
von Stubben hurried along with her. "Please allow me to
arrange for a carriage, Your Majesty. Surely you cannot
mean—"

"I can, Doctor. I am perfectly fit to ride. If you wish a
carriage, then take one for yourself and leave me in
peace."

"But Your Majesty—"

"You are dismissed. I am sure that my other doctors
are quite capable of attending me."

Von Stubben's bristly hair stood up around his pink scalp, his mustache protruding. "I am beginning to believe that the maidservant you sent away was correct about your English doctor. His eyes are the sign that he is not right in the head. I can see how his presence here amused you on your journey, Your Majesty, but I pray you, allow him to deliver his message and be gone!"

Elisha stared at him, for the first time in full light. His left eye revealed flitting shades. Not so strong and malevolent as those that clung to murderers like the mancers, and yet the doctor had lives on his hands, too. For the first time, Elisha feared to see his own reflection. How many dead must he be carrying? He rubbed his eye and banished his other sight. "The physician does make a point, Your Majesty," Elisha said, causing a little stir among the party, and tipping his head, his fingers tracing the cross-shaped scar that parted his hair. Given that his enemies knew their destination, it might be better to circumvent their trap and simply never arrive at Bad Stollhein. "My changed eye is the result of surgery—but that's not what I meant. I will be staying only to see Your Majesty to the baths, then I must continue my journey. Your need for care will go on, and you must have someone to see to the baby—"

"I would rather have you."

Drawing back, Elisha gave a little shake of his head.

The empress set her shoulders. "Since you came, I have been less troubled by my pregnancy."

"Herbs, Your Majesty. Such tonics as peasants rely upon," said von Stubben. "I myself could have prescribed such things if I had not thought them beneath you."

"No," she snapped. "It is not merely that. He does not fear to touch me. He does not retreat from me, but stays by, and even as he speaks to Katherine, he is alert to my worldly needs. His, Doctor, are hands that heal."

"You are being taken in by his scars, Your Majesty."

"So be it." She stared down her nose at him, until the physician finally swept a bow and stomped away toward the village, jostling the boys who held the horses. "Now," she began, turning to Elisha, "you will stay. Until this child is born."

"Your Majesty, you do not understand—"

"No, Doctor, you do not understand. I am the empress here. You wish my husband to hear your tale. I wish you to attend me. If you do not, I can simply order that your journey is at an end. Right here." She pointed to the ground at her feet, the soldiers growing still, hands to their sword hilts.

Elisha's shoulders stiffened. "How long must I stay, Your Majesty?"

"A week at most." Empress Margaret's lips curled into a smile. "A woman knows these things, Doctor."

Elisha bowed his head, the fur cloak dragging him down. At his left breast winked the goldsmith's pin: a ram trussed for the sacrifice. Why did she show her steel? Why now? On the barge she had been firm, but always gracious. What had changed but the presence of the soldiers? Perhaps her steel was not a weapon, but armor against enemies she knew were near.

Accepting the offered horse, Elisha found his place in the procession, not far from the empress, a purple cape draping her dappled mount. His lonely ride to Heidelberg had been along narrow trails and through the thickest trees he could manage without dismounting, the better to hide from pursuit. Now, they rode wide paths, sometimes paved with ancient stone, that passed through villages of huts where peasants emerged to bow and to wave. Empress Margaret cast a few coins out to the poorest, and accepted sacks of chestnuts and peasant loaves of dark bread. After a time, Katherine slowed her mount to ride beside him, cocking her head at him. "What was it you wished to know?"

"Have you always been with the empress?"

She blinked at him a moment, probably expecting a more engaging topic. "My family and the royal house of Bavaria have been allied for years. It is the emperor we serve. Please, don't take it ill—I am happy to accompany her Majesty. My mother was in service with Emperor Ludwig's first wife, Queen Beatrice, before her untimely death."

Beatrice the mother of Thomas's wife, Anna. Elisha nodded for her to continue.

Katherine gave a shrug. "Even during Beatrice's reign, there was a rival emperor, but Ludwig took care of him promptly. It was a few years later, after he'd married Her Majesty Empress Margaret that he tried to name his own pope." Her voice dropped a little, and he reined closer to her to listen. "We almost broke with him then, in spite of his patronage. That's when he became excommunicate."

"I heard about that." Elisha tried to fathom the power it took to proclaim a new speaker for God. Ludwig, already possessed of earthly power, tried to claim dominion over Heaven as well, or at least, over Heaven's vicar on earth.

"The arrangement did not last long. It seemed rather unlikely to, without the approval of the cardinals, after all."

Ludwig was even more mad than he seemed. "And your husband?" he asked lightly.

She stared off toward the forest. "It was an advantageous match, given his salt holdings." Her presence chilled, and her hand rose absently to her chest, to where her husband's shriveled hand lay bound beneath her breasts. "There were four children. One died young." She crossed herself.

As he studied her profile, he saw the flitting of that slight shade beneath the edges of the darker shade of the child's father. He wanted to know more, but the questions were those he dare not ask in the air.

"He died in a mine accident, killed by his own salt." Her hazel eyes caught his glance. "Years ago, we dug out an older section and found a few miners in bright clothing with ancient tools—mostly worn away by the salt, of course, but likely they had been there for centuries, crushed, like he was."

"Strange to be killed in a place known for healing."

"Quite. The healing baths are simply runoff from the process of dissolving the salt to refine it," she said with a conspiratorial air. "We are fortunate to be blessed with hot springs as well as mines."

"A very healthful combination," said the physician Emerick, spurring up at Katherine's other side. "Salt is also efficacious in the prevention of witchcraft. So perhaps your new companion, with his unusual eyes, would be averse to such a place." A hint of humor bubbled through his presence, his broad-lipped smile showing a flash of teeth. "I theorize that it is the very structure of salt, not to mention its purity of form, that prevents the intrusion of the diabolical."

"We have a church carved into the mine, Doctor. Dedicated to Raphael, the angel of healing." Her lashes dipped over her eyes, but her glance was for Elisha, and heat rose in his body.

"I understand you have come from England not merely to speak with the emperor, but also to explore the means by which your queen might be healed. Perhaps a shipment of the margravine's salt might be efficacious in that regard." Another smile. Elisha began to wonder if the young doctor himself wished to pay court to the wealthy and influential widow. "Describe for me her condition, sir, and I shall see if there is any knowledge I might impart. I am a graduate of Padua, you know."

In the distance, another steeple rose, dwarfed by the mountains which drew slowly nearer, but it was Brigit's lovely face that overlaid the clouded sky. "She lies like one asleep, her breath steady, her eyes in movement, though they do not open. Her skin is warm"—soft, creamy beneath his rough fingers—"her pulse slow, but even. She gives no response to voice, touch, or pin prick." Though her presence still warmed to his. Elisha swallowed. "She takes nourishment—soups, almond milk— nothing that must be chewed."

"The king must be quite distraught."

If any conversation were calculated to separate him from Katherine, this would be it. Thomas. If the king were distraught over anything, it was Elisha's own absence that worried him, but the lingering state of the

woman he had newly married also prevented him mar-
rying again, to get the heirs he still needed. "She was
struck down during an act of treason against the crown.
It's fair to say the king's feelings are mixed at best."

"Then why feed her at all, if I may be so bold? Surely
it were best to let her pass unto the Lord's judgment."
Emerick used expansive gestures when he spoke, sweeping one large hand about and expertly guiding his horse
with the other.

Both looked to Elisha, and he carefully controlled his
presence, projecting disinterest as he replied, "She is
with child, Doctor." His child, though the world would
know it as Thomas's. A son, Elisha already knew; then
his horse snorted as he gave an involuntary jerk on the
reins. His son would not merely be claimed for the king's
son, but for his heir.

"Dear God!" Emerick said, crossing himself as Katherine did likewise, but her face now remained studiously
blank, her gaze lowered, and Elisha knew he had revealed too much. "Well, then, Doctor, it seems that every
effort should be made to rouse her. If she was engaged
in treason, might it not be a demonic attack? The lingering effect of a satanic influence that held sway over her
during a time of . . . well, of female weakness, if you'll
pardon my saying so, Margravine."

"Some females are weaker than others," she replied,
but neither she nor Brigit would qualify as weak.

"What about the urine?" Emerick asked. "And do
you know the sign of her birth?"

The leather reins bit into Elisha's grip, and he forced
himself to relax. This was his story, after all, the one
meant to conceal his deeper motives—he should be prepared to discuss the matter, especially with other medical men. He took a deep breath. "Urine, clear. Her birth
sign: Scorpius, I believe." He imagined the charts of the
body, each organ governed by one of the signs. On every
chart the scorpion ruled the genitals. That would suit
Brigit's fire, and her allure.

Emerick, given a worthy medical problem, began a
recitation of poisonous plants that might be the cause of

such a state, not to mention various other maladies. Elisha, who had brought about the state himself by magic, allowed the words to flow over him, adding a grunt of recognition or a sound of inquiry from time to time. Katherine rode stoically between them, ignoring Emerick's gestures and invitations for admiration. By unspoken consent, they managed to slip his interest after the break for nuncheon, but this move placed them close to Empress Margaret and to Agnes, who was regaling her majesty with ribald songs that muted any attempt at conversation. At last, they reached the market town where they would spend the night, the royal entourage taking over the manor of a local lord who had gone off on other business. As the lord's servants rushed about their preparations, Elisha stepped up to Katherine's horse to help her down, his hand upon her waist, her face too close to his. She smelled of oranges and cinnamon.

"Is it true that the salt mines inhibit magic?" he asked through the contact.

"It can be contained there, but you cannot reach beyond. They hate the mines. Too many of their tricks don't work down inside."

"You can't open the Valley?"

"What valley?"

"The Valley of the Shadow of Death."

She frowned at his words, but he sent her the sense of what he meant, and her face cleared. *"Yes, exactly—the dark road, they call it."*

A few grooms approached, saw their near-embrace, and scurried away again, eyes wide. Elisha stepped back, breaking the contact, considering. Not every magus could reach beyond the skin, except with direct contact—even if that contact meant a scrap of flesh or bone from a murdered victim. Even then, the strength of the contact depended upon the power of the talisman itself—for the mancers, apparently only murder would do, whereas, thanks to his sensitivity and his medical learning, Elisha could forge contact with life, with strangers, with distant places and people of whom he had little knowledge. Most could establish contact through water, some through rain, a handful through fire or earth. But salt was an element he had not tried. Such knowledge could be useful. For the first time, he looked forward to visiting the salt bath for its own sake.

By the manor steps, the empress dismounted with a stumble and a groan. Extending his senses, Elisha edged closer into the throng of servants from the manor. Margaret looked flushed as he approached and she caught his eye. "A private room, yes? For our . . . for . . ." She shook her head vaguely, her arm sliding to support her belly as her face crumpled in pain.

"Emerick!" Elisha shouted, and the doctor looked up from the far side of the yard. "Your Majesty, don't worry over the room."

"I have promised," she hissed, pushing herself erect once more. "I won't—" A gasp, and a shake of her head. "I must—"

Pain pulsed through her presence, an ache focused at her back, radiating outward. Elisha pushed by the servants and took the empress's elbow. "Your Majesty, you must rest."

"I'm here, Your Majesty. Sweet Mother!" Emerick stopped short at her other side, rising from a bow. "Are you quite well?"

With one hand, Elisha pulled off his cape and dropped it to the steps at the empress's back. As her knees buckled, he eased her down to sit upon the padded step, supporting her back. "Contractions?"

"No," she breathed, "not yet. Just . . . pain. Weakness."

"Bleeding?"

She shook her head, shivering.

Emerick fussed behind him for a moment and returned with the long cape the empress used on horseback. He flung it over her, wrapping her gently. "Is it time?"

Elisha shook his head. "She says not."

"She may be mistaken. Have you checked for signs?" Emerick lifted her wrist, pinching it between his fingers to test her pulse.

With a sense of bemusement, Elisha realized he no

longer needed to resort to such obvious tools. "It is her tenth child, Doctor. I think she knows the signs."

The empress smiled faintly. "Rest, yes."

"And something to eat," he said firmly. "You've barely eaten the last few days."

Emerick's brows rose. "Truly?"

"She pushes things around on her plate and casts them in the river when she imagines we don't notice."

"I thought you had eyes only for Katherine."

"If that were so, Your Majesty, I was not doing my duty," he told her. Her head rested against his chest as she tried to deepen her breathing, her dark hair rippling from beneath her traveling veil. "May I touch you, Your Majesty?"

She let out a breathy laugh. "Rather late for that question."

Elisha reached down along the brocade of her surcoat to her waist at her back where the pain throbbed. Gently, he rubbed, as if he could stroke the pain out of her body, applying his strength and his comfort. Her furrowed brow eased, and after a moment, her eyes fluttered open again.

"We have prepared a chamber, Your Majesty," said one of the servants, head ducked and hands clasped.

"I'll bring up the herbals," said Emerick. "We should elevate your feet, Your Majesty. Are you able to rise, or shall I organize a party to bear you to your bed?"

"Would that I could simply float up the stair, as I shall float at Bad Stollhein." She sighed. "But I think I can walk."

With Emerick's help, she rose and let a servant take her weight. The doctor accompanied her up the steps, asking questions, murmuring comfort. A good man, if a little unwilling to trust the female sex. Elisha picked up his cloak and dusted it off, adjusting the pin as he draped it over one shoulder. The ladies bustled past in the wake of their queen, Katherine among them, a fist pressed against her talisman and her face set in fear. There would be no private talk tonight, likely not with either of them.

"Doctor?" said a voice from behind, and Elisha

turned to find an aged woman approaching him, head cocked. Her glance flickered to the cape at his shoulder, then back to his face. "I was told to bring you word."

He walked with her to the edge of the yard as the grooms led horses away and the place emptied out but for them and a scattering of golden chestnut leaves. "What news?"

"My son's boat plied up the river not long before yours, with the rabbi's message. I heard your party were to stay here and come along to wait. So. There's a flagellant group come down to Augsburg—that's between here and the baths."

Elisha swallowed his curse. They knew through Katherine or Bardolph that he had volunteered to come on this journey. Now between the empress's trust and Katherine's need, he hated to leave before seeing to their safe deliverance. "Do you know the family of the Margravine at all?"

The old woman nodded. "My other son is a foreman at the mine. The old lord was not so kind, but his wife is a sound manager."

"Their children?"

"Twin boys of about twelve summers, and a daughter perhaps sixteen. Pretty girl, smart, like her mother. Long dark hair." The old woman's hand spiraled down the side of her face in imitation of the girl's flowing locks.

Sixteen, long, dark, flowing hair. Elisha's throat went dry as he envisioned a corpse, half-flayed, a girl her mother might not have recognized. Unless her mother were a witch. Or a necromancer.

Chapter 21

✦

"**D**octor?"

Elisha shook himself. "Thank you. Did you have anything else to tell me?"

"Only that about the flagellants."

"It was just what I needed." He managed a smile for her, but her flat stare showed that he had not convinced her. She bobbed a curtsy and shuffled back through the arch. Elisha bounded for the stairs, skidding on the marble of the floor, attracting the attention of a servant with a basket of bread. "The empress? Where does she rest?"

"At the back, on the left." The servant tore her gaze from Elisha's mismatched eyes, and he hurried away again.

Naturally, his haste did him no good. Her majesty was bathing, Agnes told him, with Katherine in attendance, along with some others. Agnes batted her eyes at him, making some remarks about his sudden urgency to see the margravine, but when his impatience did not yield to her humor, she grew solemn, and took him away to dine and find his own quarters. She would send Katherine when she could, and Elisha had little choice but to wait, or to intrude upon the rest he himself had prescribed. As he wrapped up in his cape, on a pallet of straw among the porters and other royal attendants, Elisha tried to dispel the dead girl's image. What troubled him was something more. When Katherine revealed her children's disappearance, he assumed it was to do with him, because he had not killed her, as an inducement to seduce him. But the girl was already dead before he turned hunter that night, before they sent Katherine as his distraction. Why kill their hostage early? Why would they have taken her in advance? What, in fact, had Katherine been repenting that night when he found her on her knees, in search of death?

He woke to her approach, picking her way across the hall, unerringly toward him in spite of the gloom imposed by the dying fire. Sinking wearily before him, she said, "Hold me," and he drew aside the cape to take her to his chest, her head resting upon his arm. He made out the glint of her eyes in the darkness.

"How fares the empress?"

"Better, but the pregnancy pains her again." Katherine sighed. "This should not be happening."

Elisha stroked the hair from her face, sending her comfort, and maintaining close contact. "This has been a difficult pregnancy, has it not?"

"Yes," she said, her teeth clicking shut on the word. She cringed away from him—minutely, but to his awareness, as clear as a sudden torch against the darkness.

Gripping her shoulder, Elisha murmured into her ear, "Katherine, what have you done?"

"Nothing!" she protested against his skin, turning her face, her eyes squeezing shut. *"Nothing . . . lately. They want her sick. They want Ludwig trapped by worry for her, and for the baby. Like you, they thought he would stay with her. It was she herself who convinced him to come later, to meet with Charles first."*

"What have you done?" he repeated inside of her, the tension rushing his body.

"Herbs, and touches. I spoiled some of the treatments— but I stopped. I couldn't bear it, as the baby came closer to due, to think I might be the death of a child. I couldn't do it anymore. I threw away the ruined things. Someone must have given her something else, something new and awful."

"This is what you repented in the church, what you feared someone would overhear." She expected punishment, but not from the Lord.

"I know I am weak, Elisha. I did stop, I swear it. Please don't hate me—don't abandon me, or my children."

As open as she was in that moment, she did not miss the flash of his regret, and she grew still, then turned to face him, placing her hand upon his chest. *"Elisha. What do you know?"*

"I do not know, Katherine, but I fear. The night that I turned hunter, I followed Bardolph to a place of slaughter, a stone in the forest."

"I know the place. It's where—where I did the one."

"They had a girl there, a victim." He lay his hand upon her cheek, refining his memory, muting the horror, imagining the girl, her height and build, her flowing locks, the touch of her blood.

She buried her face against his chest and screamed, hands in fists at her mouth, the sound resonating through his ribs, echoing in his scars. Elisha wrapped her in his arms, his face pressed against her hair, clinging to her through the rocking of her grief. Her tears burned with her shame. She feared to kill the child of another, expecting they might kill her. Instead, they turned her dread against her, slaying her own child.

The mancers—Eben—had sent Katherine to seduce him, with the understanding that she could save the lives of her children. But they already knew that he knew the truth. They sent a broken tool, one they could no longer control, and they knew it. She believed she was to distract him, but the truth was more subtle. A trap, baited with this wounded woman and her children—assuming the boys still lived—set with the flagellant commander to direct his strength against Elisha. But where and how would the trap be sprung? Tears: water and salt. Like the baths that flowed from a place where magic could not penetrate. The salt mine church of Saint Raphael, a destination where the flagellants would follow their master, seeking to enhance their punishment: salt upon their wounds. Good Lord.

Knowing what he faced, he could step off this path and dodge the trap completely. But Katherine's sobbing echoed through his bones. Could he leave without

knowing if her other children were alive or dead? Could
he leave the empress to carry her baby into mancer
hands? The mancers knew his answer; they counted on it.
Bardolph had finally convinced them that Elisha was not
simply a rogue necromancer, and his failure to kill Katherine had confirmed it. The barber could be brought down
by his compassion. It was the flaw he could not overcome.
Elisha closed his stinging eyes against the night.

He need not enter the trap unarmed or unaware. His
knowledge gave him an advantage; it had to. He remembered Isaac's words, that God's righteous might be so
frozen by their compassion that they must shelter for a
thousand years in the palm of the Lord. The Lord's
hands had never seemed to him to be that comforting.
As Mordecai once told him, the Lord created every man
blessed and cursed in equal measure, in Elisha's case, by
precisely the same thing: his blessed, cursed compassion.

Around them, people snored softly, and someone in a
far corner by the door entertained a quietly giggling
companion. Katherine's sobbing shuddered to a silent
despair. As he lay with her, Elisha hated her for what she
might have done to the empress and the baby, admired
her for trying to defy the mancers, pitied her for what
she had lost, feared with her for what remained at stake,
and realized that he had halfway come to love her.

After a time, he released her, tucked his cape around
her, and assured her he would return. She remained lost
in grief, and gave him no reply. He returned to the empress's chamber where Emerick slumped in a seat by the
door, snoring, and startled awake at Elisha's approach,
squinting at him in the light of a single candle. "Don't
you need a lantern, man, or do those witching eyes let
you see in the dark?"

They rather did, though not in the way the doctor
meant. His witching awareness, not his eyes, allowed him
to move with certainty, even in low light, as long as he
knew where he was going. Curiously, in Elisha's divided
vision, the young doctor carried no shades at all, as if
he'd never lost a patient. Just as likely, he'd simply never
gotten close enough to any of them for their deaths to

mark him in that way. Elisha kept his voice low. "We must clean out the empress's herbals, Doctor. The margravine suspects them to be tainted."

Emerick matched his tone. "Tainted? Surely not!"

"For a week, her Majesty had no adverse symptoms. Today, again she does. What's changed?"

"She moved from the barge to horseback—that alone might account for it." Then Emerick considered more deeply. "Also, she dismissed her personal physician. I was only meant to be von Stubben's assistant." Then his eyes flared, and he pushed abruptly up from his seat. "He left his supplies in the medical chest. I took the opportunity over nuncheon to check his stock and combine it with the royal chest if it contained the same herbs. Holy Rood, if I've done something—"

Elisha touched him lightly. "Let's be certain before we place any blame."

Emerick nodded and led the way quietly into the empress's chamber. Three ladies lay on pallets on the floor, with small lanterns burning to either side of the large bed—likely the lord's bed when he was at home. On a trestle table in the far corner, next to the portable altar Elisha sensed earlier, sat the medical chest. The two men lifted it carefully and carried it back to the corridor, shutting the door before spreading the contents on the floor. Emerick's long fingers swiftly picked out a dozen bottles and packets. He sniffed each one, then tapped his finger to his tongue and took a little sample of each to taste. He recoiled from a packet of sage and handed it over, shaking his head. "Good for stomach ailments indeed—this will create them." Then he frowned and slipped back into the chamber, returning with a small vial. "A cordial to encourage a strong child. We used to have a great jug of it, but the margravine spilt it a week ago and never ordered a replacement. I found this in von Stubben's things and offered it for her Majesty's use." His shoulders slumped. "She took a draught this afternoon when we paused to water the horses."

"Don't waste time in regret, Doctor. From here on, we must be vigilant."

The young man pulled up his lanky frame and gave a nod. "Indeed, Doctor. The upstart must have paid off von Stubben for his interference. I pray the poison is not too deep."

"I think not. She's been in good health while we traveled, until now. They did not want to kill her, or even the baby, just to leave her weak, unable to aid her husband, and requiring him to spend his worry on her in turn. I wonder why she took against von Stubben, though, if you've had no sign he was betraying her."

"You think that I do not trust the minds of women, but von Stubben was much, much worse." Emerick gave a rueful smile. "It seems that both her Majesty and the margravine have brighter insight than my own, in spite of all my education. I shall endeavor to improve myself in that regard."

"What more can be asked of any man?" Elisha replied.

Feeling Katherine's approach, Elisha turned as she came along the corridor, still wrapped in his cloak, her eyes shadowed and red from weeping. Emerick startled at the sight of her, then frowned at Elisha, as if he were to blame for her state.

"How fares the empress, doctors?"

"Sleeping soundly, Margravine," Emerick replied. "And yourself?"

"I have had . . . bad news. News that encourages me to move on quickly toward my home." Her grave eyes lifted to Elisha's face.

"We'll see what the day shall bring, Margravine—if her Majesty is well enough to continue. If not, I'm sure she will allow you to press on. I know that you are dear to her," said Emerick.

She smiled faintly, slipped the cloak from her shoulders and returned it to Elisha before gliding into the empress's room and shutting the door behind her.

"A fine woman of wealth and courtesy." Emerick sighed. "You are truly blessed."

"Good night, Doctor." Elisha's cloak, still warm with Katherine's presence, weighed down his arms as he returned to the hall below. By dawn, servants stirred and roamed the crowded chamber, preparing the fire. One of the first men Elisha saw was the mancer guard, yawning and stretching from a place by the hearth, the flickering shades of his victims clinging to his form. Elisha wanted to simply cross the room and administer the touch of death, but he refrained—this was the man who sent word to the others of their progress; the longer they believed Katherine ignorant of her daughter's fate, the safer her sons remained.

Breakfast found the empress much improved—if dismayed by the appearance of her dear friend Katherine—and resolved to ride quickly for the baths where the margravine could manage whatever dread affair had so darkened her mood. Empress Margaret, too, cast Elisha a doubtful look, and he did his best to be solicitous toward both women. By the time they left the manor, Katherine realized that Elisha was being blamed for her black spirits and made an effort to revive and show him favor, requesting his assistance to mount up.

In the touch of his hands upon her waist, she said, *"I must find them. You'll help me, won't you? Please."* Her face smiled down on him, her presence trembled with concern.

"I suspect they are in the mines, perhaps as bait to draw me in."

She squeezed his fingers as he released her. *"But that would mean—"* and a rush of fear that made the horse stamp beneath her.

"They sent you to bring me to them, Katherine, with your cunning or with your pain." He took her horse's head, soothing it with his hands. "Take care, Margravine."

She took up her reins, staring down at him. "The way ahead is rougher than it once was."

"Courage," he murmured.

Again, they spoke of her home as they rode, but this time she shared so many details about the mines and their operation that any other listeners quickly grew bored—and convinced that Elisha was desperate to gain her rich holdings: why else should he care about miners' slides or brine pits or the use of cow's blood to strip the impurities from salt?

When he spoke with the empress at nuncheon, inquiring about her health and offering some advice, he read in her frank looks the question of his intentions toward Katherine. No doubt, a widow of such wealth required royal permission to marry. Empress Margaret might be kindly disposed to him, in spite of her husband's enmity, but enough to give him her friend in marriage? And how, after all of this, was he to tell them he did not want her?

The mountains loomed all around them now, glowering darkly as they turned along the slopes into the town of Bad Stollhein. Katherine's trepidation grew by the moment, and she seized Elisha's hand when they dismounted, even in front of her gathered servants and retainers. *"How shall we ever find them? There are bound to be new chambers and passages—and I haven't been in the mine for years."*

"We need someone we can trust who knows them more recently." He led her forward, trying to look natural as if she merely asked his arm to take her from her horse after the long ride. *"There's a man who works as a foreman, a Jew—his mother sent me some information."*

"Daniel Stoyan? And you would trust him?" She cast him a dubious glance.

His presence chilled, and her frown deepened. *"You are margravine here. At the least you can find out what's been dug in the mine in your absence. I wouldn't doubt him merely because he is a Jew. If he proves trustworthy, he might have suggestions about where prisoners might be kept. The enemy I fear is the flagellant, the mancer who surrounds himself with living talismans, but if we can separate him from his adherents, he won't be able to use the power of their pain."*

"I will learn what I can." She released him to move forward into the welcoming embraces of retainers and bows of her servants as she directed them to the empress's comfort.

The empress herself looked pale and drawn, her face

in sharp contrast to her purple robes. "Doctors, pray attend me." Elisha and Emerick moved to her side as swiftly as the crowd of horses allowed. "I should like to descend to the baths immediately."

"It might be wise to rest from your exertions, Your Majesty," Emerick offered, delicately taking her wrist to count her pulse.

"If the bath serves to relax her Majesty, I see no reason why she shouldn't go now," Elisha said.

"Agnes and Jocelyn." The empress set back her shoulders as the ladies curtsied. "We shall go to the baths for a time before dining."

"Very well, Your Majesty. I'll see to your things." Agnes bobbed another curtsy, then slipped between the porters to take charge of a pair of them hoisting a chest and urge them into the smaller procession that split off toward a vast domed structure built against the side of the mountain. It gleamed with gold and torchlight that could not hold off the black foreboding of the forested slopes. Beyond them—far beyond—lay Rome, and Elisha still had no idea how he could get there.

A few guardsmen immediately started ahead, with the mancer in the front, crying, "Achtung! Clear the baths for her Royal Majesty!"

By this hour, few bathers remained in any case, and these readily emerged, servants hurrying with their robes and towels, bowing to the empress as she swept inside with her dozen companions. While the empress made ready in a separate room, Elisha and Emerick walked down an echoing hall to the heated pool. It occupied a domed chamber, torchlight reflecting in ripples on the brine then back again to form bands of light across the ceiling. The moist salty air tingled Elisha's nostrils and eyes. Beyond the pool with its stone dome rose a wall of salt, rosy-hued and veined like alabaster. Hollows on the walls held candles behind a thin layer of carved salt, casting a pinkish glow at the far side.

"Glows like a maiden's blush," Emerick murmured, staring about.

Elisha found a long bench with pegs above and hung

his cloak, then shed his heavy jerkin as well, his inner tunic already clinging with sweat. Damp black curls draped his forehead, and he pushed back his hair — nearly long enough now to need a tie — his fingers running along the cross-shaped scar. Between the moisture, the heat, the scent of salt and minerals, and the forlorn echo of dripping water, Elisha's senses filled with the place so it took a moment to know what was missing. He caught the drift of Emerick's presence nearby. And beyond, was nothing. No matter how he stretched his awareness, focusing on the empress or even the mancer-guard who watched the door, Elisha could not feel them. Six months ago, he knew no other senses than this — and now, the lack of his magical extension worried him, as if he'd been amputated of a limb he had not known was there.

His left eye caught glimmers of a few shades here, but even these were faint, hard to distinguish from the flickers of the torchlight except that he could make them vanish by shutting his eye. His power was not gone but diminished, subdued by the properties of salt.

"Climate warm and moist, clearly. I should recommend a diet this evening of cool and dry ingredients to provide some balance to your humors." Emerick's voice rang strangely around the chamber beneath the dome. He pushed back his velvet sleeves and wiped a cloth over his brow.

Kneeling on the damp floor by the broad stairs, Elisha dipped a hand into the murky water. It tasted of iron and salt, strong but not dangerous.

"Well, doctors? My mistress awaits." The lovely voice of Lady Agnes filled the room, overriding the drip and splash as she modulated her tone, transforming her query into a trill of music that echoed as if she were become a chorus. She smiled, and in the ruddy gloom, her homely features softened.

"Marvelous," said Emerick, then gave himself a little shake. "Indeed, my lady, I believe she may enter. It is warm, and we shall wish to monitor both herself and the infant to be sure she does not become overheated."

"How are you to monitor that in a bath, good sir? Unless you propose to do something unseemly." Agnes's eyes flared.

"No, assuredly not." He waved his hands. "If the empress will be comfortable on the stairs, or perhaps in this smaller area, I may maintain a count of her pulses, and take occasional reference to the infant as well."

"Assuredly not," the empress replied, entering at a stately pace, Lady Jocelyn carrying the train of her robe. "It is my will to drift. At the far side of the pool, the salt is stronger."

"Drift, Your Majesty? Is one of your ladies prepared to accompany you and to be sure about the pulses? This is not something to be trifled with."

"The English doctor shall accompany me." She stared at Elisha. "He shall need to strip to his hose and trews, but we shall be in full view of my retainers."

In spite of the heat, Elisha's mouth went dry, but her stare brooked no refusal, and a twitch of her eyebrows suggested she had some serious intent. After a moment, he nodded and removed his belt and tunic, laying them aside on the bench, tucking his packet of letters inside. He still carried Thomas's ring and a few hidden talismans if he needed them.

"So many scars." Agnes's ethereal voice, even at a murmur, echoed around him.

"The good doctor has not always kept such refined company," said the empress as she released the clasp of her robe and let it fall to the waiting servants. Beneath, she wore a white chemise ruffled at the throat and wrists, draping over her pregnant belly and falling a bit short of the floor. "I pray he shall gather no more scars in his sojourn among us."

Emerick retreated from the sight of the empress in her under things, turning a bit pink as he went to stand by Agnes.

"Sing for us, would you?" Empress Margaret smiled, then beckoned to Elisha as she started down the steps.

He pulled off his boots and hurried to join her. The empress placed herself, and her baby, in his hands. He took her hand upon his arm, escorting her into the water as if to a ball beneath the sea. The warm bath rose up above his hips, but the floor felt just rough enough to keep his footing. Agnes began a hymn that filled the chamber, a solemn song unlike her usual fare, but suited to the cavernous bath.

Walking steadily, Empress Margaret brought him to the far side, beneath the glowing salt. She moved a little apart from him, keeping his hand, then lay down with a sigh, her chemise floating around her, the rise of her breasts and belly swelling up from the water. Elisha sank to his knees in the water, guiding her drifting form until her head rested at his shoulder, sure to be clear of the water, her braided hair draping against his arm.

"Do be sure to monitor my pulses," she murmured, her eyes closed, her weight borne upon the bath. No wonder she was so eager to come here. She lay as if on a bed of softest feathers, steam rising gently around her, arms loose upon the surface.

"Voices do not carry from here, Doctor. With Agnes singing, none shall hear what passes between us." Her eyes opened, reflecting the strange light. "Tell me now, Doctor. What evil stalks my husband?"

Chapter 22

———— ❖ ————

As Elisha spoke, overcoming their awkward intimacy, some of the comfort of the bath seeped into his own body, weary of vigilance, sore from the ride. He left out anything to suggest Katherine's role, and minimized his own dangerous strength, but noted Bardolph and the mancer-guard as agents of the enemy. Almost, given the relaxation of her face and form as her eyes closed again, he thought her sleeping there upon the water, but her presence remained attentive and her forehead sometimes creased as he outlined what he believed about the mancer influence over Charles, and their desire to drive people to Rome, to strike a blow against the Church itself.

"Perhaps it is these sorcerers who control the madman at Rome," she murmured. "It would explain much."

"Then you do believe me." He reached along her arm, taking her wrist gently to check her pulse—a gesture for Emerick's benefit rather than his own; so close together, even the densely salty water could not prevent his attunement to her body.

"If all you say is true, then I should have you seized as a witch." Her face grew solemn, her eyes searching his.

Elisha held his breath, awaiting her condemnation.

"But there have been many strange things happening here, not least of which is the power of the upstart to gather support away from my husband. I do think there may be something unholy in this."

"The upstart is a man of great charisma, Your Majesty," Elisha said carefully. "I don't think he knowingly conspires with these sorcerers."

"In spite of what you have seen, Doctor, my husband is not an angry man. Rather, it is the recent changes that drive him to his mania. I believe he must have some knowledge of these things, but that he fears to tell me. I am merely a woman, after all."

He thought of how she had brought him here, every excuse with seeming logic and clear intent—yet quite different from her actual intent, creating the appearance of playful trust to make the space to hear him. "Your Majesty, I have learned not to underestimate women." Brigit's face and her own still form flashed in his memory.

"And Katherine? What do you say of her?"

Across the water, Emerick's raised voice began to wonder if her majesty hadn't been floating long enough now.

Drawing a deep breath of the salted air, Elisha felt he was breathing in Katherine's tears. "The margravine is a fine woman, Your Majesty."

"But you do not tarry for the sake of women?"

"My enemies—our enemies—are already moving against her, Your Majesty."

"Again, you evade my question. This urgency you carry, Doctor, I do not understand it. You think that you must go to Rome. That you, yourself, must save us all."

"Who else will?" Who else even could?

"We shall save the Germans, as your King Thomas has saved the English. As for Rome, it is the Pope who should be looking out for his city."

Elisha's anger returned the tension to his neck, and he said, "How can he, if he doesn't know the danger? Or if he himself is the danger?"

"This is the obligation of the powerful, to tend those in their care, as my husband tends his own people. Those with the worldly power of kings shall defend the flesh, and those with the spiritual power of priests shall defend the souls. You have neither."

The obligation of the powerful. Kings, she meant, and queens and empresses, the pope, the cardinals, the priests. Not one of them would see Elisha's place—it was not quite among them—yet he had traveled so far from the people he always sought to serve. He thought of Isaac's thirty-six, working quietly, wielding their power not from palaces, but from paths that others dared not walk. Their power was of the spirit, not of the world. Rulers like Thomas or Charles united worldly power to a strong sense of spiritual guidance—an ideal balance, if that guidance were not given by necromancers.

The empress let her feet sink, pushing herself to stand before him, limned in pink light and sheathed in damp fabric. She might have been seductive but for the hard expression on her face. "As we must look out for those who have stumbled. Katherine is not merely my friend, but also my husband's vassal, who holds of him great lands—and the salt that keeps our land rich. A dalliance with an underling is a fine thing upon a journey, but now she is at home, and it must end. A husband shall be found to match her station—I will not have her sullied by her infatuation with you."

Elisha's head bowed beneath this sharp reminder of his true place. "Forgive me, Your Majesty. It has never been my intent to damage her honor."

"Since seeing you, she has been all a-flutter—fainting, foolish, tearful, and hopeful by turns. You do not say what power you hold, Doctor, but whatever it might be, it lies very close to the heart."

As Elisha considered what might be said to that, her fingers pinched his chin, forcing him to meet her gaze. "You are handsome, kind, and competent. Your scars make certain women feel an urge to tenderness—and none of those things confers the right to the liberties you have taken. Men have been castrated for less. If you do not stop, Doctor, and stop at once, I shall give you to the bishop and watch you burn." She released him with a flick of her wrist that turned his face and dismissed him back to the rank of her servants.

Across the water, Agnes fell silent, and Emerick repeated his plea for their return.

"Bring me there, Doctor." The empress put out her arm in the expectation of his aid, and Elisha took it upon his own. Water ran down her body, shaping her chemise to her full breasts and belly as he led her back to the party by the steps. It made her not a figure of desire, but of stone—a marble queen draped in majesty, at every moment cold and calculating. The empress's attendants waited by the stairs, the mancer guard lurking by the entrance beyond. Katherine moved up through the others, with a stranger at her back, both looking anxious.

As she stepped from the water to the towels held by her waiting servants, the empress glanced over at her friend, then back to Elisha. "Thank you, Doctor. I shall keep my promise to you as well. My husband shall hear your words. There is no need for you to tarry any longer."

Elisha's jaw knotted, his eyes downcast, struck back to a barber once more, to live and die at the whim of others.

"He might wait a day, and speak his own message, Your Majesty," said Katherine. "My steward tells me the emperor is on his way—to rally an army against the upstart."

The empress broke her marble façade, her eyes fiercely alight. "Ludwig comes here? We must be ready." Her gaze lingered on Katherine, and she said, "You may have a moment to say your farewells." Then, to the others, she said, "Come!" The party broke before her to let her pass and swirled up the stairs again in pursuit of her.

"Emerick!" Elisha shouted, and the doctor pivoted on his heel. "Watch over her—she and the baby have enemies closer than she thinks."

"I've seen it," Emerick replied. His lips parted to say more, but he simply shook his head. "I've a feeling we'll miss you before too long. Fare you well, Doctor."

"And you," Elisha murmured as the doctor hurried after his charge.

Katherine lingered as Elisha trudged back to where he'd left his clothes.

"You'll want this," she said, holding out a towel. Her gaze traveled slow across his chest, as if it caught upon every scar before she looked into his face. He reached for the towel, but she did not let go, using his grip on the other end to pull herself closer. Her right hand slid across his lower back, stroking upward, tracing the hatchwork of scars left from his lashing. *"I've brought your Jew,"* she said into his skin, but her touch carried longing.

"Thank you." He bit off the words, ducking her glance. *"Her majesty has said she'll kill me if I dally with you."*

Far from driving her away, this statement drew her closer, her breath against his shoulder. *"So that is what she meant about farewells, but did she not say just yesterday that she needs you to tend her baby?"*

"Not as much as her husband needs your salt in his control. It was a useful ruse, but we must have done with it." He jerked the towel from her grasp and started to scrub the salty water from his hair.

Katherine slid her arms about him, her face pressed to his back, her palm pressed to the brand upon his chest, the smooth patch where no hair would grow, cut by the groove of Thomas's blade. Elisha froze, his heart thundering beneath her touch. The last time any held him so, Thomas drew him half-drowned from the roiling Thames and carried him to Mordecai, desperate to save his life. "Margravine, please," he hissed.

"My watcher remains at the door, Elisha," she said against his flesh, pleading, the fear that chilled his skin at odds with the passion she displayed for the benefit of their witnesses. *"The flagellants hold vigil in the church below. They are mounting against us, against you, and now Margaret has turned against you."* She broke away from him then, blinking back tears as she retreated. "Forgive me, Doctor. The empress has decreed that you must go." She trailed her fingers along his arm, sending, *"Go. I will find my children, somehow."*

Could he leave her? He still had no plan for how to find them, or how to break the mancers from their power, even here in the deadening salt. The mancer by the door resonated his interest, the Jewish worker—his non-magical presence not even marking Elisha's dulled awareness—studied a mosaic by the entrance.

"I should," Elisha murmured, knowing his voice would echo. He focused what awareness he could muster on the mancer by the door, then he stepped up to Katherine, dropping the towel, gripping her shoulders as he kissed her, as if he said farewell. The spike of the mancer's interest pierced Elisha's awareness. *"Do you feel him watching?"*

Katherine, startled first by his deed, then by his words, took a moment to reply. *"Faintly—as anything is felt down here."*

"The mancers. Do they share moments other than killing?"

"You mean—?" She stared up into his eyes, her face flushed.

"If they thought we would be lovers," he insisted. *"If they thought you would kill me at the height of passion, they would come for that. They'd have to be close, in order to feel it, to share in that betrayal."*

"It is just the sort of moment they revel in." Her reply felt hollow, dismayed. *"But the empress—"*

"We'll do it now, tonight. I'll talk to Daniel and find out what I can, where your children might be hidden. You go to the empress and do what is needed for her—let her imagine I've already gone—and tell the mancers your plan. Ask for their aid in killing me—but insist on seeing your children before you deliver me."

"They already think we are in league. Why would they believe me?"

He softened his hands upon her shoulders. *"Katherine, what would you do to save your children?"*

The strength of her talisman surged through her, and she need not answer.

"They will believe you. For a death like this, they will be too tempted not to."

She leaned into him. Her hand once more upon his chest. *"My Raphael,"* she murmured. *"How will you survive?"*

"Let me think on that." Elisha stroked her face and smiled, radiating desire for the benefit of the mancer, his loins tightening at her touch. How far could he go in counterfeiting love before his body betrayed him by making it real?

Katherine pushed up and kissed him again, lightly, then withdrew, gathering her skirts, already touching the hidden talisman that would summon her watcher to follow. "Here is Daniel Stoyan to speak with you. He can answer questions about the healing properties of the salts. Come to the kitchen before you go and I'll see you're given . . . sustenance." She let her eyes linger on Elisha, then cut her gaze away and vanished down the corridor, the mancer-guard stalking after. The foreman bowed as she passed, acknowledging her authority. Had Elisha truly gained an ally among the mancers, or had he just given her the way to secure her children's safety with his death?

Elisha quickly toweled himself off and pulled his tunic over his head and arms before addressing the foreman. "Herr Stoyan. Forgive me for making you witness that scene."

Daniel Stoyan took a step nearer, his hands fidgeting with a few oddments that hung from his belt. "I . . . am given to understand that the margravine needs fresh information about the mines. I assume you are the doctor I have heard about? I have been told to trust you, first by my mother, and now by the margravine herself."

Taking up the cloak, Elisha displayed the pin Isaac had given him. "Forgive me, as well, for taking you from your duties, but it's true that we need help."

Locks of gray twisted through his black curls beneath a dark cap. "To plan a tryst."

"To save the lives of children," Elisha shot back. "When was the last time you saw the margravine's children?"

"Fraulein Sonia has gone for a visit with friends, I am told."

"And the boys?"

"The whereabouts of children are hardly under my purview, Doctor."

"Sonia is murdered, and the boys are missing. I have reason to believe they are concealed somewhere in the mine, hostage against their mother's obedience to enemies of the empire."

For a moment, the man regarded him blankly, echoing, "Sonia, dead? Can it be?" Then he said, in that same distant tone, "For holding captives, it is not the new part of the mine you want—miners are there at all hours. It is the oldest parts, where the veins are no longer stable. From the church you would go to the east, bearing east at the turning. A portion of the tunnel collapsed that once led to the hillside above the lake. It's a warren of ancient rooms and broken passages. The miners fear to go there, now."

"Can you show me a map?"

"Come back to the office," Daniel said, with a gesture toward the door, but Elisha stopped him.

"My enemies have power beyond the salt—and I would not recognize them all." Within the salt, his sensitivity let him feel the mancers if they drew near. Beyond it, he lost that advantage to men with stronger attunement to this land. Elisha studied the mine foreman, his broad shoulders and strong arms. Outside the mine, any magus of power could sense the presence of the *desolati*, those without power. And within it? They were invisible. Another advantage. Elisha grinned. He did not know what the mancers had planned for him, but he could preempt their plans with one of his own. "The margravine— what would you do at her command?"

The man's downturned lips sank a bit further, and Elisha beckoned him closer, away from the entrance and deeper into the salt. "We are laying a trap, an ambush," he said softly, and the foreman leaned in to hear him. "Our enemies believe that the margravine and I are lovers, that we'll plan a tryst tonight before I'm forced to leave. They'll come to try to kill me—and they'll have to reveal themselves. If you and some of your men hid in the caverns, you can help me stop them."

"You're asking me to kill. To bring up my men and tell them to kill these people you claim are your enemies." The miner snorted, shaking his head.

"Don't think of me—think of her, and her children. Before you agree, find out if she's seen her children, when anyone saw them last."

"You asked for a map," the man prompted.

"I need to find a room, not too far in, where it might

be reasonable to—plan a tryst." He tried to say it lightly, but the idea shook him still. Most of his recent experience had been with the whores of Coppice Alley, trading their favors when they had no other way to pay him for his own service. When he'd pursued Brigit, not knowing all she could do, she delayed his passion until she knew she was ready to conceive a child. She claimed to love him, and perhaps the baby allowed her to keep a part of him even while she planned for his death. Since that night with her, he remained celibate, to guard his own heart if for no other reason. And if desire stirred him toward the king, he could pretend it was only the bond they shared through the battles they had nearly lost, and finally won together.

The foreman squatted, dipping a finger in the water and drawing on the stone. "Here's the church, and the passage out, as I said. Two turns left and one right brings you to this room, with a few little niches and such, broken tunnels, as I said. These two other tunnels are intact, one down to another level that we still work, and this, branches toward the lower mines again, and back up to the western slope for ventilation. There's a few other little chambers, but mostly narrow, and others lower down." He stared down the map he had drawn, Elisha kneeling beside him. "An eager man, one who didn't know the mines, wouldn't want to go that way."

"And one who had to keep two children hidden?"

The man's dark eyes searched his face. "He would, a man like that. There's rooms here, by the broken section, where you might still get water and air from the surface."

"Bring a dozen men at least, and have them hide around that chamber—not in the tunnels that go through, that's where the enemy will be."

"And if I don't believe you?"

"Then all you'll get is a show," Elisha told him dryly. "But if they come, we'll need help. If you can, don't touch them with your bare hands."

At that, the foreman chuckled. "Some kind of poisonous, are they?"

Elisha did not smile. "Deadly."

Chapter 23

———————— ❖ ————————

*L*etting the man depart—hopefully, organizing for the ambush—Elisha finally left the deserted bath. Outside, night loomed, with an autumn drizzle that left him shivering after the heat of down below. He pulled the empress's gift closer about him, his breath misting the air, and hurried toward the manor. Katherine's parting words had been a message, telling him to come to the kitchens where they would finalize their plans. The town's streets all wound upward, houses built like steps on the slope of the salt mountain. Some of the streets, in fact, were steps, broad terraces leading toward the fortified house at the top of the town. A bell tolled Vespers in the lower town—the empress would be dining soon, with her companions. Down a side street stood a series of low buildings, clustered about the sound of running water, and beyond that, the mine entrance. An arched door marked with glowing pink sconces of salt opened on a passage to the Church of Saint Raphael. Good.

He felt the drift of people on the streets, a stream of miners dispersing back to their homes, children scampering with messages or home from work of their own, women talking and laughing as they hurried through the light rain. The wind spoke of coming winter, and Elisha hoped to be far out of the mountains by the time it struck, although the journey would be long and unpleasant no matter what. He should find himself a map to Rome. If he were right, the mancers were planting relics there in preparation for their invasion, but he had no way of knowing which bones might lead him there. Insufficient knowledge plagued him. And he still didn't know how they hoped to cow enough of the populace and the priests to bring the continent under their control. The Empress spoke as if each nation bore its own burdens, as if each could simply vanquish its own enemies and perhaps conquer a neighbor or two if events turned that direction, turning the chaos to their own advantage. She claimed the nobles bore the responsibility of those beneath their station, but it was those below who would die to cement Ludwig's grasp on the empire.

As he approached the manor, Elisha wove himself a deflection, enough to dodge the glances of guards no doubt ordered to keep the lusty doctor from the vulnerable margravine. At the kitchen door, a server pressed a sack into his hands, whispering, "Be at the well by the crossing, at Compline," then hurried him back out against a backdrop of roasting meat, steaming pots and the clatter of knives. He did not see Katherine at all — but neither did the empress see him.

In a sheltered courtyard between manor and mine, Elisha opened his sack. He found a wedge of a meat pie, a stoppered jug of wine, and a vial that rattled with salt. To sit "above the salt" at feast, where one could sprinkle as much of the stuff as one liked, a man must be very noble indeed, and now, a barber sat outside the feasting hall, granted the salt that was the wealth of nations. He uncorked the vial, shook some onto his pie, and took a bite. The crust flaked against his teeth, the meaty aroma filling his mouth — then a shock of terror dissolved against his tongue.

The taste of blood blossomed, stinging with pain. Elisha spat out the pie, then vomited, purging the flavor of death that oozed down his throat.

Gasping, wiping his mouth, Elisha stared at the meal laid out upon its sack beside him. He hesitated, then took up the wine, taking a long pull and spitting that out as well, before drinking long from the jug. Dry and heady, it could not erase the memory of that taste. He shivered and took another swallow. Careful now, he touched the pie, searching it with his magical senses, but it was only meat, thick with the tiny deaths of animals he barely noticed. The vial of salt winked in the vague torchlight that spilled from the upper windows of the feasting hall. Taking a few of the large grains on his smallest finger, Elisha touched them to his tongue. Pain, fear, grief, and dying. He shuddered and stuck the cork back into the vial. Did the empress dine tonight on blood salt? No—such large, gray crystals would offend the taste of nobility. The salt on the empress's table would be fine-grained and white. He tossed everything into the sack and returned to the kitchen, barely remembering to cast his deflection as he neared the guards.

Inside, the flurry of activity went on, servers passing dishes to the young nobles who served at table in the feasting hall. Music echoed from the hall, and the clear sound of Agnes, singing. Elisha dodged two boys carrying a whole hog on a huge platter, and spotted the woman who had handed him his dinner. Sidestepping cooks who snarled at his approach, Elisha came up to the woman. She glanced at him and back to the bowl where she sifted flour in a white blur.

"Did you pack my supper?" he asked. She kept her eyes downcast, her face tight, then gave a sharp nod.

"At my mistress' request."

"And she chose the food?"

Dropping the sieve with a clatter, the woman took up a huge wooden spoon. "She hasn't the time for that, has she?"

"Clearly she trusts you," Elisha ventured, shifting his presence to suggest that the margravine trusted him as well.

"Something wrong with the food, that's down to the cooks."

"And the salt?" He put a hand in the sack and drew out the little vial.

"Our salt is known round the world," she said stiffly. "Nothing wrong with it."

"It tastes like blood," Elisha whispered, and the

woman turned, her hands pressed to the table. Her eyes widened as they met his, then her gaze dropped again.

"Surely not."

"Freda!" someone barked. "Get to work, or get on! Get your man out of the kitchen."

"Come then," Elisha said, seizing her elbow. "Get me out of the kitchen." He towed the reluctant Freda across to the outside door. "Tell me about the salt, and be quick before your master gets angry."

"She told me to give you the best," the woman hissed. "Like you're royalty, but I know her Majesty's warned you off, and you should be gone. As if you could hide those eyes. Everybody's heard about you."

"Stop it." Elisha squeezed her arm lightly. "I don't care if you hate me—I need to know about that salt. She wanted you to give me the best, but you didn't. What did you give me?"

"The gray. It's for salting fish, mostly, and there's an inn that takes it—not the kind of place where anyone'd want to eat anyhow. But you can't taste the blood— nobody can." Her chin rose with a sharp pride and rippled through her presence.

"But there is blood in it," Elisha said carefully.

"Cow's blood, to separate the impurities. But even in the gray, the blood's long-gone, skimmed off in the curing." Shaking off his hand she said, "Like you should be."

He gave a nod, stepping aside, then asked, "The message about the well, is that what she really said?"

"You leave her be. She deserves better."

"Agreed," Elisha snapped, "but at least let me bid her farewell."

"Farewell at Raphael's chapel," the woman snarled. "Where the priests of pain will keep their vigil—and keep you honest. Then you leave her be." She swept away from him in a puff of flour.

Blood-cured salt, for salting fish, or for a certain inn. No wonder the mancers had an interest in the margravine and her mines. He hadn't asked how they found her, how they knew about her husband—but the answer seemed plain: when her husband died, the mancers were already here, enjoying the added savor of salt that tasted of death itself. Elisha slipped out the back with a few men emptying the peelings. He returned to the old yard, stomach rumbling, and finished the pie—without salt—and drank the wine. The vial of salt he slid into a pouch at his belt. With another hour or more to wait before Katherine broke free of her guests, Elisha sat in a dark corner, legs pulled up beneath his cloak, and forced himself to rest, his senses extending through the cracked stone, the tufts of grass, the autumn rain. When he shut his eyes, he imagined the scene to follow, but it was Thomas he followed into the dark maze of tunnels, and Brigit who kissed him there with the promise of death.

Elisha's eyes snapped open. He pushed himself up and stalked away toward the church, shedding some of his deflection. The enemy must know his approach, but must not know he suspected. Instead of revealing himself completely, he allowed flickers of anticipation to brighten his presence, like a man going to his lover, as if even a magus could not contain such excitement. Candles flickered in hollows scooped into salt to guide him down beneath the mountain. He heard the murmur of prayers, startled that, for the first time in months, he heard them before he sensed their need. A handful of citizens knelt before the altar or stood regarding the cross that hung over it. Elisha crossed himself, breathing deep of the gritty air. Three tunnels led from the chamber: the one he'd come down, a broad passage leading toward the mine entrance, and the one that pointed east, deeper into the mountain of salt. What if Stoyan had not believed him, and no one hid there to come to their aid?

Just inside the church, Raphael, angel of healing, stood carved in a listening posture, hands spread, head bent, great wings folded at his back. The statue showed bands of pale salt veining the pink. Elisha knelt before him, bowing his head as if in prayer. He sought attunement, the people around him vanishing as he shut his eyes, emerging as a vague pattern of warmth in the strange emptiness of the salt. If he stretched his power, it echoed back, but weak and fragmented, as if it sifted

among the thousand crystals in the air. Instead, Elisha
gathered himself. He opened himself to each talisman, to
the silk of Thomas's lock of hair and the sting of the
earth where his brother had died, to the absurd collection of toenail clippings Brother Gilles had given him,
which had saved him from ambush once before. This
time, the Valley offered no escape for him, nor any entry
for his enemies. They must walk inside on foot, as blind
and senseless as any other men. Most of the magi Elisha
knew awakened to magic early in their lives, often as
they developed from children into men or women, like
Mordecai as a boy, realizing without being told that his
mother was pregnant. Elisha, with his late awakening,
had spent most of his life without the special senses and
skill the magi depended on, more used to being *desolati*
than gifted. With luck, that would give him an advantage
here.

The weak presence of one of the worshippers by the
main altar spiked with interest and receded, likely an
ordinary man asked to watch out for him. Good. Someone needed to send the mancers where Elisha's allies
would be waiting for them. If his allies even came. He
pushed aside that fear, instead considering what he
could do alone, or with Katherine's help. Before she arrived, the power of his dread talismans hovered beneath
a projection of anticipation and lust.

A whisper of Katherine's agitation preceded her into
the room and Elisha rose. Carrying a lantern of salt that
glowed like the dawn, she wore a hooded cape, concealing her identity from the ordinary men and women
around them—but not from the mancers who would be
looking. The hooded head turned, found him, and she
hurried over, hands already reaching so that he caught
her arms, not yet drawing her close. Lips parted, she
gazed up at him from beneath the hood.

*"They brought my son Rudolf to the feast. Both boys
were sick, they said, and Matteus still lingers in his sickness—Rudolf barely spoke, fear rolled from him, Elisha."*
She trembled. *"They took him away again, even as I rose.
I had no chance to learn more, even to touch him!"*

Sliding his hands up to her shoulders, Elisha sent, *"But he's alive."*

"He looked awful, half-dead. So pale."

"You are meant to be seducing me, Katherine," said Elisha, cupping her cheek and kissing her lightly.

"I don't know how, not so they can feel it."

"Focus on the emotion you would project. Take only that and cover the rest. Your talisman gives you the power. Let its death conceal any part of your own life."

Her presence, already shading with relief at finding him, rallied with each breath. Through their contact, he guided her, projecting his own false calm, conjuring desire, letting fear become excitement, urging her to do the same. *"Holy Mary, Elisha, if we survive this, I shall plead for the right to marry you."*

He projected what he willed, and kept the turmoil of his true emotions locked away. *"Come."*

"We should—" A brief note of surprise warmed her skin. *"—you have a plan."*

"Don't speak of it," he answered swiftly, for the thrum of pain approached, accompanied by sobs and shouts of prayer. The flagellants were coming, the priest of pain. Gripping her hand, Elisha sprinted into the old passage, as if he were fleeing before anyone could see them. By the time they passed the corner of the passage that led out of the church, the edge of the clouded power brushed Elisha's limited awareness. It had to be enough. Let them think he tried to dodge them, to seize his moment with the woman they thought to use against him.

"This isn't the way I said we'd go."

"They'll catch up." He slowed, choosing the path that Daniel had drawn out, praying Daniel and his men were already there. The walls gleamed dully as their lantern approached. A few beams, some already cracked or fallen, shored up the roof. *"One of those in the chapel was watching out for us."*

"I did as you bid me, I told them I would kill you."

He squeezed her hand. *"How?"*

"Poison. Wolfsbane." She ducked her head, her pulse leaping with uncertainty. Elisha drew the symptoms

from memory: nausea, tingling, chest pains, convulsions, paralysis, and the awful clarity of mind that lasted even as the body failed. For the mancers, it would be ecstasy. *"On my fingernails, as they suggested."* She shuddered.

The passage opened out into a rough oval with a few dark niches—tunnels that went nowhere, most of them. Elisha's heightened senses reverberated from the crooked walls of salt, disorienting him until he drew back and stopped his searching.

"At the height of passion, I am to scratch you."

"Carrying it into my blood. Clever."

"I don't want you to die." She gazed up at him. *"I want us both to live, and my sons to live."*

Blood-borne wolfsbane would take only moments to affect him, likely bypassing the nausea and tingling of the lips that were consequent of swallowing the root.

"I want that, too." He slipped the lantern from her numb grasp, noting her painted nails. *"It will take them a few minutes to find us. How many do we expect?"*

"Five or six. It's short notice, and they can't simply ... arrive here." She wet her lips. The rosy, flickering light made her face look younger, her eyes darker beneath the hood.

Setting the lantern on a ledge likely carved for the purpose, Elisha reached up and stroked his hands over her hair, letting her hood fall away, tipping her face up to his.

"Here?" she whispered, eyes darting.

"Trust me."

Her eyes closed, her smile both fond and weary. "I do, by God, I do."

A thin circlet held a pursed veil to contain her hair, and Elisha plucked it free, running his fingers through her hair, letting it tumble down over her shoulders. Their breath intertwined. He was little trained in the arts of seduction—most of his few partners had been professionals, after all, used to handling the matter for themselves. And when Brigit came to him, he knelt, bound and helpless beneath her hands. Thrusting aside the memory, Elisha caught Katherine's face and kissed her, hard, her lips parting beneath his as she moaned.

He broke away to strip off his cloak, unclasping the pin to spread it out, the rich fur inviting them. With fumbling fingers, she untied her own cape and let it drop, revealing a loose undergown, but the black stain of her husband's death still hovered at her chest, over her pounding heart. For this to work, for this to be true to those who would sense it and be drawn to the powerful tonic of passion and death, he must divide his attention, burying his thoughts, his plans, his secrets, while revealing exactly what he wanted them—through her—to know. He had to love her.

Stripping off his jerkin, dropping his belt to one side, Elisha kissed her again. He thought of the ball when he danced with Rosalynn, projecting confidence, allowing her to find her balance and feel her grace, so that Rosie's father believed he might want her. But this memory tangled with another, one much more complicated. Thomas, in disguise, witnessed the dance that stirred his own desire, but it was not Rosie he was watching.

Elisha swallowed hard, his breath and heart thundering in concert as Katherine pressed against him. She ran her hands from his shoulders down his spine. One hand slipped across his thigh, stroking lightly, then finding the ties that bound his braes and hose.

"No," he breathed. Then, "Not so soon," working to cover his lapse, stepping out of her hands, her dark nails opening to release him. "The gown."

"Oh." She smiled, swallowed. "Yes." Crossing her hands, she reached down to pluck the fabric and pulled it up, up, over her head, silk swishing down her back. Beneath, she wore a chemise tied a bit lower than her throat, and a bodice, defining her shape, lifting her breasts to press against the light fabric above. Concealing the talisman that shaded his vision. Elisha shut his left eye, repressing the shade: it would not be the first time she murdered a lover.

From the passage below, a subtle shifting of the heavy

air. From the tunnel they had used, a whisper of sound. The mancers came.

Again, she reached for the ties at his waist, sliding her hands beneath his tunic, and this time, he let her tug the knots even as he opened the ribbon at her throat and spread the fabric down about her shoulders. Surely, a lover now would unbind her bodice and free her breasts to share the pleasure—but to do so would leave her truly naked, her talisman cast aside with her clothing, and she would need it in the moments to come. Katherine's right hand found his manhood. "Come," she sighed, her breasts swelling at the edge of their confinement. She lay back before him, onto the pile of their cloaks and clothing.

Kneeling between her thighs, Elisha pushed back her skirt. Their eyes met. Salt and more parched his throat. His hand—dark and rough against her pale skin—lingered on her knee. *"We don't need to—"*

"I want to," she answered, her right hand gripping the back of his neck, urging him down, propping on her elbow, she kissed him, sending him confusion, lust and need, heightened by terror.

She risked her sons, her heirs, her position with the empress, her estates, and her legacy along with her life. What did he risk but some mad sense of honor, of devotion to what he could not have—who he could not have? And yes, in that deep place where he buried his secrets, he felt the gnawing of a new guilt: he wanted it, too.

She opened herself to him, a gulf of desire, strength, courage, and he sank between her legs, grateful for the strength of his arms to support him, for the softness of the cloaks beneath as her legs embraced his. Katherine kissed with frantic need, not the practiced passion of the whores, nor the calculated sympathy that Brigit projected. Her kiss recalled him to his old friend Martin and the two kisses they had shared: the first on the eve of Elisha's burial, Martin claiming the kiss he'd wanted for so long; the last on the day of Martin's sacrifice, Elisha's gift before Martin's spirit soared, and he worked his final spell.

Then thought was gone. His body shuddered and she moaned, her hand pulling him closer, her back arching as she clung to him. For a moment, her presence hovered, as if on a wave, caught between the swirling chaos of the death she carried against her heart and this flash of light. She glowed against that darkness, vivid as his angel, and gave a cry. Then her nails raked his spine.

Elisha trembled, gasped, threw his head back and screamed. His body rocked, his heart stuttered, and he died.

Chapter 24

❦

$\mathcal{B}$reaking open the secrets he had sealed, Elisha spilled
forth Death. He drew it out from every talisman,
from the memory of dying, from the scar upon his scalp
that marked his broken skull and the Valley of the
Shadow that ever lingered. He allowed his heart to fal-
ter, calling up the memory of every patient beneath his
hands whose operation had gone wrong, and he plunged
his life into the frigid void of death. His scream broke off
as if his startled flesh forgot he still commanded it.

Katherine's voice rose up to take its place. She jerked
and struggled under him, then rolled them both and rose
to her knees, wailing, tears streaking her face.

"Come on, hurry!" snarled a deep voice.

The familiar voice of the flagellant priest called out,
"Repent, you temptress! Repent and leave your weeping, for God has done His will through your weak flesh
and the enemy lies dead."

"Stop shouting," replied another, coolly. "Wolfsbane
won't kill him right off. He's just paralyzed. We've got a
few minutes to reap him right."

Elisha's staring eyes dried in the salty air, and he
cursed the urge to blink them—though the idea of blocking out Katherine's horrified face was temptation in itself. Why were her horror and guilt so strong? She had
known what to expect, but perhaps his execution of the
scheme surprised her with its thoroughness. Even now,
she seized and chafed his hand, magic entwining from

her talisman in dark bands that flowed along her arm as she tried to reach him. Elisha did not respond.

"Hurry up, then, the priest's beaters will grow anxious if they're without him for long."

Five. Five mancers against himself and Katherine—but his own performance left her stunned, in more ways than one. Let them get their hands upon him, they would know death. In his cold, Elisha readied himself.

The soldier leaned over them, grabbed Katherine and pulled her away. "Come on, woman. You've had yours—now he's all for us."

To the east, a rustle, a crack, then a cry that ended in a sickening thud. The Valley tore open, chaos howling from the gloom to suck down a soul. The ambush had begun.

"Holy Rood!" Shouts and screams and the tremor of feet in the salt beneath him.

A spatter of blood struck Elisha's face. The instant chill carried the sharp tang of death, and Elisha rolled, pushing himself up.

Katherine shrieked again in a rush of confusion.

The mancer soldier scrambled away, reaching for his weapon. "He's meant to be paralyzed, woman, scratch him again!"

"Who are these people?" cried one of the other mancers.

The flagellant priest reared back from Elisha, bringing up a whistle that hung at his collar, and the blast echoed through Elisha's skull.

"Idiot!" cursed the soldier. "Why'd you call your acolytes?"

"We'll need them," the priest spat back, and already, his presence brightened with the clamorous approach of his followers, eager to give him their pain.

"Margravine! Watch yourself."

Katherine flung herself close to the wall, isolated both from him and from any weapon.

Elisha leapt back as Daniel Stoyan stumbled through, swinging a bloody pickaxe. The soldier seized its handle. With a burst of power, the pick fell to rust and the handle shattered. The soldier lunged toward the miner, but Elisha sprang between them, conjuring Death. At the end of the chamber, one of the mancers lay dead, and one of the miners beside him. Four other miners wielded picks and shovels, beating at the pair of mancers only to have their weapons struck through. A mancer with a thick brow shot out his hand, clawing death into a miner who twisted and screamed as his flesh withered.

"Don't touch them," Elisha cried. The soldier sneered, and his dark shades rose up around him—twenty deaths at least, a cold army—but weakened and without a source of contact to carry his power into the miners. Even the floor they shared, carved of salt, would carry no magic.

The soldier lashed out, Elisha danced back, leading him away from Daniel and Katherine. Then he stumbled over their abandoned bed of cloaks and dropped to one knee. The soldier drew a knife that gleamed with an edge of darkness and swirled with shadow. Elisha grabbed the cloak that had tripped him and yanked it, tumbling the soldier. Elisha caught the fresh deaths around him, snatching the soldier by the throat as if he could shove the dead straight down it. The mancer's eyes frosted, his mouth gaping.

Snatching the knife from the dead man's grasp, Elisha searched the chamber. Armed now with the dead who lay about him, he felt his power constrained by salt, but not suppressed. One of the deaths the knife remembered echoed to the east; a faint, but certain, sign that another mancer here shared that crime. Elisha blew a breath and conjured it to wind, then flung the knife and let the echo of shared murder carry it home into the mancer's side.

The fellow wailed and clawed at it as the cursed blade poured forth its cold. The man's flesh peeled back, crumbling, from the wound. He conjured blackness to his grasp, only to be bashed down by a miner with a block of salt clenched in both hands. The cursed blade finished its work, the mancer's blood freezing into a stream of red crystals, his peeling skin turning black until his flesh was as twisted as any slab of salted meat. The remaining miners—Daniel along with them—grabbed stones, knives, anything that could be thrown. The mancer caught in the corner conjured terror from the talismans he carried, but the salted stones battered him until a miner stabbed him in the throat.

"Lo! And do you see the depravity!" howled the mancer-priest, his half-naked, bloodied followers forming ranks about him. "Do you see what the flesh has wrought?" He shouted, and they echoed with "amen" and "save us," their spirits given to his will. Already dripping blood from lashing themselves in the chapel, they reached for each other, linking hands, blood spiraling their limbs as the mancer at the center drew power from them. If they felt this unnatural flow, they showed no sign of it, their eyes turned in ecstasy or weeping from the sting of salt upon their wounds.

"Bring him! Bring the sinner here to me!" the priest shrieked, pointing at Elisha.

Elisha mustered his power, but to wield it, he must slay them all—he could not reach the mancer except through those he had deluded to his service, the people he had forged into both weapon and armor.

"I'll bring him!" Katherine cried, rushing forward.

"No, woman—he knows you bear him sorrow in your heart!" the priest thundered at her.

"Then take my strength, father! And let me join with you!" She reached out her hand, and the followers on that side wavered, the circle bending as she strained toward their leader. If she could reach him, she could loose the blast of death against him, but he reared back from her.

"Strip off your bodice! Shed that symbol of vanity that offers up your breasts like a whore."

He was asking her to give up her talisman, to be vulnerable to him. After the briefest hesitation, Katherine struggled with the bodice laces and let it fall, her talisman falling with it, leaving her bare of magic. "I'm ready for the whip, father," she said.

The acolytes moved toward Elisha, a dozen of them, joined in a union of pain and aimed at Elisha like a blade. Elisha edged backward.

"What do we do?" Daniel Stoyan demanded. He'd found the handle of a broken shovel, but held it uncertainly, faced with his margravine's crazed behavior and the ring of innocents that shielded the enemy.

"Don't touch them," Elisha said again, retreating another step.

"Run," said Daniel, gesturing with the handle, urging him away. But if Elisha ran, he left Katherine's fate to the mancers. Her change of heart seemed calculated to convince them she had tried her best to kill him, and been thwarted, but the priest's wild glare and the black power he sent in her direction suggested he already guessed the truth: that her fingernails were never poisoned to begin with.

Katherine straightened as if she saw it, too, and she glanced to Daniel. "Yes, let's go!" but when she tried to retreat, the priest cried, "Seize her! Let her flesh be punished and her soul revealed!"

"No!" Elisha reached for her, but it was too late. Two bloodied acolytes caught her arms and dragged her inward, the circle closing around them already.

Katherine kicked and struggled. Daniel smacked the arms of the acolytes with his shaft of wood, but they cried with evident delight and madness, welcoming the pain.

"Father!" Katherine wailed, dumped at the feet of the mancer-priest. She collapsed as if to kiss his feet, then dragged her nails down his bare calf, leaving four trails of blood. The priest's glower flickered and his hand flew to his chest. He gulped, swayed, and dropped to the ground, his body jerking and flailing, arms and legs scraping the salt, then dreadfully still, eyes staring and mouth gaping. For a moment, the frisson of power surged through the small chamber as the dying mancer strained to conjure some final blow, but the salt ground into him and his magic shredded to nothing.

The sharp web of his power collapsed with him, draining away as his acolytes' ecstatic cries turned to woe. A few of them dropped beside him. "Saint Raphael!" someone shouted, and they stumbled, shoved, and fell in their eagerness to take up his body. Some made as if to come for Elisha, then followed their master instead, leaving him with muttered urges to repent of his fleshly sins. Without the mancer's magic to hold them, their unity withered. Perhaps they no longer knew why they bore the stripes of lashing or why they honored the madman whose corpse they carried away, its rigid limbs battering the walls as they went.

Wolfsbane. Administered directly to the blood from Katherine's hand, just as she had said she would do to him.

Elisha's chest echoed with his heartbeat. Katherine knelt there still in an attitude of penance. Her bowed head twitched a little, as if to glance his way, but she did not.

The corridor back to the church echoed with shouts as the acolytes pushed their way inside. Where she knelt on the blood-stained ground, Katherine tremored, a sob escaping her.

"Margravine? My lady?" Daniel glanced around uncertainly, wiped his face, motioned for the two remaining miners to come closer. "Would you, that is . . . are you hurt?"

"My sons!" She staggered to her feet, spinning wildly, her hands spread, her nails dripping blood. "All the mancers are dead, Elisha, and where are my sons? How will they ever be found?"

Moments before, those hands stroked heat into his loins. And now? Elisha met her gaze, and her expression twisted with pain.

"I'm sorry." She raised her shaking hands, first one, then the other. "My left hand was poisoned—in case, in case—" She gulped for breath, then sobbed again. "I'm sorry."

Elisha turned away, confronted at every glance by the dead. The other two miners, pale and frightened, took their fellows, while the mancers lay where they fell, oozing blood or, in the case of the soldier, simply dead without sign of injury but for the frozen blackness at his throat. Her left hand was poisoned in case she decided to kill him after all, but she had decided to let him live. Numbly, Elisha surveyed the dead. "Thank you," he said to the miners, but they glanced at Daniel and avoided his gaze. All the mancers dead, five of them.

"There were no others you knew in Bad Stollhein, my lady? No others you expected would come?" Elisha asked.

"None," said Katherine.

The upper corridor reverberated as if there'd been a scuffle up above. If the watcher who had spotted Elisha remained, he might know another mancer, or there might be *desolati* involved, paid to keep the boys from their mother. There might be anyone—how was Elisha ever to know? They had fought to free her and her sons from the mancers, sacrificed the lives of the miners, and won nothing.

Blood oozed along veins of salt tingling his bare feet with echoes of pain. Blood, and salt. "The man who makes the blood salt, do you see him here? Or the owner of the hostel that buys it?"

"What?" Katherine's bleak voice rang with confusion and despair.

"This man's a hostler," grunted one of the miners, pointing to the thick-browed mancer.

Daniel broke from his indecision, wiping his face, and shaking his head as he looked around. "That'll be Heinrich von Deussel who makes the blood salt."

"Do you know where to find him?"

The Jew's brows lifted. "Of course—to avoid him. His work is against—" But he did not finish the sentence, with a glance at the margravine.

One of the miners, carrying the body of a comrade toward the upper corridor, halted abruptly and dropped into a bow. The sound of marching feet echoed down toward them and a pair of soldiers clad in tabards bearing the imperial eagle tramped in, swords at the ready.

"Go!" Elisha pointed toward the lower exit, the one that would lead them to the mines. "Hurry—you need to get to him." Elisha scooped up her cape and flung it over her.

"But how can you be sure?" she pleaded.

"I've tasted his salt—he's bleeding someone to make it, and you said your son looked pale. Show him your nails—it should convince him I'm dead, and he can release the hostages. Run, before he hears the truth from someone else. Daniel—"

"I'll take her." Daniel snatched the lantern with his off-hand. "Margravine. This way. If you please." They ran into the darkness.

"Halt! In the name of his majesty, Ludwig, king of the Romans!" barked the voice of the steward, Harald, as he swept in, his own imperial garb swaying with his rush. More soldiers followed, carrying torches and hurrying to block the other passages. A few crossed themselves at the sight of the bodies.

Elisha bent to a bow of his own, glance darting toward his pile of clothes. He reached for his hose, but Harald shouted, "Be still!" The point of a pike appeared in the corner of his vision, spearing his undergarments, and Elisha froze, briefly squeezing his eyes shut.

"My wife has been telling me about you and your adventures," the emperor intoned. "But I hardly expected this. By God, Man, you should be ashamed of yourself."

Elisha's cheeks flamed. There might be a worse moment to meet the emperor, but Elisha, half-naked and surrounded by corpses, could not imagine what that might be.

"Eight dead," the emperor observed. "And you without a scratch."

Not entirely true: Elisha's back stung with the marks of Katherine's nails now ground in salt. "I assume her majesty told you all that I said—that you know the nature of the enemies we face, Your Majesty. Five of these are necromancers."

"Sorcery!" cried the nearest miner. "It was awful." Then he dropped his gaze, hands knotting together in fear at having spoken out of turn.

"You were here—surely you are witness to his words." Ludwig tapped the man's bent back. "Come. Straighten up and say so."

"Yes, Majesty. It was like the room filled up with pain, with terror and death. Like that. That's what their knives can do," he said, pointing to the hideous wound in the dead mancer's side where Elisha had driven his own murders deep within. "My mate, he was just touched by one of them, and he screams and dies." He gestured at the dead miner's face, warped by the blast of death. "I want to bring him up to Raphael's, Majesty, so's the priest can lift the cursing from him before his wife sees him."

"Go on then, bring him up." The emperor nodded, and the second miner hurried up. Between the two of them, the miners lifted their dead companion and shuffled up the hall.

"Sorcery. Back in Heidelberg you were taken for blessed." The emperor's mustache bristled as he swung his heavy regard toward the steward, Harald, who had witnessed Elisha's recovery.

"Forget about me!" Elisha's fists clenched. "I don't matter, truly, Your Majesty. What matters is stopping the enemy."

"The upstart Charles cannot manage a battlefield, Barber. I see little to concern me in his quarter now." He stood solidly, as if expecting battle to be joined right there.

"These are the enemy!" Elisha gestured toward the dead mancers. "It was necromancers who slew your daughter Anna and used her very flesh as a weapon."

The light of the lantern carved deep shadows in the emperor's craggy face. "So you say."

"Every one of these men carries such abominations, to create the terror the miners witnessed." Elisha lunged and drew off the dead soldier's mantle, expecting to find the draped skins of his victims, but finding only a linen tunic underneath.

"Unhand him," spat one of the guards. "Show some respect for the dead."

"It's there," said Elisha, "I—" He broke off. He saw the shades that hovered there still, and felt the chill of death that clung to the mancer's hands, but these were things no other man here could know.

The steward Harald squatted at the dead man's head, tipping it aside to look at the mark on his neck, the clear outline of Elisha's hand branded by cold into the dead flesh. "This could be merely strangulation, Your Majesty. We should at least see if there are any other marks." He reached out one hand, methodically unclasping the long row of buckles down the mancer's chest and pulling aside the rumpled cloth. A skewed tunic pulled up from his belt, showing a wedge of tanned skin, as different from the mancer's pale flesh as could be, and at his side where even his own skin would hardly be revealed to the sun. Elisha caught the edge of the tunic and they peeled it back together. Beneath his clothes the mancer wore a tight-fitting vest stitched with braided strands of hair, strips of skin laid side by side, pale, beige, freckled, one with a tattoo, one with the dimpled center of wrinkles where it once overlaid a joint.

Harald's dark eyes met Elisha's as he grimaced and dropped his side of the tunic.

The emperor growled low in his throat.

"These are the skins of his victims, Your Majesty," Elisha said, and he continued with precision, "He used them to incite terror and to kill. He murdered all of these people, and he is not alone. A man like this slew Anna, Your Majesty, and flayed her, and wore her for a trophy."

The emperor's head swiveled to look back at the corridor. "Come!" Then he stared down at the mancer's vest of skins. "Black arts. Necromancers."

A lightness soared through Elisha as the awful moment turned about. The emperor believed him—at long last, he saw it for himself. "It's all true, Your Majesty."

The emperor glared. "I know," he rumbled. "I've known it for years."

Chapter 25

———— ✦ ————

"**What's your will**, Majesty?" said a fresh voice. Clad in rich clothes, his cursed sword hung from a baldric embroidered with imperial eagles, Eben the mancer entered from the tunnel. His round face and ruddy beard glowed warmly in the salt-stained light. "Ah. I heard a rumor you would die tonight, Barber. I'm relieved not to miss it."

Harald's shoulders sank and he kept his head bowed as he stepped back to stand among the emperor's party.

Eben slipped a dagger from his belt, but the emperor trapped his hand. "Enough. Not here."

Eben's smile slipped. No doubt he was hoping to claim Elisha's death all for himself, to add to the dozen flickering shades that pursued him. "Your Majesty must see how dangerous it is to let him live even another hour."

"With his healing powers, my lord, I doubt your blade would be sufficient," Harald murmured. But of course, he could not see the shades of death that stained the steel.

Eyes narrowing, Eben nodded. "True. You should have kept those miners as surety of his obedience."

"I should greatly prefer not to lose any more of my citizens to your feuds." The emperor waved his hand toward the remaining dead. "Especially not someone as esteemed as the margravine herself. The fact that she felt she must run from my soldiers suggests a certain lack of confidence in her safety."

So Ludwig did not know that Katherine was a mancer herself. Good. Elisha reached out and caught the haft of the pike that had pinned his clothing, pushing it back with a quick movement, and a burst of magical strength. The power of the dead lingered within.

"Majesty!" blurted the startled pikeman, but Elisha ignored him.

"Unless you have an objection to my being dressed for my trial," Elisha snapped. He snatched his braes, pulling them up, and following with his hose more carefully, binding the straps and knotting them snugly.

Inside, he reeled. Ludwig knew about the mancers, had known about them for years. Since before his daughter married Thomas? Likely. Before Charles, certainly—and the mancers slew Anna, not for her own sake, but for something her father had done, or failed to do. He was livid not because he didn't believe Elisha, but because the mancers had thrown their support behind his rival. Ludwig expected mancer power to win his own kingdom, not to be wielded against him.

He pulled on his jerkin, palming the packet of letters and tucked them again at his waist. When Elisha reached for his belt, Eben growled, "Don't let him take his things."

"You came here to look for the lady—perhaps you'd like to continue that search elsewhere," Ludwig suggested with a flick of his finger toward the exit.

"I came here to punish the one who defiled her," Eben replied, raking Elisha with a greedy stare.

While the great men glared at each other, Harald quietly gathered Elisha's belt into his hand and tucked it through his own, then draped the cloak over his arm, concealing it. He ignored Elisha's glance, standing erect once more at the emperor's side.

The emperor said, "If you think I shall abandon the margravine and her estates to your ambitions, my lord, you are greatly mistaken."

"I am not the only man here with ambitions," Eben replied, then added, with a tip of his head, "Your Majesty."

"I have gotten you the man you wanted—are you adding your marriage into the bargain?"

Beads of sweat stood out upon Eben's forehead, and he gripped the baldric, his sword twitching. "If we are negotiating, Your Majesty, we might at least go somewhere more comfortable."

And outside the mines, where the mancer could wield his magic properly. Elisha's trap had brought some of the mancers here, but they had known he was coming to Bad Stollhein—they would have prepared a trap of their own. Elisha sat to pull on his boots, letting the loose cloth of his tunic cover the mancer-soldier's fallen knife. When he rose, hitching up the band of his hose, he picked up the knife at the same time, tucking his hand under his tunic as if to smooth out the cloth and slipping the knife into the band where it ached at his hip with a sinister chill. He listened carefully, trying to see if the emperor's irritation with Eben was merely an aspect of his choleric disposition, or if it suggested a chance for Elisha to shear him from his mancer allies. "Your Majesty," Elisha began, but the emperor jabbed a finger at him.

"Quiet, Barber! There's nothing you can say that I don't already know."

Eben's smile brightened at that rebuke. To the soldiers he said, "Take hold of him, tightly. When we pass from the mines, he'll try to use his sorcery to flee."

"Do as he says," the emperor ordered, and the men finally obeyed, two of them locking their grip about Elisha's upper arms. Eben counted on Elisha's reluctance to kill them. The men's nervous tension translated through their flesh. They feared him, indeed, but they feared their emperor's wrath a good deal more. Elisha allowed himself to be taken, keeping an eye on the steward who carried his medical kit and coin purse. Once outside, he could summon the power to shake the ground. With luck, he could seize his things, open the Valley and be gone before Eben or the *desolati* could stop him. But where could he go? He needed to get to Rome, to stay ahead of the mancer plot, but the talismans he currently touched could take him only to

Brother Gilles' chest, via the nail trimmings, to a mancer's slaying ground, through the soldier's blade, or back home to England.

Lord, how he longed to go home. Then he imagined seeing Thomas's face, and he did feel shame. Thomas had children—his own daughter had been taken by mancers to be used against the crown—surely he would forgive what must be done to save them.

The emperor's entourage passed through the church of Raphael, with a small knot of miners on one side, holding vigil, and a fervent crowd of flagellants on the other, commending their brave leader to the Lord, not knowing that Katherine surely sent him straight to Hell.

Even as they mounted the tunnel to escape the salt, Elisha felt a growing chill. In the jostle of mourners and flagellants, Eben ended up directly behind him. Casting back a glance as if scratching his chin against his shoulder, Elisha noticed that Eben's hand gripped the hilt of his sword as if preparing to draw. His left eye observed the meshing of shades that came together around it, every moment more clearly, a braided strength that fused the weapon with the hand that bore it, extending Eben's power down the length of the sword. The guard's blade on Elisha's hip hummed with an answering power—the two blades had shared at least one killing. The blades shared an affinity and he could use it, if Eben did not use it first. Walking ahead of Eben, Elisha reached for attunement, finding the soldiers who marched before him along with the brooding presence of the emperor. Elisha's awareness fragmented where the salt impeded magic, but leapt into clarity as they emerged above the village.

Dropping to one knee, Elisha twisted aside, dragging one of his guards with him. The man shrieked as Eben's cursed sword slashed into him. For any other blade, the blow would be glancing at best, but this weapon carried its poison, shafts of cold and decay crackling through the dead man. Released on one side, Elisha snatched out the knife he'd taken, reaching for knowledge of the shades it carried. The Valley howled into being, blazing where the guard fell, but the roiling shade flowed to Elisha and the Valley snapped shut.

Eben plunged through where the guard had been, swinging. The sword whipped through the air, trailing a black fog of death.

"What are you doing, man?" the emperor shouted.

At the sight of Elisha's knife, Eben hesitated, recognizing it for its former owner.

Thrusting out the little knife to one side, Elisha cast a summoning, drawing Eben's blade to his through the deaths that connected them. Eben's arm turned, his face set in a snarl as he tried to control his blade. It struck Elisha's with a clang that tremored up his arm. Cold shot forth from the contact, but he warded off the attack with power from the grim, fresh death of the soldier whose blood still dripped from Eben's sword.

Both weapons shattered, the combatants stumbling forward as the tension collapsed. Elisha shot out his hand for Eben, but the lord arched away and spun, staggering, out of his reach.

The second soldier released Elisha, taking up his own sword, but wavered, uncertain whom to attack.

Eben retreated, hovering at the emperor's side. "Your Majesty needs allies against the upstart, not to mention the French and whoever else dares defy you. That man has already slain twelve of us, Majesty. Twelve who would have stood with you. You cannot allow him to escape."

"Twelve who would have stood with me? How many stand with Charles?" The emperor kicked Eben away from him like a dog.

Fury swept Eben's presence, white-hot, dispelling his usual calm. His hair and garments shivered with no earthly wind, and shades rippled around him like a flock of ravens. Elisha dove between them as the mancer regained his balance.

"Your kind slew my daughter, Eben," the emperor thundered. "You claimed you would cement my throne, for the sake of unity, but you have gone over to my rival. I would see the empire once more under a single banner, but you! You would reeve it flesh from bone."

As if the emperor's fury quenched his own, Eben drew himself up, solid once more, the shades that surrounded him gathered to his hand. "Yes," he said quietly, "we will." He raised his fist, something clenched in his grasp, exuding cold, and all around him, the night ripped, spilling mancers at his command.

The soldiers brandished their weapons, forming a ring around the emperor—and Elisha with him, more by accident than choice. As he felt the Valley tear open with each mancer's arrival, Elisha counted under his breath. Nine, ten, eleven, twelve—fifteen.

A wind rose up around them. Some of the mancers drew weapons of their own, others merely stood, hands bare and ready. Mancers ringed the soldiers. One of them, a tall man with silvery hair that rippled in the uneasy night, Elisha recognized even in the darkness: Conrad, and he had another man kneeling at his feet, but Elisha could not make out his features.

Harald dumped the cloak and held out Elisha's belt. "Have you any weapons?" the steward muttered.

Elisha wrapped the belt around him, the familiar presence of every talisman tingling, and he didn't answer, giving all his attention to the mancer army arrayed against them, drawn from every estate. Three mancers unslung bows and stepped back from the circle, preparing to take aim from beyond Elisha's reach. Inside the ring of death huddled two dozen soldiers, the steward, the emperor, and Elisha himself. The mancers would never reveal themselves unless they intended to win, to slaughter everyone who had seen them, and this time, he had no hidden allies waiting to strike.

"Are you certain about this, Eben?" asked Conrad. "That is your emperor at the barber's side." Something dangled from his hand, a pale cord that shifted in the flickering light. At his feet, the kneeling man murmured prayers. Not a mancer, a prisoner.

"Ludwig's become completely intractable." Eben stripped off his baldric, and it crumpled in his enchanted grasp, fraying to nothing and whipping away in the wind. "He must go. Hold the dark road."

Conrad gave a nod and swept the cord around his prisoner's throat, drawing it tight and cutting off the prayer.

Eben took a deep breath, and exhaled horror. The shades they carried should have been invisible, black on black, yet to Elisha's eye, they danced like flames, rising up, their eyes and mouths open pits that sucked the heat from the air. Shades grew from each mancer, flaring up into the night, the torches of the soldiers and the lanterns of the houses showing darkly through. Where they overlapped with light, the shades glistened and rippled like pools of blood. The smell of rotting flesh roiled out, along with a sound, at first so soft Elisha felt it in the hairs at the back of his neck before it reached his ears, the rising moan of the dead. Conrad flexed his arms, his prisoner twisted and struggled and the Valley soared open, the chill of coming death turning both men's breath to frost upon the air. The mancers, lost in the inky night, crouched, stabbed at the ground, and stepped away from the towering spirits.

One of the soldiers screamed, dropping to his knees, others stood their ground, but their mail and weapons rattled with fear.

"Can you see them?" Elisha breathed.

Harald bobbed his head, his throat working. "Christ and all his saints preserve us."

"It's an illusion." Not quite true, but the projections could not harm them directly—the apparitions merely focused the soldiers' fear, and their attention. Shit. How were *desolati*, ordinary men, ever to fight such an enemy?

Through his feet, Elisha sensed the torment of a dozen souls long dead: each mancer had planted a knife when he stabbed the ground, anchoring the dread spirits they had conjured and forging contact with the soldiers who shared the ground. The Valley linked these dead, its thrumming center held by Conrad's dying victim. Another presence hovered in the open Valley—Conrad's father, that warden he had sensed on the night he hunted, the one who intimately knew the paths of the dead.

Outside the circle, the archers raised their bows with casual precision. The mancers moved deliberately, with the inexorable strength of those who know they cannot lose. They had every advantage on their side from the cursed blades linked through the earth, to the warden of the Valley stretching forth his power to let that roiling horror swell into the night, bound to the writhing figure at his son's feet.

A few of the torches guttered, and the soldiers cursed and whimpered their fear.

"Take them!" The emperor shouted, drawing a sword of his own.

"How?" cried one of the soldiers. "They're huge!"

"Not the spirits, the sorcerers," Elisha answered, but someone shrieked and died behind him, the power of that death snapped up by a silent mancer. The killing had begun, and Elisha still had little idea how to counter the powerful magics arrayed against him.

Cursing, Elisha pulled free his surgical knife and slashed open his palm, gritting his teeth against the shock of pain. He seized Harald's wrist, making contact and forging the affinity of sight. Shutting his left eye, Elisha cleared away the visions, sharing this clarity with Harald, allowing him—no, forcing him—to see the living mancers, who could die, and not the terrible visions they conjured through the ground.

Harald twitched and frowned, then his sword arm straightened. Releasing him, Elisha leapt for a soldier, flicking him with blood, another and a third, making contact and sending them clarity. The soldiers he touched joined battle with the mancers, swords sparking through the air, but it wouldn't be enough—the mancers came to kill Ludwig, and Elisha didn't know how to stop them. Conrad's prisoner must be the key to holding the Valley, but Conrad himself stood outside the circle, mancers shifting between them. If he could get the emperor to safety, Elisha could more freely flex his power.

Another soldier tumbled, taken with a choking rattle, and a bowstring twanged. Elisha dropped to the ground, a stone bruising his calf. He reached back for the emperor, but Ludwig stood and shouted orders, his voice whipped by the foul wind, as if he could not hear the retching of his men nor see their terror. Elisha grabbed the stone, wincing as it jabbed his cut hand. The Valley rent for another soldier, but the vigilant killer sucked down his death and grew yet stronger.

Somewhere down the slope, horses whinnied their fear. If only they were close enough to ride.

Elisha lifted the stone, stumbled to his feet, an arrow hissing through the spot where he'd been a moment earlier. With all the strength he could muster, Elisha threw the stone downhill toward the horses, then he snatched Harald's arm and the emperor's belt. With no time to warn them or ward himself, Elisha ripped open the Valley, plunging through to the blood-stained stone.

Chapter 26

◆

The three men staggered as the Valley sealed behind them, twenty yards or so downslope from the battle where a howl went up at their vanishing. "The horses!" Elisha ran, sensing the pattern of heat and worry from the tethered mounts. "Ride, Your Majesty—you must flee!"

"Do you take me for a coward?" The emperor slapped Elisha's hand away.

"Every man they touch, they kill."

Ludwig's sword swung toward Elisha's head and stopped short. "It's you who dared touch me."

"Only to save your life, Your Majesty."

"The empress's guard, Your Majesty, thirty strong," Harald panted. "They're just by the manor."

"Go!" the emperor shouted, and the steward pulled himself up on a bareback mount and kicked it into motion. Ludwig swung his head about to Elisha. "I can't leave my men there to die, nor my enemies to prosper. You are the monster we all came here to slay—surely there is something you can do."

Elisha, already shaking from the night's exertions, stared back up the hill. Fifteen mancers, all still standing. Last time he fought so many, they linked themselves together to overcome him, and he turned their connection against them to magnify his own power. Taken one by one, any given mancer might be overcome, but only by bringing all he had to bear against that one—leaving fourteen more to attack. From the sudden spike of interest, he knew the mancers had noticed their absence. If Elisha and the emperor struck now, they had a chance. If not, the soldiers would be dead, the mancers hunting their true prey. A little above the battle, the archers took aim on the trapped soldiers, launching shafts fringed with echoes of the dead. "The archers can kill me from a distance, and I can't touch them. I can do nothing against the archers—not without bringing down the mine and your own men with it."

Ludwig's thick beard parted in a sudden, ferocious grin. "Then they are for me." He caught the mane of the nearest horse and swung himself up, brandishing his sword as the horse plunged up toward the battle. In the flaring light of torches, the emperor looked like the archangel Michael, come to slay the enemies of the Lord. He had none of his rival Charles's charm, but, in that moment, Elisha saw why men would follow him into battle, even such a one-sided battle as this.

If he would salvage anything of this night, Elisha, must follow. Cloaking himself in shades and deflection, he ran after. The guise would not last long, but it might do until Ludwig could distract the archers. Ahead, the ring of soldiers squeezed and pushed back, but did not approach the flickering shades formed by the planted knives, even though the threat came from the other side. If Elisha could strip the mancers of their magic, even a bit of it, they could be slain as other men. The unearthly moaning of the Valley led him on, and the knives, with their history of death, pierced the vale of the dead. Conrad and his father, the warden, held it open, sending power to the mancers and fear to the hearts of those they fought.

Elisha circled toward Conrad and his victim, but Eben stood as body guard. The victim still writhed, his shoulders jerking. His hands must be bound at his back. The shadows moved, and for a moment torchlight glinted on a sweat-streaked, tonsured head and caught the whites of the captive's eyes. Brother Gilles, his mouth gaping and face suffused as the cord drew tight around his throat, but Conrad did not kill him—no, he held him there on the border, his imminent death keeping the Valley open. Shit.

But murder was not the only way to open the Valley.

Dropping to his knees beside the first knife planted in the earth, Elisha steeled himself and opened to the Valley as he grasped the hilt, his cut hand stinging. The Valley groaned to his command, an effort that tightened his every muscle and made his jaw ache with the clenching. As with all magic, it was easy to create in the natural order, and difficult to defy it. Passing through the Valley, as all the dead must do, was terrible, but natural. This rending, propping open not a single door, but a dozen, defied the nature of both this world and the realm beyond: It must strain even the warden and his son, even with the promised death of Gilles to hold the gate. The chaos dazzled his right eye, but his left . . . twelve shades stretched between the blades, bridging the realms, drawing off the power of the Valley to the mancers who had killed them.

Talismans worked because of resonance, because they magnified the innate skill of the magus. These shades reflected the power of the Valley itself. Every time the Valley tried to close, sucking them in, leaving only the remnants that clung to the killers, the warden within the Valley reached back, sending the power to kill with that single touch, ripping the life of their victim into the Valley. Elisha killed by seeking the death inherent in life itself, making nature his ally in destruction, making his killing inevitable, and hideously easy.

Using the contact of his own near-death, Elisha called the pinned shades, summoning them back to the Valley not through the contact of the blades that killed them, but rather through his own kinship, the Valley that opened within when he had nearly died. They rushed through him, extinguished from the earthly plain as if by a mighty wind.

Power rebounded against him, the warden reaching back, trying to hold the conjured shades, but the warden had not killed them—he had no direct control over these shades—nor did he have Elisha's kinship with Death itself. The warden had been unprepared for Elisha's entrance, his manipulation of the Valley, achieved without killing anyone. The lashing howl of the warden's broken power knocked him flat as the Valley wailed shut, its warden thrust away, likely as staggered as Elisha himself—or even more so.

He held on to the knife as if to pin himself to the world, gulping for breath. The pounding madness of the Valley ceased, leaving a sharp silence, a single beat, then cut by the rage of the abandoned mancers and the elation of the soldiers, whooping and calling gratitude to the saints above as they joined battle. The mancers were still magi, and most held other deaths to call upon, but nothing like the horror of the Valley itself. Diminished and angry they fought on, struggling for contact with the remaining soldiers, the elite warriors of the emperor's own guard.

"Conrad!" Eben howled, "what happened?" His form crackled with cold that shocked a soldier dead.

"He broke the path to the knives. Your blades aren't strong enough, and I can't hold the Valley open alone."

Every time someone died and the Valley beckoned, Elisha reached back through the memory of his own death and snapped it shut, denying the mancers their full strength. One of the deaths chilled Elisha's hand—it was one of the soldiers he had marked before fleeing the scene. Elisha caught the power, abandoning the knife and curling his fist, healing himself, but holding his connection to the Valley. Death gnawed at his chest, eager to return him to his rightful place. Instead, he leapt through to Conrad's side and thrust out his hand.

Conrad wheeled, hauling Gilles before him, and Elisha caught the friar, sending a withering stroke along his skin that frayed the cord around his neck to nothing. Gilles tumbled to the ground. Elisha leapt for Conrad, letting the power of death precede him. The mancer, a gruesome talisman held in his grip, vanished into the Valley before they'd even made contact.

Above, the emperor's battle cry resounded over the

thunder of hooves, the shriek and crunch of a sickening death.

"Fucking barber!" howled Eben's voice over all. The Valley ripped, and before Elisha could stop the opening, Eben sprang through, landing at the nearest cursed knife as Elisha rolled to the side and staggered up. "Even if you live through this night, Barber, we've got worse for you. You can't even imagine what we've wrought."

He slashed out with his dagger, stained by a dozen deaths. Elisha stumbled and fell, rolling downhill as the tip sparked against the cobblestones, then Elisha snatched himself through the Valley, back to the bloody stone by the stable, his lungs laboring, his pulse pounding in his ears.

The mancers howled their frustration, then one of the cursed knives tumbled from the gloom to clatter to the ground nearby. Immediately, the Valley ripped again, and Eben stepped through the contact between his dagger and the knife he had thrown. Two more mancers stood with him, their own blades shimmering darkly.

"How the Hell did you get here?" Eben demanded of Elisha. "You can't pass through living blood."

Shouts echoed up the hill before a blaze of torches. Harald led the way on horseback while thirty men or more sprinted after him, armed and angry.

"My lord," said one of the mancers, with a flicker of his power to draw the eye toward the *desolati* reinforcements.

"I'll take him, you get the emperor."

The other mancers flashed away through the Valley as Elisha shouted, "No!"

In Elisha's moment of distraction, Eben grabbed his arm with one hand and sliced downward with the other. The dagger bit across Elisha's hip, grinding against bone.

Pain shot through him, the snarling cold of death blasting into his flesh from the cursed blade. He forced it back, rejecting the call of the Valley. Eben tore free his blade, twisting Elisha's arm so that he screamed, then shoving his face hard to the ground. The blade drove downward, Elisha's blood spattering in its plunge toward his spine. Desperately, Elisha cast his power outward, into the blood that marked the dagger. The blade shattered as it plunged toward him, scattering frigid shards across his shoulders.

Eben cursed and dropped the hilt before the freeze reached him.

Writhing against the ground, Elisha managed to turn and straighten his arm. Eben dug in his fingers, his power swelling, and the cloth of Elisha's sleeve disintegrated under his grasp. But now Elisha could grab him back. He jerked the mancer forward and slammed his other fist into Eben's face.

Eben's nose broke, spewing blood, splinters pushing backward, and Elisha reached for Death. Never far from him, it sprang at his command, surging through his flesh. Eben's throat produced a strangled sound, the splinters of bone shifting just far enough, then he toppled, the cold release of his demise soothing Elisha's wrenched arm and injured side. Drawing strength, Elisha forced his side to heal, pain vanishing in the chill wonder of another man's killing. He pushed Eben's body off of him, shaking out both hands, the one frigid with Eben's blood, the other stiff, its damaged sleeve revealing damaged skin beneath. He urged his fingers to close.

In the distance, wielding death, the mancers strode into battle. The archers up the hill had not launched an arrow for a long time, and Ludwig wheeled his horse among them, then plunged downward, sword gleaming as he shouted. Fresh soldiers converged upon the mancers, but Eben's companion flashed away, the Valley rent open and shut, open again, like a bolt of lightning. Eben's companion sprang forth beside the emperor's mount, and his sword slashed across the horse's throat. In a gout of blood, it staggered and pitched sidelong, Ludwig falling with it.

Elisha ran, stumbling, as the mancer raised his sword and thrust, the shades of all those it had slaughtered wreathing the blade. Ludwig shrieked, his own sword cutting the air, then tumbling down, free of the hand that ruled it.

The soldiers threshed nearer, their rush of bodies obscuring Elisha's view.

The Valley ripped over and over as the surviving mancers fled the scene. Two dozen soldiers they could slaughter, but not fifty, not prepared with the knowledge Harald would have shared. Just for a moment, elation flooded Elisha's spirit: It could be done! Armed with magi knowledge, a force of *desolati* could fight the mancers and even defeat them.

His elation died quickly; what of Gilles or Harald or the emperor?

Shaking off his numbness, Elisha ran uphill. Harald's riderless horse thrashed about and leapt a pile of corpses to clatter down past him, back to its fellows, eyes rolling with white. Two dozen or so men remained standing, dazed, glancing around to see if the enemy had truly gone.

With its tumbled bodies and the upthrust pikes that pinned a few, darkness transformed the battle into a strange forest of rounded stones and limbless trees.

Elisha cast his awareness through the earth and caught the flicker of cold that hovered over the still form of Brother Gilles. He stumbled in that direction, hauling off a dead soldier. Gilles lay face up, his chin tipped back, his throat bruised and scored and not moving. Elisha dropped beside him and caught his clammy face in both hands. Somewhere deep, the pulse still quivered, but he had no wounds to heal, no bones to set. Gilles, who believed Elisha to be holy, lay now at the verge of death. What kind of wonder-worker could not save even the true believers?

He remembered the rabbi's awe as he scribed letters to his friends, to anyone who would listen. Some of the wonder-workers, he said, could even breathe life into those who lay as the dead. Elisha brought his mouth down to Gilles. With the power that coursed through him, he reached for healing, for the urgent needs of the flesh to live, and he breathed for the fallen friar.

The body twitched beneath his hands, and he breathed again. Gilles shuddered, then his eyes fluttered open and he took a gasp. "You," he breathed. "He named you demon, the one who took me, but it was himself he spoke of." He lifted a trembling hand, but Elisha shook off his reverie.

"Rest," he ordered, and straightened away, glancing around into the night. "Steward," Elisha called, swallowing, and trying to work his voice up. "Steward!"

"Doctor?"

Elisha picked his way around the dead to find the steward kneeling by Eben's companion, taking a few deep breaths of his own. Harald glanced up. "Pikes work well to strike at a distance. But poniards will do, if you have no other." He lifted his bloody fist, still wrapped around a spike as long as his forearm.

The mancer's face was a pool of blood, pierced through the chin.

"You've done very well," Elisha said, surprised.

"I brought that point for you." Harald looked away. "I am his majesty's assassin. But too late to save him." He started up, swaying, and Elisha tucked a hand beneath his elbow to help. They moved a few paces, to where the emperor's horse lay slaughtered. Ludwig lay beside his mount, his eyes open and staring, his hand in death still reaching for his sword. His ribs lay crushed, his heart forever still.

Elisha knotted his hands into his hair. "I'm sorry."

"He should have listened to you sooner." Harald went down on one knee by the fallen emperor and said, "I wish he had heard that his son was born. The child is weak but Doctor von Stubben is with them. I—"

Grabbing his shoulder, Elisha stopped his words. "What? Von Stubben was dismissed."

Harald shook his head. "He's been with the emperor longer than I have. We met him upon the journey and he reported that you had undermined his post. He joined—"

"Shit!" Elisha turned and ran, tripping downhill and leaping the bodies to run for the manor, stumbling through the dark and empty streets. Surely, Doctor Emerick wouldn't allow von Stubben near the empress—which meant something had happened to him, as well.

By the time he reached the broad steps of the manor, Elisha's legs trembled. Only a handful of men remained on duty there, and he stumbled up to them, shouting, "Urgent news! Where is the empress?"

"You are banned," one of the guards pronounced, and they clustered in front of the door. "On pain of death, as I recall." He lowered a sword at Elisha's gut.

"The empress is in danger—someone must warn her. Where's Doctor Emerick?"

"The margravine called him away, but the empress is well-tended—put out your hands." To one of the others, the captain said, "Search him for weapons."

"You don't understand." Elisha raised his hands, but he wanted to wrap them around the captain's throat. "The baby is in danger, they're both in danger. For God's sake, let me pass."

Quick hands patted down his sides, pausing at the medical kit, rumpling the packet of letters. Behind them, the door sprang open and Lady Agnes appeared, looking pale. "It's the baby. We need Doctor Emerick."

A soldier on the lower step snapped to attention and ran down into the street.

"Please let me help!" Elisha lowered his hands, but the captain brought his sword up under Elisha's chin, forcing him back.

"How did you know about this?" the man barked.

Trying to keep his throat free of the blade, Elisha grated, "Harald the steward told me they brought von Stubben. Von Stubben works for the enemy; he's been poisoning the queen. Please."

Agnes shot out her hand to catch Elisha's and pull him up, past the startled soldiers, earning him a nick on the cheek as the captain tried to get his blade away. "Come on."

"My lady!" the captain cried, but Agnes ignored him.

Her nose wrinkled as she pulled him inside toward the back of the house. "You're covered in blood," she said.

"Tell me what happened."

"She retired after the feast, feeling ill again, and

Emerick went with her, but she seemed well enough after a bit. The emperor's riders had got here, and we expected him any minute. I sang to her—then Katherine arrived, exhausted, and said her sons needed a doctor. The empress sent Emerick, of course she would, but she started with the pains after that. Von Stubben arrived with the emperor's men, hoping to re-ingratiate himself. What were we to do?"

"You did your best. I need to wash."

"Of course." She stopped her tugging long enough to bring him to a basin stand where she poured water over his hands and he wiped off as much blood as he could.

Strange how, so far away from his own place, he suddenly found a moment so dreadfully familiar. Even as he dried his hands, he felt the cold tug of the Valley and slammed open the door. Beyond, the empress lay propped on downy pillows on a low bed marked with blood and water while a pair of women cleaned and clucked over her. "My baby," she said.

"He's with the doctor, Your Majesty," one of the women answered.

For moment, Elisha couldn't move—a familiar moment indeed. With vivid clarity, he saw his brother's wife lying there, in a pool of blood, her husband already dead, her baby dead—both of them torn from her because of Elisha's own arrogance.

The empress's eyes opened and saw him—and his paralysis broke.

Elisha ran past her to the open door beyond. In the small chamber, the balding white head of Doctor von Stubben bent over a table. He jerked upright at Elisha's approach and turned, his back to the bundle on the table.

"What have you done?" Elisha demanded, the slight black shade of the infant rising up alongside the doctor's right hand.

"I've done all I could," von Stubben stammered. "The baby was born weak, he struggled, and I—"

Elisha reached out to move him aside, and he need not touch the man for the force of his rage to be felt. Von Stubben crossed himself and backed off, glancing from

Elisha to the child's swaddled form. Elisha gathered the baby close to his own warm heart, touching its throat gently, but the lips looked blue, even in the ruddy face. A few feathers clung to the damp, still chest, reminder of its mother's vain comfort. Even that faint sense of life that lingered at Gilles' beating heart was gone here, and his breath could do nothing. He wanted to scream. Instead, he went after.

Elisha leapt into the Valley and commanded the infant's return.

Chapter 27

❖

The child's shade, so slender, not yet rich with the attachments of a lifetime's experience, swirled quickly into the Valley's glow and tumble. It did not howl with pain or fear, it knew nothing of those things, not yet, and so as Elisha reached after, he found the Valley calm, radiant, its tumult more a waterfall than a whirlpool. The Valley once opened to him that way, inviting him to rise from the flesh, and he had almost gone ... beyond. For a moment, Elisha glimpsed a web of contacts, arcing out in response to the baby or to his own presence, then, between one breath and the next, all sense of the baby was gone.

Expanding his awareness, Elisha searched, his attention bringing the flickering shades into focus here and there, the sinuous shreds that clung to his own presence, spreading. Gaps pierced the Valley, tiny places where the shades were still. He searched through knowledge, calling up all he knew of the empress—strong, beautiful, joyous; of the emperor—hard, angry, fierce, and powerful—as if to find the child through some union of its parents, but he found no sign.

Elisha howled into the empty Valley, and there was nothing he could do.

His own presence pulsed in mad rhythm with the Valley as its chaos returned, overwhelming the peace of the child's death. The place once more wailed with terror and despair. It urged him to let go whatever bonds still held him to the earth. Just as earlier he had torn the shades from that place, now the strength of the Valley threatened to tear him free and plunge him forever into this maelstrom. His heart thundered, his muscles tense against the terrible strain as if he lay upon the rack.

Teeth clenched, Elisha forced himself back to the land of the living. Turning from the Valley, he bowed his head over the child and wept. The rough edge of the table pressed into his hip, the baby's cooling body filled his arms, the power of the Valley briefly sustaining him.

"I—where—?" Von Stubben's wondering voice broke the silence, and Elisha turned on the doctor: the tool of mancers, the agent of death.

"To Heaven," Elisha said, "to see him home."

He wreathed himself in righteous fury, harnessing the child's peace and innocence. With a blast of strength from the collapsed Valley, Elisha blew forth wings. He conjured them from the downy feathers clinging from the mother's pillow, from his anger, from his grief. They towered behind him, their tips bent forward by the room's close walls, his back and shoulders aching. Elisha's cheek flared with warmth, recalling the touch of an angel's wing from the fire of his youth.

Von Stubben gave a strangled cry and fell to his knees, hands upraised and pleading.

"And you"—Elisha's word fell with a dread power— "will tell his mother why."

"Elisha?" Katherine's voice joined a clamor outside.

"Is he here? I must thank him," said the hoarse voice of Brother Gilles.

Elisha raised his head, and let the wings vanish, a few soft and tiny feathers drifting down. One of them touched von Stubben's hands, and he flinched, blinking up at Elisha through glistening eyes. "Go on," Elisha said, barely a whisper.

The doctor scrabbled away, pulling himself up at the doorframe. Katherine and Emerick stepped aside to let him return to the bedchamber, though they did not take their eyes from Elisha. Gilles stood behind them, positively gaping. "Of course," he whispered, crossing himself. "I should have seen."

Exhausted, he leaned back against the table. That had been too much, too strong. His fury had overcome him, the child's death one blow too many on this night of sorrows, and he had given them all a show he had not intended. Now Gilles would never give up his testament.

In his arms, the baby looked at rest, aside from the wrong color of its lips. Likely, the doctor had simply covered its mouth and nose with his own great, clumsy hand, not knowing the emperor was already dead and they need torment his wife no longer. "I came too late to save him."

Emerick winced sharply, squeezing his eyes shut, pressing his fingers into them. "No, it's me. You told me to watch over her—I didn't think the birth would be so soon."

"If anyone is to blame," Katherine said, "it would be me. I took you from here for my own needs." Slipping from the young doctor's shadow, Katherine came to Elisha's side. She stroked a hand over his shoulder.

"But your sons?" Elisha asked, torn between the desire of his body to give in to her comfort, and some vanity whispering that strength required him to reject her.

"My sons are well, thanks to you," she answered. "Daniel and I went to Heinrich, the old salter, and he believed my story of your death long enough to turn over my sons. Then we—took care of him. My sons are weak from bleeding, but they will be all right. Doctor Emerick assures me so."

Emerick's throat bobbed, and he said, "Yes. They're young and otherwise healthy. I've tended their wounds." He pushed off from the door and held out his arms, taking the child from Elisha. "We met Steward Harald and your friend the friar on our way back. We know . . . the outcome." He took a corner of the swaddling cloth and draped the child's face, then turned away and left them.

Gilles blinked, then said, "I should go, yes, forgive me. But thank you. And may God be with you." His head bobbed as if he were uncertain whether to bow or to cross himself, then he hurried from the room and out into the corridor beyond.

In the chamber, Margaret's voice rose to a wail, then to scathing rebuke of von Stubben, then to stern command. The Valley snarled open, but Elisha stayed as he was, the black strength of another death eddying around his ankles as the Valley seared shut. He breathed in the cold, but it gave him no urge to face whatever awaited. *"Will she slay me, too?"* he sent to Katherine's steadying hand upon his cheek. Just now, the prospect seemed both fine and fitting.

"No," she answered aloud. "It will not be so."

At the door, a man cleared his throat, and Elisha finally lifted his eyes to find Harald there waiting, looking as grim and weary as Elisha felt. "Elisha Physician, you are summoned." He held out the fur cloak, dark with mud and other stains.

For a moment, Katherine tried to keep him, but Elisha rose and followed, accepting the gift once again, though it no longer looked so regal.

"I have told her Majesty what I know of the battle down below and of his Majesty's death in defense of his crown and of his men. Von Stubben admitted his own role in the empress's ill health and in the murder of her child." Harald ushered Elisha forward, directing him toward the bed while a pair of soldiers dragged von Stubben's body across the floor, a single neat hole pierced at the back of his skull. The steward—slight and still clad in his royal finery—acknowledged Elisha's glance with the slightest quirk of his lips.

"Kneel, Doctor, so that I may see you," the empress directed, allowing Agnes to take from her the tiny, swaddled form of her son.

Little room remained at her bedside, and what there was had recently been vacated by the executed physician. With a series of precise movements, Harald stepped away, rounded the bed and stood by the door, tipping his head to Elisha to show that he was out of range to strike. So if the empress would kill him, it would not be Harald's poniard that took him.

Wetting his lips, Elisha lowered himself as she commanded. "Yes, Your Majesty."

"You rushed here from the battle where you were to die, to be at my childbed, and my men stopped you at the door."

This did not require any reply, and so Elisha stayed quiet, but she said, "Look at me, Doctor."

Pale, nestled in a tangle of dark hair, the empress regarded him coolly, though her eyes gleamed and spots of color marked her cheeks. He guessed her earlier outburst had been unusual, the remnant of her labor and her grief—but an empress did not throw tantrums or wail, even at the death of a child. Even, it seemed, at the death of an emperor.

"These sorcerers are strong. No matter your power, I am not surprised you could not prevail in battle and prevent my husband's death. But young Ludwig," she swallowed, and her hands edged together, the one covering the other, tightening. "If you had been here, you could have prevented it, is that not so?"

Elisha's knees ached. He longed to lay down his head, and half-wished she would simply order his execution and have done, however unfair that might be. "Anyone could have prevented it who knew the truth of von Stubben's intent."

"We suspected von Stubben had done something to the medicinals, Your Majesty," Emerick blurted, coming forward. "Forgive me, but Elisha does not bear full blame for this—"

"Hush," she said, lifting her hand, and Agnes touched the young doctor's shoulder to draw him back. "I agree with you, Doctor Emerick. It was I who gave the orders my men so fervently kept. Only my companion, Agnes, saw the need and the danger, and dared defy them for my sake and that of young Ludwig." She returned her dark eyes to Elisha's face. "It is as if I stood by that door myself, Doctor, and barred your way to saving my son's life."

Katherine bent her knee in a curtsy and straightened. "Your Majesty, you acted to try to save my honor. You did not know what lay at stake." She took a deep breath. "It was none of Elisha's doing that we became as lovers. I was commanded to this by the necromancers, who stole my children as hostage against my obedience. Elisha responded to me only because I begged it of him, in mercy to help me save my children, which he has done."

"They commanded you? Then von Stubben was not the only traitor among us." Empress Margaret's mask of stone descended once more.

"It was my rebellion against that allegiance that brought my punishment, Your Majesty."

"I see. I will need to consider what your involvement means." Turning from her friend with a flash of new sorrow, the empress pushed herself up, her maid leaping to prop the pillows higher to support her. "Bring me my altar, would you?"

The girl did as she was bid, with the help of another servant. The rosewood chest, marked on top with a cross, smelled of death and shifted with shades to Elisha's keen senses. Running her long fingers over the surface, the empress said, "You believe the battle moves to Rome, that those who slew my husband and supported the man who slew my child will use the Eternal City for their evil."

"I do," Elisha said, blinking away the shades, beginning to think he might come out of this with his neck intact.

She pressed on the cross and a drawer popped open at the front of the altar. Drawing it open, she moved her fingers over a series of small, silken pouches and crystal vials, laid out like a medicine chest of bones. "These . . . they are recent gifts, to aid me in childbirth, or so I was told." She made a little pile of them in his hand—four relics in silk wrappings. "From what you say, their authenticity is in question, if nothing else." Then her hand hesitated. She selected one more from the row and lifted it free, then offered it to Elisha, a clear vial containing a shard of wood about the length of his thumb. "And this. Let this protect you in your journey. It is a sliver of the True Cross, from the piece at Rome. Ludwig cut it with his own hand to be my wedding gift."

Within the cool crystal, the wood hummed with power. True Cross or no, a man had died upon it. He thought of Simeon hanging helpless in the dark over him, about to be made a martyr. Elisha closed his fist around the vial. "Thank you, Your Majesty. This is more helpful than you know."

"My door shall no longer be barred to you, Elisha Physician, if there is anything that can be done to aid in the destruction of such evil." She held out her hand, and Elisha took it upon his own, lightly kissing her knuckles, then drew back. "For myself, I can fight no more today." Her eyes fluttered shut, and she said, "Go with God, Doctor, and with my blessing."

Elisha withdrew, bowing himself from the empress's presence, and moving carefully toward the corridor. His muscles shivered with the night's exertions, but he did not know where he could find rest. Where had Gilles gone? Probably to the chapel, to thank the lord for sending his angel.

Elisha's stomach churned. For a moment, he recalled his brief elation when he saw the battle was won, but the memory shone only distantly, as if he had felt no joy since childhood. He came to the continent to share his knowledge, to gain allies in war against the mancers, but the ally he sought was already a mancer prize. Elisha failed him, and failed his family. Rome awaited, stocked with savage relics, taunting him, but would it be only another failure?

Katherine emerged behind him, shutting the door softly. "My Raphael," she called, and he hesitated.

"Come." She walked up to join him, close enough to touch. "There will be a bed for you tonight—what is left of the night, in any case. And then, to Rome?" They walked to a narrow stair and climbed two floors to a broad loft, where they passed silently through a phalanx of slumbering servants to a smaller room at the back containing a rope bed with a straw mattress. "It's a recovery room for the injured, but it should do. I'll find you blankets." She rubbed at her arms in the raftered space, then dug into a chest by the wall to find blankets.

Elisha sank onto the bed, resisting the urge to simply collapse. He had taken to sleeping on graves, allowing the dead to conceal him. How long had it been since he had been offered a bed? But he forced himself to focus a little longer. "Do you know anything else of their plans?"

"Something is due from Kaffa." At his blank expression, she continued, "That's a trading port to Cathay. You don't suppose they are importing oriental necromancers?" She shuddered and dropped a pillow at one end of the bed, then let her hand stray to his shoulder. *"I should like to stay with you."*

"I could use your help in Rome," he answered, though the drift of her emotions told him that was not what she meant. Her hand grew heavy, hanging onto him, or anchoring herself.

"I can't." Her lips trembled. *"Elisha, I wish I could go with you into danger, but to do so, I would have to abandon my children again. They've already taken my daughter, I must protect my sons. As soon as they are well enough to travel, I must find them a sanctuary before I can help you defeat the enemy."*

"How will you hide?" He tried to stop the surge of ferocity that accompanied this question, but she flinched and drew back. In the air, he continued, "They know you, Margravine. They know now that you've lied. They won't rest until they've slain both you and your children. Any place the mancers' relics are, you are not safe."

"Then I must find a place without relics. A place unstained by death."

Silent, Elisha dropped back onto the bed, the rafters dark and soaring overhead.

"Yes, I know it's madness—impossible! You don't have children, Elisha, how can you know how it feels to lose them? To know that you, yourself, have put them at risk? What would you have me do, bring them to Rome to fight the mancers?" She thrust up her hands, displaying the sharpened nails, now washed clean of her deeds. From her left hand, swirls of shadow rose like smoke to accuse a killer. "How would you be safe in my company? It might have been you tonight." She closed her right hand, the left outspread as if it still carried the poison that might have killed him instead of his enemy. "I will find a way to continue the fight, but I dare not go with you, Elisha. No repentance would save me from that crime."

Chapter 28

❖

$\mathfrak{M}$ancers stalked Elisha's dreams. He stood in the Valley, holding it back with all his might, while the warden of the Valley, that faceless presence he had sensed whenever mancer blood mingled with that of their victims, rose against him, towering and dark. Sometimes, it was Katherine herself who assailed him, fulfilling her nightmares, raking her poisoned nails across his face, weeping all the time. Then he heard a baby crying, and he ran through a dark forest, but he could not find the child, and he startled awake, snatching at nothing.

For a moment, he thought to rise and leave for Rome right then, but the idea made him all the more weary; he did not even speak the language, nor had he a long voyage like the one that allowed him to learn the German tongue. Still, he must go, and soon—to cut through the web of mancer intention and spoil their plans.

That returned him to the idea of the Valley. They could not simply leap through from place to place—they could not even use living blood, but must depend upon the greater power of murder. This thought comforted Elisha in an awful way, for it meant that they must make contact with their fellow mancers first. They must find and recruit each other, travel by horse or river or on foot to forge the rings of their chainmail conspiracy. No wonder it took time for them to build this far, to seize their captive thrones and plant the relics that would yield their harvest of horror.

Last night as he worked to manipulate the Valley, Elisha observed the flaw in their power. Back in England, he met a group of magi so devoted each to a single talisman that they became indivisible from it: *indivisi*, whom the other magi accused of madness. To be so attached to a single thing, while it gave them great power over that thing, also made them vulnerable, like the iron magus who rusted to death. They thought, in fact, that Elisha was with Death, indivisible from it, but his affinity seemed more subtle than that, a delicate awareness of the threshold between life and death. Because of his devotion to healing, he saw more, knew more, used more: while the mancers drew only upon darkness, Elisha remained capable of holding the light. They ignored the opposite of their strength, while he relied upon it. He did not know how that would help him—a hundred mancers sucking in the pain and fear of a dozen murders could rout a battlefield without an army resilient enough to fight back. Elisha's hand brushed over the talisman he wore about his neck, the earth of England, and wished he could talk to Mordecai about all of this to sort through what he knew and to devise a plan for Rome.

He felt her presence and sat up, groaning at the aches that assailed his body, as Katherine entered, her eyes too wide and lips compressed with worry. When she saw his hand fly to his side, to the slash he had healed, her face softened to sympathy. She came to sit by him, setting down the lantern she carried. "I felt you wake." Her right hand spread upon the thick wool of her robe, the nails still edged with a hint of blood. "It took a moment to realize it was you. I shall need to scrub harder so that I am not bound to you." But she gazed at her nails as if that were the last thing she wanted.

"I'm sorry to wake you." He pulled the blankets a little closer about his hips. "We both need the rest."

Katherine reached out and caught his hand. "There are other ways to calm the mind and flee the fears of night." The heat of contact rushed through him, her desire captured in the sweat of her palm and the pressure of her hand, and he tried not to respond in kind.

"True, but the Church has not lifted its ban on opium."

Her hand stroked his cheek, turning him gently to face her, her fingers working through his hair, tracing the cross-shaped scar and the pockmarks that had been holes into his skull. Her touch, just there, poured through him, a cascade of emotions that tightened his chest and burned into his loins. *"Let me give you this, Elisha, once more, without fear."*

The lantern gilded her silvering hair and made an enticing darkness between her parted lips. He stood too often on the threshold now, using his knowledge to force back death, but only rarely able to embrace life.

Elisha met her eyes, then pulled her closer, his hand sliding beneath the robe, finding her skin hot, damp, naked, without the chill hand of a dead man trapped between them. Without fear. He kissed her, gripping her back, her hair tumbling over his hands. The vial of England pressed into his chest. Without fear, but not without shame. Could a man atone for what he did not truly repent?

Elisha found the vial with his hand and tugged it to one side, sliding it to dangle against his back. Then they tangled in each other, casting a deflection against the senses of the world and the confusion of the heart, and Elisha let himself be lost in gratitude for her gift.

He slept at last without dreaming, and long after Katherine had left him, woke to daylight glowing gray through the arrow slits in the end wall. The building creaked as people rose and built up the fires, fetched the water, performed all the hundred tasks a manor required every day.

Almost refreshed, Elisha dressed and walked back down to the Great Hall. Here, he found a day board spread with slops—trenchers of bread soaked in the juices of last night's meat, accompanied by a light wine and heaps of apples. Elisha ate heartily, not knowing when he would find another meal. By day, his clothing looked disheveled, even his rich cloak looked like something he had stolen from a grave, but it would have to do. He could take a few minutes to brush out the worst of the mud and blood, and hope that Rome was dark and

damp this time of year. In order to set about his plans
there, he must live as quietly as possible, attracting no
attention, avoiding mancers unless he must confront
them. There would be no mancer-hunting, no raids of
mancer-lairs to liberate their victims. If he caught their
eye too early, he would be killed or forced to flee before
he could stop them.

Harald found him finishing his meal and took him to
a private alcove, asking every question he could think of
about mancer tactics, powers and places, his hawkish
face utterly focused, the courtier vanished beneath an
assassin's intensity. He took the news of Bardolph's true
nature with a grunt of anger. "Bardolph could not be
found in advance of this journey—he had been sent to
Lord Eben, but Eben sent him on without consultation.
I thought it strange that his Majesty so readily accepted
Eben sending his royal messenger on another mission."

"Another mission? You know no more than this?"

"Nothing. Eben was not a man to speak freely, though
his manner always suggested that he did." Harald
propped his hands on his knees and pushed himself to
his feet, covering his wince, but not well enough for a
doctor's eyes.

"Have you been seen to?" Elisha searched the steward's presence and found him weary, battered, deeply
bruised by his fall from the horse during the battle.

Harald shook his head. "We'll be resting here a few
days—I'll be tended. I did not want you to go before I
know all of what we face."

Smiling grimly, Elisha said, "I wish I knew all of what
we face. I fear these civil wars are only the symptom of
something greater. The margravine will return when she
finds safety for her sons, she'll help you."

Putting out his hand for Elisha's, Harald said, "God-
speed to Rome."

Then nothing held Elisha back but regret for the
deaths that had happened here and fear of what was to
come—neither of which would improve with age. He
moved through the manor, where servants wiped tears
from their faces as they worked, and spoke in low tones

for fear of disturbing the widowed empress as she lay
upon her childbed, in mourning. The miasma of grief
haunted him, but at the same time, he knew these two
terrible deaths were small compared with the mancers'
plans. They must be a spur to try harder, not to abandon
the fight.

From the steps outside, a figure rose abruptly, the soldiers stirring—more of them since the day before—but
the figure's monkish robe and contrite demeanor made
the guards settle again. Even so, Gilles nested his fingers
together, slid them apart, nested them again as he waited
for Elisha to approach.

"You might have sent word you were waiting," Elisha
said.

Gilles separated his fingers again. "I hate to intrude."
He glanced away, and Elisha thought at first that his moment of tenderness with Katherine after the baby's
death had embarrassed the friar. Then he noticed that
Gilles's face might be averted, but he still flashed his
gaze toward Elisha, his eyelashes fluttering as if he gazed
at something too bright to be studied directly.

"How did you come to be in Bad Stollhein? You said
the man who took you prisoner came to you."

"He was a guest of the emperor, Doctor, an important
man who had heard the rumors of what happened in my
chamber, when you were healed by the relics." Gilles
chuckled. His voice still sounded strained, his eyes
haunted after his role in the battle. "Well. I have never
been to Rome, and I should dearly love to go, and so it
seemed a blessing that this man had heard of the relics
entrusted to me. Of course, it was you who interested
him, your story, of which I know little enough." He
forced his hands apart. "And of course I had swooned at
your ravaged appearance, so my testament offered little
yet again. Still, he said he had need of someone to assist
him in an important ritual, and of course, I agreed." His
tonsure glowed slightly pink as he stared at his sandaled
feet. His voice fell very low. "I did not know he meant to
tempt me to Hell itself. I should be there still, if not for
you."

"As dedicated as you are to the saints, Brother? I doubt you'd be there long." Elisha found a smile.

"I will pray on that. Indeed, I have been praying all night." He lifted his eyes again, round and gleaming. "You cannot tell me more of . . . of your purpose?"

"My purpose is to break the rings of demons who prey on men like you."

Gilles straightened. "I pray that one day I will be found worthy to assist you. The empress, the widow, that is, has asked that we continue our work and craft a reliquary worthy of her husband's memory, God rest his soul." He crossed himself. "I pray this service will aid me in whatever penance must befall. The demon came to me, and I succumbed."

"You needn't blame yourself, Brother. These demons will look and act like anyone else."

"The same could be said for angels."

Elisha did not know how to answer that, so he replied simply, "Peace be with you."

"And also with you," the friar said, and Elisha felt certain his gaze followed until Elisha could no longer be seen.

Chapter 29

— ❖ —

While most who were abroad at that hour went down toward the church or the market, Elisha walked up the hill, until he found a quiet corner where none would likely disturb him.

Rome awaited, but the idea of consulting Mordecai—and passing on what he had learned—had taken hold. Rested now, thanks to Katherine's comfort, Elisha could muster the strength for more than one journey. As he uncorked the vial and sprinkled a little of the earth of London into his palm, he knew he was delaying his real task. But if he could take advantage of Mordecai's knowledge, why should he not?

Steeling himself against the memory of his brother's death, and casting a deflection against the stealthy awareness of Conrad's father, Elisha opened the Valley and slipped inside. The Valley this time felt personal, thrumming with the betrayal of Nathaniel's suicide in the wake of his child's stillbirth and—he believed—his wife's own death. Elisha passed with relief into the low, familiar workshop, its fire banked, a few candles glinting from the votives people left there to honor the man they claimed as God's chosen king, a healer, a martyr risen from the grave: Elisha himself, in the guise of Saint Barber.

Shutters covered the windows, and a new wooden door filled the frame, with gaps of weak London sunlight edging around it. Nathaniel's shade sat at the center of the room, slitting his throat and dying. Elisha's eyes burned as he blinked the shade away. He felt a whisper of movement, ducked and turned as a man rose behind him, sword drawn. Allowing the tip to rest at his heart, Elisha raised his hands, smiling down the blade at Madoc, once his captain, then his bodyguard, and now the self-appointed guardian of his shrine.

"Is it you, and not some skin-clad killer?" the man muttered, glaring back at him.

"I walked at the wheel of a siege tower, Madoc, and you commanded me to fall and feign death when the bombard shattered the tower."

Madoc withdrew his sword and shoved it back into its sheath. "If you'd've stayed dead, it might've saved a world of trouble."

Elisha's good humor fled. "If I'd've stayed dead, Thomas would not be king, and England would be ruled by the skin-clad killers."

"True enough. Shall I send for the king, then?"

"No," Elisha answered, too quickly, wondering if Katherine's scent still lingered on him. He took up the vial again to scoop back in the precious, tainted earth. "I haven't much time. I need to go to Mordecai. Has he left the means?"

Madoc's beard ruffled as he pursed his lips. "His Majesty won't be pleased to miss you."

"Nor I him." Despite the shame that brought sweat to Elisha's palms, he longed for the sight of his king, that rare smile breaking across his face, his blue eyes blazing. His keen gaze always saw a little more than Elisha meant to share.

With a brief arch of his bushy brow, Madoc turned away to count off the votives until he found the one he was after. "Glad to see you well, in any case." He held out the carved object. "I am allowed to tell him you came? That you're still alive?"

Elisha's hand closed over the votive carving of an arm, feeling the warmth of the hairs hidden within, a talisman left by his mentor in Madoc's care. "Tell him I'm well, tell him I'm sorry." Tell him Elisha had allowed his father-in-law to be killed and taken a mancer as his lover. Once, for the sake of her sons, yes, but twice? The second time had been all for the flesh, all for Elisha, and he knew it, worldly powers egging him on to worldly temptations.

"Tell that saucy nun Sabetha I said 'hello.'"

"I'll do it," Elisha said, then he stretched his senses, searching, concentrating on the lock of Mordecai's hair. His wrist ached as he conjured his memory of the day he healed the surgeon's hand and summoned him back from the brink of death. Elisha drew himself through the Valley. Because he made contact through life, and not through death, the passage felt narrow, somehow both sharp and tenuous, as if he might be drawn off course like a traveler forced to leave a forest path, never to return.

His head ached when he emerged, trembling, into the hall of a certain lodge on the Isle of Wight where he once stayed with Mordecai in exile.

"It worked, then," Mordecai pronounced dryly, looking up from a book.

"Only because I'm a sensitive. It's good to see you."

Mordecai's presence welled with the warmth of their friendship. "Queen remains stable. Eats what we feed her, dreams, sometimes. If I have contact I sense her dreams. Baby keeps growing."

Elisha couldn't help the flinch at the mention of the baby, his arms weary again as if with the slight weight of Margaret's dead child. Mordecai slid his book away and indicated a seat. "Bad news festers in you, Elisha."

Sinking into the chair, Elisha told him. He left out the depth of his relationship with Katherine but shared everything else, everything he could think of, in case the knowledge sparked some insight from his mentor.

"Been to Kaffa," Mordecai said, and drew out a map from the heaps of documents on the table, pointing to a region across two small seas. "Long time ago. Barbarians rule the area, but the merchants of Genoa control the city, trading from there across the world. Strange peoples, spices the English never taste, diseases your physicians have never heard of. Anything could be shipped out of Kaffa. Armies, weapons. Heard they were besieged last year and pelted with corpses."

Elisha shuddered. "That sounds like mancers, but I don't see how a bombardment of corpses would help them destroy the Church."

Sometime during the narrative, Sister Sabetha came down the creaky stairs. She startled at the sight of him, then quietly settled across the table, her thick fingers interlaced as she listened. "Cursed unholy monsters," she muttered, when Elisha spoke of the battle and the hostage children in the salt mine. She pushed off to pour a round of cider for them, which Elisha accepted gratefully, his throat sore from talking. Mordecai examined the letters from Jacob and the rabbi, his grizzled brows furrowed over the pages.

"Do you believe it?" Elisha asked.

"Baal Shem, a wonder-worker. Men will order the world according to their knowledge. Should have thought of it myself, but I've been too long from the lore of my own people."

"It's a tale that gives them comfort, nothing more."

Mordecai passed back the pages with a tip of his head. "Same could be said for your Christ."

"Fine, granted—I'm not that either." He covered his scarred hands. "It's a useful story if it brings me aid, like finding Daniel Stoyan, but that's all."

The surgeon drew back into his chair, touching one of the scrolls he wore at his waist. "From the first, Elisha Barber, you have denied yourself to be anything remarkable."

The scars stood out at the back of Elisha's hands, pale against his work-darkened skin. "I used to think I was, before I'd ever met you—before I knew anything of the magi."

"You?" Sabetha said. "Unremarkable?" She snorted. "Maybe in your mad world of witchery, everyone can appear from nothing a thousand miles away, or heal a woman with a thought, or make the earth shake so hard a man can't even stand. Maybe that's all so much

porridge to you, but it's not to me. Not to anybody else I
know."

Elisha thought of the baby, but he said, "Everyone?
No, Sister. The travel—that takes a connection through
life or death."

"Contact," she said brightly. "Yon surgeon's been telling me about that. And knowledge, yes?"

"Right. The mancers travel through murder. They
need a strong contact between where they are and where
they're going. They might have less knowledge of the
end point, but they know the murder intimately and its
power overcomes the distance."

"So they fake up relics by hacking people to bits." The
nun crossed herself. "The devil's own—they must be."

"A sensitive magus, one with a knowledge of life and
death, like myself or Mordecai, could travel through contact with life. We deliberately chose a very slight
contact—hair—to be sure no others could follow me.
Speaking of which—" Removing the furred cloak, Elisha
stripped off his bloody tunic and crossed to drop it into
the fire, prodding it with the poker until the flames
caught.

"Give over." Sabetha stood up and made a grabbing
motion until Elisha handed over the cloak. "You'll not
want to burn this. I'll get it cleaned up for you, and bring
you a fresh shirt."

"Thanks," he told her.

Her annoyed look suggested her reluctance to leave
the conversation, but she went, draping the cloak over
her broad shoulders and prancing in her imitation of a
courtier as the door swung closed behind her.

Mordecai glanced up, toward the silent member of
their little household: Brigit. "Will you see her?"

"I should." Elisha sighed, drained his cider, and
pushed himself up, Mordecai trailing after as they
mounted the stairs. Pushing open the chamber door, Elisha still expected to be struck by her presence, that seductive blend of mystery, magic, and desire. Instead, he
felt nothing. Lavender overlaid the faint scent of urine in
the air, but it was nothing like the miasma of sickness at

a hospital. Mordecai and Sabetha tended their patient well.

As Elisha drew near the bed, he sensed the warmth of life, and the curious overlap of one life upon another: the baby that grew within her swelling belly. Brigit's chest still rose and fell, her hair in red-gold trails upon the pillow had grown notably longer since he'd cut it months ago. Her eyelids flickered when he touched her arm, but her eyes remained mercifully closed. To look into those vivid green eyes, knowing he had riven the soul behind them, would be his undoing.

"I've been researching her state." Mordecai laid his olive-skinned hand on Brigit's forehead, the strength of his healing presence swelling around him. Elisha's left eye saw the wisps of shadow trailing the surgeon: patients he had lost, his own slain family, like strands his presence tethered to the earth. When he touched Brigit, the strands briefly faded, as if banished by a glow Elisha could not see although he felt the rising focus of Mordecai's interest. "I have found little of use. There are fairy stories of princesses who sleep for years and wake again, and your nun tells stories of saints who rise from such apparent death. We found a narrative of Hildegard von Bingen, describing trance states and visions she received from them, although they were of short duration."

Brigit's beauty grew a little thin; the soups they could feed her sustained her life, but she did not flourish. Still, her lips looked rosy and almost expectant, and Elisha knew how the princesses in those tales awoke. According to the tales, the king, her husband, should kiss her, and her eyes would open. The image repulsed Elisha in an instant. Thomas married her in a moment of despair, needing the heir she secretly carried, grateful for her apparent rescue of him, and terrified of Elisha himself. None could know Brigit's full treachery until the day in the chapel when she had evoked the spirit of her dead mother and tried to use it to break or kill all the aristocracy of England. Oh, no, if Brigit had a true love to wake her, it was power alone could offer that kiss. If her sleeping form could be brought together with sufficient raw magic, Elisha had no doubt that the lure of power would draw her back again.

Elisha's fingers lightly wrapped her wrist, feeling the pulse there, slow, but steady. Should he have killed her then, sacrificing the life of the baby to ensure that the mother would never rise? *"The baby?"* No. His baby. Brigit would make any sacrifice in service to her dream. Thank God he had not had to sacrifice his child to stop her.

Mordecai lifted his hand, his moist eyes meeting Elisha's glance. "What will you do when you get to Rome?"

"I have to locate all of their talismans and find a way to steal them from the churches, or to destroy them, all at once, and without the warden of the Valley knowing I'm there, if at all possible. Sometimes I feel his presence in the Valley. If he is all his son and the others say, he could readily destroy me."

"Could mark the relics, keep contact with them as you find them, keep yourself secret as possible."

Elisha considered. "I can't use blood, it could give them the means to trace me and make contact in turn." He stared down at Brigit's still form, trying to think of another way.

"Hair, then. Like the talisman that brought you here. Should be slight enough."

"Good idea."

"Are you the only one who can travel in deaths he did not make and lives he does not know?"

After a moment, Elisha said, "So far as I know."

"Unless there are thirty-five others as your friend Jacob claims." Mordecai's presence shimmered with humor.

"Hush," said Elisha. "I didn't come here so you could tell me stories. And I still get twice as many wonders as you do."

"And you still don't think they are enough," said Mordecai in the witches' way, sending his gentle thought to brush upon Elisha's awareness.

Shaking his head, Elisha drew back his hand from the still form between them. "Even if I go to Rome and ruin their relics, somehow, without them finding me, it still leaves the mancers to scheme again. Rome is not the end of their design. They need to topple the Church itself. Even if I can stop them in Rome—I cannot stop them forever. And they still want Brigit. They're searching for her; they have some role they think she could fill in their plans."

Mordecai bowed his head gravely. "Then I will do everything in my power to shelter her."

"I should go. I'll return your talisman to London on my way." At least they had sketched a plan for how to manage the relics of Rome, dangerous though it would be. And the timing should allow him to find the mad tribune, Cola di Rienzi, to see if he, too, were one of the mancers' playthings.

As if Mordecai could sense his worries, he said, "If anyone could work this wonder, Elisha, it would be you." The surgeon raised his right hand, allowing his sleeve to slide back and reveal his wrist, ringed by faint crossings, the sutures Elisha once used to bind his failing life. *"You have always had good hands, Elisha."*

Elisha smiled faintly, but he turned away.

Chapter 30

◇

 n the screens passage, Elisha found Sabetha wearing the now-brushed cloak, but she glanced up and sighed when she saw him. "Gave this up when I chose the veil, didn't I? As if I'd've had a chance for it anyhow." She passed him a clean tunic which he slipped over his head, then reluctantly handed over the cloak.

"Never thought I would, either, Sister." He stroked the furry edging and ran his finger over the golden ram Isaac had given him. Things too fine for a barber. Too fine for a killer.

"I trimmed off the torn fur, but you'll hardly notice." She eyed the luxurious garment. "You move in the company of emperors now. Can't say as I envy you, though, facing them, night after night." She shivered and led the way back to the hall with its crackling fire.

Night after night—and he hadn't even spoken of his dreams. "Thanks for tending her. Them, really."

Sabetha rubbed a hand along the wimple at her forehead. "Well, it's mostly no trouble, is it? Don't know if I want her to wake or if I don't."

Silently, Elisha agreed.

"Yon Jew's teaching me to read—he tell you that?" She pointed to a wax tablet, likely the same one Mordecai used to teach Elisha a few short months ago. "It was him that worried me, to tell you the truth." Sabetha squared her shoulders, prepared for his taking offense. "I've heard all kinds of things about the Jews, all my life.

I said yes because you were asking, and because the princess was going home to her Da, but I figured your Jew was as likely one of the devils as one of us." She cocked her head, frowning. "He's a bit prickly, but I never seen him do nothing demonic."

At that, Elisha chuckled. "You've seen demonic when you were traveling with me, yet I'm the one you trust?"

"Back with the Mother Superior, everything was clear, see? Witches, evil; Jews, evil; pederasts, evil; heretics, evil. A beautiful face meant a beautiful soul." She scratched absently at her back, perhaps reminded of the wounds where Brigit struck her with a rake, a dozen stab-wounds Elisha healed as he fled with her through the Valley. "It's not so simple as I thought."

"Sometimes, I wish it were," he murmured.

"God be with you, Barber."

"And also with you." He took out the vial of earth from the workshop, and opened the Valley back to his brother's workshop in London. Even as the howling snapped shut behind him, Elisha felt the sudden heat and a surge of joy: the strong, brooding presence of the king. He should have known Madoc would go to the king. Immediately after this thought, guilt stabbed at his conscience and Elisha swallowed hard, preparing to face him, but before he could work out how to greet the man who was both monarch and friend, Elisha heard a girl's voice call out his name. Then Alfleda's arms wrapped about him, and the joy won out.

Elisha pulled the girl close and swung her about, her golden hair tickling his face. "Such a welcome! I hardly expected to see you here, Your Highness." He set her down at arm's length, taking in her bright blue eyes, cheeks filling out after her two years of grief and confinement. Tall and lovely, even for a child of eight, Alfleda spun a little circle, displaying a gown of winter wool with a purple hood. She grinned at him and giggled.

"I overheard—I wasn't meant to, I know, but when that hairy man comes, I always hope he might bring word of you!" She tipped her head down, rubbing her cheek across his scarred hand, the contrast between her innocent, rosy face and his own rough knuckles made all the more apparent.

Behind her, Thomas rose slowly, firelight adding gleams to his eyes and shadows to his dark hair. His own expression moved from a father's indulgence to a mingled longing and fear. "I could not keep her away, Elisha. I do not think she could believe us truly reconciled until she saw us together." Almost, he smiled.

"Come, Father—give him the kiss of peace—then I shall be certain!" She grabbed her father's hand and tugged him closer.

Thomas lost his smile, but his gaze never left Elisha's face.

"He's done that," Elisha told her. "On the battlefield."

The king reached out and took Elisha's hand in a grip as if to pull him closer, but he merely wrapped Elisha's hand in both of his, pressing over the ring he had given. The heat of that contact was almost too much and Elisha dropped his gaze, looking to the child instead. "Here—" He plucked the carved votive containing Mordecai's hair from his belt and offered it to her. "Find a place for this, would you?"

"Yes, of course! It's not a very good one, is it?" She moved away to search among the tiny nails for a place to hang it.

"I know you did not wish to see me," Thomas said softly. "Madoc tried to make it sound as if your urgency would not allow it."

"It's not that," Elisha protested, even as his stomach clenched—Thomas knew him too well to miss the lie.

The king released him, folding his arms below the chain of his office. "Then what is it, Elisha? For all we've been through, I would at least hope for your candor." But the disappointment that carved the corners of his mouth suggested he hoped for more than that.

Elisha swallowed again, uncertain what to do with his hands. At last, he said, "Emperor Ludwig is dead. Forgive me."

"God rest him. A hard man but a good one." Thomas

exhaled sharply. "Why does his death require my forgiveness?"

"I went there to track the mancers' plans, and to warn him, Your Majesty, but . . ." Here he stopped, wondering how much to say. Did it matter anymore that Ludwig had been the mancers' pawn? That Thomas's marriage to Ludwig's daughter had likely been part of their plot? Anna and her father were both dead now, both at the hands of the emperor's erstwhile allies. In the far corner, Alfleda gasped over some trinket she discovered.

"Shall I order you to tell me what you know?"

That brought Elisha's chin up, solidifying Thomas's dual role into one: He was the king, and Elisha was his agent. As king, Thomas required the truth, no matter how it might wound him as a man. "The emperor had been served by the mancers in the past, Your Majesty, but they found him difficult, as you say. They sponsored the upstart, Charles, and this convinced Emperor Ludwig at last to reject them. By then, it was too late, and they were willing to sacrifice him. I failed to protect him."

Thomas gave a regal nod. "What was the disposition of your army?"

Narrowing his eyes at the king, Elisha replied, "Only me, the emperor, and a man of his who turned out to be very capable. That man brought back a company of soldiers."

"And the enemy?"

"Fifteen necromancers, drawing strength from the Valley itself, through a pair of mancers who are adept at manipulating its power."

"Good Lord!" Thomas's voice drew Alfleda back to his side, clinging to his hand, her eyes wide.

"It's less than I fought here, for England," Elisha pointed out. "And I lost the emperor—the man I should have saved."

"He would have wished to die fighting. What else?" Thomas prompted.

Now, they came to it. Here, in this place where his brother died over the loss of his child, grief still echoed from the walls and the stained earthen floor. Elisha's hands hung at his sides. "I also lost his baby, Your Majesty. The empress Margaret went into labor during the battle, and the child was slain by an agent of the mancers, not realizing Ludwig himself was already dead. I—tried to revive him, I even—" He swallowed and shook his head. He had even taken the form of an angel in his grief and madness. "I failed."

"Elisha, the baby was murdered."

"I should have been able to do something." He raised his hands, the scars white against his clenched fists. "What is this power for, if I can't even save a child's life?"

A knock sounded on the door, and a voice called, "Everything all right in there, Your Majesty?"

"Yes, fine." The fire popped, but the flames sank low, drawing shadows down the king's lean, handsome face.

Alfleda nudged her foot across the dirt. "You saved me," she said softly, her hair falling forward.

The king stroked a hand over his daughter's golden hair, letting his palm rest lightly on her lowered head. "Isn't that why you turned away from God, because He allows babes to die?"

On the wall, a few tin crosses winked in the dying light, crosses like the ones his brother made. "It's also why I became a witch, because I could not save a baby's life."

"At least you hold yourself to a high standard," said Thomas, with that edge of dark humor Elisha recalled so well. "Neither you, nor God, can save them all. At least *you* are trying."

Elisha let out a tremulous breath. "Then why can I not succeed?"

With a sudden rush, Alfleda pulled away from her father and came to Elisha, catching his fist between her hands. "You will," she said earnestly. "Next time, I'm sure you will."

The next baby could well be his own, Elisha realized with a sick dread. The mancers were searching, not even knowing what a treasure they might find.

With a shock of heat and the full strength of his presence, Thomas brushed his fingers through Elisha's hair, tracing the scars where his cracked skull had been opened. "For all your power, Elisha, you are just one man. I pray you will succeed next time—and I know that you won't stop trying." The king's sharp gaze shifted away from Elisha's face. "The hair is coming in white."

Elisha held very still, barely breathing. "It's a common effect after head trauma."

"I was looking for fresh scars. They must be well-hidden."

Elisha thought of the Empress Margaret, telling him that even his scars could be found attractive. He always felt exposed before Thomas's gaze. "Not very," Elisha whispered, and Thomas smiled gently, withdrawing his hand.

"We pray for you," Alfleda blurted. "Even though you don't like God very much. We pray for you here and at the chapel, and sometimes in the big church, too."

"Thank you," he told her.

"I pray you come home safely," Thomas said, touching a warning finger to his daughter's lips, and she turned a little pink, embarrassed at her interruption. "I fear you'll die over there, and we shall be left with nothing, not even a stone."

If Elisha died over there, there would be no grave: the mancers who slew him would dance about with his bloody bones. For a moment, he thought of staying, never again leaving English soil, no matter what came of it. But if he did, how much blood would flow in the streets of Rome? "Thank you for your prayers," he said, though the words felt hollow. "I do need to go."

Thomas gave that regal nod once more and stepped away. "Fare you well, Elisha." Alfleda hugged her arms about Elisha's middle, then moved to her father's side.

Elisha took out the relics Margaret had given him. The bone chips might be part of the mancer network, but he could not be sure they led to Rome, so he focused on the vial of the True Cross, working free the lead seal to make contact with the shard of wood. Some pilgrims, he knew, had taken bites of the cross as they leaned to kiss it, but the emperor had boldly taken a knife to it.

At his touch, the wood chilled so sharply it stung his fingers, and the shade of a tortured man vented his pain. He deflected his own presence with every talisman he carried, praying he could deflect the warden himself. This passage must be swift and direct, as careful as he could make it, stealthy, to slide in under the very notice of the warden who served as the master of Rome.

Elisha took a deep breath and opened the Valley, taking the time to still the maelstrom and soothe the howling. Sensing the pull of the Cross—shards of the same wood here and there that pulsed to his call—he stepped inside, drawn toward the largest, as if he could hear the man dying. Leaving the familiar grief and the steadfast friendship of his home, Elisha stepped a thousand miles away, to Rome.

Chapter 31

———❖———

Elisha crouched, holding his deflection in case of prying eyes, dank air filling his nose and throat. A single thick candle burned nearby, with the rank odor of animal fat, but the space pulsed with shades and shivered with the echoes of the dead. The dirt beneath his feet felt strangely familiar though he had never been here before; it resonated with layers of history like the earth of Jerusalem. The thick beam stood behind him, looming in the shadows, reminding him of Simeon, but he did not know who had died here. Steeling himself for what he must feel, Elisha opened his awareness fully to the relic and placed his hand upon the beam. It stung with cold, but it lacked the fresh horror of the recently dead. Unlikely the mancers had forged this one.

Elisha drew back his hand, unsure how to feel about that: it was a comfort that they had not crucified this stranger, but someone had, years ago, a legacy of brutality linking present to past. In a niche carved in the wall hung a nail as long as his hand, rusty with old blood. Just for a moment, Elisha thought he could serve with mercy as an executioner, drawing death with a touch, swift and painless. Even a criminal deserved better than this.

Weak light revealed a stone staircase that rose before him. He stepped over the low wall that surrounded the beam. Beyond the enclosure, the ground felt foreign again, and Elisha realized the earth itself was a relic, carried from Jerusalem and spread beneath the cross.

If the mancers could use only the relics of those they killed, they must be placing dozens of their own fragments. The ones Empress Margaret gave him could serve as a beginning, but if he used one of those relics to cross the Valley within the city, that would draw the attention of any mancer who shared in the kill, including the dangerous warden of the Valley itself—Conrad's father—and startle anyone who worshipped at the tainted altars, thus drawing the notice of the *desolati* authorities as well. Stalking up the stairs, Elisha entered the dim space of a church with few windows, and those high up in the rafters. Ranks of columns rose out of the murk. At the end of the nave, a small door stood open, shedding some light on the plain granite. Elisha walked toward the door, still expecting to see priests or penitents. The place echoed with emptiness, except for the shades that stained the crosses.

Elisha emerged into a crumbling courtyard surrounded by a brick wall. Browning grasses protruded between the stones here, though a smooth trail marked the line between the church and the gate to the outside world. A campanile rose overhead, its growing shadow indicating late afternoon. Here, at last, he heard voices, a group of men muttering among themselves in a rapid, unfamiliar tongue. On the other side, a huge curved structure interrupted the wall, partially built into the church enclosure, but the rest tumbling into ruin beyond, like a great round of bread that had been chewed by a thousand rats. Shades roamed thick upon the ground here: shades of people clad in nothing but leather, shades of soldiers in jagged skirts with round shields, shades of women, children, ordinary men. If the mancers ruled, how many fresh shades would join them? Elisha blinked the vision away.

At the far end, another courtyard opened. That must be where the Bath of Constantine would be found, and the tribune with it, taking his daily bath. Should he approach directly, or trail after?

A trumpet blast froze Elisha where he stood, his muscles instantly taut. He pivoted slowly, expecting arrest or command. Instead, the party of men he had been hearing stood to attention in two rows fronting a low octagonal building. The man at the end of each row held a short brass trumpet, but their clothing lacked the arms and ornament of royalty, and even the trumpets looked small and battered.

Into this array stepped a dark-haired man of about his own age, a wreath of leaves upon his head and a swath of white fabric draped over one shoulder atop a coat of armor. Thomas's garden held a statue that looked like this, a sculpture of some ruler a thousand years dead. One of the guards waved toward Elisha, beckoning. Direct approach it was, then. The guard who hailed him chattered in his rapid tongue, and Elisha focused his awareness, trying to glean some meaning from the fellow's words. He looked pleased enough, if a bit confused as Elisha failed to respond to what was evidently a question.

Elisha pointed to the church. "I went to visit the Holy Cross," he replied in English, then crossed himself. "I am looking for the tribune of Rome, to pay my respects."

The man in the laurel wreath pushed through his guards, flapping his hand to hush Elisha's interrogator. In quiet, distinct Latin, he asked, "Are you a pilgrim?"

Relieved to hear a language more familiar, thanks to Mordecai's teaching, Elisha said, "I am."

The man's wreathed hair glistened with water, and it dripped a little over his eye as he studied Elisha. "I could see you are not a Roman. Where are you from?"

Evidently, they had not recognized his language. Good. "Bavaria," Elisha answered warily.

Breaking into a grin, the man repeated, "Bavaria!" and switched into German. "You have come from the emperor? Excellent! I am Cola de Rienzi, the tribune of Rome."

Elisha bowed, hoping that was the appropriate honor for a man of such dubious station. As he rose, Cola reached out, fingering the fur that edged his cloak, then snatching Elisha's hand. He ran his thick fingers over Elisha's palm, but lingered on his calluses, rather than his scars.

Elisha twitched at his touch, but did not pull away—
as Cola muttered in Italian, the contact enabled Elisha
to understand his words. "A working man. The Emperor
sends me an envoy like myself, only recently cloaked in
majesty." He grinned again, more fiercely. Elisha smiled
back, uncertainly.

Cola wrapped his arm through Elisha's and said carefully in German, "Come to my home, honored guest."

"Thank you," Elisha replied, letting himself be towed
along. The tribune's favor could well allow him entry to
places otherwise locked, and the tribune's recent rise to
power suggested mancers at work, though he did not
sense any among this group. The men of the guard
showed the usual faint shades of fighting men with
blooded swords and battles to their honor, though some,
including Cola himself, lacked even those.

When they reached their tethered mounts, Cola ordered one of his men to walk so that Elisha could ride.
They crossed a landscape of tight buildings interspersed
with broken ruins, some ancient like that oval building
by the Church of the Holy Cross, and others with scorch
marks still recent and mounds of rubble pushed aside
from the narrow streets. Everywhere he looked, new
buildings incorporated bits of the past: columns, carved
stones and the occasional stone coffin lid constructed
into houses and shops. And everywhere he looked stood
the churches. They passed at least twenty close up, and
glimpses down the tangled ways showed dozens more
towers and crosses in the distance. Elisha's heart fell.

No wonder Gilles wished to come here: the city must
be stacked full of relics—more saints than citizens, given
the emptiness of the streets. Clusters of people gave half-
hearted cheers and waves as the soldiers rode by, and
Cola waved back, clearly delighted, only to fall to brooding as they passed a huge round ruin fortified with new
walls. He smiled at Elisha, transforming his worries into
an expression bright and open. "Does the Bavarian follow after?" he asked in his studied German.

Elisha hesitated. "His wife hopes to make the journey,
for the Jubilee, at least."

"But this remains two years away! As you can see, we strive daily to prepare for that glorious time, but the beneficence of your emperor would encourage so many lesser kings to recognize what we have already achieved."

A city of ruins and rats. The tribune needed more than an emperor's recognition to make this place ready for thousands of pilgrims. "I fear I bring sad tidings, Tribune. Ludwig the Bavarian is dead."

"È morto!" Cola crossed himself, his brow furrowing as he looked away. "But the Holy Father is close with this Charles, who is named emperor, and the Holy Father is one of our supporters. It shall be well. Simply, we shall make an embassy to Charles instead." He glanced sidelong at Elisha. "But you have still come."

"Ludwig's widow still wishes to make her pilgrimage, but she fears for her safety. I have come to be sure that she may travel here freely and unharmed." Margaret and all the others coming for the Jubilee would be safer if Elisha could root out the mancers before they knew what he was doing.

"Since the tribune has come, we are all safe!" cried one of the guards, twisting in his saddle, his German sharp and clear. "He has expelled the wicked barons and brought peace at last."

Cola raised his fist. "Many are firm in their support of the great Republic. Imagine what shall be the greatness of Rome when all the world acknowledges us!"

They turned a corner beneath a huge palace, and the breeze carried a familiar putrid scent that curdled Elisha's stomach. Alongside a set of broad, stone steps, three corpses hung from a scaffold, one nearly rotted to bone, the others more recent. To Elisha's left eye, unnatural shadows edged their decaying flesh, remnants of their humanity, and his awareness hummed with the dread strength of the dead. The wind pushed their dangling feet and the hair that mercifully covered their faces, dark liquid dripping to the wooden platform below. Like the rest of the city, this fresh stain overlaid the old, along the shadow of the scaffold, broad enough to carry six men. The local mancers must hunger for this place.

"Come, honored guest. Let us show you the hospitality of Rome." The tribune tossed his reins to a waiting boy and slid down from his mount, smiling again, waiting for Elisha in the lee of the scaffold. "Tell me, how many of the seven have you seen so far?"

"Sorry?" Elisha tore his gaze from the dead men.

"The seven great churches of Rome which the Holy Father has decreed necessary to complete the pilgrimage. No doubt your queen shall wish to visit each. You shall help me to draft my condolences for the queen, and I shall have the maps and guides brought to you. Captain Rinaldo shall accompany you! As you see, he has the ease of language." He pointed to the young man who spoke German. Rinaldo gave a short bow, but his presence chilled, his dark eyes focused on Elisha. A more partisan chaperon would be hard to find.

Switching to his native tongue, Cola said, "Rinaldo, this man is a liar. I need to know why he's really here. Don't leave him alone." He smiled, his tone light and cheerful, though the contact of his hand upon Elisha's shoulder carried his suspicion along with his meaning.

"Sì, Tribuna." Rinaldo bowed sharply, also smiling.

Then to Elisha, the tribune said, "If you rout any bandits or barons from the churches, we shall hang them on the steps." He gestured toward the scaffold and grinned. "In the meantime, we eat!" Cola marched up the steps, his trumpeters once again sounding, his servants hurrying forward to see to his needs, his white drape slithering through the shadows of the dead.

Over a meal of marinated olives, dry cheese and local bread, the tribune regaled Elisha with stories of his army's victories—signs that God approved of his cause. Cola reverted to the local dialect while Rinaldo translated, allowing Elisha to connect the unfamiliar Roman language with one he knew. He listened to the narrative, searching for evidence of mancer intervention, but finding none. In conclusion, Cola pointed to the emblem of a dove painted on the wall of the high chamber. "See, this dove is the sign of God's pleasure in all that we do."

A door swung open to admit a tall man in a clerical robe. Elisha flinched as the man turned, for taut skin permanently sealed his right eye socket. The one-eyed priest glanced at the dove, then back to Cola. He moved carefully, as if he feared to fall, or simply to fall apart. "Have you enjoyed your bath, Tribune?" he inquired in sonorous Latin.

"Indeed I have. It is refreshing to the body and brings clarity of thought."

"Certes," the priest drawled, "but a bath may do the same without despoiling a holy place."

"Despoiling, Father Uccello?" Cola braced his hands upon the table. "I draw my inspiration from the empire, and what better inspiration than Constantine himself, who brought the light of truth to his pagan realm? They name you 'the Silent One.' I suggest you live up to it."

For a moment, Father Uccello froze, then made a visible effort to soften. "He bathes in the baptismal font of the Emperor Constantine," the priest explained, echoing Lady Agnes's breathless gossip. "An old argument." His lips smiled, but his single hazel eye did not. It flicked from side to side, matching Elisha's gaze in one eye then the other, taking in the difference between them.

Elisha offered his hand in greeting—and for the chance to make contact.

Father Uccello's smile crimped as if he held it by force of will alone. Finally, he put out his hand, and Elisha held his breath. The man seemed, at first, to have no presence at all—but it was a deliberate self-effacement, not the hollow feel of a mancer cloaked in the power of death. "Well met, Father Uccello."

"Not long a student of Latin, I see, but you have come to the best place to practice." Breaking the contact, he folded his hands carefully into his sleeves. "You are the man who would survey the seven churches? It is not possible. Half of the seven have no archpriest to oversee them—they are in haphazard condition at best. Of the others, two are in the hands of the Colonna. Until the wise tribune ceases to hang their kin, I doubt they shall be allowing visitors. I suggest you go home and tell your queen to stay in Bavaria—or perhaps she wishes to travel to the Holy Land and try her luck with the Saracens; they may be more accommodating."

Cola burst to his feet, shooting out his finger to jab the priest's chest. "You, Father, are a coward." He spoke in Italian, but his fury projected his meaning for any magus to receive. "Your family cannot supplant the Colonna, despite decades of trying, and so you speak as if they cannot be bested. I have beaten them before, and I shall do so again, even without your aid. Tell the Holy Father to come to Rome! Tell him to send us the funds for repairs and for battles, and we shall be ready for the pilgrims. It was I who suggested the Jubilee to begin with—myself and Petrarch—and the Holy Father agreed. Why now am I no longer supported?"

Elisha thought the hanging corpses by the steps and the worried faces of the citizens suggested a few reasons, but he seized upon the fact that the Jubilee had been Cola's idea, the event the mancers planned to use to draw their victims to the city. "Pardon me, Father, Tribune," Elisha said, sending his words with a suggestion of calm. "Perhaps I can begin with the churches that are open."

"You should begin your pilgrimage at Saint Peter's Basilica, Dottore," said the priest. "My family, the Orsini"—a pointed look at Cola—"maintain it well, and I think that your safety can be assured on the route to get there. I shall obtain permission for such a visit. The churches of the apostles are vital to obtaining the indulgence for yourself."

"That had not been my intention," Elisha said carefully.

The priest made a soft sound of interest. "Have you no sins worthy of pilgrimage, Dottore?"

"Father, if I tried to lift all of my sins, the queen would be a long time in waiting," Elisha replied lightly.

"Most men are reticent to admit to any sin. Your humility does you credit." The priest's smile widened. "There is no easy path to absolution, but the Church of

San Lorenzo is not fortified, perhaps we may begin there." The priest at last pinched up his robe a little and settled onto a chair. While older than Elisha, the priest seemed too young to have developed the problems of the joints that all of his movements suggested. The meal resumed, but each stab of a knife to spike an olive or slice a wedge of cheese seemed to heighten the tensions. When the Romans showed Elisha to a chamber where he might rest—along with the avid Rinaldo and a couple of other guards—they expressed indignance, if not surprise, at his tale that his belongings had been stolen on the road.

Cola muttered in his own tongue that even a Colonna thief would have taken the rich fur-lined cloak and Elisha's gold ring, and Rinaldo merely nodded, trying to look sympathetic for Elisha's benefit. In spite of their suspicions, they found him bedding and expressed enthusiasm for his project. Their conversation shaped a landscape of Rome in Elisha's mind, the palaces of Orsini and Colonna barons and all the minor nobles who divided between their two wary camps. Their struggle to claim the city since the Pope's departure had battered Rome almost beyond recognition, with the brave citizens caught between. Until Cola rose up ready to lead them to victory. Or, he would be, if he had the money and supplies he needed. To which camp did the mysterious warden of the Valley belong? Did he hold power both worldly and magical, at the head of one of these warring households?

The idea that he might be mistaken for a mancer himself had begun to take root, suggesting a plan that could ease his way here, if he could reassure the local mancers about his purpose and still keep them at arm's length. At all costs, he must beware the warden. Any mancer strong enough, sensitive enough, to hold the Valley open for so long was indeed a force to be avoided. He could not afford to let his urgency destroy the very secrecy he needed.

As it happened, any travel beyond the palace was put

off while Cola and his meager army confronted the
baron who had barricaded the vast oval structure they
had passed—il Colosseo, Cola named it.

From a balcony two days later, Elisha and the members
of the council watched as Cola ordered a few more exe-
cutions. As an executioner draped a noose over each
man's head, one prayed, one pleaded, two others shouted
defiance—urging the vengeance of God upon the tribune. The air stank with fear and rot. The executioner
kicked the first one over the edge. Bone cracked as the
condemned man's head jerked back, and Elisha flinched,
his hand rising to his own throat.

"Such is the treatment of the enemies of the Republic," Rinaldo murmured, watching Elisha's reaction.

The Valley opened, but the cold dread of the first
criminal's death slid aside, drawn off by an unseen
strength as blood spattered from his mouth to the ground
below. A mancer had marked the gallows slates and si-
phoned the power of those who died. Another degrada-
tion of the condemned men, and one that few but Elisha
would ever recognize.

The second criminal kicked and strangled, until Cola
raised his hand, and a pair of women broke from the
crowd, running up to pull on the hanged man's legs, mercifully snapping his neck rather than leave him to choke
to death.

"The tribune's justice upsets you," Rinaldo observed.

"I have too often known justice to go awry." Elisha's
hands ached from clutching the rail. He scanned the
crowd, looking for the flicker of shades that marked a
mancer's wake. What mancer could resist such a feast of
fear?

Two men, distant from one another, wore the signs,
one in the black habit of a monk, the other in workman's
garb, leaning on a shovel as he watched, eyes wide to
take it all in. A few half-hearted cheers rose from the
crowd. Most merely stared, mouths drawn tight.

The weeping man, given his shove, kicked and gurgled
a long moment, but nobody came to tug on his body as

he swung back and forth, his bowels releasing, until he finally twitched into stillness.

The workman mancer emanated a thrill that reminded Elisha of Morag's pleasure in the power of the Valley. Would the Germans have warned their allies who to watch out for? Elisha sealed his presence beneath his skin and transformed the shade of his eyes, making them both appear gray. It was a projection only, the flesh would not conform easily to his will against nature, but the markers of the barber they feared must be concealed. The shock of white hair, the scars upon his hands, he erased. If the mancers spotted him, they'd see only a dark-haired stranger.

The executioner repositioned the knot before knocking the last man down for a sharp break. Scattered applause and cheering greeted this last execution, then Cola made a little speech in the local tongue. Rinaldo led cheers for the tribune until they echoed from the stone buildings all about, and the crowd drifted back into the haunted streets.

"Now will we have the peace to make our visits?" Elisha asked, turning away from the dangling dead.

With a gesture of dismissal, Rinaldo explained, "There may be reprisals. For several days, at least, we should remain inside the palace. Among the tribune's first pronouncements, he made a law that no murderer should be suffered to live, no matter the circumstances of his birth. A noble law, but there are still those who do not understand that order is maintained only by strength." He aimed a finger at Elisha. "Don't go anywhere. I must join the tribune for counsel. If you will excuse me." With a nod, Rinaldo dismissed himself—no doubt to tell his master that their visitor was among those sickened by this mode of justice. How far could their suspicion grow before Elisha found himself once more at the end of a noose?

The yard and steps emptied. After the last of the populace filtered through, a pair of guards closed the tall gates, barring them with a huge beam.

Two mancers now, Elisha would recognize on sight,

and he had evidence of a third. He pushed away from the rail and descended to the piazza below. The executioner directed a team to haul away the older remains of the criminals that had been cut down to make room for the new. The workman mancer helped with this gruesome task, pushing a barrow out through a smaller gate as Elisha approached the scaffold.

Death stained the stones beneath and fresh blood now dripped down to join it, mingling with even less appealing fluids of the dead. A sensitive mancer could use his own blood to mark the area where a dead man's blood might fall, then use that contact to gather the power of the criminal's death. Another sensitive—the warden of the Valley, a man who knew the paths of death almost as intimately as Elisha himself, and apparently could employ violent deaths he had not actually committed. That was worrisome indeed, narrowing Elisha's few advantages. Worse yet, how was Elisha to remain unnoticed in the city with another sensitive as its master?

The workman mancer returned to haul away another body, but he paused, his stare aimed directly at Elisha, and a hint of his magical scrutiny snaked out. His eyes narrowed as he turned away with the body, leaving one more for a final load.

The workman returned for the last body, and Elisha started to walk away, but the man called, "Here, sir, you seem at ease with the dead—give a hand, would you?" The fellow waved an arm, his voice cheerful and pleading, at odds with the heavy weight of his stare.

At ease with the dead. Elisha's heart raced, but he concealed that as well. He should have known any foreign visitor would not escape notice in such unsettled times, especially one who had not been seen to arrive by any ordinary means. For a moment he thought to ignore the workman mancer, but if Conrad and Eben's conversation could be believed, this man and all the Roman mancers followed the warden of the Valley, Conrad's father, as their master. Better for the warden to be aware of him, but think him no harm, than to associate the stranger with the enemy. Every death that touched him he drew up like a cloak of shadows, recalling the mancer-archbishop of England, Jonathan, and the skillful projections he used to intimidate other magi and those who risked contact. Elisha made a mancer of himself, steeped in sorrows unfeigned.

He gripped the talismans connected to Rome, conjuring a thread of cold. "Of course, let me help you."

The mancer grinned. "Thank you kindly."

Together they lifted the last body, and Elisha felt the unmistakable tingle of contact, an inquiry made along the very flesh of the dead man as they placed him in the barrow.

"Who are you, then?" the mancer demanded, wary, but not yet ready to strike.

"Please tell your master who marks the gallows that the English are returning to strength. I am here to make us ready for Rome."

"He mentioned a stranger passing his gateway, better for you that you've been honest than to keep secrets." He offered a crooked smile, but his presence gave a pulse of hostility. *"Know this: we don't share."*

The workman referred to the Valley as the warden's gateway, as if it were his private road. That disturbed Elisha, but he was careful not to let it show. *"No need. I shall go about my work and be gone."*

"I should do likewise." With a bob of his head, the mancer released the body. Elisha stepped back as the man heaved up the barrow's handles and trundled away.

Elisha stood trembling, his throat dry. Had he just made peace with the enemy, or had he cast himself upon the waters, unable to swim?

Chapter 32

❖

When the nightly skirmishes between the tribune's men and their enemies ended, and another corpse joined the rotting ones upon the scaffold, Elisha, Uccello, and Rinaldo rode out of the city at long last so that he could carry on his mission. The need to proceed cautiously was one thing—but to make no progress at all, except in his language skills, was quite another, and he chafed under the enforced stillness.

A vast cemetery spread around the Church of San Lorenzo, full of the quiet presence of the dead. Here and there lay murder victims, and others unjustly killed whose shades shimmered with the echoes of their earthly pain. The mere presence of so many dead at first piqued Elisha's interest, but while the mancers appreciated the resonance of such a location, especially for working magic, ordinary corpses were of little use without the mancers' personal involvement in the deaths. Among the gravestones, a mancer moved, his presence chilling the relics Margaret had given Elisha. The mancer's head rose as the party rode by, sharp eyes tracking them. He made no move to follow or speak, but that chill lingered. The warden's eyes were on him, through his companions if nothing else. The thought brought Elisha's breath up short, and he forced himself to play his role, projecting a strength he did not feel, and concealing the signs of his own identity as he always did when he wasn't alone. Cola's spy threatened execution if he were

revealed to be an enemy—the warden's spies promised so
much worse.

Inside, using Latin as the language they shared, Father
Uccello told the tale of San Lorenzo's martyrdom and
revealed the stone on which the saint was laid out after
his grisly martyrdom—and the iron grill on which he had
been burned to death, with a section of burnt flesh still
attached. His closely controlled presence shivered a little
at that, and he studied again Elisha's mismatched eyes.
"Burning is now a favored punishment for witches.
Thankfully, they rarely frequent Rome. There are too
many holy things here for their comfort."

His stare alone reduced Elisha's comfort; it made Elisha want to blurt out his secrets, to reveal the terrible
witches already at work in Rome, and the destruction
they would bring down upon the city and all who traveled there. Breaking the Church itself, just as the rabbi
had said.

Elisha turned away and continued his pilgrimage
from altar to altar. Excitement surged through him as he
felt the brush of a familiar shade. On taking a careful
stroll through the church, he located two relics shared
with the cache given him by Margaret. The second fragment occupied a large reliquary overseen by a pair of
stern monks who relaxed only when Elisha dropped a
few coins in the box for candles and lit them, thinking of
his mother's piety, his brother's tithing, his own king's
abiding faith. He lit one candle for his stillborn nephew,
another for Queen Margaret's murdered boy, and forced
the memories aside.

Another mancer, a thin, severe woman dressed in
black, looked up from a nearby altar, her eyes, and her
other senses, upon him, stalking him. Elisha offered a
polite nod, and she turned away.

Under the guise of tucking back his hair, he plucked
a few strands and caught them at the base of the elabo-
rate reliquary, sensing the layers of other dead the vessel
contained.

To use the hair against him would take a highly

sensitive magus, one with knowledge of Elisha, like Elisha's use of Mordecai's hair to reach the Isle of Wight. Such a subtle marking would pass beneath the notice of most mancers, and serve to give him warning in the meantime if others used these relics to open the Valley. He could link all the relics in this way and pull them from the churches through the Valley, as he fled the scrutiny of so many mancers. He could finally go home.

In addition to the two victims whose talismans he carried already, the church held three more items freshly forged by the mancers—three more shades he could pursue and one day lay to rest.

The next day, they rode again, but from a different gate, through an empty country toward the church of San Sebastiano, accompanied by a small party of soldiers in case the bandits emerged. A pair of mancers working in a field stretched their senses toward Elisha, making his skin crawl. Though he clamped down on the sensation immediately, a growing unease gripped him, translating to his horse who stamped and snorted, startling at shadows. While the entire city of Rome teemed with shades both new and old, this broad avenue paved with ancient stones carried legions of the dead, quite literally. If Elisha did not blink them away, his party passed through troops of soldiers clad in the metal skirts and plumed helms of the ancient Romans. The fresh shades of recent travelers moved among them, along with strangers in the garb of distant lands and Northern climates. It should be warmer in Rome, even in November, but the chill reached Elisha through his fur cloak, as if cold permeated the land.

"You seem unwell, my dear sinner," said Father Uccello, eying him. "Don't fear—the church is just ahead." He pointed past a series of old stone buildings.

Between stood two small churches Elisha could see already. "Which one?" he asked, hoping his relief didn't show.

"Not these—these are merely entrances to the catacombs. San Sebastiano is a bit further, across that field."

"Catacombs?" Elisha formed the unfamiliar word, trying to get a sense of it.

"For many centuries now, it has been unlawful to bury the dead within Rome. Such a ban is necessary in a city so large as Rome. So the dead are here, beneath us. We encourage the people to use the new graveyard, as at San Lorenzo, but many will still follow the old ways." He turned his palm up in half a shrug.

Drying fields and small farms surrounded the older structures, some with smaller houses built into them. Elisha said, "There are no gravestones."

"No, the catacombs are caverns, dug out for miles. Rather than graves, there are shelves for the dead to take their eternal rest. Many of our martyrs are interred below." Father Uccello crossed himself.

Elisha stared at the ground as they rode, his mount's hooves treading through dim shadows that rose like a mist from the very earth. He wished he could stopper his awareness completely and set aside his unease, but, especially outside the city walls, he needed his vigilance. Since he had spoken to the workman, mancers appeared everywhere—serving in the tribune's hall, working the fields, tending the graves—and he'd begun to think the conversation had been a bad idea after all. He could feel their attention upon him.

His unease increased as they rode, his stomach churning and shoulders tense. He envisioned ranks of the dead down below, some disintegrating with age, some just begun to rot, piled together on beds of stone. "May we stop, please?" Elisha reined in his horse before the other men even answered, in front of a small church.

Father Uccello reined in as well, sitting stiffly as if riding triggered that old injury Elisha had observed in his movements.

"You wish to enter here?" Rinaldo's lip curled, and he remained on his mount as Elisha slid down and let one of the other soldiers take his reins.

Elisha shook his head, but approached the small building slowly, leaning one hand on the doorway as if weary, and let his awareness stretch down below. He need not reach far: blood marked the lintel—the same blood he noticed at the scaffold. When someone brought their dead here for interment, the mancers would know, and come to reap fresh talismans. Then, too, if the mancers of Rome manufactured false relics of their own, it would be in a place like this, where the miasma of dread would keep most people away, and the remains of their activities could simply be left among the other corpses when they had ripped both life and strength. What better place to conceal their brutality than here, in the halls of the dead? No wonder they stared, watching him greedily. Were they envisioning his own dismembered corpse and skinless face?

Elisha paced away from the chapel, leaving the mancer's mark far behind. He wasn't ready, not for that. The entire purpose of revealing himself to the workman had been to avoid having to meet the master.

In the grassy verge, a tumbled marble slab lay. He started to sit on it, until he made out its length: a sarcophagus, absent its body. A little way down, a few more stones emerged, the bases of ancient columns, and he perched on one of these, facing San Sebastiano over the rough fields and monuments between. Now that he focused his doubled vision, Elisha found gaps and streams among the shades that lingered here. They had not died here, so the forms remained indistinct, but the gray pall gathered thickly in some areas and not at all in others. Slowly, he climbed to stand upon the fragment of column, breathing carefully and gazing out over a map of the catacombs below, a webbing of the dead. Closer to the chapel and beyond it, sharper shades emerged, dark and cold with recent death. No wonder the master of Rome stood warden of the Valley, for he lived in a web of death, its pathways and crossings as dense and worrisome as the dread Valley itself. "Do the bandits use the catacombs? To hide in, I mean?"

A shrug. "Only if they are brave or foolish. They might be crushed in a collapse, or possessed of evil by staying with the dead." Rinaldo shuddered theatrically.

"The dead have no cause to linger, Captain," Father

Uccello said. "Their spirits rise or sink as befitting their
state of grace upon their deaths." His single eye stared at
Elisha.

Near the recent interments, trails remained in the pall,
as if the living disturbed the peace of the dead when they
descended into the caves. Between this chapel and the
taller tower at San Sebastiano, the shadows roiled. It
must be easy, in the chaos that was Rome, to take a victim from the streets and bring him here to suffer and die
and rot among the thousand bones that lay below. He
thought of the moment he shared with Thomas, the
king's fear that Elisha would be left without even a stone
to mark his grave, and the thought made him jittery.

"Nor have we cause to linger—let us ride on," Rinaldo urged.

Sick with dread, Elisha re-mounted, and pressed onward, hurrying through his prayers, three watchful mancers tracking him at every moment until he fled the
church at last, retreating from the warden's web for the
precarious safety of Rome.

The next visit—a long ride along the river—brought
them to a fortified monastery and basilica with a wall so
long it encompassed a small village of its own. Passing
the holy doors, complete with Rinaldo's uninspired com-
mentary and Father Uccello's dour silence, they began a
circuit of the vast church.

At each altar, while Rinaldo prattled, Elisha prayed
again, spreading his awareness with caution, especially
when the priest hovered nearby. When he found one of
the mancer-relics, he marked it with a few hairs and
moved on. A chill edged his right shoulder, and Elisha
drew back both his hands and his slender awareness,
burying his inquiry beneath his mask of piety as the
mancer-monk he had last seen at the execution walked
by with a measured tread, like a jailor or a ticking
clock.

"If you wish to make confession here, Dottore, it will
gain your admission to the tomb of the Apostle," Father
Uccello told Elisha in Latin when he finally rose from his
knees. He gestured toward the older stone structure

across from the eastern door, the subterranean chamber where the remains of the Apostle Paul were said to lie.

Were there mancer-relics even in the apostle's tomb? Elisha had only one way to access it to find out, though the idea of Confession made him hesitate.

"When was the last time you confessed?" the priest prompted.

"Easter," Elisha told him. His brother had escorted his greatly pregnant wife, Helena, into Saint Bartholomew's and Elisha followed after, watching for the tell-tale signs of labor, praying that his brother would speak to him, accepting his aid and his abject apology. Four days later, his brother was dead.

The priest's single eye bored into him. "Come, my son, even I can see the sins weigh heavily upon you."

And on that point, at least, Elisha had to agree.

Chapter 33

❖

Father Uccello went off to speak with the resident priest and take a purple stole from his hands in spite of the other priest's glare. Glancing at Elisha, with a nod toward the wooden confessional booth, Father Uccello made a show of draping the stole about his shoulders as he entered the other side. Even the confessionals of Rome were built on a grand scale, perhaps to impress the great lords when they came on pilgrimage.

Rubbing his palms against the skirts of his tunic, Elisha entered the darkness of this cave within the church and knelt down, feeling his breath so chilled it should mist the air. He wet his lips and said, "Bless me, Father, for I have sinned." If he were to speak his every sin, there could be no end to his penance.

"I understand you are a stranger here," replied the priest in Latin, "but it is expected that you should confess in a tongue in which the priest is also fluent."

"Forgive me," Elisha mumbled in the same language.

"You spoke from memory, in the language of your home. English," the priest said sternly. "I learned some of the language from William of Occam when the emperor was in residence, but I did not expect it from you."

Elisha's fingers bound together in his lap. "I told the tribune I came from Bavaria. I did not say I was born there."

"What brought you to travel, then?"

A grate of ornately carved wood separated them, so that Elisha could hear the other man's voice and the occasional shift of his robes, but could make out only the vaguest outline of his form. He maintained his deflection, but it would not hold if he were pressed on issues where his feelings ran strong, and he did not know where the mancer-monk had gone. The wrong magic, the wrong projection, could get him killed.

"You rebuke me with your silence," said Father Uccello. "This is Confession, not the inquisition. Very well. Tell me your sins that I may absolve them."

"I have taken the Lord's name in vain, several times," Elisha told him, and he thought of his last confession, before the results of his arrogance caused his brother's suicide. "I have succumbed to pride." He closed his eyes, but his brother's image waited there and he opened them again. "And to despair."

The priest sucked in a breath, and Elisha clamped down on his own emotions. "That is a grave sin, my son. If you wish to speak more of it, I will listen." For a moment, they merely breathed, then Father Uccello said, "I wear the confessional stole, I will hold in confidence all that passes here."

Elisha gave an involuntary snort.

Beyond the screen, the priest's voice warmed. "Admittedly, it is likely the tribune will ask."

"You are in an awkward position, Father."

"More than you know," the other answered. "Have you anything else to confess?"

Staring at the screen, wishing he could ask the priest's confession in turn, Elisha said, "And I have lied."

Father Uccello gave a single, short bark of laughter. "It is well you have come to the Eternal City, my son. If you undertake the pilgrimage, you will receive your indulgence—even if you do so under the auspices of your duty to the queen."

Could any pilgrimage lift the sins that still haunted his heart?

To the east, a door slammed open and a voice bellowed, "Orsini!"

Beyond the screen, Father Uccello's silhouette pulled upright, worry piercing him.

"Father?" Elisha whispered. "Would they violate the confessional?"

"What would they not do?" the priest murmured.

Footsteps pounded down the aisle, and the same voice barked, "Calm yourselves, Brothers, we're not armed."

The door of the confessional flew open, and Elisha scrambled to his feet, summoning power that burned below his skin.

The man outside—large, handsome and clad in crimson velvet embellished with a crowned column—squinted back at him. A fighting man, clearly, by the shades that clung to him, but no mancer. He slammed the door and stomped to the other side. Elisha pushed free of the confessional just in time to see the intruder slam open the other door and reach inside. With a swift movement, he pulled Father Uccello out, his hand clenched around the priest's upper arm.

"What are you doing in there? You are an Orsini in a Colonna stronghold," the big man snapped. "You have no authority here."

"I am a priest in a church, my Lord." Father Uccello floundered a moment to get his feet under him, his face white. "I have more authority than you."

The lord's dark eyes widened and his nostrils flared. "You tell your keeper the Holy Father has had enough of him." He pushed his face close to the priest's, unable to intimidate by height alone. "I suggest you all vacate the palace and flee for your wretched lives."

"My Lord Colonna," Rinaldo began, starting forward, but a little ring of Colonna retainers moved up to block him, and Rinaldo stiffened, his tribunal finery and rough features standing out among the forest of guards.

The lord did not spare a glance for Rinaldo, but kept his stare focused on the priest he held. "Don't think you can hide at the Basilica San Pietro. It, too, shall be ours." With the last word, he drew his hand up and back.

Father Uccello danced a moment on his toes, his mouth gaped in a silent scream. His shoulder popped, his arm suddenly too loose as his body pulled downward. The priest's eyes gleamed with tears. Elisha sprang to his side, sliding his arm about the priest's chest, taking his weight. He seized Colonna's hand with his own, sending the strength of his fury and pulled it free.

Colonna grunted and yanked back his hand, shaking it.

Landing hard on his feet, Father Uccello stumbled from Elisha's grasp, swaying, his good hand cradling his elbow. Still, he made no sound, but the moment had shattered his control, and his presence radiated pain and terror.

"Who are you?" Colonna snapped—and Elisha realized they had been speaking in Italian, but he had understood it all. His days of near-captivity with the Romans had done him some good after all.

In German, Elisha snapped back, "I came from the Imperial city to see if Rome is free of bandits and tyrants. I see that it is not."

Colonna shook his head, waving one of his men forward. "What does he say? What is this man?"

"My Lord," said a monk, rather timidly, hands clasping and unclasping as he bent himself near double. A few other monks hid behind him. "If you have delivered your message, that is, San Paolo is meant to be holy, a refuge—"

With a growl and a wave of his hand, Colonna turned away. His cloak swished around him, followed in its arc by his retinue of soldiers, who marched after him out of the Holy Doors.

"Bold words, Dottore," said Rinaldo. "I am pleased you support us—and so shall be the tribune."

Ignoring him, Elisha moved into the gloom beyond the confessional, searching the darkness. "Father Uccello?" He spread his senses, the barest suggestion of his presence, and immediately the pain throbbed in his own shoulder. Pivoting, Elisha dropped to one knee before the dark cave of the confessional. "Father."

"Don't worry over him," Rinaldo called from the far side. "It happens from time to time, and he takes care of it."

Elisha wished he could slap the soldier: Rinaldo could not feel another man's pain. Instead, he schooled himself to calm, seeking the strength of healing. "Father, let me help you."

"Leave me," the priest whispered.

Elisha edged forward and made out his form, on his knees, leaning against the wall, still cradling his misshapen arm. Dislocated—more than once, from what Rinaldo said—and Colonna had known where to grab and how to wrench. Anger returned, but Elisha forced it away. "Please, Father—you don't need to suffer like this."

After a shuddering breath, the priest murmured, "The Lord will provide."

"Certes," Elisha said, "He provided you a doctor."

Again, that single, sharp laugh, breaking near a sob. "Come, Dottore," he gasped. "Do your worst."

Elisha edged into the cramped space. With swift fingers, he loosened the priest's garments, then carefully drew his robe away from his shoulder, guiding it down, taking over support of the injured arm. The confessional stole still draped the priest's left arm, and Elisha glanced from it to Father Uccello's face. "We are still in the confessional, are we not?"

A hard swallow followed by a tiny nod.

"Then you are bound not to reveal this."

The priest's ruined eye faced him. With a careful shift of his head, a sliver of Father Uccello's good eye became visible, fixed upon Elisha's face.

Mastering himself, Elisha drew upon his talismans of peace and joy, letting them swell in his compassion, and warmth spread through his hands. He shifted one hand beside the shoulder joint where the skin, muscle, and tendon strained, and sent his healing, suggesting wholeness, strength, peace. With a deliberate, practiced movement, Elisha took the priest's arm and guided the bone back in place, ending with Father Uccello's hand clasped against his own chest, Elisha's left hand still sending its warmth into the damaged joint, and his own shoulder throbbing with the affinity as he worked to ease the tendons and encourage a deeper strength.

The priest stirred and carefully took back his arm, bringing up the robe to cover his exposed back and

shoulder as Elisha withdrew. Father Uccello's every joint
was weak, aching, and bands of scar tissue wrapped the
priest's wrists, his ankles, too, no doubt. Elisha could
have relied on simple medical skill, but no mere manipulation of bone and muscle would soothe the fear that
paralyzed the priest. The comfort he sent would help, but
the injuries were too old for him to fully heal, and the
effects of torture went deeper than the flesh. Someone
had bound Father Uccello on the rack and stretched him
till his shoulders wrenched from their sockets.

"I feel . . . better." Father Uccello's eye squeezed shut,
and he sighed. "Then you are a witch. God help me, so
was I."

Startled, Elisha lay his hand gently on Father Uccello's back, as if monitoring his breath, but he felt none of
the resonance he expected from another magus, even
now that the priest's formidable armor had been
breached. At that moment, the both of them open, too
surprised to stay guarded with each other, Elisha sensed
the spike of another man's interest. The mancer-monk —
and now he knew about Elisha's healing.

"Damn it!" Elisha pushed himself up and shed his deflection, stretching his awareness in all directions. Rinaldo
stood off by the door, supervising the Colonna retreat.
Three warm presences by the altar—monks. Another
moving rapidly away, accompanied by the shivering chill
of a familiar shade. Elisha groped in his pouch and found
a silk-wrapped relic that went cold even as he touched it.
The dark pull of the Valley spread beneath his fingers, the
presence of the mancer-monk dissolving into it. No!

With the relic clenched in his fist, Elisha pulled back.
He seized the mancer's presence and felt himself stretched
as if he tried to steer a team of mad horses. At his back,
the reliquary, too, hummed with its connection, and his
hair quivered where he had marked the base. Drawing
upon the other relic contained in the reliquary, doubling
his contact with the fleeing mancer through the murder
the man had shared, Elisha summoned the man to him.

Giving a yelp, the monk fell against Elisha inside the
confessional. For an instant, their eyes met, and Elisha's

hand went cold as the mancer conjured his power, but Elisha wrested it from him, clamping his palm over the other man's mouth. *"Do not interfere with my business. Surely you were warned."*

"You're not one of us, not at all. Who are you? What are you really?"

For a moment, Elisha considered killing him outright. A monk, slain in a confessional, with a priest as witness. Damnation, indeed. He let his hand grow so cold that the monk's face twitched and shivered. *"I am the master of England. Do not make me your enemy."*

"No, of course not." His presence shivered as he reached for power enough to warm himself against Elisha's icy threat.

Elisha released him and the monk fled into the Valley, surely going to tell his master Elisha had lied.

Father Uccello cowered in the corner of the confessional. "What happened? Who was that?" The priest clawed up the wall until he could stand in the cramped space, turning his good eye to see what was going on. Elisha's heart thundered; he had to go after the monk, but he had to give the priest some answer.

"One of the monks wanted to see if we were through with the confessional."

Father Uccello tucked his arm back into his sleeve, frowning down at it, surprised by its sudden ease of movement. Again, the priest turned his head. "Then where did he come from and where did he go? Not by the door."

Elisha set his hand gently on the priest's chest, holding him back, hoping for his silence. "Please, Father," Elisha murmured, as near to a prayer from his heart as he had given since he came to Rome. They stood face to face, the priest taking advantage of the several inches he had over Elisha to stare down at him in the narrow door.

"Are you above a few more lies?" Then Father Uccello's voice dropped so low it rumbled through Elisha's bones. "Or will you kill me, too?"

Chapter 34

Elisha's own joints felt weak, his muscles aching like iron strung along a frame too fragile to hold. "No one is dead, Father, not today."

"I felt the cold and heard the howling fiends of Hell, and then the man was gone. If not dead, then—"

Carefully, Elisha reached out, and the priest flinched back, but could not retreat from Elisha's hand moving toward his throat. Elisha took up the dangling end of the confessional stole and draped it back down the priest's chest. "We are still in the confessional, Father."

"Sorcery." Father Uccello's mouth twisted as if he would vomit, and his chest shuddered. "Devil's spawn."

So quickly the healing was forgotten—but the healing had been a mistake, unwanted by the patient, drawing unwanted attention to the healer. Curse his stupid instinct. "You said you used to be a witch, Father."

The priest escaped Elisha's hand and the close atmosphere of the confessional to stumble into the church. He stripped the stole from his throat, the ends trembling in his outstretched fist. "There shall be penance, Dottore!" His gesture made the purple cloth bounce and snap through the air. Then he turned on his heel and stalked away, his stride more even than ever before.

Elisha caught his breath. There seemed little purpose in leaping through the Valley right then in pursuit of the mancer. Either they would come for him, or he would make contact with them to reinforce the lies he needed them to believe. A liar, just as Father Uccello had said. He meant to fight the mancers, must he become one of them to do so?

"Dottore?" Rinaldo's voice echoed, and Elisha jumped.

"Ah, forgive me." The soldier smiled at him. "But you have earned your visit to the apostle's tomb, in spite of the interruption of your confession. I gather you and the father have concluded it?"

"For now," Elisha said. He wanted nothing more than to leave. "But the father is still shaken from his confrontation. Perhaps we should return to the palace and come another day?"

Rinaldo shook his head lightly. His manner with Elisha had relaxed since the Colonna intrusion. "Things shall not improve for our leaving the city walls, especially since you have supported the tribune against the Colonna. We should make a quick visit to the apostle's tomb now and hurry home, in case we are not able to leave the city for a time." He draped his arm across Elisha's shoulders, escorting him, as a friend now, toward the tomb of the Apostle Paul.

"Three openings lead in, two for the viewing, and one to pour drinks for the apostle." Rinaldo chuckled at this, and Elisha managed a smile.

Shivers of power and weakness alternated beneath his skin as they walked, leaving the dim area of the confessionals. Would it be more dangerous for the monk to tell his story to his leader, or for Father Uccello to tell his story to the tribune? Already, Cola distrusted him and set Rinaldo to spy upon him.

Rinaldo continued, "Can it be that my lord Colonna has affected Father Uccello for the better? I have rarely seen him look so vigorous. Or did you give him some medication to aid his recovery?"

"I know some methods for injuries like that. Do you know what happened to him?"

"It was during the last visit of the Emperor Ludwig— God rest his soul—" Each man crossed himself, then proceeded down an ancient stair toward the apostle's tomb. "My father was a soldier for Ludwig—it is why I speak German. You will know, of course, that the emperor proclaimed his own pope. This was twenty years ago, now. Naturally, there were many in the clergy who did not wish to bow to the emperor's candidate."

A candelabra on either side lit the narrow chamber. Gesturing toward a small, square opening in the sandstone wall before them, Rinaldo said, "Here we have the Apostle."

Elisha obligingly knelt to look through, but the presence of the ancient dead, even such an important corpse as this, could not deflect his attention from the problems of the living man, and of the missing monk. "Father Uccello resisted the emperor's will?"

"Many priests and monks simply abandoned the city, but Father Uccello is also Orsini, and they will never give ground to the Colonna, and so . . ." Rinaldo shrugged, a carefree gesture that emphasized the easy, natural movement of his shoulders. "Attempts are made to convince him. 'Il Silencio' some call him still, 'the Silent One,' for he will answer not at all, even at the rack."

Emperor Ludwig, the mancers' early favorite, the grandfather of King Thomas's beloved daughter, tortured priests. Elisha felt ill as he started for the stairs. "Can't the tribune do anything about the Colonna and the Orsini?"

"He does try." Rinaldo led the way swiftly back to the horses. "They have been at odds for centuries, vying to dominate Rome. It cannot be solved in mere months."

In a city where a priest could be assaulted during Confession, what effort could possibly suffice? The holy authority that once held the city had broken down. It was a portrait in miniature of what would happen if the mancers succeeded in breaking the Church. The priest himself waited outside, but did not look at Elisha as they mounted and rode for the Capitol. A hesitant rider on the way to San Paolo, Father Uccello now settled gracefully in the saddle, and Elisha envisioned the constant pain of his injuries dispelled to a quiet ache. Would the priest's belief in the confessional sacrament prevent him from revealing Elisha's sorcery? Heaven only knew.

Back in the palace, Elisha excused himself as quickly as he might. He had a mancer to meet.

In a disused chapel in the palace, he hid his letters, his medical kit and most of his talismans, keeping those less personal and ranging in a circle around him the mancer-made bits he'd linked to Rome. At the center of this ring of death and fear, Elisha attuned himself. From the meager possessions he had accumulated in Rome, he took out the map Rinaldo had given him showing the pilgrimage churches, including the distant San Sebastiano, center of the web of death that was the catacombs. Elisha longed to wait until the morrow, but that only gave the mancers more time to plan. Better to face them now. It might be their home, layered with the dread power they forged, but any island of the dead was home enough for him.

He began by searching, sending his awareness beyond walls, touching first one and then another of the relics he carried. Among them, he found the one that linked him to San Sebastiano and the mancers of Rome. It gave a cold tingle at his touch.

Cradling the fragment of bone, Elisha sent the barest whisper of thought along the paths it carried. The warden was sensitive, possibly as sensitive as he. If the mancer could sense him at all, it would be a kindred spirit who called him. A slender shock of cold returned his touch, and Elisha spread the Valley wide before him, the howls of the dead framing a direction, an invitation from the gatekeeper himself. He felt a curious pull to the south, a growing reservoir of power that threatened to draw him off-course. Intriguing, but not enough to deter him tonight. He stepped through madness toward the catacombs, where two mancers expected him. Only two. Good. They did not anticipate trouble then, or else they had the means to summon up the others as need be. The passage, with the warden's power reaching back toward him, felt as comfortable as stepping into a bath.

He emerged into a cavern carved with pillars and arched overhead with mosaics that glittered in the light of candle-stands at each corner in his line of vision. Close and moist, the room held bones in niches along the walls, the skulls placed at the fore, a hundred blank stares aimed at him. Rough openings led out in several directions, structuring the webbing of the dead he had sensed from above ground. In a wooden folding chair with lions at its arms, an old man waited, regal in his silver beard and hair, his eyes pale and sharp. The resemblance to Conrad was clear. He wore fine garments with the shimmer of expensive thread. They seemed lightweight and practical at the same time, leggings ending in a pair of close-fitting boots worn with thick-heeled wooden clogs to keep his feet from the muck of city streets. Beside him, an embroidered robe hung from the head of a figure carved into the wall. "Brother," he said in Italian, inclining his head and offering a similar chair. "Good of you to join me."

Elisha dredged up a smile. "Latin is a better tongue for me, Brother, if it suits you." He accepted the chair, feeling awkwardly underdressed.

"Certes. I would like you to feel at ease. Given the short notice, I was unable to arrange for a meal. I hope you are not disappointed."

"No, the tribune feeds me well, when he is able."

The mancer's eyes crinkled with a smile. "You do not find Rome at her best, I fear, but we, of course, have other means."

Elisha's left eye revealed swirls of darkness that caressed the mancer's feet and shifted along his chair, like fawning pets come to beg for his touch. Less distinct than the true shades of the dead, Elisha had noticed these same kind of tendrils drawing power toward the priest from his flagellants, and the horror of the dying toward Elisha himself. The echoes of death roiled out around the warden along every path and hall, but those in the second opening on the left were disturbed, like fog stirred by the passing of a ship; the sign of the living who had moved through the warden's web of power. The second mancer waited there, his presence nearly erased by the conjuring of the dead. When Elisha stretched his awareness in that direction, he could barely find the man, like a patch of deeper darkness, misted in fear. Elisha quieted the drumming of his own heart.

The warden's courtly manner and overly civil speech reminded Elisha that he himself had at one time been a king. He thought of Thomas, wearing majesty even without a crown, and conjured up again that part of him. "How could I fail to be at ease in such a place, Brother? Forgive me for worrying you at such a time. No doubt you have more important concerns than guests."

With a slight raising of his hand, the other replied, "Our associate has already disturbed me tonight, with unlikely tales of your behavior. If anything, I thought you might keep me waiting. Thus, you find me pleased at your prompt attention to the matter."

"As I told your man at the tribune's palace, I have no wish to become further involved with your affairs than I must, but I do assert the right of England to claim her place among the Chosen." Bardolph's name for them.

"Brother Tigo said that you claimed to be the master of England. I know your land has recently experience some turmoil." A tip of his head.

"There was another claimant who divided our cause. I have taken care of her." Elisha folded his hands together.

"And yet, my associates have been wondering what you've been doing. You have not brought any relics, after all. In those places you've gone, they find nothing changed." The mancer watched him keenly.

"If I'd been up to anything interesting, you'd have noticed, wouldn't you?" Elisha pointed out. "Just as I found your mark upon the gallows. It's not as if you need to personally kill a man for his death to have meaning in your practice."

His companion relaxed slightly. "There are very few who can make that claim. Perhaps only two?" He tipped his head again, and Elisha tipped his in turn. His throat felt unbearably dry, his palms itching. "Certes, none of my associates are so skilled, and Brother Tigo, I fear, is more blunt than most." The remark ended on a trailing breath, as if on a question.

"He inserted himself into my ... negotiations ... when I had not the time to explain."

The pale eyes flared just a little, and the mancer's quiet tendrils of interest insinuated themselves into the miasma of the dead. "Negotiations? Do tell."

"You do want the Pope to come here, do you not? To attend the Holy Year in person and to bring his many thousands."

"Even without the pope, they will come." Taking his gaze down to his perfect oval fingernails, the mancer said, "I understand that my intimacy with the paths of the dead makes me useful to the French and the Germans, but at times I am not certain what I shall gain in return. Rome gives me a fine banquet, I have a bold son to carry on our traditions. It is he, really, who wishes to join in the spoils of this game, though it means I hardly see him anymore." He flicked a glance back up. "I thought the English had withdrawn from the field."

Elisha suppressed his knowledge of the warden's son and focused on the man's curiosity. "I was nearby when Jonathan fell."

"There is a man we shall miss. There are few enough of *us* as it is, even among the Chosen." He emphasized the word, joining himself, the dead archbishop, and Elisha in a brotherhood of power, then he gave a genteel sigh. "The Germans did not think there was any promising material left in England, though."

"The Germans don't know as much about England as they think."

"My son tells me they are still pursuing the absent English queen. And he nearly met that barber everyone's been speaking of."

"I found the barber unremarkable," Elisha said, carefully mastering his emotions. The warden had no direct knowledge of Elisha until now, and he prayed that ignorance would be enough to leave him unrecognized.

The mancer's fingers slid along the wooden lion beneath his hand, lingering on the teeth. "In sooth," he said, drawing out the sound, "at first, I thought you might be that barber. Certes, Brother Tigo's tale would seem to support that conclusion."

"And now?" Elisha let the power of death flow through him, his skin shimmering with darkness.

"You wear the raiment lightly, as if it were silk, and you had only just come to town, yet you were immediately aware of me. This suggests the great depth of your knowledge. It is rare indeed that I meet someone as aware as myself." The mancer's eyes crinkled. "But some of my adherents are impatient. They grow restless waiting for the Holy Year, and they will not accept the more cautious pickings as I have done."

Marking the gallows to steal the strength of the dead. Elisha swallowed. "It's a long time to wait, I agree."

"It would have been even longer without the poet and the tribune waxing eloquent about the glories of Rome," the mancer drawled.

What poet, Elisha wondered, but he could not ask without revealing his own ignorance. "The tribune's behavior of late is turning his allies against him, hence my negotiations. Perhaps working more directly with the Church or the barons will yield a better result."

"Very wise. The Germans have been getting hasty themselves. They should have kept the Salernitan under closer control."

The Salernitan? Another mystery Elisha noted.

A rat scampered along the edge of the room. The warden casually expelled a crackle of power. The rat convulsed and died, its leather tail thrashing into stillness. "But we need not discuss politics, when there are more useful pursuits."

"What did you have in mind?"

With a smooth movement, the mancer rose, beckoning, and led Elisha toward the second arch. "I noticed you noticing our companion. I do try so hard to find the right companions in this lonely work of ours. They were instructed merely to observe." He shook his head, his silvered hair stroking his shoulders. "Any man so quick to betray one of the brotherhood cannot be trusted."

They walked silent among the dead into a second, larger chamber, this one hung with oil lamps, light shimmering upon the instruments that lined its walls: hammers, knives, saws, probes all beautifully polished and sharpened, ready for the brutal surgeries they would perform upon the broad table at the chamber's heart. Beyond the table, a great wooden wheel leaned against the wall, with the mancer monk chained out upon it, sweat beading his tonsured head and a silver pin sealing his lips.

"Distasteful, isn't it. Men of our sensitivity forced to such a course. I have expended much effort to ward this chamber so that we need not feel the full effects of our work. My studies suggest that those who indulge their own ecstasy during the harvest may dilute the finished talisman. I wonder if you feel the same?" He arched an eyebrow, then continued, "As for this one, I have given him a lesson in patience." The mancer gestured gracefully. "I think he now understands the value of restraint. I do not usually share, but after all, my brother, it was you he sought to betray."

The warden watched him as if casually, no stray emotion escaping his carefully forged presence. But Elisha guessed what this was about: That barber, the one who was taken in at every turn by his compassion, what would he do, in a moment like this, with an invitation to murder? The warden waited to see, to know for certain what manner of man Elisha was.

Elisha let his heart go cold and reached for a knife.

Chapter 35

$\mathfrak{T}$he warden inclined his head. "You will wish to remain clean, especially if you must go among the *desolati* tonight. I keep a supply of garments on hand." He displayed a few clean robes in shades of russet, like dried blood.

"You are a most generous host," Elisha replied, taking up one of the garments. A small collection of bones and other relics formed a line upon a chest nearby, along with two human skins, rippled at their edges, and a monk's cassock all folded neatly. The monk had been stripped of his talismans. Elisha looked away, resuming his consideration of the knives arrayed upon the walls. Any surgeon would envy such a collection. "In Germany, they do not clean their knives, but prefer to let the signs accumulate, making them talismans in themselves."

The warden curled his lip. "I cannot abide sloppiness. Only the insensitive require such crudity."

Elisha selected a long, slender blade with a smooth horn handle that fitted his palm. As he wrapped his fingers around it, the bound mancer whimpered, and his master swelled with power, a rushing of shades that tingled over Elisha's skin. The warden felt all that passed within this chamber, the place hummed with his presence, like a web trembling at the touch of its spider. Interest pricked the web as other mancers stirred, some near, and some far, bound to the warden by the brutality they shared. All those who had been watching him. At the

slightest twitch of their master's anger or fear, the cata-
comb would flood with mancers and Elisha's mission
would be over, Rome ceded to the mancers to terrorize
the pilgrims and tear down the Church relic by relic. If
Elisha refused this offering, or turned his skill against the
warden himself, he would, in moments, be confronted by
the gathered strength of all Rome and beyond.

Slowly, as if considering his choices, Elisha approached the wheel. A few hammers of different sizes
rested nearby, waiting to break limbs.

The captive writhed against his chains, grooving his
flesh. Two sharp paces, and Elisha stood before him, staring into the mancer's damp brown eyes. The remnants of
murder clung to the monk, flickering shades of a half-
dozen victims. Elisha braced the mancer's chin with his
left hand, a gesture firm, yet gentle—the only comfort he
dared. Then he drew on the mantle of Death, letting the
Valley within his breast beat with that dark power, shedding all sign of his humanity. The hovering chill of Death
swelled and pulsed with the leaping fear of the man beneath his hand, but Elisha no longer cared. His power
encompassed the mancer's skull, the vessels that carried
his blood, the sweat that sheened over his face, all concealing the mystery within, the fragile organ that, once
damaged, could never be made right. Knowledge filled
Elisha with eagerness—the knowledge of the fragile life
he held before him, the knowledge of the power to come
with its destruction.

With a swift and calculated blow, he plunged the knife
into the mancer's eye.

The black pall of Death rushed free in an instant, a
cold that shocked his hand and feathered his cheeks with
frost. The power cascaded through him, and Elisha
gasped, his body quivering, charged as if he stood too
near when lightning struck. The Valley remained shut, all
the cold and the panic streaming from the dead man
straight to Elisha's frigid heart.

The warden let out an appreciative sigh, accompanied
by the frisson of satisfaction along every thread of Death
that linked him beyond the chamber.

On the wheel, the mancer's body sagged, his head pinned upright by Elisha's blade as the tension left the stretched limbs and terrified face. Elisha gripped the hilt a moment longer, blood oozing from the pierced eye, until the mancer's face relaxed.

At last, he released his grasp, drew a deep breath and stepped away, not yet turning from the corpse that he had claimed. He drew off the borrowed robe, returning the garment to its hook, spotless.

The warden leaned in to examine Elisha's work. "I have never seen a harvest so smoothly made." He studied Elisha with frank admiration, and a knot of fear that hid at the back of Elisha's throat dissolved beneath the mancer's wonder. "You are an artist of death, my brother."

The subtle sting of self-loathing followed immediately after. Perhaps it had been a mistake to shed the aspect so soon. "I know you abhor a mess."

"Do you wish to take anything more?" The warden wafted his hand toward the corpse, but Elisha shook his head.

"Thank you, no."

"Because you require nothing. Exquisite." The warden's eyes gleamed. "The others will think it a gift."

Elisha met his sharp and pale gaze. "And a warning, as it was meant to be."

"I doubt any others will interfere with your remaining negotiations, nor shall they defy my commands. Neatly done, Brother." With an elegant sweep of his hand, the warden bowed.

Elisha accepted his obeisance with the slightest tip of his head. If he moved, if he spoke, if he broke the careful blank of his expression, the awful power that curled within would shred him from the inside out.

"I am so sorry I must let you go, but if you think we are better served to bring the Pope to us, then your negotiations must take precedence." The warden gestured for Elisha to go before him, and Elisha urged himself into motion, feeling brittle as ice. "I am not without influence myself, provincial as I am. I shall do what I can."

"Thank you," Elisha said again, though the words felt thick upon his tongue.

In the smaller chamber, the warden donned his embroidered robe, folding back the cuffs. Then he tipped his head, silver hair brushing over gold-worked flowers. "Brother Tigo told me the Orsini priest was present during your confrontation."

Elisha smothered his shaft of fear, and gave an approximation of the Roman shrug. "He may have seen something he shouldn't, but it was the confession, after all. I don't believe there's any danger in that quarter."

"Perhaps no." The warden opened his palm. "But it may damage your hopes with the Orsini."

"He is still sworn to take me to their stronghold, at San Pietro. I think I can rectify any damage at that time." Elisha gave a tight smile and a slight bow of his head. "But I do need to go, by your leave."

"Certes, Brother. Until we meet again."

Elisha raised his hand in farewell and drew open the Valley with a whisper of strength. It stood no longer as either an arch or an obstacle, but shimmered like a curtain of mist to be parted with a breath. Silence, the tumble of shades around and through, and he stood in the disused chapel deep within the tribune's palace, alone as he could ever be. He gathered his things and returned to the bedchamber he shared with the tribune's guards, empty save for him.

Drawing the warmth of an ordinary darkness into his chest, Elisha banished the Valley to where it hid, lurking like a tumor barely caged by his ribs. Slack-jawed, he stared up at the ceiling, his hands clenched together to keep from trembling.

By God, what had he done? What had he become?

The monk was a murderer, several times over. If any man deserved to die, it would be him. Collecting himself, Elisha shut his eyes. His right hand felt again the plunge, the jellied resistance of the eye, the pressure as he pierced the braincase, the crack as his blade thrust through the mancer's skull. The quickest kill he could imagine making. The cleanest harvest the master had ever seen.

Elisha dropped to his knees. He dragged the chamber pot from beneath the bed and vomited, his throat and nostrils seared. He pushed the pot away, eyes stinging.

He bought himself time to save others from the mancers' blades, but with what currency? Other men came to Rome to be cured of their sins; Elisha merely compounded them.

Once, Elisha held up his hands as the only thing he had any faith in. Tonight they slew a helpless man and bore no trace of blood, as if the crime had never been. He no longer knew his own hands.

Restless, he longed for sleep, but the power he stole from the dead man moved within his chest and the distorted face haunted his vision when he closed his eyes. He wiped his face on his sleeve and flung open the door, stalking down to the well to draw some water. It could not wash away the bitterness. He braced his hands upon the stone, letting water drip from his face and fingers. At his back, music and shouting filled the great hall, the raucous sound of men celebrating, but echoing with the fear of the doomed, soldiers on the verge of battle, not knowing when it would come. Elisha drank another draught and ran his wet fingers through his hair, shaking it back. Ignoring the guards and the drunks who cluttered the stairs, he pushed back into the hall.

"Rinaldo! Captain!" He called out over the sounds of the revelers.

The tall young soldier glanced up, breaking away from his conversation to approach, his face furrowing. "You don't look at all well, Dottore."

"There is a man, a provincial lord who comes to Rome frequently. He's taller than you, with long silver hair and a beard, perfectly trimmed." Elisha's hands sketched the mancer's height and figure and he forced himself to stillness.

"Count Vertuollo? But usually it is his son who comes to treat with us. How did you hear of him?"

"Rumors," Elisha snapped back. "Orsini or Colonna?"

"Either, neither." Rinaldo gave that rolling shrug so typical of Rome. "His allegiances are never clear."

"Whoever he's with, whatever he does, Rinaldo, he's the enemy, do you hear me?"

"Dottore . . ." Rinaldo touched his shoulder, and Elisha jumped back, certain that Death would meet that contact with brutal force. The captain put up his hands, patting the air in a soothing gesture. "Come and have some wine. It will help to settle you."

"Nothing will help," Elisha murmured, "not tonight."

"Herbs? Or women?"

"No," he said, shaking his head. "Tomorrow . . . until tomorrow." He turned away, back to the chamber he shared with his ghosts.

"Get some rest, Dottore!"

Nodding vaguely, he found his way down the halls to his narrow door and shut himself inside. Meticulously, he replaced his talismans. The vial of earth from his brother's death he hung at his throat and Thomas's golden ring upon his finger. The scrap of cloth Martin had given him, his first talisman, he kept close to his heart, held inside his tunic with the pin containing scraps of toenails that had taken him to Brother Gilles. The dozen or so talismans he had taken from mancers or received from Margaret he concealed as well, placing the shard of the True Cross in his boot for the morrow.

As he placed each one, he invoked the peace of the dead. Not all were restless, not all howled their agony into the Valley, or vanished into a sorcerer's breast. Biddy went with purpose and with joy, and Martin rose with laughter. Duke Randall died of a witch's vengeance, but knowing he had not been wrong about Elisha after all, and the Emperor Ludwig died in battle, facing a foe he could never defeat, but facing it boldly, for those who would follow. And the mancer Elisha slew . . . he dare not send comfort or release him from fear, but he gave him the best death he could, swift and nearly painless. Somewhere in the catacombs, the mancer's fellows would pull his skin and break his bones and make merry of his murder, all the while knowing any of them could be the next. Elisha's hand took the life, but left whatever dignity remained.

Thomas had remarked upon his standards: that Elisha imagined he and God could save everyone, that Elisha, at least, was trying. Trying was not good enough for God, he knew, but it was enough for his king. In the end, it was all that he had. He drowned in the sorrows of his past, and remembered the strength of Thomas's hands, bringing him to the surface of the water, bringing him home. With the image of Thomas's face before him, and the vial of English soil clutched in his hand, Elisha allowed himself to be comforted and finally found his rest.

Chapter 36

❖

Just as Rinaldo predicted, the tribune's recent victory had only spurred on the barons, and they were not allowed to leave the palace again for almost a week. Restless as the lions at the Tower of London menagerie, Elisha stalked the halls and tended every injury or medical complaint he could discover, pulling the teeth of aged retainers and soothing the aches of washer-women. Cola busied himself with grandiose plans for an imperial reception which left Elisha wondering if Charles served as the emperor in this vision, or if it were Cola himself who occupied the throne. Rinaldo seemed to regard Elisha as a new partisan of the tribune—so perhaps he had escaped the shadow of the noose—but Father Uccello remained distant. When they saw each other at all, Father Uccello aimed his sharp hazel eye at Elisha, his presence so controlled that the look alone revealed the depth of his emotion. Since his meeting with Vertuollo, Elisha sealed his own emotions, smothering his compassion. But the need to play the mancer stifled him, and he worried over what Vertuollo would do with his newfound regard.

A few days after their trip to San Paolo, Rinaldo, flushed with excitement, caught Elisha's arm. "You and Father Uccello seem angry with each other—what's happened between you?"

"He was embarrassed to need my help after Baron Colonna abused him at the church, that's all."

"Are you sure? It seems more than that." His grip

shook a little as if trying to cajole answers from Elisha. "Does he seem more ... partisan to you? Closer to his family?"

"I imagine that being assaulted by the enemy during a confession might put a man in a foul humor. Why do you ask?"

"Nothing, nothing." Rinaldo let go immediately and backed off. "It is only the tribune is eager to bring the families together, to heal the rifts, not to allow them to fester." He flashed a grin, then hurried off, leaving Elisha mystified by the whole exchange.

They were all at table when the Orsini messenger arrived, announcing that safe passage could be made between the palace and the Orsini territory around San Pietro. "Then we may visit?" Elisha asked.

Father Uccello set down the chunk of bread he had been dipping in oil and said, "Indeed. And the sooner you seek for repentance, the better off you shall be."

Rinaldo glanced from one to the other, but neither spoke any more about it. The captain's odd questions about the priest came back to Elisha's mind, but still meant nothing to him. He was heartily sick of the politics of Rome, especially when the warring families kept him from finishing his task. Entry to San Pietro was a great step forward, and Elisha drained his wine and made ready.

Together, they rode winding streets down to the river and up again beyond, crossing a broad plaza toward San Pietro, the seat of the Holy Church and the greatest cathedral in Rome. In contrast to the grand towers and intricate sculpture of the cathedral at Cologne, San Pietro squatted at the back of a square plaza, colonnaded, and stocked with a handful of wary guards. Soldiers challenged them at the outer gate, and again when they stopped to dismount. Above the arched entrances, a mosaic showed the apostle Peter in front of a huge boat, apparently walking on water. Bits of gold sparkled with the last rays of the sun, but patches of tile were missing, and the entire building listed slightly to one side.

Inside, a few boys hurried to light candles for them, but these illuminated little in the way of painting, sculpture, or gilt work. Even as this party of fire-bringers moved ahead of them, Elisha felt the weighty silence of the dead. They lay all around him, beneath graven images set into the floor and altars by the walls, deep in layers and crowded into common tombs, as if so many sought burial here that they had to be crammed in like herring in a barrel.

"All of the popes are buried here," Rinaldo whispered as they moved through the gloom. "And the apostle's grave is below. We shall need time to see it all." He crossed himself reverently.

Elisha nodded. Time, indeed. Relics, bones and shadows cluttered every niche and stone. Where before Father Uccello had told the tales of the saints at the churches they visited, here he maintained a frosty silence as they proceeded on the tour. The priest conducted them with a gesture or a word. His gestures, endowed with a healthy grace since Elisha had healed him, had become circumscribed, as if his new ease of motion disturbed him. Moving from one pool of candlelight to the next, the visit took on a solemn air, almost punitive. Elisha knelt at every altar, planting a few hairs to mark the false relics as he found them. San Pietro had many, displayed about the church, most with altars, but some with tombs or other graves. Elisha had a distant relationship with the Church ever since he watched the burning of the angel, though he continued to observe the proper rituals. Now more than ever, kneeling at an altar, forming the words to familiar prayers, felt like lying, over and over. And the fact that lightning failed to strike him down convinced him, more every moment, that God had no interest in the morality of His creations. But Elisha knelt, he prayed, he marked the relics on behalf of every believer who would come after him, every *desolati* the mancers would crush into terrified submission.

At last they approached the high altar, over the tomb of the apostle himself, and descended the curving stair into the crypt. The tombs of various popes, with statues and paintings of their occupants, surrounded the apostle, each figure illuminated briefly by their torch-bearers, as

if they passed through a room of sleepers, hands pressed
together in prayer. The sense of them rose in Elisha's
awareness, a focused atmosphere that reminded him of
the mancer's catacombs, but rich with faith from the
dead interred there and from the offerings left by the
living: old candles, bunches of flowers, bits of clothing,
and votive charms. The frescoes and carvings featured
chains and keys, affirming Saint Peter's role in binding
and loosing, and showed scenes of his torture at the
hands of the pagan Romans of many years ago. Elisha
glanced at Father Uccello and wondered if he, chained
and nearly martyred for his adherence to the Pope, felt
especially close to Peter. By the gleam of the priest's hazel eye, Elisha thought it might be so.

Father Uccello glanced back at him. "This chapel rises
above the bones of the Apostle. It is called the Chapel of
the Confession."

"Then it is fitting I share it with you," Elisha said. For
a long moment, their gaze held.

"Does the father, too, have sins to confess?" Rinaldo
asked, leaning a little forward, but Father Uccello drew
himself up with an intake of breath as if he would spout
a sermon of brimstone enough for them all. "Forgive me,
Father," said the captain, but his face in the flickering
light looked strange. Rinaldo crossed himself, gave a
short bow and retreated out of their circle of candlelight.

Releasing the anger that had animated him, the priest
sank to his knees, hands pressed together. After a moment, Elisha joined him. This side of the priest's face
showed no sign of the disfigurement, and Elisha wondered if his eye, too, had been taken by Ludwig's tortur-
ers in their attempt to bend him to their will. Father
Uccello intimidated him with his formidable demeanor
and his depth of will, and Elisha ached to think of the
pain that presence concealed. Surely, the fact he still
cared showed he had not entirely lost his footing among
the decent people of the world, in spite of what he had
done in the catacombs.

"The captain seems to have taken against you, Father," Elisha remarked.

"The captain allows worldly trifles to come between himself and the Lord," Father Uccello snapped, then he sighed. "Perhaps I have allowed this as well. I had intended to show you the welcome of the Orsini and how well we maintain the Apostle's church." He stared over his prayerful hands. "I know not if I must atone for my inability to do so."

"Your unwillingness, you mean, because of what you saw and what you felt at San Paolo."

"Because you are a sinner born and willingly made, and until you repent of it, you shall never be saved nor see the Kingdom of Heaven."

"I have too much work to do here on Earth, Father, to be concerned overmuch about Heaven."

The priest gave a sharp exhalation. "You have no concern then for your immortal soul."

"You worry for the souls of others, Father. So do I. This thing you think you know about me, I use it in service to others."

"A godly man would not use it at all. He would fight every temptation to do so."

Elisha's hands pushed against each other as if he could crush his doubts between them. "I cannot fight what I am, Father."

"Then you are not fighting hard enough."

Elisha's lips parted, but he thought of the monk upon the wheel and the knife Elisha had thrust through his eye. Had there been another way? He could not fight what he was—could he fight what he was becoming? Hands pressing together, he remembered his first glimpse of Katherine, kneeling, tearful, before an altar very much like this, praying for forgiveness or release. He left England to hunt the mancers and learn their plan. How, when he faced such a remorseless enemy, could Elisha himself afford remorse? He slew them alone in Heidelberg, and joined together with Katherine and Daniel to kill them in the mine, and now he knelt at prayer in Rome undisturbed by his enemies because Count Vertuollo had asked him to kill, and Elisha had obeyed.

By the chapel's entrance, Rinaldo scuffed his feet, no

doubt eager to return to the palace and the work of
fighting men. Only two more churches of the seven, and
Elisha, too, could shake off the weight of this unwelcome
tour and turn to the problem of destroying the relics he
had found.

Rising, his knees aching, Elisha crossed himself once
more, and, after a moment, Father Uccello did likewise.
The priest led them back up the curved stairs into the
quiet sanctuary of the vast cathedral.

When they reached the door, Father Uccello paused
and said, "Captain, I should like to join my family for
this evening, but I shall return to the palace and the
tribune's council on the morrow, unless there is any objection?"

Rinaldo glanced around the piazza where his small
troop of soldiers waited, with Orsini men stationed all
around. "Very well. I will send you an escort."

"Thank you." Father Uccello inclined his head and
joined a pair of men who walked toward a round barrel
of a building topped by an angel that stood alongside the
river.

Rinaldo flashed that grin again, one without humor or
joy, then led Elisha back to their horses.

The next day, although Rinaldo sent the soldiers for Uccello, he insisted the conditions were not good for travel
and they must stay close to the palace, subjecting Elisha
to another frustrating day in close quarters with the restless captain and a handful of men who had not accompanied the tribune on his latest escapade. The morning
after, Rinaldo brought out a book of Petrarch's poetry,
expounding on the poet's devotion to the cause of Rome,
then regaled Elisha with readings, poems of love, and
heartfelt tributes to the glories of the past.

Elisha had already heard far too much when he decided to simply cut in to the next break as the captain
searched for a page. "Look, do we need to wait for Father Uccello in order to visit the other churches?"

Rinaldo gave a jerk as if Elisha had struck him. "No,
no, it's not that. San Giovanni belongs to the Colonna,

and they do not care for you. As for the other, Santa Maria Maggiore has no archpriest just now—"

"Doesn't that mean you can simply get the key? Or are the streets still unsafe today?" He had been aware of shouting earlier, but no more than the usual riots.

"You would not wish to go without the stories of the saints and all of the relics. There is only so much I can tell you."

"Didn't Father Uccello return yesterday, when you sent the soldiers?" But the priest had not come to any of the communal meals. Was he that dismayed by Elisha's sorcery?

"Yes, of course, but he is indisposed." Rinaldo gripped the poetry book against his chest. "But we could find another priest, perhaps. Shall I make inquiries?"

Elisha pushed off the bench where he had sat through the poetry reading, extending his senses, concentrating on the agitated captain. "You've been with me all morning, since breakfast, how do you know Father Uccello is busy?"

Rinaldo's presence rang with righteousness, deception, and fear. "There is council business, of course, things he has not been addressing since he has been touring with you."

"Cola rode out on Thursday. He's not even here to meet with the council."

Rinaldo lost all attempt at a smile. "There are many kinds of business."

With a swift hand, Elisha snatched away the book and seized Rinaldo's shoulder. "What business?"

Rinaldo ducked his head, a vein leaping at his throat. "There was a monk found dead after we visited San Paolo. He had a wife, and she says that some things were stolen, some relics which he always carried. A monk with a wife! Imagine it." Rinaldo gave a high-pitched chuckle. "When the Holy Father returns—"

Cold washed over Elisha, his skin prickling. He thought the mancers would shred the monk's body for talismans: Instead, Vertuollo had it returned to the monastery. "Why haven't we heard about this death before now?"

"The body was not found right away, and of course,

the monks must first speak with the Colonna, who are their patrons. It has taken some time before this matter came to the attention of the tribune. He must stand for justice, do you see? When he is asked by the Colonna to arrest an Orsini, well, he must be sure of the truth, and so far he has had no answers. Questions must be asked, they must be answered, but—" Rinaldo silenced himself before he said more.

Il Silencio—"He's arrested Father Uccello?"

"We must be seen to be even-handed, do you see?" Rinaldo shoved against Elisha, breaking free of his grip. "We are blamed for persecuting the Colonna, and they say we would allow an Orsini to escape even murder—but it is not true!"

"Where is he? Where are they holding him?"

"Do not concern yourself with our justice, Dottore. You have no right to interfere."

"In the torture of an innocent man? Good Lord, it's not a right, it's a duty."

"How say you that he is innocent? He returned to the confessional while you and I went to visit the apostle's tomb—he was seen by the other monks, and it was they who found the body, but only after our party had gone." Rinaldo widened his eyes as he stared at Elisha. "This is how we know it was not you, Dottore. If Uccello had found the body, he would have reported it—unless he killed the man himself."

Elisha's chest tightened. If he confessed to the killing, his mission was through, whether by his own arrest, or his identification by the mancers. And if he did not? Never had the struggle between body and soul, between world and spirit, felt so acute. "Where is he held?"

"It is a matter for Rome, for the tribune."

"Father Uccello promised me a penance, and he has not given it." Elisha stared down the other man, projecting his anger, if not the reason behind it. "If you don't let me see him, you stand between my soul and its salvation."

Rinaldo searched his face and finally gave a nod. "Very well, Dottore, for the sake of your soul."

Chapter 37

As they hurried through the palace corridors and outside, down to the prison in the depths of the hill, Elisha considered he should be grateful they had not simply hanged the priest out of hand. But then, if the priest were already dead, Elisha need not face his choice. That thought, rising unbidden, brought bile to the back of his throat as Rinaldo explained their way past the soldiers and inside.

The walls echoed with layers of pain, and Elisha winced as he entered their shadow. Low voices emerged from the gloom beyond the pools of feeble light from the few windows, and they came into a tall room decked with chains and smelling of vomit and urine and blood, together the distinctive scent of men's despair. Shades of those who died here lingered in manacles on the walls or on the machines of torture, their translucent forms caught in distorted postures that no undamaged body could attain. To one side, a half-dozen men clustered around a long, low table: a priest with a rich cassock, a man in Colonna livery and another in Orsini, a few men in the tribune's tabards of blue, one of whom held a slate poised for writing. Chains wrapped from a windlass to a man's feet, blood oozing beneath the shackles, the rest of him concealed by the crowd.

"No, he's not dead," said one man in Italian, prodding the prisoner with a long needle. "A man cannot die on the rack, not really. The heart requires greater trauma to cease. You see? He shows pain."

"Wake him, then," ordered the man with the slate. "The tribune needs the truth."

The slap of flesh on flesh resounded as Elisha pushed his way among them, catching the hand that struck the priest before it could land a second blow. Already, a trickle of blood marked Father Uccello's lips, his head limply resting against his grotesquely stretched arm. His broken fingers curled against his bloody palms, and one ear had been cut from his head.

"Ah," said the man as he pulled his arm from Elisha's grasp, "this must be the foreigner who claims he is a doctor." Italian again, meaning that Elisha was not meant to understand him.

By the long robe and kit of supplies the fellow carried, he was, indeed, a doctor himself. Elisha's jaw clenched. The insult sent him straight back to the days of his barbering in London, when the physicians and surgeons sneered at him even as he did their dirty bidding. In English he said, quietly, "May your penis rot and drown you in your own piss."

The other doctor frowned at him. "What does he say? Who here speaks German?" but from the table of the rack came a single, sharp exhalation, the ghost of Father Uccello's laugh.

The priest's face ran with sweat, his scarred eye toward the side where his tormentors clustered, forcing him to twist his neck if he would see them at all, but making the blood from his missing ear flow down into his eye and mouth.

The others parted for Elisha as he circled the top of the rack, the torturer glowering at him through his hood, his hand on the windlass though he did not crank it.

"Father." Elisha lightly touched the priest's cheek. The hazel eye fluttered open, but his face twitched away.

"Please don't touch me," he breathed, and only Elisha's magical awareness caught the words, so quiet, and so damning.

Elisha withdrew his hand. By now, Rinaldo had joined them, bowing, apologizing, explaining about the penance owed. Elisha's muscles drew ever tighter. Across the way, the young priest in his stiff, gold-embellished chasuble listened gravely, and said, in accented Italian, "Indeed, if the confession was interrupted, as you say, that could have some consequence for both men's souls."

The torturer and the doctor shared a look as if to dismiss anything the priest might say, but the tribune's magistrate gave a sigh. "It is the tribune's great wish that the Holy Father shall return to Rome, that is why these things must be carried out with such care."

"We did not turn his body over to your justice so that his soul might be at risk," said the young priest. He reached beneath his chasuble to produce a purple stole, likewise edged in gold. "We should allow the sacrament to be completed."

"But if the priest is a murderer, does that not bode ill for the soul of the foreigner?" asked a portly fellow who wore the badge of the Colonna.

"He is no murderer, nor thief, but a man of God!" A tall man, brightly emblazoned with red and white Orsini stripes, loomed over the Colonna representative. "Your philandering monk earned the doom of the Lord for his iniquities—no doubt the relics missing were translated back to their saints to preserve them from such venial men."

"A theft has occurred and a man has died—"

"While the tribune is away to make his righteous battle, I am the arbiter of justice," the magistrate insisted.

Elisha ignored their squabble, drawing inward, sinking to his knees by Father Uccello's strained right arm. He clasped his own hands together to keep from strangling the mad combatants or clapping their heads together with the force they deserved. "Leave me to my confession—I beg of you," Elisha said in German, his voice firm. The arguing men faltered, glancing his way as Rinaldo repeated the request in Italian.

Colonna man clearly, understood his words without translation, bristling at the request, but the Orsini representative made a gracious bow of his head. "Dottore, come to San Pietro when this terrible business is done and help us to mourn for our lost cousin."

As if Father Uccello were already dead. If Elisha could help it, he would not die. And yet . . . Elisha's eyes burned. He could stop it all right now, simply by claiming the murder and producing some stolen relics as evidence. He could condemn himself instead, cutting short his mission and damning the city of Rome and all the pilgrims who would come there to terror, torture and death.

"Our churches are open to you, Dottore," the Colonna man barked in German, "as to any representative of our noble emperor. Truly, you should have come to us immediately, for our longstanding friendships with the North."

Raising his hand in a gesture for silence, the young priest said, "Who receives entrance to San Giovanni is up to me, my lord." He let his gaze trace Elisha's face and figure, then reached out the purple stole and coiled it on Father Uccello's skinny, bare chest. "But if your penance should demand it, then you may come." He tucked his hands beneath the chasuble and retreated carefully, aiming a dark-eyed glance at each of the others until they accompanied him across the chamber. At the back of the group, Rinaldo herded them onward, leaving Elisha alone with the man he had condemned to die.

"Bless me, Father, for I have sinned." Elisha's voice trembled as he spoke, and he squeezed his eyes shut. Over the tortured form of the priest, the warring families had given him just what he needed: access to the sealed churches. That knowledge rested like a blade that cut his heart with every beat. To earn the lives of thousands, of all of those pilgrims who would follow, Uccello would die. Perhaps that was the Christian way.

Again, that short, sharp breath as if of laughter. "My son," the priest whispered, "there has never been such a sinner as you."

Father Uccello's eye blinked fiercely as a trickle of stinging sweat edged among his lashes. Elisha reached out to wipe it, but the priest said, "Please, don't."

Once more, Elisha drew back his hand, slowly, pained by the effort to restrain his instinct.

"A liar you are, but indeed a healer. No other man would be so willing to touch." He took a slightly deeper breath, the purple cloth rising and hitching downward. "When they bind a man like this, they take from him the most intimate freedom. They chose when to touch, with what, how often, and how hard."

Images seared through Elisha's memory: his own arms pinioned as a surgeon burned him repeatedly for answers he could not give; Katherine's daughter, bound, slaughtered, and flayed; Thomas, finally freed from his chains, but struck with terror at Elisha's touch. Since Elisha witnessed the death of his first witch, and the more so since he discovered the sorcery within himself, he had dedicated his hands to healing, and now the priest denied him.

Father Uccello sighed, "None but my mother ever touched me in the name of love."

"Father," Elisha began, but what could he say? The one thing that must be said—that Elisha himself was guilty—must not be spoken.

"You wish a penance from me? You would reform yourself, witch? But I have not the strength nor freedom to burn away the devil's mark." He tried to wet his cracked lips, to no avail. "It was my mother who burned it from me, and gave me up to God, so the Devil would not find me. I wish to God that I could do the same for you."

The old scar stretched against the priest's lean face. Elisha swallowed hard. "Your eye?"

"Was once as blue as yours, witch."

"Yes, I am a witch," Elisha whispered forcefully, "as was the monk who died. If he and his allies succeed, they will turn this city into one of the pits of Hell."

"And you and your allies would not?" A breath of a laugh.

"Magic is not of the Devil, Father, it is of the flesh, born in a man like the color of his hair."

"Or the color of his eyes." Father Uccello's remaining

eye flashed open. "More lies. If what you say were true, then my life has been for naught."

Mutilated and made a priest by his mother's superstition. Elisha's own mother once believed much the same. Softly, Elisha answered, "Then believe that I am evil—it is near enough the truth. You could condemn me with a word."

"And break the Holy Sacrament? Is this the temptation your master sends for me? No, I will not do it—not even to cast out a witch."

"I can take away the pain," Elisha said, aware that this, too, would seem a temptation, but he could not hold back.

Father Uccello let out an angry snort. "Touch me not with your foul spells." His eye slid shut, the purple stole rising and falling upon his fragile chest.

Elisha bowed his head, his forehead resting on his knotted hands, and tried to think of some way out of this. The priest would die for Elisha's secrets rather than to break the sacrament, and if Elisha revealed himself, his quest to stop the mancers would fail, for the sake of this one man. How many, then, would break and bleed and suffer? Elisha's every muscle ached, paralyzed with the choice that he must make.

Across the room, the voices of the tormentors rose a little louder, and Elisha raised his head at last. He pushed himself stiffly up and gathered the silken stole into his rough hands. If Father Uccello noticed the loss, he made no sign. The young priest of San Giovanni did, however, tipping his chin up in inquiry, and Elisha gave a nod, drawing them back. Over the rack, he said, "If a doctor must be present, let it be me."

With a mournful face, Rinaldo translated his words, and the Italian doctor snorted, shaking his head. "Very well. I have living patients to attend to in any case." He turned abruptly and left.

The others resumed their places, the hooded torturer by the windlass, the tribune's official with his tablet poised in case the priest should speak, the representatives of the warring houses glaring at each other with the buffer of the younger priest between. "I am Pierre Roger," the young priest said in his accented Latin, "Archpriest of San Giovanni. I can see you are a merciful man. Father Uccello is blessed to have you to oversee his trial."

Trial? Is that what they called this? He wished he could be merciful, taking away Father Uccello's pain, or even his wretched life, with a touch. "Thank you, Father," he managed, barely restraining his anger, or his despair.

The tribune's man tapped his stylus on his slate, and spoke in a tone that verged on boredom. "So, Uccello Orsini, did you kill the monk, Brother Tigo?"

When the priest said nothing, the official gave a slight nod. The torturer turned his windlass barely an inch, and the prisoner's arms stretched with the crackling sound of torn cartilage.

Elisha winced, stifling a cry on behalf of Il Silencio. If Elisha would face these next few hours, he must not feel. He drew up the strength of Death, the chill that rose within him, flesh and bone. In his old practice, when he operated on difficult cases, Elisha used to hum his mother's songs, using the sound to focus his mind and distract himself from the pain that he must cause in surgery. Now, sorcery filled that need, smothering his feelings, detaching him from his surroundings. The first time he had done it, allowing Death to overwhelm him, he almost had not returned. Without Brigit's touch, he might have lost himself to the dreadful silence of inhumanity. He refused to go so far again. Instead, he layered the cold carefully, building up his armor, letting himself be present, but absenting his emotions and the long years of reflexive compassion. He heard the official's pointless questions, the creaking of chain, the tearing of muscle, without response. Count Vertuollo, the warden of the Valley, returned the monk's corpse to the confessional for this, to frame Father Uccello and ensure that he would never reveal Elisha's secrets. It was a gift, from one sensitive to another, and it sickened Elisha to accept.

Only a few months ago he had been the student to Brigit's secret tutoring. Sorcery he learned from Brigit, before moving on to desire, deceit, betrayal, and a hundred other lessons painful to recall. Lessons he seemed to have taken too well to heart.

When the prisoner's arms gave way, his neck at first arching, then allowing his head to loll to the side, Elisha lay his fingers gently at the man's throat, confirming that his heart beat still, and withdrew them promptly, noting Father Uccello's twinge at even that careful touch, but noting it as a symptom, with no need for his own response.

"The trouble is, he's been racked before," said the Colonna man.

"We started with his fingers, and the ear, and that gave no result," the magistrate pointed out.

"He may simply no longer possess the power of speech, in which case, there can be no confession. Perhaps you should try with the boot?"

"Mmm." The official swept his glance over their victim, and gave a Roman shrug. "I think you are right about the rack." He waved his hand to the torturer, who released the windlass, letting the malformed body contract as much as it was able, then grabbed one broken hand, pulling it closer to unclasp the manacle.

Elisha placed his hand on the torturer's muscular arm. "I'll do it." The torturer twitched at the chill touch of his hand, but let him take over.

To his patient, Elisha said, "I must touch you, Father. Please forgive me." With minimal contact, Elisha moved to each limb in turn and freed the catches, sliding the manacles from the ruined flesh with precision.

Without healing, and without feeling the pain that must throb in the prisoner's body, Elisha gently brought the priest's arms down to rest across his body, his battered hands cradled on his own yielding flesh. Then Elisha swept off his cloak, and draped it like a blanket over the trembling man. Father Uccello's eye barely opened, his lips parted, but he did not say a word. The golden pin of the sacrificial ram gleamed in the torchlight.

"Father Uccello never shall yield," said the Orsini man. "He is famous for his fortitude."

"What do you suggest, then? He should be freed? He should merely lie in prison while our retainers have swung from the scaffold?" The Colonna man waved his crimson arms.

While they argued, Elisha found a clean basin of water and a rag. He soaked the cloth, then brought it back, laying the corner in Father Uccello's mouth so that he could suck a few drops of moisture.

"Bene! Hang him now!" The Orsini man shouted.

"Now? But there is no crowd to witness his perfidy."

The tribune's official watched Elisha move about the prisoner, taking each tiny action to ease his flesh, if he could not ease the priest's spirit. Rinaldo, who had spent much of the time pacing some way off, approached and murmured with the magistrate, gesturing to Father Uccello's covered form.

Straightening, rubbing his back, Elisha pierced his armor just enough to apply his magical senses to listening.

"—appease the Colonna," Rinaldo was saying, "we must hang him. The tribune will understand this when he returns. If we wait and announce the execution, the citizens who attend will see what has been done in the name of justice. They may not understand, especially without the tribune to explain."

The two men stared down at the tortured man, then the magistrate nodded. "I do not believe we must continue this trial any longer. Four brothers of the San Paolo abbey testified that Uccello Orsini was the last to see the dead man alive, and who but another cleric would know to search for his relics?" He stood firmly and announced, "I find Uccello Orsini guilty as charged, sentenced to be hanged, sentence to be carried out immediately." To the torturer, he said, "Have you a rope?"

"Si, Signore. Already waiting." Tossing aside Elisha's cloak, the torturer bent to gather up the prisoner. "On your feet!"

Father Uccello's chest rose and fell with a short, sharp breath, his cheeks hinting at his ironic smile.

Once more, Elisha intercepted the torturer. "Lead the way. I will bring him."

"Get him up, then." The torturer stepped back, pointedly waiting.

Still, Elisha took a moment to replace his cloak about his shoulders, pushing it back to keep his arms free. He knelt at the side of the bloody table, meeting the gaze of that single eye. He reached out and gathered Father Uccello in his arms. "You wished me never to touch you," he murmured, "and yet someone must. Maybe you would prefer their brutality, but I cannot abide it."

As if these words broke open the seal of memory, Uccello's awareness drifted back, and Elisha's acute focus on his patient, along with the close contact, carried the memory into Elisha's flesh more vividly than anything but a witch's sending had ever done. In the vision they shared, Uccello lay again upon the rack, his flesh stronger, younger—just as shattered—while voices rose around him.

"This gains us nothing." Emperor Ludwig, his dour face framed by hair more black than gray, loomed into Uccello's half-sight. "He won't support us, not me, nor my pope. And he's only one."

"As you say—he is only one. Others might," an urbane voice answering, with a different accent. Not German, not Italian. Uccello turned his head weakly. "He should not see me," the man barked. "I should not even have come here."

"Von Stubben, hold him," Ludwig snapped.

The doctor caught the priest's jaw and forced him to look the other way, his good eye pressed against his imprisoned arm, but not before Elisha glimpsed the stranger who had spoken, a man with a florid face and liver-spotted tonsure, clad in the robe of a bishop.

"Too many kings still oppose us, and we cannot dominate the Church this way, with a foreign pope and a campaign of torture," Ludwig continued. "Why did I ever listen to you?"

"Because we gave you ascendance over your rivals," said the other man, very carefully. "Because without us, you are merely the Duke of Bavaria, and barely that. If the other rulers will not accede, then we will replace them

*with those more tractable, and we will find another way to
bring the Church to heel."*

"You never will, Renart. I haven't, none of my predecessors have."

*"None of your predecessors had the Chosen to support
him." A cold, hard voice. Renart the mancer, the master of
France.*

*Ludwig gave an exasperated sigh. "If you would topple
the Church, you'll need more than a pope—you'll need a
miracle of Biblical proportions," he added with a harsh
chuckle.*

The words reminded Elisha of the rabbi of Heidelberg, pointing out the power of the Church, suggesting
how great an effort would be required to overcome it.

*"Your Majesty," von Stubben ventured. "Shall I bring
back the torturer or the executioner to finish him?" His
hand still pressed Uccello's face down, just as he had,
more recently, smothered a baby with that very hand. His
other hand roved over the priest's scarred eye socket, tracing the bone, pressing at the center, pressing again, harder.
"I should welcome the chance to open up a scar like this,
for a better understanding of the healing of such a
wound." He clutched the priest's head in his hands with a
hideous greed.*

Elisha burned with Uccello's silent fear, but at least
he knew that the foul doctor was dead. Harald had killed
von Stubben too kindly.

*"No—let him go. Let him serve as an example of im-
perial power every day he lives and breathes. There's an
army approaching, and I must withdraw. Thank you for
coming, Renart, but I'm afraid we're done here." Footfalls
pounded away, receding as Ludwig departed.*

*Other footfalls drew nearer, and Uccello's battered
body tensed. "Biblical proportions," Renart muttered
softly.*

"Your Grace?" von Stubben said. "What is your will?"

"You heard the emperor," said Renart. "Let him live."

"I heard him, Your Grace, but I know whom I serve."

*"Good man, von Stubben. See you keep it that way."
Renart's hand, stinging with cold, settled on Uccello's*

bound ankle. "Another man, I might have to cut out his tongue, but you," Renart's voice sank low, into the flesh, "you won't say a word, will you? You know how to keep silent."

His fingers traced along Uccello's leg, up and up, feeling the pulse jump at the inner thigh. "Oh, but you would be so delicious to take."

Uccello's memory gave the words a sexual cast, his stomach roiling with terror, but Elisha knew better. Renart's hand followed the line from the priest's belly, taut with fear, to his sternum, to his throat, to the tip of his chin, the line Renart's flensing blade would follow if he sliced open the priest and peeled off his skin. Where the mancer's fingers moved, the priest's flesh flared with cold as if he had, indeed, cut deep. The mancer's presence swelled with a sick pleasure at Uccello's response.

No wonder the priest fought against sorcery. No wonder he fled Elisha's touch. As he carried the priest up the stairs in procession, Elisha's armor sank away, warming his arms, allowing Father Uccello to feel the beat of his heart, using his strength to banish memory.

"You are a very devil of compassion," said Father Uccello, in words that Elisha knew only through the contact they shared. The priest channeled the last of his strength into his neck, refusing himself the comfort of resting his head against Elisha's shoulder.

Long rays of sun stretched their shadows upward, Elisha's form tall and dark, the priest's dangling feet drawing downward, the Pieta in silhouette—except Mary bore her son down from the cross, while Elisha carried Father Uccello to his death. They mounted the steps to the gallows, a scant few workers ceasing their tasks to turn and see, the mancer workman among them, gazing with hunger. Elisha stopped at the edge, and carefully let down Father Uccello's legs, his feet settling on the wood, though Elisha still supported the his weight as the executioner prepared the rope.

Brilliant sun gleamed in Elisha's eyes as he waited, embracing the man his own silence condemned to death. Tears burned, but he did not let them fall, though his blinking increased, and he tried to blame it on the sun. The priest's heart beat steadily—his legendary fortitude maintaining him—but his presence fragmented into spirals of fear, pain, weakness, worry, everything he worked so hard to keep from revealing with his keen wit and powerful faith. Elisha wished the priest had been a magus: he would have given much for such an ally.

Wood creaked as the executioner approached. He dropped the noose over the priest's head, tightening it against his throat. Elisha's heart raced. At his own execution, he had been convinced of rescue, not resigned to death by his own virtue.

"Shhhhh," breathed Father Uccello, and Elisha met his eye. Golden hazel, damp with pain, the priest blinked back at him, then he bowed his head to Elisha's shoulder. With his final words, the priest released resentment, even letting go the fear that Elisha's compassion was merely a temptation of the Devil.

In a voice that echoed through Elisha, flesh and bone, Father Uccello said, "Te absolvo."

Chapter 38

❖

For a moment, he clutched Father Uccello against him, but the executioner nudged Elisha's arm, and he had to let go and step away.

Knees buckling as if he moved to prayer, the priest sank gracefully from the platform. Rope creaked, bone cracked. No cheers, no applause, only the voice of Father Pierre, murmuring prayers.

Elisha stood rigid, his back to the open square, waiting. The Valley swirled open beside him, more brilliant than the glowing sunset. Father Uccello's shade roiled outward, shedding darkness, shedding fear and pain and worry, such a singular glow that Elisha gasped as he felt it rush through him. No sense of betrayal clung to the dead man—that burden was Elisha's alone—then all sense of Father Uccello vanished into the wild Valley, and Elisha could breathe again. Count Vertuollo's blood marking on the pavement below shivered in Elisha's awareness, but he would gain no power from this death. Doubtless he expected Elisha to claim it for his own.

Immediately, the Orsini man demanded the priest's body be cut down so they could take it for burial. The executioner, used to keeping the corpses on the beam until their example was made plain, refused, and another argument began. Ignoring them both, Elisha laid his cape upon the scaffold and reached out to the swinging corpse, catching it in a one-armed embrace, cold against his own cold breast. Now, Father Uccello had no choice but to submit to his touch. Still, Elisha handled him gently, cutting the rope high up before he laid the priest upon his cape. He removed the noose, but kept it close. The cape itself, stained with blood and tears, resonated with death and would be a fine talisman. Elisha wished he could set it aside after putting it to such service, but he might need its strength one day.

The executioner noticed what he was doing and pounded back up the stairs to shout at him in Italian, but Elisha reached to shut the priest's single eye and wrapped the body with regal fur.

"Dottore," said the sonorous voice of Father Pierre, and Elisha glanced at him, the priest's face level with his own for he still knelt upon the platform. In his accented Latin, the young priest asked, "Is this a part of your penance?"

Father Uccello had given him none: but his absolution in the face of Elisha's unrepentant guilt was penance enough. "Yes, Father."

The young man's dark eyes rested on him, then he gave a slight nod. "I will smooth the way."

"I thought you were with the Colonna."

His handsome face furrowed, and he shook his head. "I am with His Holiness, the Pope. The Colonna cannot dictate to us, not really. And Lord Colonna has already ridden out, which shall make things easier."

"Thank you."

Pierre inclined his head and moved on, stilling the virulence of the executioner's words with a lift of his hand. Young, he might be, but he had the maturity of grace.

"Here—" Rinaldo appeared on the platform, carrying a swath of white cloth and knelt at Elisha's side. "This is better."

Together, they wrapped the body of Father Uccello in the white shroud, while Rinaldo muttered explanations. "The tribune regrets this, you know. We delayed as long as possible to make our inquiries. He had no alternative, faced with such a murder. And with the need to show his strength, he could not bend the law, even for a member of his council like Father Uccello—no, especially not for a member of council." His hands worked too fast, brusque as if he tried to distract himself with extra movement. "Did Father Pierre say that the Lord Colonna has gone out?"

"He did." Elisha hardly needed his magical senses to note Rinaldo's agitation in asking, or his excitement at hearing the Colonna leader had left the city.

"Perhaps now we shall have some peace and be able to forward our plans. At least you may visit the churches, eh?" A brief flash of teeth in imitation of a smile.

"I think Father Pierre will smooth the way there, as well."

"He is ... a man of influence," said Rinaldo ominously. "Given his parentage ..." a shrug, then, noticing Elisha's stare, he continued, "Rumor is that 'Holy Father' is more than a title to Father Pierre. Before the Pope took the name of Clement VI, he, too, was called Pierre Roger."

Elisha replaced his cape on his shoulders, tucking the hanging rope carefully at his back to burn it later. If Father Pierre were indeed the pope's bastard, he wore it well; such a rumor could give a man infamy rather than influence.

Father Pierre moved away into the city while the Orsini retainers brought up a few horses and loaded Father Uccello's body on one of them. Elisha and Rinaldo watched the silent procession depart through the broad gates into a city grown dangerously quiet as well. Was Rome itself the target? Would springing a hundred mancers through tainted relics to terrorize the pilgrims be enough? Certes, that would subvert the very meaning of the relics, transforming prayers from saintly to demonic intercession.

"May we visit San Giovanni after supper?" Elisha asked, eager to finish his mission in Rome, the more so since he had shared that chilling vision with Father Uccello.

"It is across the city, Dottore. Why not remain another night and ride there in the morning?"

"I have spent weeks here already, without making my

report to Queen Margaret. Besides, Lord Colonna thinks he controls San Giovanni, doesn't he? With him away, it might be easier to see it now."

"Very well, Dottore. Let us finish our visits and return you to your queen."

After supper, they rode swiftly through the streets to San Giovanni where an altar boy was convinced to fetch the archpriest, in spite of the glowering presence of four armed soldiers at the entrance. If Father Pierre thought it strange they came so soon, he said nothing, but conducted them gracefully through his domain.

Like the others, the Church of San Giovanni showed its age, as decrepit and rat-infested as the rest—the skittering of claws preceded their torchlight as they made a circuit of the church. Ahead, as if they herded the rats toward Hell, something gleamed whenever the torchlight passed between columns. When they had visited several side altars, and Elisha left his mark on two of them, they emerged from the gloom to the glory of the main altar, a marble table rising up from the scuffed paving and topped by a canopy of silver. Torchlight glittered from its rich embellishments: stones and enamels and images of saints. Dazzled, Elisha stared up at it until Father Pierre, smiling at his reaction, urged him forward, and he stepped up beneath the gleaming dome.

"Is it not glorious in celebration of the Lord?" The priest spread his hands. "We are blessed indeed that it has escaped both fire and thievery."

Elisha nodded, allowing his senses to unfurl, his hands raised as if he could feel the blessing. The dead pulsed above him, a jostling host of saints and martyrs. "Glorious," Elisha echoed. He hoped his own interventions would not serve to destroy it.

They followed the priest from the main church to a side hall containing a set of broad stone steps. "The Scala Pilata," Father Pierre intoned, "which brought our Lord Jesu Cristo to the hall of Pilate." He crossed himself, and the others followed. "They may be mounted only upon your knees, as befits our humility before the sacrifice of the Lord."

Elisha suppressed a groan as the priest bent his knee, and Rinaldo joined him. "The pilgrim who so climbs the stairs is granted an indulgence, a freedom from his present state of sin," Father Pierre informed them, glancing up at Elisha. His dark, earnest stare brought Elisha, too, to his knees, and together they climbed until Elisha's knees and back ached, his mind humming with the sound of the priest's Pater Nosters. All Rome determined to sway him from sin—or to tear him apart when sin could not be avoided. Every moment he spent in the city was a penance.

Rain fell steadily when they emerged, exhausted, into the night. "Thank you, Father," Elisha said.

Father Pierre reached out, taking Elisha's hand between his. "Thank you, Dottore, for your service to Father Uccello. No man, even an enemy, should go to his grave without such an attendant."

The intensity of the young priest's words and the fervor in his touch left Elisha speechless. The truth dragged his shoulders down, and rain seeped along the back of his neck, over the scars of his own hanging. Elisha nodded and turned away to mount his horse, his breath catching in his chest. Grateful for the rain to match his misery, he signaled to Rinaldo his readiness.

Rinaldo and Elisha rode back through the rain, finding the gates thrown wide and thronged with the shouting, jostling soldiers of the tribune's army, finally come back to Rome.

After sliding down from his mount, Rinaldo hurried off into the crowd to find his master—but not before ordering their companions to escort Elisha someplace to warm up. And not to let him out of their sight. As it happened, his keepers' goal and the captain's coincided; the tribune celebrated his own return in the capitol's main hall, a huge fire lighting frescoes of grapes being harvested and maidens dancing. They reminded Elisha of his one dance with Rosalynn, before she became—so briefly—queen, and died. Elisha shivered as they led him toward the hearth where every prop and table already bore a dripping load of cloaks and hoods.

He stripped his wet over-garments, draping his cape where he could keep an eye on it, but the shivering did not cease, even as he stood too near the fire.

"My good doctor," boomed the tribune, his voice, as ever, so much stronger than the man. He spread his hands to Elisha. "I hear so many tales—it seems I've missed quite an exciting time in Rome." For a moment, his face bore no expression, then split into a grin. "Of course, it is always exciting in Rome! We suffer the birth pangs of a new nation."

At the tribune's shoulder, Rinaldo lurked, dodging Elisha's glance.

"My captain tells me you are a liar, he thinks you understand our language very well indeed," the tribune went on. "But I have heard what you did for Father Uccello, and I cannot believe you are not also a good man."

After a moment, Elisha said, "Thank you."

Cola raised an eyebrow that nudged the soggy laurel wreath atop his damp curls. "You don't deny it?"

"Being a good man?" Elisha said. "Oh, yes, I do."

At that, Cola tipped back his head and laughed aloud. "Should I trust you for your service to Father Uccello? Or should I rack you for your secrets? How can I know these things?"

Over his shoulder, Rinaldo's face paled, as if they shared in that moment the vision of Father Uccello's body, stretched beyond healing.

"We share a goal, Tribune, that of making Rome safe again, for her people and for her pilgrims," Elisha said.

Cola laughed again. "Rinaldo! You claimed he spoke our language, but it is a poor version at best." He folded his arms. "Dottore. You say we share this goal. So far, you have stood with me, with the people of Rome. Would you swear an oath to this?"

"To defend the people of Rome? I would."

"And me?"

Elisha took a deep breath and composed his words carefully. "The cause of Rome is larger than any one man."

The tribune pursed his lips, then nodded slowly. "In-

deed. Well said." He waved a hand and a servant poured
them sweet wine, warmed over the fire. "To Rome."

"To Rome!" Rinaldo cried, raising his goblet, and others around them took up the call, shouting or drinking.

Elisha, too, drained his mug, the sweet heat soothing
his throat and sending tendrils up through his aching
skull. He absently rubbed at the scars beneath his white-
streaked hair and considered getting roaring drunk for
the first time in years. "Forgive me, Tribune, Captain, but
it's been a long day and I need some rest."

"Of course! But you deserve more than to share a
room with the guard. We shall make up another chamber
for you. We have now a little room we had not before."
The tribune grinned in a way that made Elisha nervous.

When he was shown the room, he found his concern
justified. It was not the dungeon as it might have been
if he had truly lost their trust. Instead they gave him the
austere, windowless chamber that once belonged to the
tribune's councilor, Father Uccello. A crucifix graced
the wall over the bed, the weary, wounded Christ hanging over him. No, they did not send him to the dungeon—
not yet—but this room was a weighty reminder of what
could be.

Chapter 39

❦

The next morning as Elisha ate alone in the dining hall, Rinaldo thundered down the stairs, still gripping the rail as he called, "Dottore!" though Elisha sat only a few feet away. "Do you still wish to attend Santa Maria?" His thin face suffused with anger, knuckles whitening.

"Yes, but—"

"I hope that now is a good time."

"Yes." Elisha followed eagerly in Rinaldo's wake. One more church, and then Elisha must determine how to strip the mancers' power here and break their plan forever.

Rinaldo walked with a vengeance, boots pounding the stones, and it took no magic to sense his mood. Overhead, blue threaded the clouds as the rainy weather broke at last, but it had grown so cold that a few white flakes drifted down around them and lingered on the damp stones.

Rinaldo snorted at the sky. "Santa Maria Maggiore was founded on such a day, when a miraculous snow fell, showing where the Virgin's church should be built. She is also called the Lady of the Snows." He snapped out each word.

"If you'd rather not escort me, Captain—"

"I am assigned this duty, and I am fulfilling it. This, at least, is a task that still makes sense." He darted a glance at Elisha as if daring him to deny it.

For a moment, they pounded along without speaking, Elisha puffing to keep pace with Rinaldo's long strides as the church came in view, its broad plaza pitted from missing stones. "It's good to have a task like that," Elisha ventured carefully, "especially if other things seem nonsensical."

"Have you heard what he has done?" Rinaldo stopped and swung about before the doors of the church.

"Only that he led a great victory."

Rinaldo's lips compressed, and he pointed up again, this time, at the campanile that towered over the graceful church. "Santa Maria has the highest tower in all of Rome. Perhaps in all of Italy. It is not to be missed. The tower is just complete—well, nearly so—before il Papa has gone to France." He hammered on the door until a bleary-eyed old priest emerged. "Come." Rinaldo grabbed the old man's lantern and clumped off into the gloom, Elisha hurrying to catch up. Pointing to each altar as they loomed up from the darkness, Rinaldo barked, "A Colonna family chapel," or "Dedicated to the Virgin of the Snows," barely pausing long enough for Elisha to cross himself. Whichever mancer watched the palace must have missed their speedy exit, for they shared the church with no one. No matter: Anyplace in Rome where the dead lay, there, too, lay Vertuollo's power.

Elisha's attunement needed to be a hurried process, but he had grown accustomed to tracking the fresh relics and now it seemed they cried out to him from the moment he let his senses unfurl. They whimpered with pain, fear and grief, animated by their captured tortures as he marked them. Elisha thought of Father Uccello and prayed that the Orsini would keep his body safe until it could be buried, rather than allow it to be hacked to bits by those eager to taste the betrayal of the priest's wrongful death. Perhaps it was these thoughts, together with Rinaldo's agitation, that lent an ominous weight to the day. Elisha felt that death mounted around him, lingering nearby, the Valley echoing close to his heart, his old injuries throbbing, from the piercings in his skull to the wrist he used to create affinity with Mordecai when he

performed that miraculous healing. His breath misted
the air and he caught himself rubbing his arms, grateful
for his fur-lined cloak as Rinaldo hurried him from relic
to relic with the dizzying pace of his swinging lantern.

"At last, the tower," Rinaldo announced, and Elisha
wished he could beg off climbing to the top—he was no
longer sure if Rinaldo even believed the excuse he had
given for making these visits. In an especially shadowed
corner, the captain pushed aside a grille and mounted
the steps in the base of the tower.

By the time they emerged into a stone portico near
the top—Elisha a few paces behind—Elisha's legs ached,
and he gasped for breath.

Rinaldo slumped, arms folded, against the low wall
opposite. "Apologies, Dottore," he muttered. "I realize
our visit has been too quick. It is only that I am in a state,
as you must have noticed."

Elisha waved this away, bracing his hands on his knees
to catch his breath.

"A great victory, you said." The captain sighed. "Our
first great victory in quite some time, and he taints it with
his fervor. In his excitement after the victory he had two
dogs brought to him at the river. He asks one of the
priests to baptize the dogs, to name them after our enemies, yes? It is an insult and a jest—the army laughs.
Until the tribune has those dogs hanged as if they are
criminals." Rinaldo's head sank as he continued the
story. "He makes himself appear the madman. The prisoners he has taken are afraid, of course. They think this
will be the fate of all, even of the barons he has captured"—he pushed off from the wall, standing boldly,
then—"and the barons, they should be punished for
their crimes, it's true! But there is so much fighting, even
among the council, that he doesn't keep the prisoners.
Last night, he gives them pardon, and they all go home.
To what? To make war upon us again, of course!" With a
wild gesture he spun away, then both hands gripped one
of the pillars as his head rested against it.

Rinaldo's tension spread through the air, seeming to
add a chill to the wind that stung Elisha's cheeks. But no,

this was more—a sense of death approaching. Deflecting the other man's emotions, Elisha breathed in the Roman autumn, drawing down the coming winter in spite of the clear blue sky, and he knew it was not only Rinaldo who disturbed the day: that sense of foreboding had not left him. Spreading his senses, Elisha turned a slow circle, taking in the city below him.

The tower of Santa Maria showed Rome in all her tattered glory, the dark thundering river as it gathered the hundred churches in its broad arm, leaving the angel's round castle to defend San Pietro on its distant hill. Ruined palaces and broken homes marred the tight alleys and cluttered the piazzas, including an expanse of rubble where a few columns still thrust up from the grass over some ancient place. Il Colosseo gaped to the sky not far away, with the city wall beyond it, dividing the city of the living from the vast catacombs of the dead. To the South, a sense of spreading darkness, the mantle of death creeping onwards, with no sign of the cause. And there to the east, where browning fields and overgrown vineyards capped the rolling hills, the ancient road filled with a shifting mass. An army.

Elisha reached out and seized Rinaldo's shoulder, turning him and pulling him close, in spite of his protest. Rinaldo reeled, Elisha's hand supporting him until he could prop himself on the rail. A few distant banners flickered against the sky and both men leaned closer, peering into the distance.

"Colonna?" Elisha murmured, as if they could hear him.

"Sì," Rinaldo breathed, then squared his shoulders and crossed himself. "Si, Colonna. They own estates in that direction. I'm afraid we must cut short our visit."

"Certes," Elisha replied, but they were already running for the stairs, Rinaldo stumbling onward until Elisha caught up the lantern and came along behind to light the way.

Halfway down, Elisha nearly fell as the sharp slice of the Valley cut his awareness. Rinaldo steadied him, frowning, barely waiting for Elisha's nod before starting down again. This had not been the cold, howling external ache of a death, but a subtle, calculated intrusion like a surgical slice.

"Ah, Captain. I was told you would be here." The cultivated tone of Count Vertuollo rolled to meet them as Rinaldo clattered, breathless through the grille at the bottom of the stairs. "Careful now, the floor is uneven."

Forcing himself to slow, Elisha mastered his own breathing and strolled from the grille, offering a tip of his head in greeting. His heart still pounded, and Elisha turned his awareness inward, slowing his pulse, demanding that his body reflect a calm he could not feel. The mancer stood with his hand on Rinaldo's shoulder, supportive or sinister, Elisha could not be sure.

"I was not expecting you, Don Vertuollo." Rinaldo swept a bow, but his glance darted toward Elisha, who instantly regretted his earlier warning against the count. Hopefully, the mancer would not take Rinaldo's agitation personally.

Vertuollo smiled. "I went to pay a call upon the tribune, but I heard that Santa Maria might be open and wished to pay my respects to Our Lady as well."

"As you say, Don Vertuollo. I fear we cannot stay to accompany you." In the lamplight, Rinaldo looked pale, glance darting toward the door where the old priest scowled.

"No? A pity—especially when I have just given my support to bring the Holy Father home. Myself, I have said we should simply go to where he is . . . but I have lately been convinced otherwise." His hair gleamed like honed steel.

Rinaldo squared his shoulders, tearing his eyes from the door. "È vero? Then you have my gratitude and that of all true Romans, Don Vertuollo."

"Alas, I don't believe that my fellow barons are united with the tribune in his bold cause." The count opened his palms. "But I did appreciate his recent magnanimity toward his noble prisoners."

"A victor can afford to be generous," Rinaldo replied stiffly.

"You don't agree with his ... generosity? It takes a great lord indeed to be lenient with his enemies."

"Generosity should come after the victory is complete, Don Vertuollo." The captain's hands tremored at his sides, betraying his eagerness to go.

"Perhaps if he had made an example or two, then the people would once more come together." Folding his hands at his back, Vertuollo nodded slowly, with a murmur of consideration. "I shall pray upon it."

Elisha's throat went dry. Pray. Only in English, so far as he knew, could the word be "prey" as well, a meaning Vertuollo, in Italian, could not intend. Could he?

"But I shall keep you no longer—I see you are on an urgent mission." With a beatific smile, Count Vertuollo dismissed them, giving Elisha no more than a glance, but his presence radiated excitement, and, as Elisha passed, Vertuollo sighed, "Farewell, Brother."

As they hurried through the streets, Rinaldo tossed over his shoulder, "You've said he is our enemy, but you never said why you think this, Dottore. If he has given his support, then surely—"

"No, Captain," Elisha snapped back, jogging to keep up. "A man may fight beside you, may support your cause, for reasons that have nothing to do with honor or justice." And a mancer that sensitive did not come out of his way for a church, but to deliver a message. On the surface, his support seemed genuine, a commitment to the peace of Rome, in the hopes of bringing home the Pope. He spoke as if Elisha had convinced him of this course, the glory of a Holy Jubilee, returning wealth and vitality to a decrepit city.

Sometimes, Elisha caught glimpses of what Rome had been, what it once more could be, but the mancers would use the Holy Year to torture and terrify thousands and bring the Church under their control. Vertuollo spoke of examples and enemies. Thank God he did not know Elisha was among them.

Within an hour of the warning they delivered, bells across the city rang, calling her citizen-soldiers to arms.

Word spread of the Colonna army, and the citizens came, more worried about the barons than about the tribune's erratic behavior. The mob gathered near the gate of San Lorenzo, named for Cola's patron saint by happy coincidence that the tribune was pleased to acknowledge in a rousing speech before the open gates. Any reasonable tyrant would close them, barring out the enemy, but Cola stood so convinced of his own righteousness that he merely shouted louder as the army approached. The Colonna paraded along the wall in all the trappings of nobility, horses decked with mail and silver-fitted bridles, knights in armor, ranks of men-at-arms in the matching Colonna livery. Elisha watched from the shadow of a damaged palace, his back to the stone, the presence of death almost overwhelming now, the shades of the dead flickering among the crowds of the living as if they should soon all be one. Rinaldo stood with the rest of the tribune's army, clad in blue, decked with stars, swords gripped in their shivering hands.

"They think still to oppress us, my good citizens! Do you see how they seek to intimidate? But we are not afraid! We have conquered them before, and so we shall conquer them again!" Cola raised his fist to the sky, drawing a ragged cheer from the crowd.

Off to one side, a number of knights and nobles who remained in the city sat upon their horses, Count Vertuollo among them, drawing Elisha's awareness. All other eyes were on the tribune, in his absurd ancient armor, bare-headed but for the crown of laurel. A few other mancers lurked among the crowd, supporting their master, or simply hoping for their own spoils. The warden lifted his head, shrugging back his cloak as if the afternoon grew too warm for such a thing. Something flashed white, and a dove—symbol of the Holy Spirit, and of the mad tribune—circled overhead.

As the dove soared, people pointed and shouted, calling out prayers, and their cheers grew deafening with sudden conviction. Through it all, an insidious glee crept among them, kindling excitement and the urge for battle. Count Vertuollo extended his influence through the webs of the dead that underlay the very earth of Rome, sending a suggestion that became compulsion as it matched the desires of those it touched. Blood-lust stirred the citizens. Cola's speech had primed them for it, and the dove's flight clinched their conviction, a sign that this desire was sent by God and no other to inflame their spirits for a holy victory. Only Elisha had seen Vertuollo release the dove.

Beyond the gate, one of the young Colonna lords kicked his horse, galloping through the arch, his sword raised to the sky as his horse reared and he called for battle, his face flushed with bravado. The crowd surged forward, cutting off the young man's retreat even as those outside shouted for him to return.

Among the ravening mob surrounding him, the black presence of a mancer flickered with a half-dozen bound shades. Elisha felt again the jittery strength of the mancer he had slain and taken into himself. He wondered if the other mancers—no! Not *other* mancers. He was not one of them. He pushed off from the building, banishing the eagerness for battle that mounted within. He did not want to see the bloodshed, to feel the deaths about to happen here. He could draw off the deaths and deny their power to the mancers lurking in the crowd, but that would only make them angry; even Count Vertuollo encouraged his followers in such pursuits, taking strength where it would not be missed.

Swords clashed, clubs rose and fell, and the young lord in Colonna red screamed as his horse reared once more. Then the horse thundered away, its saddle bare, and Elisha clutched his chest as the Valley ripped open to suck down the soul. The fevered roar of the crowd and the terrible screams of the dead merged into a wall of sound towering up around him.

Elisha plunged into the crowd, angling for the place of first combat. Already, the citizens pushed hard, their few mounted knights galloping ahead, breaking the Colonna parade ranks like a spear point followed by the shaft of armed and angry men. Count Vertuollo was not among the cavalry—having done his part, the master retreated from the massacre that he helped create.

Projecting chill absence to ward off approach, Elisha
moved across the stream of humanity, citizens sidestepping out of his way at his aura of menace, for all the
world as if he were a mancer himself. His hands alone
stayed warm, all of his compassion gathering there, all of
his healing knowledge carried against his skin. Elisha
was a doctor, even Vertuollo knew that, and he would
play his part, walking that line between serving life and
drawing strength from death.

The Colonna lord lay dead, mouth pooling with blood,
half-stripped already by those eager to despoil those they
saw as their oppressors. Nearby, a laborer reeled, his head
bloodied, and Elisha snatched him, pulling him aside to
bind the wound with a strip torn from his tunic. The fellow
grinned his thanks and pulled away, snatching a stave
from the ground and swinging it about him as he whooped
a war cry. A small group in Colonna red cut through the
crowds, horses snorting, working toward where their lord
had fallen. One of the citizens took a shovel to a knight's
spine, and he arched back, tumbling from his horse. The
Valley swirled open, and Elisha caught the flash of wicked
glee in the shovel-wielder's face, the corpse-tending
mancer, like Morag, creating his own clients.

Bone cracked nearby and Elisha spun. A group of Colonna pages bore down on a wounded man, his arm
clutched against his chest. Elisha grabbed the sword from
a fallen guard, blocking a blow that would have killed, anchoring himself with the power of the dead all around him
so that the page's arm tremored with the rebound of his
blow. Citizens filled the gap between and Elisha hauled his
patient out of the way. A simple break, an easy matter to
deaden the pain and twist the bone back in place, binding
his arm to his chest with a strip, but this man's presence
sizzled with the lust for blood. He took Elisha's borrowed
sword in his off hand and leapt back again.

Appalled, Elisha watched him go, and watched him
fall, blood spraying in an arc to stain the white column
that marked the Colonna livery. As the body twisted
away from the sword, his mouth gaped open and he
screamed Elisha's name.

Chapter 40

◆

Elisha leaned as if to go to him, but the Valley, so near the surface here, already carried the shade away. Had he heard rightly? Surely not—the man could have no idea who Elisha was.

Shaking himself, Elisha edged back to the fringe of battle, thrusting his arm in low to drag out a youth in danger of trampling. This one, at least, had the sense to retreat when Elisha had bound the gash in his thigh.

Then it happened again: a woman with a cross bow staggered, shot through by an enemy archer, draping Elisha's arm, staring up at him, her shade rushing through him as she whispered his name.

Recoiling, Elisha let the body fall; his hands shook.

A spear aimed at Elisha's head parted his hair as he stumbled aside, then dodged another thrust. He scrambled out of the way, fetching up against the corner of a tower. Mordecai's words echoed in his memory, advising him to wait at the hospital rather than go out to the battlefield, for it was easier to tell the living from the dead. At the San Lorenzo gate, they felt so eager for the fight that even those he rescued converted too easily from one to the other. If he stayed, he'd get himself wounded in service to those who'd rather die than abandon their cause. Better to wait behind lines and help those wise enough to seek out aid. If he retreated a block or two, he could set up a makeshift field hospital, ready at need.

He turned the corner, waves of citizens pressing

forward and he the only one moving the wrong way. Another death howled behind him, and it howled the shape of his name.

Elisha froze, his eyes wide, as the breath caught in his throat. Again, the shriek of the wounded became the howling maelstrom of Death, and again, the beating sound called his name, an eerie, drawn-out wail that sucked at him, flaring through his talismans, stinging his skin and taunting his ears.

Fighting for breath now, Elisha shook himself. His fingertips scraped the stone of the house at his back and found purchase, clinging to the cracks as he mastered his senses, clamping down on his awareness, reeling in his presence and inverting it, projecting his absence, a deflection woven of the terror that gripped him and the numb pressure of Death that battered his pierced skull. His wrist throbbed.

The crowd still pressed forward, but they curved around him, squeezing together rather than brush the absence he made of himself. He launched himself away from the building, snugging his cape tighter, head down and shoulders hunched as he ran for the tribune's palace. His breath came in clouds that fell in tingling shards upon the ground. The wrongness of the air pained his lungs.

A ghostly child ran into the street, tumbling beneath the hooves of an unseen horse as he came up, but when the shade ran again, its blank eyes met his, and its mouth formed his name. A shade fell from a tower above, twisting in the air and struck Elisha with a whisper of his name. At the next block, he dodged through an ancient battle—every shade he glimpsed froze in its repetitions of death as he passed, and every one of them called out his name. Never before had these ancient shades possessed any animation but to repeat their own deaths. What force drove them now?

He clamped his hands over his ears and staggered on, keeping his left eye closed against the dead, but still he felt them, and tears stung at his eyes. When he stumbled to the servants' entrance, the startled guard there took one look and opened the gate, letting him fall inside. Elisha rocked on his knees, gasping for breath.

"Dottore!" One of the servants stood over him. "Are you well? What has happened?"

Elisha shook so badly he could not answer. His teeth chattered. He did not know what was happening, but who else knew so much about the dead? Had Count Vertuollo inflicted this upon him? Or was it some effect of the man whose death he swallowed? Had he grown too close to the Valley now to ever escape it? But this was not the chanting summons of his own impending death, no matter that it pained his skull, reminding him of the desperate surgery that one time saved his life. Thomas's strong hands and stronger need had kept him in his body then; that, and the strength of Mordecai's magic. The thought of his mentor seized Elisha's skull with a pressure that made him cry out.

The servant grabbed his arm, tugging him away from the gate and supporting him as they gained the balcony. "I'll bring help," the servant told him, hurrying away again.

Elisha sank to the stone of the balcony, his fingers wrapping his right wrist, feeling for the stitches from the old surgery that linked him with his mentor. As if this memory were a talisman of death, the Valley swept open. The world vanished as knowledge swept over him, and his own screams were swallowed in the vastness of sound. Mordecai. With one voice, the dead called out for Elisha. With Mordecai's voice.

Drenched already in despair, Elisha let the Valley take him, but this was no journey across the lands—it went within, cutting his spirit, his heart, his memory.

Trembling, he crouched in the maelstrom, lashed by the pain and fear of those who passed this way. Gone were the comfort of Biddy, the aching joy of Martin Draper, the surrender of old age, the righteousness of Father Uccello, the severed innocence of Margaret's baby—even that sense of Brigit's lost soul lingering in the Valley was overwhelmed.

Elisha raised his head and forced his eyes to open, his

mind to open. The scars in his skull pulsed with knowledge. His eyes glazed with tears as he cradled his wrist.
"Mordecai," he whispered, and a shade rushed over him,
cold and urgent, a jumble of images that reminded him
of the French magus dying in his arms, struggling to order his thoughts and send the message Elisha must hear.

A familiar stone house, a refuge on the Isle of Wight,
crossing water — a feat that took great strength, even for
him. Three in the house, then four, then ten. The first intruder arrived with a movement that stung Elisha's back
like an arrow's strike. Blood contact. Mordecai's fractured memory cried out, his voice echoing Elisha's own
despair as if he feared for Elisha's death, but despair
twisted as the intruder spoke: not a mancer, a woman,
soothing, interested, then outraged. Mordecai's confusion welled, damped by caution. Sabetha, former nun,
current nursemaid, came near to Mordecai, her contact
suffused with surprise, wonder, guilt. Guilt? For a moment, he felt the brush of fur, the dark marten of his
cloak, cleaned and repaired by Sabetha during his brief
visit. She trimmed a scrap from the torn lining, and
slipped it into her sleeve, a scrap of the luxury she longed
for — not knowing the tiniest spot of his blood might provide a vital contact for his enemies.

Despair surged again, but Elisha forced himself to focus, pushing away the pulsing demands of the other
dead, summoning Mordecai. The Valley roiled with the
memory of the passing mancers, trails converging on the
memory. Mordecai was sensitive, strong, capable, and utterly overwhelmed. Cursed blades tore his flesh. He
learned enough from Elisha's tales to deflect the fury of
the gathered deaths, but a knife need not be talisman in
order to kill a man, even a magus. Mordecai fought them
from his panic: he had never had to face them before,
had only Elisha's advice to guide him. It wasn't enough,
it could never be. Mordecai fled for the fire.

Mordecai's knowledge infused the moment, Jews in
other times and other places, choosing the flame rather
than be slain by their assailants. Mordecai poured his
strength into fire, denying them his body, defying their

rage. With meticulous need, he bound his memories. Even as the Valley opened to suck down his spirit, Mordecai wove it with his memories, suffusing it with himself so that Elisha could be warned, directing the strength of his dying to that end, sending his voice before him, to cry to Elisha's heart.

But that was not all he did with the power of his own death. With all the anger he could muster, Mordecai set fire to that house, lest his own skin be stripped by Elisha's enemies. He prayed for Sabetha's escape, and for Brigit's burning, for her to be consumed before the mancers found her. The flames hurt, searing Elisha and Mordecai both. As the spark of his own life vanished, Mordecai felt his failure. The intruders found Brigit to take her away.

Elisha forced his jaw to unclench. Brigit, like her mother, spoke in fire. Even in her terrible silence, her being longed for life. Just as Elisha once called through the rain and summoned Mordecai to save him, Brigit's flesh called through fire. At its slightest touch, the mancers came, and Mordecai felt his loss in the swelling triumph of those who took her.

As the flames soared, devouring his body, Mordecai bound his memory into the Valley itself, pouring his strength into the warning it must deliver.

Mordecai spent the last of his power, the last of himself there might ever be, to quench the pain in his broken flesh and spare Elisha from experiencing the full horror of his death. It was that small mercy, so precisely Mordecai, that broke Elisha's heart.

Chapter 41

---

lisha came to himself, weeping, the heels of his hands pressed so hard against his eyes that he saw redness and stars, a private canopy of grief. He rocked against the stone parapet, his breath hot and ragged, tremors still shaking him.

"What's happened?" a voice floated on the winter wind above him.

"I don't know. I believe he was at the battle, helping the wounded."

"Is he hurt? He's bloody enough."

"I don't know," the servant repeated.

"There's no doctor to call; he's it. Wait with him—perhaps the fit will pass and you can learn more."

Cramped around his horror, Elisha could not imagine rising, marshaling his legs to somehow support him. The trembling stirred even his bones. Shivering waves of release emanated from the center of his being as Mordecai's bound shade, its message delivered, dissolved into the Valley. Hollow and aching, Elisha crouched in the cold, tears soaking his ripped tunic, his wrist and skull—reminders of those healing skills they had shared with each other—no longer throbbing. Snow sifted from the evening sky, far too pure and beautiful. It clung all over him, his flesh still too cold to burn it off. He shifted to rise, but his trembling knees would not support him and he caught himself on the wall. Too many days of fear, of nightmares stalking him both night and day, to reach this terrible climax. Mordecai, dead.

Elisha reeled, clutching the stone. Brigit, taken, and his baby with her. What would the mancers do with such a prize? What could they not do? He must search until he found her, fight until he took her back, or slew her in the effort. Snowflakes speckled his hands and melted like the Virgin crying.

"Come inside, Dottore." The servant brought him through the doors, slowly. They paced the corridor to his tiny room where he tumbled onto the bed.

He woke remembering Mordecai, after the first time Elisha took on the aspect of Death to stalk a battle. He had woken then, startling a serving girl, and it was Mordecai who came, summoned by their bond. *"A poor nursemaid I make,"* the surgeon had said. Elisha's eyes burned, but he had no more tears.

He woke again to the sound of voices, the tribune and his captain standing over him. Elisha kept himself as if he slept.

"I fear we are done for here," Cola murmured. "The dottore's affliction seems the last sign. I thought that God was with us today. I think now . . . it was not God who urged that battle."

"Don't speak so, Tribune," Rinaldo answered, but his voice was low, the protest rote. "Go speak to the men, let them hear and see you. Perhaps then . . ." but the words trailed away.

"You have always been most loyal, Captain. You have my thanks."

The door creaked and the tribune departed. Elisha let his eyes flutter open. "What happened at San Lorenzo?"

Rinaldo's thin lips twisted into an ironic smile. "Another great victory." He pulled up the vacant chair. "Most of the Colonna are dead."

"Isn't that what you wanted?"

"Peace is easier to make with the dead, it's true. But their ghosts shall haunt the living. The citizens robbed a Colonna priest and left him dead and naked in the

vineyards, a man who never had borne arms until yesterday. Janni della Colonna, the lord's young son, was
stripped and slain inside our gates. And Baron Stefano
was overmastered with grief. They hacked his body as if
they had him in a butcher's shop. This was no battle, Dottore, it was a slaughter."

Elisha nodded. He had witnessed Baron Colonna's
cruelty toward Father Uccello, and could not bring himself to mourn, but the slaying of boys and priests and the
defiling of vineyards went beyond the needs of battle. In
the few months he had lived in Rome, he saw the faces
of its people move from righteous fervor to deadly fury.
Count Vertuollo might have nudged that fury into such
terrible bloodlust, but it was Cola who led them into the
carnage, and they would not forgive him.

"Romans killing Romans. It was not meant to be like
this." Rinaldo gazed down at his knotted hands. "At the
height of battle, our standard broke, as if God had left us
to wallow there in Hell. I think it is not long before the
last of the barons rally against us." He took a deep
breath. "In the morning, the tribune took us back there,
to the puddle where Stefano died. In that bloody water,
he made his son a knight of this victory." He spat the last
word, as if it were a curse, then he lifted his eyes at last.
"You should go home, Dottore. There is no more to do
here. You have seen the churches and touched the bones.
Tell your queen . . ." He shook his head. "I don't know
what you should tell her. I pray by the Holy Year, that
Rome shall again be safe for her. But God only knows if
that shall be." He pushed against his knees and rose.

"I'll need maps, and a horse," Elisha told him.

Rinaldo bowed briefly and departed.

Elisha pushed himself to the edge of the bed and sat
up, groaning. He needed to search, to find Brigit. He
needed, too, to finish his mission here—he had marked
the tainted relics, but he still needed to destroy them for
good. Rubbing away the sleep from his face and drinking
the last of the cold broth, he struggled for attunement.
When he drew up his strength to assault the relics, he
would need to act fast. Too many mancers held the flesh

and bone of these victims. If he moved without precision, they would be on him. From his sleeve, he plucked out one of Margaret's relics, the finger bone of a tortured man.

Could he simply draw the relics to him? No, they must be destroyed. What then? Fire, perhaps.

For a moment, Mordecai's dozen wounds streaked Elisha's memory, followed by heat. He gasped, dropping the bone as he turned aside the memory, and a breath of cold reached back. On his feet in an instant, Elisha spun, braced.

The silvery shape of Count Vertuollo stood by the door. He gave the slightest nod. "Ah, my brother. I feared you would not be ready for visitors." He paused, brows lifting. "After that exquisite outpouring of grief."

Elisha swallowed, banishing all emotion, all sense of himself back beneath his skin. "I appreciate your sympathy," he replied, thankful that his voice didn't tremble.

"Ha!" Vertuollo gave a slender, sharp smile, his eyes crinkling. "Sympathy. Oh, that is rich. Your . . . friend? . . . made quite an impressive showing for one who'd never before entered my gate. I might like to have known him."

The wound of Mordecai's death still stung, in spite of his defenses. "I'm not sure you would have gotten on."

Vertuollo's face lost all hint of humor. "They seem to think that you are my problem now, since you have sojourned so long in my city. What has he been doing, they inquire? Looking for me, I assume, seeking to insinuate yourself into my good graces. Did you learn what you wanted?" The pale eyes widened. "No?"

Elisha drew up a breath, and Death rose with it, tingling beneath his skin as if it frosted his veins.

Vertuollo sighed lightly. "I like you, Brother. You have skills even my son cannot share. You know the traumas of our sensitivity in ways few others could understand. And what, exactly, do they think I can do about you? You expect me to kill you, yes? Is that even possible?"

As ever in this man's company, Elisha felt at a loss, the mancer's civility at odds with his casual inquiry. Count Vertuollo liked him? Good God—that damned him more surely than any inquisition. "The Germans tried. Several times."

"You see?" He gave a turn of his hand, too cultivated to adopt the Roman shrug. "The French, well, one expects them to be ignorant, but the Germans have known you—they should cease to underestimate what you might do."

"When they slight me, Brother, they're slighting you."

"Precisely." His eyes crinkled. "You allowed the priest to hang, then stole his essence. You slew that fool who thought to betray you to me. You . . ." he shook his head slightly. "I can't kill you—even if I tried. Even in your grief, just now, I could not surprise you."

"I doubt you came here to compliment me."

Vertuollo tipped his head, acknowledging the point. "I am content with Rome. It is a good country, rich, beautiful. It is enough, and it is mine." Power crackled through him then, the tendrils of death wreathing his hands, draping his shoulders like a cloak of darkness. "Death is not the only unpleasant fate for such as you. You are a strong man, a good man—whatever that is worth—and you cannot possibly succeed. You cannot comprehend the forces arrayed against you." For a moment, he regarded Elisha with a steady, almost pitying stare. "Go home to England, Brother. Go home and drink the wine of your own vineyard."

With an unfurling of the Valley, Vertuollo was gone.

Elisha sank onto the bed, heart pounding, and tried to catch his breath. Before he'd even retrieved the bone from the floor, footfalls thundered down the hall, then Rinaldo's agitated presence cut his awareness followed by a banging on the door. Elisha pushed himself up to draw back the bolt.

"Dottore! Praise Mary, I've found you." Rinaldo caught his arm. "There is an army gathered against us—we have to go."

"I need to take care of—"

But Rinaldo shook his head fiercely. "It is Vertuollo's son who leads them. He says they must expel the tribune and all of his council—especially the foreigners. Come, Dottore!"

Shit. Vertuollo paired his curious warning with a terrible threat. Elisha should have expected this sort of subtlety—stirring innocents to move against him. He knew how to counter a direct attack, but to fight off the very citizens he had been working to save? He thrust his few possessions into a satchel and hurried after Rinaldo through the emptying palace. They met the tribune at the great lion stairs before the palace, where once he hung his enemies. Once more he wore banded armor of an ancient style that barely contained his growing belly. He stared down at the helmet in his hands. Ringing over the city in urgent waves, the bells of Sant'Angelo called the citizens to battle. Already their cries rose up after each stroke of the bells and torchlight glowed.

"The mob is coming." Cola held up the helmet, its crest shivering a little in his hands. "I shall depart as a warrior. One day, I shall return here, and they will once more adore me." So saying, he placed the helmet on his head, his eyes gleaming in the narrowed view. Mounted among a small company of knights, Rinaldo once more at his side, Elisha rode out as the madman abandoned Rome.

For a few days, they wound through the mountains, until they finally fetched up at a small monastery where Cola and his men intended to rest and decide what to do.

Elisha roamed the monks' peaceful graveyard, considering his own path. When he was a child, his mother had wanted him to join a monastery—hoping the religious life would cure him of the impression the burning angel had left within him. If he took vows, he could tend the graves of the peaceful dead, and never again know the horrors of the mancers' world. Except that the mancers' world was growing. It would consume Rome and all of her pilgrims. It would consume the Pope and all of those who followed him, devouring both secular and spiritual realms at a single blow. And Elisha, at peace, would be powerless to stop it.

At peace among the dead. *"How could I fail to be at ease in such a place?"* he asked of Vertuollo in the

catacombs of Rome. The mancers who stole Brigit knew
she had been important to the mancers of England if not
to Elisha himself. They knew he'd gone to considerable
trouble to conceal her from them—they would go to
equal lengths to conceal her from him. How? Not the
obvious way, by relying on the negation of death for life:
Death was one area in which their enemy was their
equal. In fact, he had shown all of them, time and again,
his power drawn from that source. He'd been assuming
they would want that strength as well, that they would
need the dead to succor themselves and defend against
him, but they also had Count Vertuollo's advice in this.
By now, they knew Elisha was more sensitive than almost any of them. No matter the care they took with that
power, they must expect him to be yet more capable of
discovering it. So they would avoid death completely.
They would look for a place where none had died.

Elisha sat on a bench near the little graveyard chapel,
taking a deep breath. Good God. That could be anywhere. Couldn't it? If they used all possible caution, they
would travel by sea, knowing that the combination of
salt and water would make it all but impossible to find
her that way. Clearly, they avoided using the Valley or he
would recognize her presence there. How was he ever to
find her?

A few flakes of snow drifted down to settle on the
leaves and the cross before him. Elisha blew out a breath
that ruffled the fur of his collar. A bloody scrap of this
very cloak had enabled them to find her. He frowned,
running his palm over the softness. Even then, it would
have taken a sensitive, someone who knew about the
cloak, who might be able to search as he could across
such a distance. Count Vertuollo? He had only recently
learned the truth of Elisha's identity, but sensitives like
them were hard to find.

Then Elisha's breath caught in his throat. Gretchen,
Queen Margaret's maidservant, beloved of the mancer
Bardolph. She bore him a grudge both for the damage
he had done to her lover, and for his and Katherine's
collusion in having her expelled from the Queen's

service. Elisha squeezed shut his eyes and searched his memory, the visions that Mordecai had left him. The one who appeared at the lodge on the Isle of Wight, the first to arrive, was no mancer, it was a magus, a woman. Damnation. Likely, until she arrived there, she didn't even know what the mancers were looking for. Instead, she performed a scouting mission, possibly looking for Elisha himself, and discovered the sleeping queen, the woman supported by the mancers of England. Likely, they assumed the child she carried was Thomas's, the unborn heir to the throne. It wasn't Elisha they were attacking, not yet, but the throne of England. They knew him to be its defender, and hoped to distract him with the battle of San Lorenzo: making a mess in the city of Rome, a mess that Count Vertuollo would have to clean up. No wonder he grew so angry with them. But where did these revelations leave Elisha? Gretchen had been the messenger that drew the enemy to Mordecai's refuge. A sensitive magus married to a mancer, with the blessing of her family. She had one of the arrows that nearly killed Elisha, and Sabetha had kept that scrap of fur from his cloak. A mancer, even a sensitive, could not have traveled through living blood like that—they needed a magus who still cared for the living.

Elisha lifted the latch at the chapel door to let himself inside and shut it behind him. Drawing on the moisture of the drifting snow, Elisha conjured the door to swell into its frame, ensuring he would not be disturbed. He lit a pair of candles, leaving them beneath the altar-table to shield their light. For this, he did not even need the maps, but sorted through his talismans until he found the one he sought: the knuckle bone of Bardolph's father. With a few breaths, Elisha sought attunement, spreading his awareness.

Finally, he opened the most slender inlet to the Valley, hardly an opening at all, but merely an acknowledgement that it was there, always with him. By the time Vertuollo's interest quivered inside the Valley, Elisha had emerged in the silence of the unfinished church at the heart of Heidelberg.

Chapter 42

❖

Straightening his cloak, Elisha cast a deflection and moved swift and silent through the wintery market to the sign of the Unicorn. Thick snow draped the rooftops and piled in the corners, and he gave thanks for the warmth of Margaret's gift. What must the Empire be like now that Ludwig was dead and Charles ruled at last? That mancer victory weighed heavy on his mind. At least he and Ludwig had made them fight for it. Margaret would be in Bavaria, her husband's stronghold, while the surprisingly capable Harald learned how to hunt mancers with Katherine's aid.

The unicorn sign swung above him, and Elisha redoubled his deflection. Seven people in the common room, two moving among them and away; three more above, two sleeping, and the last one was Gretchen. He withdrew his senses before she could become aware of his interest. The door popped open, and a thick man muttered apologies as he stepped around Elisha.

Elisha moved inside, letting the door swing shut again in the breeze with a little flutter of snow. With deliberate speed, he walked the common room, raised a hand to the serving man as if bidding him goodnight, and mounted the creaking stairs. All the way to the back, beyond a door that marked the family's home, and inside it without a cry of alarm.

Gretchen spun at the click of the door, a hand flying to her throat where a string of glass beads glinted. She cast a deflection, smothering her thoughts and emotions, any sense of her that might help him, though her face simmered hot with anger. "You monster—what are you doing here?"

This greeting left him briefly speechless.

She drew a deep breath, and Elisha pounced, snatching her hand and snapping her into the Valley where her scream joined a thousand others, unheeded by mortal ears. The sound hitched upward, terror flooding the contact as she stared around them.

"Will you do to me what you did to her?" Gretchen's eyes welled with tears, but her arm tensed to steel as if ready to strike. *"Will you steal my soul and leave me a living casket to carry a child?"*

Elisha reeled with horror, almost releasing her, but she could not get home without him, not unless Bardolph had been much more open with her than Elisha believed. *"No, Fraulein, no more did I intend that for her."*

"So it was an accident that Britain's queen collapsed at the moment she came into her power? That sorcery sustains her at the king's need? When the child is born, what then? Will he kill her and marry again, or simply rape her to get another?"

The images she conjured sickened him, but his fury fought the bile down again. *"You know nothing of the king, and nothing of her but the lies they told you. She would have slain half England to take that throne. Her power burned every lord, lady, and noble child, Fraulein. You don't know what you're talking about."*

"Then why save her? Why not kill her, if she were the evil you claim? Let the king get himself a new baby on a new bride."

The words beat at him like the howling madness of the Valley itself. He clenched his jaw and sought the strength of death to hide his heart even as Gretchen's whoosh of breath showed he was too late—her sensitivity had revealed him. She gripped the beads at her throat. *"It's not a royal babe at all—it's yours. Holy merciful Virgin, what depths does your wickedness not know?"*

Elisha mastered himself, forcing back the guilt along

with the swirling chaos, forging them a place of stillness from the heart of pain. *"Where have they taken her?"*

"As if I would tell you. They shall bring her back from where you left her." She thrust up her chin. *"Go on, then, kill me. What else do monsters do?"*

What, indeed? If he released her, how quickly would she go to Bardolph and tell him the truth about the child? And yet, too many innocents had died already. *"Where's your husband? I presume you've married him by now."*

"I would never betray him."

He focused his senses on her as she writhed in his grasp, her enchantments stinging at his skin, then submerging as she sought a way to defeat him, but an edge of white showed at her eyes, and her awareness fractured. A part of her struggled against him, while the rest trembled in terror at the place he'd brought her. What if he left her? If he let her go, right now, and conjured himself away, she would not be able to reveal him. Cold threads seeped in through his skull and the warden's interest stretched in his direction. Elisha was running out of time.

Her breath shuddered in her chest, a cloud of white against the flickering dread around them. "Don't leave me," she whispered, and she seized his wrist in her hand.

Elisha hardened his heart against her, forcing himself to feel nothing. "Tell me where to find them."

Gretchen's throat worked, and she brought her eyes back up to meet his. "No."

Will battled fear within her flesh. Gripping the vial he wore at his throat, Elisha pulled her through the Valley and stumbled into the darkness of his brother's workshop. He thrust her away as she stumbled, spun and faced him. "What—"

But he must move fast if he would return to Heidelberg before the paths faded. Elisha fled her astonished gaze, stranding her in England for his friends to handle. She had walked the Valley before, at least once on her own when she entered the manor on the Isle of Wight and brought the mancers who slew Mordecai. She might do it again, when she realized what had happened, but it would take her time and trouble to get back without a powerful contact. Hopefully, it would take her long enough to return that he'd be gone on his quest.

Elisha repeated his journey from the Church of the Holy Spirit back to the Unicorn, surprising the same server he'd waved to before. "Forgot something," he called to the man's frown, as if that explained everything.

Unfortunately, a search of the chamber where he'd found Gretchen revealed a few items of her clothing, but no talismans at all—certainly no bits of bone or scraps of flesh to link her to her lover. For a moment, he perched on the bed, so angry he could shred the mattress down to its straw. He risked himself, revealed the one secret he could not afford his enemy to know, for what? To terrify a magus and abandon her thousands of miles away? Nothing personal remained here. Likely, she didn't even live here anymore, but only returned home for a visit. It must be close to Yuletide, or even beyond. What did mancers give at Yule? Relics of their victims? Holy bones and holy blood, wrapped in the glory of gold to honor the Magi's gift. Elisha pushed himself up and, before exhaustion overtook him once more, slipped back through the Valley for the tiny chapel he'd left behind.

He awoke to someone banging on the door and calling, "Dottore! Is it you in there?"

Elisha scrubbed his face and realized he must have been snoring. Outside, Rinaldo tried the door with a rattle of the latch and a groan of wood and stone. "Just a minute," Elisha called out.

"Are you well? We have missed you at dinner."

"Aye," but the assent came out on a sigh of frustration, and he dragged the door open, expending a bit of magic to encourage the door back to its proper fit.

Rinaldo stepped back, regarding him in the gloom of the lantern he held. "We shall go on to Napoli tomorrow, the tribune has decided."

"Napoli?" Elisha shook his head dully. He had no idea where to go himself.

"To the south. Queen Giovanna of Napoli is an ally of the tribune, and he hopes her favor can restore him."

To the south, where a spreading darkness loomed in Elisha's awareness. "Why not go to the Pope?"

Rinaldo drew himself up as if physical effort were needed to keep so much control. "The Holy Father has rescinded his support. He may have granted his assistance to the barons at the end."

"I'm sorry." Elisha met the soldier's gaze with the weariness of recognition: The tribune's dream was a noble one, but his pursuit of it had gone badly awry.

"Will you accompany us? It will bring you close to Salerno. They have a fine medical school perhaps of interest? You shall not be able to pass the Alps until the spring, in any case."

The home of the Salernitan Vertuollo had mentioned? "Perhaps." It was as good a plan as any, though it left the task of Rome undone. He gathered the few things he had brought to the chapel, then stepped out to accompany Rinaldo.

His visit to Gretchen had probably revealed more to her than it had to him—she seemed to possess no relics nor talismans of any kind. The only thing she had of any interest was a beaded necklace, and that had shown no signs of mancer taint . . .

Elisha laughed lightly. For a time he had forgotten that a talisman need not be torn from an unwilling victim or forged of misery and death: It need only be personal, especially for a sensitive magus who could call upon its secret strength. When Gretchen's hand flew to her throat, he took it as a sign of fear—but in fact, it was the natural gesture of a magus reassuring herself of her talisman, something she reached for whenever he mentioned Bardolph. "Rinaldo. If a man could go anywhere at all to purchase glass beads for his lady, where would he go?"

At that, Rinaldo gave a snort of surprise. "Venice, of course—where else?"

"Of anywhere in the world?"

"Venice—I tell you true. You have not been long in

Italia, you do not know all the treasures she holds, and for glass, it would be Venice."

"Then I'll go to Venice."

"To buy glass?" Rinaldo held up the lantern to guide Elisha inside the dormitory.

He shook his head. "To search for a lady."

In the morning, beneath a wintry sky, he rode down again with Rinaldo and the tribune. He asked as many questions as he could about Venice, especially its churches, gathering knowledge to aid him in travelling there, and thanked them for the horse. He considered riding all the way to the Mediterranean Sea—if the mancers truly found a hiding place beyond the paths of death, he couldn't use the Valley to pursue them—but riding all the way would take time he'd rather not spend. Instead, he rode for a couple of days, as far as Assisi, where he sold the horse and found shelter at a small inn. The ride also gave him a chance to rest before traveling the Valley again: he would need all of his skill to deflect Vertuollo's notice the next time he passed that way. The battle and Mordecai's death left him drained.

In the little private room he hired, Elisha spread his map again and considered all the Romans had told him about Venice. Cola and Rinaldo, excited by their new friend's journey through their country, described the great churches and monuments of the powerful trading city, a city made of islands and canals, drowned by storms and visited by every merchant or majesty who could make his way there. Elisha laid out one by one the mancer relics he'd taken from those he had killed and used his awareness to search north, toward Venice. He visualized the great Basilica San Marco they had described to him, not quite believing the opulence they imputed, and felt a faint resonance beneath his hand as one of the bones found its match.

Elisha wrapped the other talismans with care and organized his few possessions. The journey must be fast, his contact with the mancer relics as brief as possible lest his passage be marked. Caution and urgency warred within, but urgency won this skirmish: he had no idea how long it would take Gretchen to return from England and find her way back to her husband's side to tell him the truth about the baby. Every time he thought of her, his heart ached. Was it better for her to die in service to a cause she misunderstood, or to live just long enough to understand her mistake?

Centered, his awareness honed to a keen edge, linking himself with that distant place, Elisha slid through the Valley and emerged on the other side in a glorious dazzle of gold. The shiver of the Valley only just reached him as he sealed it once more. The passage had been so very easy. He knew the Valley of the Shadow, as intimately as once he knew the streets of London, as deeply as he knew his own heart. He remembered the expression of approval on Count Vertuollo's face as he examined the mancer Elisha slew. Such clean and tidy horrors. Elisha felt he stood between a pair of distorting mirrors: Gretchen on the one side, a sensitive, a magus who genuinely believed she worked for the good and could not understand why Elisha did not; on the other side, Vertuollo, who called him 'Brother,' and remained astonished that Elisha was not more like him.

A few candles at the altar that held the tainted relic lit the side chapel where Elisha emerged from the Valley. Before him, the Basilica San Marco opened in magnificence. It was all that the churches in Rome might have been, all that Cola wished them to be again, carved, embellished, gilded, and brilliant — and crowded. People moved past the entry to the chapel where he stood, praying and grumbling.

He pushed out into the crowd, not shrinking from the brief contacts that helped him to interpret their dialect. It rang in his ears with echoes of both Germany and Rome.

"—the harbor! How does the doge expect us to survive?" snapped a woman in a crinkling gown of silk as she swept past with her companion. "It will be a long enough winter without anything new to wear. No Sicilian fever is worth such a bother."

As underdressed as he had felt in the Flemish port where he first crossed the Channel, it was nothing to this. For a moment, he imagined his friend Martin Draper reveling in the vivid colors, the flowing skirts, the sleeves cut with intricate dagging, the twinkle of gems and the sheen of pearls, the occupants every bit as dazzling as the church itself. It was a cloth merchant's paradise, and his chest ached at the thought that Martin could share not even the memory. He won free at last into a broad plaza that could have enveloped the entirety of Saint Paul's back home in London. A towering campanile of brick stood to one side and the famed bronze horses stolen from Constantinople loomed overhead. How Cola crowed about that victory even though the Crusades were long past. Elisha kept his awareness spread about him, very like the ladies' long trains, ready to give notice if any mancers approached.

A man carried a tray on a strap about his neck, calling out to the passersby and holding up flashing bracelets. As he approached, Elisha recognized the beads, brightly colored spheres of glass.

"Scusa!" Elisha waved the man over. "Can you direct me to the harbor?"

The vendor squinted at him and cocked his head. "Scusa?" he repeated in turn, but with that Venetian accent.

Elisha tried again, more slowly in his Roman dialect, and the vendor heaved a sigh that made his merchandise roll and click. "Signore, the harbor is closed. There is no point in going!"

"Closed? For how long?"

A shrug. "Who knows? The doge, he closes it, he opens it. He believes every rumor he hears."

Shaking his head, Elisha tried again. "For how long has it been closed?"

"A month, maybe."

"No ships," Elisha sighed, more to himself than to the vendor. Another waste of time.

"Just the one. Here, this is a beautiful piece! Surely, your wife never saw such a thing." He held up a long string of beads winking in the patches of sunlight.

"One?" Elisha caught the end of the necklace, examining it, trying not to get too excited.

"One ship, ten days, maybe two weeks ago. It's why they're all so angry, Signore. If the doge can allow this one, why can he not allow the rest? Me, I don't mind—if they want to shop, then they have to buy from me, that's all." He grinned, his breath reeking of rotten teeth. "You are a visitor, I'll give you a good deal."

He thought of Mordecai's description of Kaffa, a rich trading port that must be something like this. "Do you know the cargo?" Elisha asked, then cursed his haste. "I'm waiting for a shipment to take home, and I hoped—"

The vendor exploded with laughter. "The harbor is closed, and you hope the only ship to land, maybe, perhaps, carries what you ordered? It would be a miracle." He tugged his end of the necklace so the beads slid along Elisha's fingers, then leaned in closer. "I have a cousin who works the docks, but he's a drunk. Perhaps his information is no good."

"My wife will want the matching bracelet."

The grin spread. "Then you judge if this is a miracle. My cousin tells me that the cargo was but a litter carried by silent attendants." Putting a finger to his lips he said, "It is a great mystery. Someone who wishes to travel in secret? Who knows, eh? One of the sailors told my cousin the passengers are very queer and quiet about it, but this sailor has taken a peek beneath the curtains before the lot of them headed north." His chubby fingers picked among the beads and fished out a bracelet. "For you, Signore, only ten for both."

Elisha opened his purse. "Ten seems very dear."

"Your wife is not worth so much to you? Perhaps your mistress then?"

Elisha burst out laughing, shaking his head. Margaret's fur cloak and Isaac's golden pin gave entirely the wrong impression of his status. "Three, maybe."

"You are cruel! And I am a poor glassmaker. I should go find other customers." He tossed the items back into his tray and turned as if to go.

"You don't know the meaning of cruelty until you've

met my wife," Elisha said, the words a jest, the reality not at all funny. Brigit was the closest he had ever been to marriage. Elisha shook his purse, and the vendor sighed dramatically.

"Five then, signore, but you drive a hard bargain."

Sorting the coins, Elisha said, "So, what did your drunken cousin claim this mad sailor saw?"

The vendor rubbed two of the coins together, producing a low metallic susurrus. "A lady most fair, and asleep beyond rousing. A lady, pale and still like a saint, who never rose the length of that voyage." He crossed himself and glanced at the heavens. "As if we need another saint!" They shared a chuckle over that, and he coiled the beads into Elisha's palm.

For a moment, as the vendor strolled off, crying his wares, Elisha imagined Brigit's pale throat and soft wrist adorned with the vivid beads of glass. Thomas's small gold ring winked on his finger as he slipped the beads into his purse and pulled it closed. He came to seek a lady—and he'd almost found her.

Chapter 43

❖

When Elisha approached the canal, he caused a stir among the boatmen who leapt up, pushing and blocking each other and calling out for his custom, but he strolled along the row, allowing his extended senses to suggest whom to trust. Toward the end, an older man sat with one hand dangling in the water, stirring up ripples from time to time, seeming disinterested in the entire process—except for the alert set of his head, his controlled breathing, and his deliberate contact with the water.

He glanced up as Elisha's step hesitated, dark eyes meeting Elisha's, then lowering with a tip of deference. "Hiring, signore?"

"Please. I've heard Venice is hard to navigate for visitors."

"You've heard right." The boatman straightened and took up his pole. "Where do you need to go?"

"North," Elisha said.

The man raised his eyebrows, his worn face falling in rounds of loose flesh, then he nodded. He steadied the narrow boat with the pole on the outside, one foot on the bench, one still on the stone step. At last, he offered Elisha his hand to climb aboard.

Drawing back all sense of death, Elisha allowed the tingle of magic to warm his flesh and accepted the offered hand. *"Well met,"* he murmured through the contact.

"We'll see," the other man replied in kind.

Once Elisha was settled, the boatman pushed off, carefully poling his craft between the others and deftly turning it. A few shades touched the old man's presence, but in the way of old men everywhere—he had seen his share of death, but had caused none.

"Where do you need to go?" he asked again once they were clear of the other boats and he had taken up a more traditional oar to bring them around the large island.

"I'm seeking a caravan that would have left the city a week or more ago. Travelers only, no trade goods, but they would have had a litter to carry an ill woman."

The boatman's presence thrummed with fear. "Strange cargo."

Elisha kept his awareness spread, his presence undimmed. "Indeed. Someone told me she was a saint."

"A saint!" The boatman snorted, shaking his head. "Not among such company."

"Necromancers," Elisha murmured. In England, the mancers had been merely a rumor until he uncovered their plots; in the chaos of Italy they were known and feared.

Another dark look from those circled eyes. "You're not the first to ask about the caravan, foreigners all."

"How many?"

"Of me? Half a dozen. The others have had more."

And a number of mancers already in the retinue. Two dozen? Three? Elisha's shoulders slumped.

"Never had so many in the city at once—Praise Mary and San Marco!—and praise the saints again that they didn't stay."

Elisha replied grimly, "I have to find them, to know what they're doing."

"Evil," said the boatman. "But far from here." He crossed himself.

"Not this time. They're working together. Mancers from France, Italy, Germany—God knows where else."

The fellow pursed his lips and looked away, squinting at the far shore, doubt radiating from him. "They're like nobility. You don't offend them, they don't make trouble for you. Best just to keep out of their way."

"You said yourself they were foreigners—whatever evil they're making won't stay away."

The boat nosed out from the shadow of an island monastery into a chill wind, and Elisha bundled his cloak tighter. "You'll need that." The boatman tipped his head at the furry garment. "Bought boots, they did. Tall boots, and baby clothes."

Baby clothes? But why clothe a child you meant to kill for a talisman? Unless they planned to use the child against the presumed father. The baby was a royal heir, as far as anyone else was concerned. Elisha's jaw clenched. They had failed to take England through Prince Alaric, then through Brigit. With the royal heir in their grip, could they succeed? How would Thomas react when he learned Brigit was gone, and the baby with her? He could marry again and get new heirs, as Gretchen insisted, but not one so blessed with sorcerous potential as Brigit's baby would be. For a moment, he imagined Gretchen herself, kind and determined, utterly believing the lies of her lover. What if a royal prince might be raised that way, fully trusting the mancers who surrounded him? Did the mancers follow Brigit's own inspiration when she rode in to rescue Thomas from a captivity she had forced upon him? They could send an emissary with the baby: glad tidings, Your Majesty, for your child lives! Tainted by mancers' care and ruled by mancers' power. No longer satisfied with manipulating the kings of other lands, if Thomas could not be bent to their will, they could forge a king of their own. *We have made kings before, and unmade them.* Jonathan's words, his threat to Alaric on the night the prince would die.

"Where they go, I must follow," Elisha said aloud.

"North, then. I know the road they took from here, so I can avoid it." He shook his head again, the loose flesh waggling, and plied his craft among the islands to a thicket of docks on the distant shore. The boatman waved away Elisha's payment. "You're climbing the Alps in winter, fool, you'll need that coin to pay a different ferry." He indicated his eyelids, as if he placed coins there to pay the ferryman of death.

"At the least, you have my thanks."

Still shaking his head, the boatman pushed off and turned away.

In the village that supplied the caravan center, Elisha used most of the coin to purchase a sturdy horse—not as fine as the beast he'd sold in Assisi, but strong enough for his need, and cheap because the hostler expected to make few sales this time of year.

He loaded its saddle with food for the journey. He couldn't bring himself to sell the warm cloak, in spite of its rich and distinctive appearance, and purchased a second one instead, a threadbare castoff with a hood and hem to cover him head to toe, his lighter city boots exchanged for a rugged pair as tall as his knee. He wrapped strips of wool about his hands to keep them warmer. So equipped, he was ready for his search. He expected secrecy, the casting of deflections to guard the caravan; instead, the villages he rode spoke of nothing else. Who was the saint? How was she preserved in all of her beauty? Where did the monks and nuns of her procession take her, and why now? More than one villager had given up his or her home to follow the mad procession north, into the mountains in the dead of winter. Mad, indeed.

Elisha wove his own deflections, dodging the eyes of magic and projecting the anticipation he felt in the villagers all around him. As he rode steadily northward, the land and the wind both rising sharply, he encountered more and more travelers on a road that should be deserted at this time of year.

"—a vision, that's right. Of a chapel built in the snow. I'm not so credulous I'd believe in a saint with no miracles, but a job in the winter time? That, I'll take." The speaker patted a bundle of carpentry tools slung over his shoulder.

"Like as not, it's just another rumor. Lot of strange stories about," his companion grunted. "Did you hear about the ships of death down at Genoa?"

The carpenter snorted. "If all the sailors died, how'd the ship get to Genoa?"

A woman stopped short in front of them and turned back, her eyes glittering. "It's the end times, is what it is. There've been signs."

The two men shared a look over her head, and kept walking. The end times: the predicted apocalypse from the Book of Revelations, in which famine, death, pestilence, and war would sweep over the land, slaying a third of all people. He remembered little else of that volume from his long-ago days at church, but it fit. If the mancers had their way, indeed—those days of darkness were coming. Scorched earth and bloody rivers. Ludwig's words echoed in his memory: To bring down the Church, they would need a miracle of Biblical proportions. Preachers focused on the parting of the Red Sea, but the plagues of Egypt were miracles, too.

Elisha kneed his horse, weaving through trees or on narrow tracks to move past the walkers. He would pass one clump of travelers, only to come upon another group some way up the road; or join a makeshift camp that grew by night with stragglers. He wrapped his cloak tighter, huddled next to his horse, and conjured up every image of warmth from his talismans of joy, Thomas's ring and Martin's strip of cloth. It snowed in London once in a while, leaving enough to shuffle through, and it had lately been cold enough to freeze the Thames. A year or two ago, at the urging of a few of the whores he tended, Elisha skated the frozen river with broad cattle bones bound to his feet, a slippery prospect that left him bruised and laughing, innocent joy of a sort none might ever know again.

In the morning, mounted again, he passed a few lingering shades, freshly risen from the frozen dead. The next night, he pressed ahead of the struggling mass, his horse breaking trail in the fresh snow that filled the tracks of others who went before. In a protected hollow, he laid a fire, lighting it by summoning the dry heat that opposed the snow. The next to arrive had a cooking pot, and each succeeding traveler added something until there was enough hot pottage to share around the make-shift encampment. Elisha sat vigil that night, a stranger's child resting against his leg, the whole gathering keeping contact to stay warm. And it was his strength that warmed them, a quiet thrum of power focused through Thomas's ring and shared among them—not so much that it was strange or miraculous, but just enough that none of his companions should die.

Dawn rose slow, creeping gold among the peaks and towering, dark trees, and Elisha was glad of his company, missing the close-set houses and rough-paved streets of home. Would he ever see London again?

His horse snorted and stamped, shaking off its blanket of snow and waking a few of the travelers. The child at his knee stirred and rolled over to blink up at him. "I dreamed of a place with so many houses I couldn't see the sky, so many people I could hardly breathe, and a great king who loved me." Then she pushed away from him, frightened, until the man on her other side woke and caught her.

"Calmi, cara. It was this man who made our fire." The father smiled, then said, carefully, "She is a fanciful child. Forgive me if she offends."

"Not at all," Elisha replied, thinking of Alfleda, Thomas's beloved daughter, and of Thomas.

Much as he wanted to keep them warm every night, he could not linger at the pace of weary villagers but pressed on, joining another group, then a third, then riding up a steep slope, his horse, too, beginning to tire, and into a valley touched with springtime.

Chapter 44

Deep between snowy peaks, broad enough for meadows, a camp of hundreds already gathered, laying out the lines and cutting sod in the shape of a cloister that spread from one end of a chapel that rose in their midst. From the dense green grass sprouted tiny flowers in blue and yellow. The pedestrians around him gaped and crossed themselves and cried tears of rapture when they saw the greening valley, many falling to their knees in prayer. Elisha, too, wanted to weep. His right eye saw the valley as his fellow travelers did: a miracle.

His left eye saw the truth. Among the joyous, worshipful pilgrims, dozens of necromancers worked, dark and joyless, to manufacture this false spring. Their cold power settled low, like mist in the valley, while the place thrummed with the strength of their enchantments. Clad in the rough gray woolen robes of Franciscan friars or Poor Clares, they tapped no talismans of death, but those more personal, those of childhood, of love, of a hundred things Elisha was sure they no longer understood, coaxing an unseasonable warmth. Tendrils of rotten power spread; the warmth here was that of an infected wound.

Drawing up magic through the more innocent of his talismans, Elisha refined his projection. He matched his eyes, making them the steel-gray of the left instead of the vivid blue of the right, then subtly changed the contours of his face. He could not hide beneath the power of death, not when the mancers themselves worked so hard to eradicate it, and this loss left him feeling exposed, a knight having left behind his armor. But what then? Even if the mancers did not see him, how would he get close to Brigit or learn the depth of their plan? They already countered many of his tactics by not linking themselves in power, by not working the Valley or even carrying the relics they forged. By creating the impression of the miraculous, they summoned hundreds of people who would support them, and they spread the rumors of holy events. In doing so, they surrounded themselves with innocents, an audience of believers, armoring themselves against his intervention with others' lives instead of deaths. They would know that he had risked his own life to save Katherine's children—what could he do if he feared to harm these others? On the other hand, he had also killed Brother Tigo and allowed Father Uccello to die, and they must know that as well. Did it seem strange to them, this betrayal, or did it mean nothing at all to a group for whom the betrayal of innocents was their custom in trade?

Then came the idea that froze him as if he remained outside the enchanted valley. They deprived themselves of Death because they thought to cripple him. But he knew Death. He was no necromancer, not a worshipper of death, but *indivisi*. He knew Death so intimately that he could no longer be separated from it. He was not merely its deliverer or its exploiter, he fought it, knew its coming, succumbed to its cold touch—and chose to return again. They built their cloister openly, daring his presence because they believed him yoked to the dreadful talismans they, themselves required. They failed the first rule he ever learned of magic: they failed to know him at all.

Elisha grinned and allowed his deceptions to fall away. He didn't need their tortured victims to open the Valley, he carried it always, close to his heart. At need, he could summon it, summon himself away from their traps or conjure himself the strength to defeat them. At last, he had an advantage over them. Vertuollo must be keeping aloof from the others if they did not know the depth of Elisha's affinity.

He unwrapped the bindings from his hands and chafed them, the scars at their centers showing white and smooth against the ruddy skin. The mancers forged the atmosphere of holiness in their clerical robes—Elisha, too, could play that stage, claiming the spiritual power that so many declared on his behalf. He stripped back his hood and, rather than hide beneath deflections, he projected rapture. Dropping the reins, he encouraged his mount forward, sending it joy, the delight of good grass and an end to winter. The horse pricked its ears and shook out its mane, trotting eagerly down the steep trail. Slowly, the train of murmuring, praying supplicants became an entourage, drawn by his delight.

The first mancer he passed, a man with narrow eyes like a weasel, startled at his appearance, reaching for a pouch, then aborting the gesture to cross himself instead. He gave a whistle, and a few heads turned, especially those freshly tonsured or wimpled, their flat eyes staring as Elisha rode nearer, weaving among the makeshift tents and hovels.

A stout mancer in the garb of a nun stood on the steps of the chapel, arms raised, her voice carrying over the crowd, over the rapping of hammers and the grunts of workmen. "—and there appeared a great wonder in heaven, my children, a woman clothed with the sun and the moon under her feet, and upon her head, a crown of twelve stars! And she, being with child—yes, my children! The Lord sends us this sign, this woman, just as John foretold!"

Elisha frowned, the horse slowing as his projected joy faltered. The voice sounded familiar, as did the words she spoke: the Book of Revelation. And the miraculous woman, being with child? Good Lord—she meant Brigit. No wonder the mancers were so pleased to find her.

"You hear the rumors of dread, but I say to you that this dread will burn from us our corruption and iniquity! It will be the fire of justice and of the Lord's righteousness that will scour us! If you repent and submit to the Lord's will, you will be saved! Repent! Repent!" She thrust up her fist and the crowd before her took up the chant. It rose all around him, and the nun swiveled toward him, her long face grim and fearsome, her eyes close-set like a hawk's. "And suffering will purify your soul."

She was the stout mancer from England, the one he had allowed to escape when he rescued Thomas. He should have killed her before, but she had done him no direct harm, and he had not then possessed the urgency to slaughter mancers wherever they were found. She had not appeared at the final battle for the British throne, or rather, what he had assumed was the final battle. Now that they controlled the presumptive heir to the throne, they might have a new plan. But the nun's words suggested something much greater than England at stake, if they would convince these people that Brigit's child were foretold in the Bible itself, the mighty leader of men who would appear before the Apocalypse, an event the mancers seemed ready to create.

He squared his shoulders. "Where is the queen, Mother, so that I may honor her?"

"Honor?" she thundered, filling her voice with power. "Kneel, Sinner, and honor first your Lord!"

Elisha slid down from his horse, managing with surprising grace and walked forward, though around him, many others knelt as she demanded, and the chants of "Repent" faded away.

"Oh, arrogant sinner, surely there shall be—"

"You would deny me, Mother?" he asked, quietly. He projected his voice with a thrill of magic, endowing it with resonance beyond himself, then he spread his hands, his palms displayed. Silence spread around them, but for the frantic alert whistles of a few of the mancers, like mad birds trying to get the nun's attention. Elisha smiled gently.

"Deny you?" she replied, and her voice, too, had fallen. "I do defy you—that ever a sinner like yourself should be granted an audience with the crowned one!" A wind rose around her, rippling her garments, and she raised up a wooden cross.

Around them whispers began. Elisha's presence, his

projection, and the scars on his hands elevated him in the eyes of the audience—the audience the mancers brought here for their own purposes, now serving him instead. Would they listen to the nun, or support the stranger in their midst who presented himself with holy majesty?

Elisha mounted the lowest step, and the nun's deep-set eyes darted, looking for guidance from the others, although they could not reach her before he did. He pressed his advantage, step by step until they stood together before the door, she facing out, eyes wide and jaw clenched, he staring at the fresh-cut wood. "Thank you, Mother," he said.

"No!" howled a woman's voice from the crowd behind him. "Don't let him! You can't let him!" Gretchen's voice, raw and anguished, as she rushed toward the chapel.

Ignoring her, Elisha pushed open the door. Thank God Gretchen hadn't had time to warn them, to prepare them for his approach, or surely they would have a stronger defense. What had they expected from their armor of humanity, as willing to believe his projections as their own? Still, his skin tingled, his muscles tightening. He celebrated that they seemed to underestimate him, but he should not make the same mistake of them. He had assumed the mancers were acting out of ignorance about his strength—what if they simply had another plan in waiting, one he couldn't see? This would not be the end of it, unless he moved quickly before they were able to re-group against him.

Candles lit the chamber before him, and braziers reduced the need for the sorcerous spring that warmed the vale outside. An altar as long and low as a bed occupied the end of the chamber. Two men turned at his entrance: Bardolph, who startled so badly he knocked over his chair, and a well-fed fellow with liver spots showing on his tonsured scalp. This second man looked familiar, but older—Elisha placed him from Father Uccello's memory: Renart, the French mancer complicit in his torture and God knew what else.

"Elisha! By God, my prayers are answered," cried a woman leaping up from her place by the altar. She stumbled, her steps hampered with a rattle of chain, but her arms still stretched to him. Tears streaked her face: Sabetha.

Elisha broke between the men and seized her arm, sending a ripple of cold Death along her skin. She gasped and tremored, but the chains at her ankles cracked with cold, and she clung to him with a grasp of need and gratitude. "They killed him, Elisha, you must know. If there was anything I could've done — but there was a girl, and she knew all about you." She sobbed, her voice breaking.

With a shake of his head, Elisha silenced her. On the altar before him Brigit lay, her face pale and lovely, her breathing as soft and steady as ever, her great, round belly nearly due. A golden crown of stars rested on her head, just as the Book of Revelation predicted, along with a cloth-of-gold gown gleaming like the sun. A pair of moon-pale slippers peeked out beneath. They clad her in the raiment of prophecy. Now they need only make it come true.

"Bardolph!" The door slammed open and Gretchen staggered inside. "It's his baby, Bardolph — the baby is his!" She fell into her husband's arms, gasping for breath, and too late.

Elisha scooped the slumbering Brigit against his chest and reached for the Valley that hovered always so close to his heart. The Valley groaned open, painfully slow, as the mancers sprang toward him. Given his intimacy with death, he expected the opening to be as easy as the last time; instead, he strained, teeth clenched. He conjured power from every talisman he still carried and cried out as the Valley ripped for him — for all three of them, Sister Sabetha who clung to his arm, the woman he cradled against his cold breast.

For a moment, the terrible madness of the Valley shrieked around them as if they stepped from a church into a battlefield. Brigit's body resisted, his arms trembling as he tried to carry her through — but through to where? He reached along the Valley to England, to his brother's workshop, but the Valley pushed back against him and he swayed beneath its defiance. Even beyond the two women he clung to, Elisha did not stand alone.

"How long can you hold, Brother? How long can you stand so open?"

Count Vertuollo's voice echoed all around him, thrumming as if it channeled the myriad howls of the dead into a choir and he its master. He stood, silhouetted by a hundred flickering shades. Hands spread, face illuminated by the queer light, Vertuollo waited, his posture echoing the risen Christ, bringing a message not of redemption but of ruin.

"No, Brother. Today, no living man may travel here." He shook his head, almost sadly. "There is no road for you." He raised his hands, his shades clamoring around him as his power surged and sliced straight for Elisha's heart.

Elisha twisted away, wrenching his focus to shut the Valley he had opened and snatch the women back with him. They would flee into danger, yes, but away from a much greater threat. At the same time, he flung up his defenses: warmth, heat, friendship, the magic of Martin's laughter, the memory of Biddy's sacrifice. Death was not always evil, not always cruel. But the Valley would not close: Vertuollo held his gateway, coolly in command of the mancers' dark road. In the midst of death's realm, in the face of its master, Elisha struggled for the powers of life. Sabetha pressed herself to his side, his left arm wrapped in her grasp as she cried out.

Trapped in the Valley, he fought in vain. The wave of power slammed into them, a torrent of searing cold that shocked through him.

Clutched against his chest, Brigit's body convulsed, and Elisha felt a rush of wetness. For a moment, he stood paralyzed—had he just lost his son? He'd never considered the risks. He prayed it was only her water breaking, not the blood that foretold an abortion. He clung tighter, even as her body jerked in his grasp and he thrust back against the waves of cold that Vertuollo set after him. His muscles shook with the effort, desperate to extend what little protection he could conjure, but here, in the warden's domain, it was not enough. His knees buckled, and the howling around him pierced his concentration. Elisha twisted, trying to shield Brigit and the child she carried.

Sabetha's eyes flared, glancing to the woman she had tended for so long, then she lunged past him, the living heat of her body thrust between the warden and the unborn babe.

Sabetha writhed and twisted, wailing. Her flesh withered, her eyes bulging as Count Vertuollo's power thundered against her, full-force. With one sharp twist, she broke free of Elisha, breaking their contact. The black power of dying ripped from her huge eyes and open, howling mouth as her body shredded under the onslaught of the terrible cold. Her living form disintegrated into the chaos of the Valley.

With Sabetha's anguish echoing in the chamber around them, the Valley snarled closed, leaving Elisha and Brigit on the outside, back in the chapel—with mancers all around.

Chapter 45

❧

Elisha crumpled to the floor, Brigit sprawled across his knees as he fought for breath, that horrible wail still filling his ears. Possibly only Vertuollo would ever have the power, the strength and the knowledge to bar the Valley against him. Elisha would have to kill him. He was damned if he knew how. Brigit's crown of stars rocked gently near the altar and one of her slippers lay nearby.

"Well, I do hope your wife knows something of child-birth?" Renart asked Bardolph in accented German.

The force of Elisha's conjuring left him panting and shivering, and Renart's soft chuckle stung like salt against a wound.

"Get away from her! Let her go, you monster." Gretchen reached toward Elisha, conjuring a sharp heat to her fingertips. Elisha winced, his hand flying to his head, fingers resting in the divots where his skull still felt vulnerable to intrusion. His lungs burned, his left hand trembling and white with frost. Brigit lay with her head in his lap, her red-gold hair tossed about her. Her lips parted with a gasp, and her green eyes opened.

"Brigit," he breathed, the most sound he could make.

She groaned softly, but her face showed no sign of recognition as her body clenched. Her eyes squeezed shut and slid open again, focusing through him, as if he weren't there at all.

Gretchen seized his shoulders with the force of her fury, but Elisha resisted. "Help me lift her."

"Get away," she growled through his skin, but he could feel her holding back her power, afraid of hurting Brigit and the baby by forcing him.

"Help me lift her." Elisha tore his gaze from Brigit's face to meet Gretchen's fierce glare. "The baby's coming."

"Holy Mary!" The woman hesitated, then shifted, taking Brigit's legs while he raised her head and shoulders. "This is your fault, monster."

"Do you think I don't know that?" He smoothed back Brigit's hair—still silky; Sabetha must have bathed her and washed out her hair. Dear God. Her pulse beat strongly beneath his probing touch.

The braziers by the altar where they lay her warmed his face and hands, but fell short of heating the chill that built behind him. The door opened and three more mancers came through, muttering together. Bardolph and Renart pushed through, interposing themselves. Elisha dodged their touch, keeping the altar between him and them.

"Do you know anything of childbirth?" Bardolph asked, catching Gretchen's hand with a brief squeeze.

"A little." Dark eyes studied Elisha.

"Just cut the bitch and take the baby," said Renart. "We'll have our symbol and a martyr in the bargain." His hands hovered over Brigit's taut, heaving abdomen, but Elisha knocked them away, a brief shock of power passing between them. The cold of the mancer's presence shivered with streaks of eagerness.

"You can't just kill her, Renart," said the stout nun. "A thousand pilgrims are out there waiting for this miracle."

"We'll blame it on the dragon, Revelations, end times—isn't that what you've been telling them?" Renart pushed back his sleeves and found a knife.

"No." Elisha dragged up what strength he had, focusing it into his hand, ready for the fight. If the mancers got their hands on the child, all was lost: Vertuollo would let them take the baby anywhere, and Elisha could not follow.

"Leave her alone!" Gretchen's heat flowed now, a shock in the room full of mancers. "Don't touch her."

"You must control your wife, Bardolph." Renart grabbed Brigit's skirts and yanked them upward, baring her belly, letting the cloth tumble over her face.

Elisha snatched the knife before it descended. The blade bit his hand and blood oozed from his palm. He bent his will to its destruction, but the blade had been tempered in torture, and his heart lurched.

"You don't know the queen, Renart," Bardolph stammered at last, apparently becoming aware of the difficult place he'd made for himself. "If she wakes, she's very powerful. At least, we have to try."

"Bardolph!" Gretchen cleared the layers of linen and golden cloth back from Brigit's face, but left her legs free. "Of course we do."

"You need to initiate her, Bardolph. It should've been done months ago." But Renart's narrowed gaze remained on Elisha's face, his strength pushing back, pain shooting up Elisha's arm, doubled by the memories of torture the blade contained. "What better time than now? What better blood?"

"Help me, Bardolph." At the end of the altar, Gretchen bent Brigit's knees, propping her feet, and set a trembling hand on the round belly.

Elisha's fist clenched around the blade, his arm trembling. "Would you let them cut her open?"

Bardolph touched Renart's wrist lightly. Though the touch was focused and direct, Elisha's raw state left him open, his senses flung wide, and he felt the words as Bardolph spoke. *"He knows her as we do not, Renart. If she dies now, even by your hand, he wins; her essence will go to him."*

"He has already lost," sent the other mancer, but he drew back, and Elisha released the blade. "Let him aid— if anything goes wrong, we'll have him to blame."

"No," Gretchen insisted. "He's the one who made her like this." She moved to block Elisha's hand, and he sent her his urgency.

"Fraulein, it is my child."

She thrust up her chin, then relented, but her power still pulsed just beneath the surface.

"If you're so worried, girl, take his talismans." Renart examined his knife, edged with Elisha's blood, and its gleaming blade reflected his smile.

Heart and breathing still uneven, Elisha held out his arms as Gretchen searched him, her probing senses stroking over his skin. She took his medical kit and tossed it aside, along with all it contained. His jaw clenched as she found one after another of his hiding places. The relics of Rome, cold with death and sharp with pain, she found easily, discarding them into the brazier with a shudder of revulsion. His letters followed, Thomas's, Jacob's and the rabbi's words curling into smoke, the nail trimmings of Saint Lucia went to the floor, Thomas's ring she wriggled from his finger and set aside. All the while, Brigit groaned, a low, inhuman sound devoid of the emotion it should carry. All the while, Renart blew cold breaths along the blade of his knife, over Elisha's blood. Elisha exchanged his own life for that of the child—once the birth was over, they'd have no more use for him.

From Elisha's boot, Gretchen pulled the little pouch containing Queen Margaret's shard of the True Cross, then Brigit's belly heaved, and she gave a sharper cry. Elisha flinched.

With a cry of her own, Gretchen startled, overbalancing, and he knelt to give her a hand. "Hurry, Fraulein. There are lives at stake."

She jerked her arm away and reached for his throat, pulling the cord of his pendant over his head. Still on his knees, he lunged for the dangling vial, the vial of English earth, stained with his brother's blood. She pulled it up, leaning toward the brazier, but Elisha said, "No. Please, Fraulein. Please don't."

Renart held out his hand, and she dropped the vial into his grasp. He slid it into his sleeve and Elisha winced—the mancer had seized his only way home.

"That's all of them," said Gretchen.

Elisha swallowed his fears and moved along the altar.

As if in a dance, Gretchen gave ground, and he followed, ending with the two of them shoulder to shoulder at Brigit's side. Elisha lay down his palm, winced as the cut stung, and forced his hand to heal, though he trembled with the effort. Defending them against Vertuollo's assault—even with Sabetha's sacrifice—and then facing Renart had left him weak. Knowing that he could not conjure from the Valley left him shaky and exposed. Vertuollo had to be expelled, but first he must attend to Brigit and the child she carried. Again, he pressed his hands against her, feeling the shape of the baby, feeling the rush of relief to know it had dropped, its head already in position. Brigit's body lurched beneath his touch and she groaned.

Gretchen gave a sob, her face nearly as pale as Brigit's.

"We'll need warm water and cloths to clean and wrap the baby," Elisha told her softly.

"Water," she repeated, too sharply, then shook herself, relaxing her hands.

"We've holy water right here," said one of the onlookers, holding up a large jug.

"The Lord shall—" the nun began, but Renart cut her off.

"You wanted a miracle—of course we'll use the holy water." He waved for the jug to be brought up, and leaned closer himself, his hair brushing Elisha's as they examined Brigit.

"Stay back and let us work," Elisha said, his muscles already quivering with tension.

"Yes, very well. Bardolph, you, too." Renart gestured to the other, withdrawing a few short paces.

Gretchen accepted the jug, cradling it against her and setting it down by her feet, steam already rising from the mouth of the jug as she channeled her nervous strength into the small sorcery of heating the water.

Moving down beside her, his hands resting on Brigit's knees, Elisha thought of his first lessons in witchcraft. It was hard to force the body to something unnatural, but easy to encourage it to what it was made for. Healing. Dying. Giving birth.

He knelt, checking to confirm that Brigit's body was

ready for this. "Send her comfort, Fraulein, and encourage her to push."

"Are you sure?" Her hands fluttered over the other woman, not settling, but Elisha reached up and caught her wrist, guiding her hand down to rest on Brigit's abdomen, just above the womb.

"Yes, I'm sure." For a moment, their eyes met. *"Your body, too, knows life. Share that knowledge—rejoice in it—and it will help her to relax."*

"What about Queen Margaret's child?"

He snatched back his hand, the reminder chilling him. "I wasn't there in time to prevent that." A trickle of blood started and he called for a cloth, but the mancers, the dealers in death, only briefly fell silent, glancing from one to another, then to Renart and Bardolph.

"I suppose one of the peasants might offer something," said Bardolph.

With a growl, Elisha stripped off his own tunic to staunch the flow. Already, the baby's head crested, the heat of its life and its urgent need warming his careful fingers.

"Push!" Elisha cried.

Gretchen and Brigit wailed as if with one voice, sweat and tears streaking Gretchen's face. The moments stretched, the baby's head appearing amidst the blood as Gretchen entwined her strength ever more closely to Brigit's form, encouraging her from within. The room grew hot around them. Elisha braced Brigit's feet, memories flashing through him. He had been a prisoner, bound and waiting to die, when she came and offered herself. No, not offered: She came and took what she wanted. Something like this had always been her plan: that Elisha's death should make a talisman of his child's birth. And they would never let him live. How would they kill him? Avalanche? That would smother him and force him to spend his strength fighting for breath and hope. Cut off his head? Or would he live long enough to work some spell against them? But what spell could he work without the Valley, and without killing the hundreds gathered outside?

The mancers wanted this child as their symbol, a living talisman to bind those witnesses together, the thousands who would hear the tale from them, a miraculous birth they could manipulate to their own ends, a mancer-child baptized in its father's blood. New life, born to the service of those who celebrated death, lifted from the hands of a dead man. The talismans of death were powerful indeed, reflecting the horror of the dying, giving strength to those who forged them. But in spite of his murders, his cold, his betrayals, he was no mancer, enslaved to slaughter. Even now, with the threats that hedged around him, his hands guiding a child into the world felt more natural than any action he had taken since he left England.

Death and birth: two ends of the same strand. Opposites. No wonder Brigit's body resisted passage into the Valley—even in her twilight state, her body held too much life to pass easily through that place of shadow. Brigit's laughing voice echoed in his memory, his first lessons, the most basic laws that governed the use of the power he knew. Knowledge and Mystery, themselves representing the Doctrine of Opposites. *"You defend the border of life and death, and your choice at any moment might tip the balance,"* she had told him, the first night he had glimpsed the full power of Death. Elisha opened himself to the knowledge, to the mystery, to the pain that rang in Brigit's body and the hope that blossomed in his own. With every strength he'd ever employed on behalf of a patient to fend off death, he gathered to himself the tools of life.

Brigit gave a wet convulsion and the child slid into Elisha's hands. Power flooded his body, a charge of light and wonder. Heat washed through him, springtime in the winter indeed. Elisha's head shot up and he drew the rush, channeling that torrent through his flesh and blood—and his blood along the edge of Renart's knife blazed with the sudden heat, shattering the mancer's cold blade.

"Now! Take him now!" Renart shouted, though his voice trembled with surprise.

Bardolph leapt around the table, knife drawn, but Elisha's spell was not yet spent.

The blood that marked Brigit's bare skin transformed her cry of pain into a gasp, a word, almost a name. The blood that fell upon the floor gave a heave and cracked the wood, and still the power swelled and rolled along the paths that he had chosen. The ground shook, and the Valley tore open at his heart as every relic in Rome marked by Elisha's hair, gave a spasm of life's power that death could not deny. The Valley swelled through him, connected to his every sign of life, rebounding against the will of the warden who tried to bar Elisha's way. Vertuollo knew Death, but this was a tide beyond his reckoning.

Count Vertuollo's shriek of fury stunned Elisha's ears with a blast of cold as the churches of Rome shuddered and broke. The warden had bound himself so tightly to his purpose that Elisha's strength exploded against him and all that he held so close. The chamber pitched and rocked, a roiling clash of magic that shattered earth all the way to Rome itself, tearing free the tainted relics and crushing them to dust.

At his side, Bardolph stumbled, his arm smacking the altar. Elisha fell back, clutching the child against him. His other hand found the floor to keep them from hitting too hard. The warmth of Thomas's ring pressed into his palm. Bardolph charged down at him, bent upon his death.

Gripping the ring, Elisha swung his arm up to block the mancer's blade. Somewhere behind him, Gretchen shouted.

For an instant, Bardolph was caught once more between them, hesitating, and Elisha seized the knife from his hand. A swift cut severed the umbilical cord, the hilt of the blade pressing the ring into his palm. Then, as the world cracked and broke around them, Elisha focused on Thomas. In a blaze of Life, he conjured himself and his baby away.

Chapter 46

❖

───────────────

Elisha stumbled on a familiar smooth-tiled floor lit by the glow of stained glass from peaked windows that framed a small altar. The king's chapel in his quarters at the Tower. And the king himself knelt there, hands pressed together in prayer, eyes flashing open, then shut with a tiny shake of his head, then open again, bright blue and staring.

Elisha stared back, his son cradled close in his arms, his heart thundering, a bloody knife still gripped in his hand. Suddenly aware of what a terrible picture he presented, Elisha shook free the blade, letting it clatter to the floor.

With the sleeve of his tunic, he wiped the baby's face, staring down into his deep eyes, the infant brow furrowing as he tried to make sense of the huge new world. The exhilaration of victory washed Elisha's skin and he grinned for a moment, but the grin soon faded. He left a world in turmoil, innocents dying, mancers waiting to claim their lives. He could not simply leave that place behind—nor could he return there with a child.

"It's you," Thomas breathed at last, then he rose and clasped Elisha's shoulders, the heat of his grip stunning after so many days of cold.

"Thomas." Elisha drew a shuddering breath.

"Your Majesty?" Pernel's voice preceded his entrance, starting to bow, then stopping completely.

Giving the servant a brief smile, Elisha said, "The queen is delivered of a son."

"We'll need blankets, water, and a doctor," Thomas ordered, and Pernel managed another bow before he rushed from the chapel.

Thomas cupped Elisha's cheek with his hand. "When we heard about the Isle of Wight, and Mordecai—my God, Elisha, what else have I prayed for than that they did not find you, too." His eyes searched Elisha's face, then glanced down again to the baby, a smile lighting his features. "He's beautiful. Brand new."

Elisha nodded quickly. "He'll need a wet-nurse—ask Helena. If she can't, she'll know someone."

"You speak as if you are not staying?"

Elisha shook his head. "I can't—not yet. I'll try to return as soon as I can. This," his throat worked as he looked down at his son. "Not yet," he said again, very softly.

Thomas's hands shifted, bringing them to lean over the baby, their heads resting gently together. "Then I will go on praying."

"I have to go," Elisha murmured. "Brigit is waking."

"Dear God. Will you be all right?"

"This gives me strength. As do you." Elisha drew himself away from the king's warmth. Thomas reached out for the child, but Elisha couldn't move for a long moment. The baby's heart thundered against his own breast. Life where, for so long, he had harbored only death.

Gently, Thomas said, "He will have the finest of care."

Taking a deep breath, Elisha placed his child into the arms of his friend. He withdrew two paces, and retrieved Bardolph's knife. He would need it where he was bound.

Thomas cradled the baby against him, bouncing slightly, the habits of fatherhood never lost, but his eyes remained fixed on Elisha. Elisha did not trust himself to speak. For a long moment, he considered staying. Rome was broken, its relics destroyed—what more remained of the mancers' plans?

He did not know, and so he must return. Brigit's blood

still slicked his palms, and through it he conjured himself
back to her side in the mancers' chapel, ready to save, to
heal, to wield the strength of life, for as long as it would
sustain him.

Immediately, the floor pitched and he stumbled,
nearly falling, but righting himself in an instant, senses
extended. The mancers' vale rang with shouts and
screaming, and sawdust hovered in the air in the trembling structure. The forces he had brought together, the
vibrant strength of life, the terrible chaos of the Valley,
still sent their tremors through the earth. Pain and terror
leapt around him. Four of the mancers lay dead, crushed
when half of the building collapsed. The broad altar
thrust up at a sharp angle, its thick edge atop the ruin of
Bardolph's chest, his eyes open, but unseeing as blood
dribbled from his mouth.

"Returned from Hell, are you, you Devil?" cried Renart, holding up a golden cross. "And what have you
done with the baby you've stolen?"

Elisha hesitated, for a moment mystified by the mancer's posturing, then he saw the press of faces beyond the
broken wall and shattered doorway, the villagers who
clustered around the false nuns and monks, pleading for
salvation from God's wrath. The cold wind of the Valley
swirled around them, shades flickering from the broken
bodies of the fallen.

"It was not God who broke this place and cracked the
earth to swallow up your fellows. No! It was Satan—and
there stands his messenger." Renart jabbed the cross in
Elisha's direction. "False stigmata he bears, given by a
demon, to sway you to him! The end times are upon us,
my children!"

Renart, clothed in the raiment and the word of God,
faced him with a grin of triumph. Elisha himself, bare-
chested, bloodied, gripping a knife instead of a cross,
could think of no way to defend himself from such madness, but he had a witness.

Through the blood of the new mother, Elisha reached
out, sensing Brigit's warmth, and that of the woman who

held her. *"Gretchen—fraulein, will you support me? You know that he's not what he seems."*

"Neither are you," she answered, *"and my husband is dead."* Her words echoed with grief.

"I'm sorry."

"You are only sorry because it means I will not help you."

He flinched and glanced at her. Gretchen knelt with Brigit in her arms, the shimmer of magic tingling all around them as she protected her charge from the rumbling earth. Then Brigit moaned, lifting her head. With a shaky hand she smoothed back her red-gold hair. Worry creased her face as she glanced about. Briefly, her gaze rested on him, green and bright, and strangely distant. Without recognition, she searched on. Elisha remembered loving her, hating her, fearing her, holding her, stopping himself from killing her—

The Valley tore open at his back. In the same moment, pain struck through him, as if the chaos of his emotions could pierce his flesh. The blow carried guilt, betrayal, release—a sharp, familiar death. Elisha staggered, coughing blood, and caught himself on the upturned altar.

"He's ruined Rome! Now we'll never get the *desolati* to come," shouted the newcomer as he jerked the knife from Elisha's back for a second blow. Conrad, his urbane voice transformed by fury.

"Papa!" shrieked a young girl from the crowd outside. "He's killing the nice man! Make him stop!"

Elisha dropped to the side, gasping for breath, and the knife hacked into the wood instead. Plain silver hilt, long, strong. The blade Elisha had used to pierce the mancer-monk's skull.

"My father trusted you," Conrad said.

"Shut up, boy," Renart muttered through clenched teeth, glaring at Vertuollo's son. "We have witnesses."

That fine nose and broad brow—Elisha would have known him anywhere for the count's flesh and blood. Would his child look like himself, or like Brigit? It was spring in the meadow; why did he feel so cold? Gretchen stared at him over Brigit's shoulder. Something dark and poisonous roiled within him, a deeper cold unlocked by the mancer's blade. Then he closed his fist around Thomas's ring and forced back the assault.

Conrad's shadow loomed over him, reaching for him, but another mancer stopped him. "What about the rest of us?" asked the mancer, in the dialect of Rome—the gravedigger Elisha had seen, his form edged with a flicker of shadows.

"Yes—aren't you going to share?" demanded another mancer, pushing past the onlookers. Elisha's vision blurred, the pain spreading, but he dragged his senses back, drew in his awareness, swallowed his strength to find the wound and force the flesh to heal.

"All righteous shepherds share in the kingdom of the Lord!" Renart cried, his voice carrying a warning as he tried to preserve his air of holiness in front of all the *desolati* witnesses.

Elisha spat blood, wiping his mouth. Conrad, projecting a bit of his father's chill power, said, "This man is mine, and his death is my father's."

When the blade struck down again, Elisha was ready for it, striking back with the deadly power that flowed in his veins. "Holy Mary defend me!" he shouted and the blade shattered, its wielder's curse becoming a scream that choked into nothing. Conrad reeled, his body shuddering, fingers clawing the air as his skin withered to the texture of old leather, his blood gone still in his veins. The body clattered to the floor, the black strength of Conrad's dying streaming to Elisha's hand.

The nearest mancers stumbled back from him as Elisha staggered to his feet. He gripped the altar's edge and thought of Isaac, desperately calling upon the Holy Family, defying his own religion to save his life. "If my cause be worthy and my need be just, Holy Mary heal my wounds." He cried out as the flesh knit too fast, the blood streaming back, slowing to a trickle, easing to nothing but a scar that ached with every breath.

Renart gaped at him, the cross wavering, the greedy mancers hesitating.

"Do not play at miracles with me, Renart," said Elisha very softly. He let Thomas's ring slide down onto his finger and closed his scarred hand around it. "You will lose."

"Kill him now—take him now, while he's still weak," the gravedigger insisted, but Renart put out his hand, the cross pressing against the other mancer's chest.

"No!" shouted the little girl again, rushing through the broken wall to Elisha's side. Elisha recognized the child he had befriended on the snowy trail to get here. Her father trailed after, while the other villagers crossed themselves.

"And deny the count his vengeance?" Renart glanced back to Conrad's twisted form, then to Elisha. "You really think you've won, don't you? I'll be there, when you see how wrong you are." Renart's lips twisted once more into that grin as he retreated. "Come, my brothers and sisters—we must away!"

Elisha vaulted the altar, dodging broken slats as the mancers hurried out, pushing their way through the crowd. Outside, people still wailed, still called for aid, and the ground gave another tremor, smaller this time, but some of the cries ceased while others rose to screams of agony. One of the mancers stopped by a fallen woman, dragging his fingers through her blood, his presence brighter with relief, and Elisha pounced, catching the back of his neck with a grip of ice. The mancer hung limp in his grasp and Elisha lay him aside, keeping his eyes upon the others.

"Weak, did you say?" Renart observed.

"Most reverend father! I bring the relics of the Chapel of Saint Anne! Let us pray," cried a nun, striding the green meadow with a golden casket carried before her. Bits of salt flaked off the casket—they must have packed it in salt to conceal it from Elisha's notice. The mancers gathered uncertainly, looking to Renart.

"Go," said Renart. "Go. No need to spend ourselves for nothing."

Like dogs called to supper, the mancers ran for the gilded case, one after the next. The reliquary gleamed

with gems and reeked of murder. They pushed open
the lid, plunging in their hands for their talismans, and
the Valley pulled wide, a roaring space of darkness. The
nearest villagers cried out, confused and chilled, and
unseeing as the mancers slid through, the gathered
shades receiving them with wild howls and swelling
fear. The villagers huddled, all entreaty for the aid of
the false clerics dying upon their lips. Even if they did
not see the Valley, they could not help but feel its
power. And the Valley itself . . . the Valley had changed.
It felt vast and dreadful, far greater than the intimate
doom of any given gathering of the dead. It thrummed
in his chest, pulsing like a second heart, but one in dangerous excitement, ready to burst.

Renart vanished with the rest, still smiling, and the
Valley sealed itself behind them, though the patch took
a long time to clear, like smoke still furling where a torch
is snuffed.

Elisha's limbs trembled, all the strength he had gathered to fight them keeping him on edge, his breath panting mist into the cooling air as the first flakes of snow
began to fall. A few hundred people remained, some of
them injured, and all would be cold. He shook himself,
dispelling the cold within. "We'll need to break up those
boards and build fires," he called out. "You!" he pointed
to a thickset man with an axe. "Get started. We'll need to
free anyone who's trapped and see to the wounded. Are
there any barbers or surgeons here?" Two men and a
woman—defiant against the men's stares—came forward.

"I studied at Salerno," she said, meeting Elisha's gaze.
"The scuola is open to all who would pass the examina-
tions."

Salerno . . . Vertuollo had said they let the Salernitan
act too soon. Vertuollo knew Elisha, more so than any
other mancer, perhaps more than any other magus aside
from Mordecai himself, and the count had stated that
Elisha could not fight them. For better or worse, Vertuollo assumed Elisha to have strength equivalent to his
own—the power to hold a city and its mancers under his

sway—and he did not believe Elisha could win. Elisha had focused on Rome, but that was not all of their plan. Something else was coming, something they believed he lacked the power to defeat. Distracted, Elisha looked back to his newly recruited healers. He reached out to her, welcoming her—and sensing only a *desolati*'s fear and courage. She could not be the Salernitan he sought, but perhaps she could point the way. "We'll need all the help we can get. Thanks."

He let the sense of Death retreat as he focused on the living, fetching his warmer clothes from the pack his horse still carried.

By nightfall, the worst of them were seen to. Elisha made no more obvious miracles, but he gave a breath of magic here and there to tip the balance in favor of healing. Those who had traveled up with him whispered the stories of fires that did not die and shed warmth far beyond their circles, and Elisha began to believe that he had won, no matter what Renart might say. He had destroyed the false relics they planted, brought down the churches they would have used to terrorize and decimate the masses at the Jubilee, and broken the Roman circle, casting its leader from his own gateway and slaying his son. Surely that was a chink in their mail that they would not soon repair, though the idea of facing Vertuollo's fury gave him pause. He had stolen back the baby they hoped to use against him. Brigit had awoken, but seemed vacant, the ambition and purpose which always animated her lost in her long sleep. If that power revived within her, Elisha would have cause to tremble, but for now, she was merely another lost soul. He had overthrown their plans for Rome, and their claims to righteousness in the apocalyptic vision they had been working toward. He had undone the apocalypse. Hadn't he? Then why was Renart still so confident?

That uneasiness kept him up as night fell, circling the fires, checking on his patients, daring, at last, to venture toward the intact corner of the broken chapel where Gretchen sheltered with Brigit.

The two women hunched over a brazier, warming a

bowl that smelled of herbs. Good. Then Elisha swallowed. They brewed healing herbs for Brigit—was it good, indeed? He knelt outside their small circle, hiding the bloody floor where Bardolph's body had been pinned. Bardolph and Conrad's corpses were gone, hauled away by sympathetic villagers who still held Brigit in awe and her handmaiden by extension. "Fraulein. How is she?"

But it was Brigit who looked up, beautiful by the firelight—so like the first time he had seen her. "Sir," she murmured. "I feel so . . . empty."

It took a moment for Elisha to understand her, it had been so long since he had heard his native tongue. "I'm sorry," he said.

Gretchen glanced at him sharply. "Are you?" She shot out a hand and grabbed his wrist. *"Are you apologizing before you kill her?"*

Cold power ebbed beneath Elisha's skin, gathering at his scarred palms. *"You don't know what she is capable of."*

"Now?" Gretchen gave a harsh laugh. *"Neither does she. I will not let you take her. Or will you kill me, too?"*

Elisha's shoulders sank.

"I thought not." She released him with a little push. "I will take care of you, Lady. There is a convent close by where you can heal. I won't let anyone hurt you. Not him—not anyone."

Bracing his hands on the floor, Elisha rose up to one knee, gazing at Brigit's vacant face, unable to find the spark that had so long been her presence. He might walk the border of life and death, but it was she who had lingered there too long. What knowledge might she now possess?

Outside, Elisha breathed in the ordinary chill of night in the mountains. This place was beautiful, with an austere strength both compelling and foreboding. Was it time, at last, to go home, to hear the music of his own tongue echoing from the narrow streets of London, and to feel the familiar stroke of a winter's rain? Did he dare to travel the Valley now, when its warden must be in a fury? He must stay at least long enough to see these pilgrims safely out of winter's rage, now that their mancer clergy had abandoned them.

He cast about for a place to find his own rest when a shout from the pass drew his attention. A lantern's light wove a tricky path down the slope, its bearer stumbling, running, calling out. Elisha and the woman physician moved toward the bearer.

"The holy one! The saint! Is she here?" he coughed and bent double, gasping for breath as they came upon him. Elisha caught the fellow's arm to steady him while the woman took the lantern and held it up.

"Is there a priest?" the man gulped between phrases, unable to get his breath, and his arm beneath Elisha's palm felt too hot, his eyes bright and his red face streaked with sweat that plastered down his lank hair.

"We're healers, we can help the fever," he began, but the man shook his head, nearly toppling over with the movement.

"It's all of them, the village, struck down, my wife," he broke off again, and Elisha sent him strength and comfort, but the runner wobbled and his knees collapsed under him. Catching the man, Elisha took the lantern from his grasp and eased him down into the mounting snow. "Please," the runner mumbled, a bloody froth blooming at his lips. The lantern wavered, its light showing the man's stricken face, not merely bright with fever, but tracked with a crimson webbing of veins.

"Oh, no," the woman breathed, backing away.

"Sir," Elisha began, but already the heat beneath his hand stirred with an unnatural chill, and the breath that last escaped the man shimmered dark as the Valley opened to receive him. "No!" Elisha kept his grip on the stranger, but he could not battle a death he did not understand. "You know what this is," he began, turning to find the lantern's light retreating, the woman doctor hurrying away so that he must run to catch up with her. "What is it?"

"I know only rumors," she said. "Towns in the south where dozens grow sick, where black bulges mark their bodies and there is no cure to save them."

Ships of the dead, the harbor closed for rumors—the map to the south spreading with the paths of death. A plague of Biblical proportions ... "What can we do?" he called after her.

"Pray!" she shouted back. "And hide."

Elisha's uneasiness fused into a weight at the pit of his stomach. Death was coming to the vale which had, until so recently, been innocent of that stain. Here, then was the foe he could not vanquish, the reason for Renart's joy. Pray, or hide. He knew he could do neither.

Overhead, snow obscured the stars. In the gathering gloom, Elisha found his horse, his cloak still draping its withers, and readied himself for the storm.